BOOK ONE IN THE DARK BLOOD SAGA

DARK BLOOD

CALEB JAMES

DSP PUBLICATIONS

Published by

DSP PUBLICATIONS

5032 Capital Circle SW, Suite 2, PMB# 279, Tallahassee, FL 32305-7886 USA
www.dsppublications.com

Dark Blood
© 2016 Caleb James.

Cover Art
© 2016 Alan M. Clark.
www.alanmclark.com
Cover Design
© 2016 Paul Richmond.
Cover content is for illustrative purposes only and any person depicted on the cover is a model.

ISBN: 978-1-63476-839-9
Digital ISBN: 978-1-63476-840-5
Library of Congress Control Number: 2016901426
Published June 2016
v. 1.0

Printed in the United States of America
∞

This paper meets the requirements of
ANSI/NISO Z39.48-1992 (Permanence of Paper).

The boundaries which divide Life from Death

are at best shadowy and vague.

—E. A. Poe

CHAPTER 1

Wednesday, July 4, 1998

MILES'S SIX-YEAR-OLD legs churned as he chased Amos, his golden retriever puppy. The boy and the dog flew down the sandy lawn of Grandma Anna's house, its borders hedged by tangles of beach plum and wild rose. Overhead, the sun shone through clouds of spun sugar. Grandma Anna was inside the white clapboard house with Mother and little Maya. Father had to work the holiday in Boston but had promised there'd be a long weekend where they'd drive to Provincetown, go out on a whale watch, and handpick a box of saltwater taffy at Cabot's.

Amos turned, stopped, and dropped the drool-covered red rubber ball. He pawed the ground and nudged the toy with his nose. He barked. It was a game, and Miles knew if he approached too fast, Amos would grab the ball in his mouth and race off.

He inched forward. "I'm not going to take the ball. Nope, not me. Not interested. Who'd want that stinky thing?" He skimmed his red sneakers forward like the ninjas he'd watch on TV with Grandma Anna. His eyes and the dog's locked. The space between them narrowed from ten feet, to nine, to eight. The animal's lustrous red-gold fur sparked in the sun. Muscles in his back twitched as he tracked Miles's stealthy approach.

"I don't want the ball. It's slimy. Who'd want a ball like that?" Ninja sneakers slid forward, seven feet, six feet. Boy and dog focused on each other and the game. Five feet, four feet. "I don't want it." Three feet, two feet. "Uh-uh, not me."

As though each could read the other's thoughts, Miles and Amos lunged for the ball. The pup was closer and faster. He gripped the prize between his teeth and raced down the hill with Miles in pursuit.

Caught in the moment and the ecstasy of flight and pursuit, neither Amos nor Miles saw the heavily laden burgundy Dodge Caravan as it turned off Highway 6A.

Likewise, the driver was distracted by his oldest daughter punching her little brother in the arm. It had been a miserable six-hour drive with no AC, three children, including the new baby, and his largely unresponsive wife, who suffered an emotional meltdown after giving birth three months earlier. He did not see the dog or the boy. What would become seared into his memory was the sequence that started with his daughter's scream—*"Daddy!"*—followed by a dull thud and single surprised yelp as the two-ton vehicle going thirty-five miles an hour made impact with the dog. The animal flew for what seemed an impossible distance.

His pulse jumped as he slammed on the brakes. He saw the dark-haired child racing toward them as he broke through a beach plum hedge, and for a split second he feared there'd be a second impact. Tires squealed as they burned rubber and ground fine white sand into the asphalt. He spotted the red dog in the rearview mirror, not moving save for blood that pulsed from an open wound onto the hot tar. From the angle the dog lay, it was clear his neck was broken.

"Don't look!" he barked to his family, who stared in horror at the unfolding tragedy. "Shit," he muttered.

His wife turned, her lip trembled, her mouth opened into a scream: "No!" He saw condemnation in her eyes.

I didn't see him. This wasn't my fault. One more sin that would be laid at his doorstep. He opened the door, not certain what he was supposed to do. "Kids, stay in the car! Don't look."

His feet touched the pavement, his attention riveted on the dying animal. He wanted to warn the little boy away from his pet. "I'm sorry," he muttered. "I'm so sorry."

Up on the hill, two women emerged onto the porch of the two-story white house, a few hundred feet from the accident. The younger held a toddler's hand while the older, dressed in black, her silver hair in a bun, started to jog toward them. She screamed at the little boy who crouched in the middle of the road, touching the dog's unmoving head, "Miles, *no! Don't!*"

What happened next the man would never understand and would never forget. As he stood frozen, the little boy lay next to the fatally wounded animal. He knew he should intervene to pull the kid away, but there was something so tender in how he wrapped his little body around the puppy.

The woman's screams grew as she ran on arthritic knees.

"Miles, don't! Stop! No! Please, God, stop it. Now!"

All the man could see was the child, his body fused to the dog's, moving his lips as though singing. His hands fluttered across the dog's fur;

they blurred like hummingbird wings. *There's something wrong with this kid. This isn't normal.* The boy was drawing designs across the dog's body. He trilled his fingers impossibly fast, first this way and then that.

And then it happened. The animal convulsed. His hind legs, which at first glance the driver thought were broken, kicked back. They were synchronous and straight. He found purchase on the pavement with his front legs. The boy rolled back on the asphalt. He stopped the freakish movement of his hands, and for a moment the man wondered if he'd been hit as well. The kid's face was flushed and smeared with blood, his striped shirt was drenched in it. His green, green eyes stared, unmoving.

The dog stood up, shook his head, and then his entire body, starting from his tail and ending with his fuzzy golden nose. Blood whipped off the animal in all directions; the droplets sparkled like garnets.

The dog turned to the boy. His broad pink tongue licked the kid's face from chin to forehead.

The man held his breath. He stared at the blood on the boy's chest. *Don't be dead. Please God, don't be dead.*

"Amos." The boy recoiled from the dog's tongue bath and threw his arms around the animal's shoulders.

"Miles!" The woman had made it through the hedge to the road's edge. She looked from the boy and dog to the man standing ten feet from the minivan.

Her eyes were a vivid green like a cat's, like the boy's. She glared at the driver. He felt her rage and fought back a childhood memory of a fairy-tale witch. "Get out! Get in your car and get out!"

He wanted to argue, to say he was sorry, to give her his insurance information, to….

"Leave!"

He looked at the boy and the dog. He saw the steaming pool of blood on hot asphalt. Too much of it for the boy and dog to be unhurt, for the dog to be alive… *but he is.*

"Leave now!"

He could almost feel the words of a curse about to be hurled in his direction. Of course that was a ridiculous thought, and he pictured the boy's hummingbird hands. The kid stared wide-eyed at the woman. Maybe it was a trick of the summer sun, but his eyes glowed as though lit from inside his skull.

"I'm sorry," the man finally said.

"Get out," she said as she walked to the child.

"Okay."

He turned back to his van. The hood had crumpled under the impact; an inch higher and the windshield would have shattered. He got into the vehicle. His family, for the first time since they left Norwood, was silent. His wife's teary gaze was fixed on the ruined hood. He put the Caravan in gear and looked in the rearview mirror. The old woman in black pulled back her right hand and struck the child across the cheek. It looked far harder than any well-deserved spank he or his wife had ever administered.

He thought of getting out, but then he thought of witches and curses and of the two-thousand-dollar-a-week cabin he'd rented to bring some fun to his family. He'd have to get the hood fixed…. *You'll say you hit a deer. You should call the cops… and say what? The dog's okay.* He looked from the mangled hood into the mirror as the old woman, gripping the child's shoulder with her long fingers, disappeared through the hedge, the barking dog trailing behind. *He shouldn't be okay. He wasn't moving. Too much blood. How can he be okay? But he is. Get out of here.* And he drove away.

CHAPTER 2

ANNA WARREN felt the energy in her grandson's body as she hustled him into her house. The foolish dog trailed behind, his fur matted with still wet blood.

Like so much in her life, she cursed his parents' decision to buy the damn thing. As if a puppy would make Miles forget his grandfather, her beloved Henry, not yet three months dead. Her head pounded from the run and from the persistent migraines that shrouded her world with pain.

Her daughter, Rachel, appeared in the kitchen door with three-year-old Maya clutched to her chest. "Miles!"

The little girl wailed.

"Shh, Maya, it's okay. Amos is okay."

The toddler pulled her head off her mother's breast and looked at her brother, Amos, and Grandma Anna. Her face lit up when she saw the dog. She squirmed from her mother's arms and raced across the space. Before she could reach either Amos or Miles, Grandma Anna's firm grip held her back as the bloody dog tried to wiggle past.

"No, child." Anna looked across at Rachel. "I need to talk to the boy. Get her out of here, Rachel."

"But, Mother, we have to call the vet. Have Amos looked at."

Anna struggled to retain her composure as she held the three-year-old from the dog, grasping the back of the boy's bloody shirt with her other hand. "The dog is fine. We are not taking him anywhere."

Rachel's focus shifted from the dog to her son. "Miles, are you hurt?"

The boy seemed dazed. He looked from his mother's worried face up to Grandma Anna, whose strong hold dug his shirt into his neck. He gulped as he felt her anger. His cheek tingled from where she'd slapped him. He had never seen her so mad. She'd never, ever hit him. "I'm okay."

But he didn't feel okay. His body pulsed like electricity, his fingers tingled, and he thought about his violin and Grandpa Henry, who had taught him to play… who was dead.

"Amos was going to be dead. Like Grandpa." Tears tracked down his cheeks. He knew he'd done something bad and that Grandma Anna was furious with him. "I'm sorry. I didn't want Amos to be dead."

"Quiet, child!" Grandma Anna pulled back harder on his shirt.

"Mother, stop that. You're hurting him!"

Anna eased her grip. "Rachel, please take Maya outside. I'll get Miles and Amos washed up. I'm already filthy. No reason we both should be."

Rachel paused, so used to doing as her mother asked. But Miles was her son… her responsibility. "Yes, Mother. Come on, Maya, let your brother get cleaned up, and then we'll all go for ice cream."

"Upstairs," Anna ordered as she released her hold on Miles's shirt. "Take Amos with you and get him into the tub."

"Yes, Grandma."

She watched as her beautiful grandson headed up the stairs, the dog at his side, wagging his lush tail. Her pulse pounded behind her temples, the pain like an anchor, the product of too little sleep and too much coffee— at least two pots a day, sometimes much more. It was the only thing that worked, the migraines a small price to pay for holding back the nightmares. As she heard the water start to run, she stared back through her life at decades of wrong choices. *I should never have married Henry. I should never have had a child.*

A man's voice whispered inside her head, *Anya. Anya.*

"No. We will not go down that road." And with practice borne of a lifetime, she imagined steel shutters inside her head cutting off that familiar voice with its deep, warm tones. "We will not go down that road."

She took a deep breath and headed upstairs. *You should never have had a child… and you did. The damage is done. It should have died with me.* Her thoughts skittered over dangerous memories. Most too painful to touch. Some like the moment she first saw Miles and he opened his eyes, green like hers, like her father's, like all of those born with the gift that was a curse.

The voice was more persistent than it had been in years. *Anya.*

She knew what it wanted, what it always wanted: first her and now the boy. "No."

The door to the bathroom was ajar. Inside, Miles had gotten the dog into the tub and was lathering the ridiculous creature with baby shampoo. The lather was pink with blood as boy and dog got soaked.

Wordlessly she sat on the tub's edge and helped wash the dog's fur clean. "Take off your shirt, Miles. It's ruined."

"I'm sorry, Grandma. I didn't want Amos to die."

The voice inside pounded with the beats of her pulse and her migraine. *Anya, Anya, Anya!* She looked at her grandson and knew what needed to be done. "Miles, I am going to tell you a story. It is for you alone, and you must never repeat it. Not to your sister, not to your mother or father, to no one. Do you understand?"

"Yes, Grandma."

She looked at the child as pink lather and water swirled down the drain. The dog repeatedly shook itself, soaking her and the bathroom floor, spattering the bleached-white towels on the rack. She grew quiet.

"What's wrong, Grandma?"

"Everything, child. I'm going to have your mother take Maya and Amos back to Boston. The story I have to tell you will take time."

"Okay." His lip trembled. "I didn't want him to die."

Anna shivered as the water soaked further into her dress. She thought about the man in the van with his children. *He saw, he knows, he won't forget.* She drew breath and knew that being kind was not an option.

"Miles, the thing you did was very bad. It doesn't matter that Amos is alive. He is just a dog. If anyone finds out what you did, they will come and take you away. They will lock you up and do unspeakable things. They will hurt everyone you love. Tonight I will tell you a story. It is not a nice story, but it is a true story. If anyone learns what you did today, bad men will kill everyone you love."

As her words landed on the boy, he grew still. Even the dog stopped shaking off water as steam filled the room and clouded the mirror.

She leaned over the tub and gripped his shoulders. Her gaze held his. She could feel his fear and shame. "You are to do exactly as I say, Miles. But first you will make me a promise, and it's a promise for life. Do you understand?"

"Yes, Grandma."

"You are never to do what you did with Amos ever again. Promise me."

The boy hesitated.

She tightened her grip. She dug her strong fingers into his flesh. "Promise!"

"Grandma...."

"Promise you will never use that gift again. They will come for you, Miles. They will kill everyone you love—your mother, your father, Maya. Promise me!"

His eyes bugged wide with fear. "I promise, Grandma."

Anna let his words register. *A child's promise, what is that worth? I must make him understand. I must make him afraid.* She wanted to hold him close, to tell him how much she loved him and how much she feared the horror that followed the gift, like the moon followed the sun. *No, this is no time for gentle words. I must make him afraid.* "If anyone knows what you did, they will take you away, and they will kill us all. Do you understand?"

The boy shook. "Yes. Yes."

The dog licked at Miles's tears as Anna reached in and pulled the animal out of the tub by the long fur of his neck. She grabbed one of the now pink-stained towels and roughly dried the boisterous pup. Her still-sharp hearing caught her daughter coming in through the kitchen door. "Rachel," she called out.

There were footsteps up the stairs and a tentative knock on the door. "Mother?"

Anna passed the dog to her daughter. "My migraines have gotten much worse. I hate to do this, but if you could take the dog and Maya and give me a couple days alone, it would help. I need quiet. But leave Miles. He'll be good and can help around the house."

Miles, now wrapped in a towel, looked at Grandma Anna. Her usually tidy black-and-gray bun was undone. Long strands of hair stuck to her neck and the wet fabric of her dress. His gaze landed on her right wrist, almost always covered; there was an angry red scar that vanished beneath her soaked sleeve. He looked up at Mom and wondered if she knew Grandma Anna had just told her a lie.

"Is there anything I can do?" Rachel asked.

"No, dear, I just need some quiet."

"Of course. Would it be okay if we came back with Joseph Friday evening?"

"Yes, I should be fine by then."

"Mom, I don't know why you won't see a doctor about your headaches."

Anna nodded. "There's nothing they can do, dear. Some things just can't be helped."

Miles listened to the grown-ups. He shivered with fear. He didn't want Mom to leave. He wondered why Grandma Anna lied. He wondered about her lie and the scars she hid. And there was more, a tingle in his belly and a lightness in his fingers. If Grandma didn't have a headache, he'd go play Grandpa Henry's violin, which was his now. Only her headache was a lie, or at least part lie.

"I'll get us packed," Rachel said. She took the dog and left.

Miles reached a hand to Grandma Anna.

She looked at it and shook her head. Her eyes widened with recognition. "Don't even think it, boy."

"I could make your headaches go away."

And for the second time in his young life, she slapped him. "Go to your room and wait for me! Already you break your promise."

Too stunned to cry, he stumbled from the bathroom, shut himself in his bedroom, climbed into bed, and listened to the sounds of Amos, Maya, and Mom piling into the car and driving away. He waited for Grandma, hearing the steady lull of the ocean. Night started to fall, and while frightened of what was to come next, he grew tired and drifted to near sleep.

A man's voice with a funny accent called out from inside his head, *Miles. Miles, come into the lake.*

Chapter 3

Tuesday, October 20, 2015

MILES MOVED through the now quiet cancer ward of Mercy Memorial Hospital in New Orleans. His short white coat designated his status as a medical student. Its pockets were stuffed with stethoscope, alcohol wipes, nitrile gloves, a lined flip pad, and the manuals he and all medical students carried, along with smartphone apps that could in under thirty seconds let him know which antibiotic could be used for a gram-positive infection in someone with renal failure, or what antihypertensives to avoid using with a psych patient on lithium.

It was going to be a long night. He didn't mind, having just had a lively, albeit tasteless dinner in the cafeteria with his best friend, Luke, and two other classmates. Collectively they'd be manning the overnight shift on the medical and surgical wards. But now he was back on the oncology floor, the lights dimmed for the night and the charge nurse nowhere to be found, likely off with the married respiratory therapist with whom she was rumored to be having an affair.

He pulled the worn flip pad from his pocket, the page already turned to the evening's tasks. Each lab to be drawn or checked, vitals to be recorded, and notes to be written were designated by the patient's initials and a series of check boxes of what had to be done. He heard running feet… little feet. *That's not good.* Visiting hours were over, and there were no children on this floor. He smiled at the thought of an escapee from pediatrics. He'd round them up and bring them back… although the kids were the toughest. Because children rarely came into the hospital unless they were bad sick. Even now, while it wasn't an every-second thought, it was a constant effort to keep the thing inside of him silent.

He strained to catch the sound again. There were voices, hushed as though aware they shouldn't be here. They came from the far end of the ward, the end where his patient, Antoine Dey, forty-two years old with stage-four hepatocellular carcinoma, would die tonight.

Miles tucked the pad away and headed to Antoine's room. A little boy not more than three popped his head out and stared up at Miles with large brown eyes. He bit his lip and ran back into the room. Miles followed and saw Antoine's wife, Lila, lying in bed beside her emaciated husband, holding him and singing softly in his ear. The little boy, Jasper, crawled up, nearly snagging one of Antoine's IV lines in the process.

Lila turned at his approach, her lovely face streaked with tears. "I couldn't leave," she said.

"It's fine," Miles said, knowing if the nurse were here, she'd have kicked her out long ago. "You stay as long as you like."

"Hey, Doc." Antoine opened his jaundiced eyes. His pupils were barely visible from the low light and the heavy doses of morphine that no longer controlled the pain of being devoured from within.

Jasper, fascinated by the drip inside one of the tubes, pulled at the infusion of last-ditch experimental chemo running into his father's PICC line. The tubing pulled free, setting off an alarm.

"I got it," Miles said, moving in to replace the line as the charge nurse, her pastel scrubs rumpled, appeared in the doorway.

"They shouldn't be here." She looked from Miles to Lila and little Jasper. "This is no place to bring a child."

Antoine, his throat parched, his lips cracked, said, "I asked her to stay."

"We have rules," the nurse replied. "You need to leave." She looked at the line Miles had reinserted and checked the tubing before restarting the IV pump.

Little Jasper tugged at Miles's sleeve. "My daddy is sick. You're a doctor. You make my daddy not be sick."

Lila gently took Jasper's hand and gathered up her oversized pocketbook. She leaned back in to kiss Antoine. Her lips hovered over his as if her breath might blow some life back into her dying husband. "I love you."

"You can come back in the morning," the nurse said. "Visiting hours are from ten to one. And then four to seven. But you have to leave now."

Miles looked at the nurse and wondered how someone could become so hard. He knew, as did she, Antoine would not live to see morning visiting hours. But with the boy here, he would not say the things he wanted to, like *what harm would it do to just let them stay and be with Antoine as he passed?* No, probably not the best thing for the boy, but dying alone in a hospital hooked to tubes and toxic chemo…. This was not a good death.

The nurse stood by the door, arms crossed, as Lila and Jasper left the room.

Jasper again grabbed Miles's hand. "You make my daddy not be sick. You promise."

Miles crouched down on his long legs to meet the boy at his level. He struggled to hold his emotions in check. He didn't want to lie to the child, who was about to lose his father, and he didn't want to think about the conversations he'd had with Antoine, whose greatest fear of dying was that he was leaving his wife and two young sons with no financial cushion. There was no life insurance policy or retirement accounts for the self-employed plumber, just a mortgage, car payments, and bills that came with crushing regularity. And on top of all that would be medical bills, which no amount of lowest-level Obamacare would cover.

Jasper tightened his grip on Miles's fingers. "You promise me, you make my daddy not be sick!"

"Jasper," Lila whispered, "we have to leave."

The little boy shook his head no. "You promise me!"

Miles looked up at Lila and then down to the tiny hand with which Jasper gripped his fingers. He felt the familiar tingle and knew he needed to hold it back. After the tingle would come the thing inside his gut, like a python wakening and uncoiling. He heard Grandma Anna's ferocious warnings, pounded into his head year after year. *They will lock you up and kill everyone you love.*

"You have to leave now," the nurse repeated, clearly impatient and wanting to get back to whatever, or whomever, had caused the crumpling of her scrubs.

Jasper would not let go. "Promise me! Make my daddy not sick!"

And in that moment, Miles knew what he was going to do. He nodded and gently squeezed Jasper's fingers. "Okay… I promise."

"You can't break a promise," the boy said as his mother eased him away by his other hand.

"I know." Miles let go of the boy and stood up.

TWO HOURS later all the check boxes in Miles's flip pad were filled. Blood was drawn, labs checked, X-rays and doses of chemo ordered for the morning. As he completed his tasks, many of them so routine as to require no thought, others critical, he forced himself out of the struggle racing in his head to make sure he accurately calculated doses of potentially lethal chemo. *You cannot be doing this.* He'd spent a lifetime repressing the gift that was a curse—at least according to Grandma Anna, who'd done her best to scare it out of him with stories of her murdered family and the scars on her wrists. He knew she'd been in a concentration camp, that there had been tattooed numbers on her arms. There were stories she told and much she held back. At times her storytelling was trancelike, as though she'd been transported back in time. He wanted to call her now, knew it was what she would want. He also knew what she'd say. *Do not give in to it.*

Finishing his last notes on the computer, he pictured little Jasper with his liquid brown eyes, and Lila, and there was a baby as well. He smiled— Baby Moses—named without irony by the intensely religious Lila. She'd be home now with her children and her mother and the Virgin Mary. They would pray through the night for a miracle.

Miles started to tremble. He looked at the note he'd been writing. *Good enough.* He flipped to the signature page, signed it, and logged out. It was 10:00 p.m. The charge nurse was again missing in action, the unit dim and quiet save for the ding of monitors and the inflation and deflation noises of automatic blood pressure cuffs. He desperately wanted someone to talk to, and there was no one. Not Grandma Anna, and not Luke, who would think him insane. Or Jenna, Luke's girlfriend and Miles's good friend, who had no issues with his being gay, but how did you break it to someone that you had a freakish ability to heal?

He looked over the edge of the nurses' station at Antoine's room. The door was open and the curtain drawn over the glass wall. *There's no one around. And you don't know what the fuck you're doing. You don't even know if it'll work.*

Without thought he was on his feet. Grandma Anna had fought hard with him over his decision to become a doctor. *"You're playing with fire, boy."* His parents hadn't understood her fury, or her willingness to cough up the tuition for music school but not for medical school. She had done her best to isolate the secret. The message had been clear: *"Tell no one."*

He crossed the unit and felt the familiar tingle in his fingers. It was a part of the gift he liked, as it gave his fingers tremendous dexterity and nuance on the violin. It was his own secret, one he never told Grandma, for just as she had his dog taken away when he was six, she would have done the same with Grandpa Henry's violin.

He paused at the entrance to Antoine's room and looked in. *Is he still alive?* He paused and watched and waited, all the while not stopping the tingle, wanting to see what might happen. *Just let it go a little.* Antoine's breath caught and he coughed. The sound was like dry leather cracking apart. The cough blossomed, and some dark liquid dribbled from a corner of his mouth.

The tingle spread up Miles's arms, and his fingers needed to move. *Just a little, see what will happen.* The thing in his belly started to wake. Like a giant snake. *Just a little more.* He moved inside Antoine's room. His eyes met those of the dying man.

"Hey, Doc. Thanks for not ratting me out."

"I'm not a doctor yet."

"Yeah, you are. This shit they're giving me isn't working, is it?" With effort he pulled a tissue from the box on his bed and wiped the blood from his mouth. He inhaled and then stopped, frightened to reignite the cough.

Miles's fingers moved beyond his control; they fluttered as if playing notes on a flute. *Shit!* He thought about trying to stop it, knew he was at the point of no return. He pictured Jasper: *"You can't break a promise."*

"Fuck it," he muttered as his hand crossed the space between them and found Antoine's.

At first Antoine said nothing, too lost in pain, regret, and drugs. "Holy shit, what's happening? Your hand, it's like fire! Your fingers…."

And the thing, the giant snake in Miles's belly, uncoiled and rose through his body. His last thoughts before it all went black were *I will not break a promise.* And then he pictured Grandma Anna and knew he had indeed broken his promise.

CHAPTER 4

Dr. Gerald Stangl, a world-class researcher and tenured professor, thought nothing of long nights at the hospital on the inpatient psych unit. It was a part of his life's work and passion. The same was true for the Stangl men before him, all doctors, scientists, and truth seekers. It was work his son, Calvin, would continue whether he liked it or not. Tonight, like every second Tuesday of the month, was his turn to round on Mercy's thirty-bed inpatient unit for mostly indigent patients with severe mental illness, compounded by out-of-control drug and alcohol use and social and medical problems that ran the gamut from homelessness, arrests, and poverty to AIDS, morbid obesity, and active TB.

As he wandered from room to room, shaking hands with the patients, sitting at their bedsides to hear how they were doing, it was hard not to draw comparisons to his own lavish facility on the shores of Lake Pontchartrain. Well-heeled patients, including numerous celebrities, readily coughed up two grand a day for treatment and respite from lives that to the casual observer appeared blessed but in reality were sink pits of anxiety and depression. And just like the patients here, the rich were no strangers to addiction. The only differences being single-malt whisky versus rotgut, and endless supplies of narcotics from accommodating doctors versus street heroin laced with something bad.

As he left the room of two women—one with bipolar disorder, the other with schizophrenia, and both being treated for alcohol withdrawal—he tapped the screen on his laptop. One more patient to go. *Saving the best for last…. Louis.*

As Gerald entered Louis Drake's private room, he let the familiar shock at seeing the seventy-year-old's face have its effect. "Hi, Louis."

"Doc, they said you were on tonight. You got to let me out of here. It's all a mistake. They think I'm crazy. I'm not, you know. I mean, you know that. Just get me out of here."

Gerald nodded and pulled a chair up to the bed. His gaze took in the lines and planes of Louis's face, like looking at Grandpapa Oskar. "So why did they haul you in tonight?" And like dropping into a soothing tub, Gerald let the man's ramble wash over him.

"It's the dollars. They took them from me. They always do. They know they have power. They say you get your belongings back when you leave, but they're never the right ones. They mess with us that way. They think I don't know. They think I can't tell. It's always changed."

Used to Louis's delusions, Gerald dipped in a toe. "What were the dollars saying?"

Louis's water-blue eyes brightened. "You understand. None of those morons do. That's why if they've got to lock me up, it's got to be on the second Tuesday of the month."

"You know my schedule?"

"It's all written down." Louise raised a hand and pointed to his forehead. "It's all written down. You just have to know how to read the signs."

"And the dollars tell you this?"

"Yeah, the big eye on the top of the pyramid. It's got a lot to say. Eyes are the mirror of the soul, and the pyramids contain the truth of everything that ever has been and everything that ever will be. The eye lets you see that." He dropped his voice to a whisper. "But you got to know how to read the signs."

"You haven't lost me. So what did the dollars tell you? What's so important?" Prior to coming on the unit, Gerald read through Louis's admission packet. This stay was almost a carbon copy of the dozen or two preceding hospitalizations. Louis, who had schizophrenia with a decided mystical twist to his delusions and the prophesying voice in his head, would stop his medications, usually as soon as he left the hospital. Within a day or two, he'd be down on Bourbon Street, panhandling and getting drunk. Social workers from the health department would try to intervene. They'd find him apartments, which he would promptly abandon. They'd bring him sandwiches, which he'd refuse, believing they'd been tainted, or at the very least sprinkled with the psych medications that robbed him of his voices.

Louis rubbed his hands together, eager for this time with the only doctor who ever listened. "Good stuff is coming. Something powerful has landed in town. I can feel it; the eye was spinning. It knows something good, something from deep inside."

"The eye?"

"No, listen, from the pyramid. Deep down it's shooting up. It's walking around. It's here. It's old and it's pure. It's holy."

"You're starting to lose me. What's holy?"

"They took the dollar, otherwise I'd show you. It's in the eye, but it's spelled out in the letters and the numbers. They tell the story. Get me my dollar, and I'll show you."

Gerald smiled, having been down this road before. While Louis, with the face of Grandpapa Oskar, was his favorite patient, spending an hour or more listening to delusional interpretations of what the serial numbers on a dollar bill meant was impractical. Gerald's gaze tracked down to Louis's right foot, which was sticking out from the sheet. "What's going on there? Let me see."

"It's nothing, Doc. It's good to let some blood out. You know that. You guys are supposed to bleed us."

Gerald pulled a pair of gloves from his jacket, turned up the bedside light, and examined an angry wound on Louis's big toe. Pus oozed from a crack in the skin, and around the opening was a thick band of warm, red flesh. He grabbed his phone, flipped to the flashlight app, and looked closer. Angry red streaks tracked over the top of the foot. "This is infected."

The older man winced as Dr. Stangl examined his foot.

"Has anyone seen this, Louis?"

"It's nothing, Doc."

"Louis, you know that I would never hurt you. I'm telling you this is bad, and if we don't get it taken care of, it's going to get a lot worse."

Without waiting for a response, Gerald rang for the nurse. He kept his voice calm, but he was furious. This should not have been missed. Yes, Louis was a frequent-flyer psych patient, but he deserved a thorough admission physical. They hadn't even bothered to look at his feet. *How can they not look at a homeless man's feet?* He clearly had an infection, and considering the amount of time he spent in hospitals, it would be with a resistant strain of staphylococcus, the kind of thing that, if not aggressively treated with intravenous antibiotics, would rapidly spread. Some incompetent fool had nearly cost Louis his foot… or worse.

Gerald's anger coursed like fire in his blood, but as he'd learned to do over a life filled with things to be mad about, no one would ever see. The corners of his mouth stayed fixed with the hint of a smile. He would get this taken care of…. *And someone is going to pay.*

As the male nurse entered, Gerald kept the fury from his voice. He'd deal with the admitting doctor in the morning. He rattled off orders. Louis's foot needed to be immediately cultured and an infectious disease consult initiated, stat.

The nurse looked at Louis's foot and nodded. "Looks like MRSA."

"Yes. As soon as ID gets here, page me. Tell them to go ahead and write for whatever they need, but I'm thinking he's going on IV vancomycin, and probably Bactrim and a cephalosporin."

"Doc, it's nothing. The dollars would have told me."

Gerald looked at Louis dead-on. *Grandpapa.* "Louis, the dollars brought you here. You keep telling me that everything is connected. They brought you to me because it's the second Tuesday of the month. You're where you need to be, and you have got to do everything I tell you so you don't lose your foot. Do you understand?"

"Yeah… and you're starting to get it too. You just have to listen to the dollars. It's fate. We're just walking through the steps."

Gerald eased slightly. At least Louis was agreeing with treatment. Yes, that could change in a heartbeat, but maybe connecting treatment to his delusions—not something he'd ever recommend—would work.

His cell rang. He pulled it out and saw the number for the resident on call. Quite possibly the same one who admitted Louis earlier that evening. The one who let him up to the psych unit without adequate medical clearance. Gerald looked at Louis and nodded. The man might be barking mad, but as he took the call and listened to the resident on the other end, he realized the schizophrenic man wasn't so far off. Gerald was a man driven by fate; things did not happen by accident. His anger toward the hapless resident vanished as he realized much more important events had started to unfold.

"Slow down," he told the harried young woman.

"I just don't feel comfortable evaluating one of the medical students."

"Who is it?" Gerald asked, wondering, hoping, and wishing for a single name to come back.

"Miles Fox."

His smile broadened. "I'll be right down."

Louis looked up at his favorite doc, the only one who listened and really gave a shit. "Good news?"

"Very. I need to go, Louis. We'll get your foot straightened out." He got up and headed toward the door. He looked back at the doppelgänger of his grandpapa. An idea formed. "You know, Louis, I'm the director of Lakeshore."

"Yeah, you're the big cheese, got lots of mice in traps."

"There are some cottages on the grounds that used to house the doctors. If I got one fixed up for you, do you think you'd stay?"

Louis's gaze narrowed. "Like a mouse in a trap? A head case on a ward?"

"No… like a guest."

"I could come and go?"

"If you still have a foot."

"Let me see what the dollars say."

"Good enough." And feeling like he'd done all that could be done, he headed toward the elevators and a meeting with Miles Fox that had been years, decades, and come to think of it, centuries in the making. He thought of Louis's mousetrap and of a dark-haired eight-year-old boy he'd evaluated fifteen years ago. *Not so much a mousetrap… but a hound bringing down the fox.*

CHAPTER 5

MILES AWOKE, or more accurately, floated toward consciousness like a disoriented swimmer who'd lost his sense of up and down. *Where are my clothes?* His throat was parched, his lips dry and starting to split. His head pounded like he had a hangover, but he hadn't been drunk; he'd been on call on the cancer ward. *Why do I feel stoned? Where are my clothes?*

His hands, his whole body, felt leaden as his fingers sought purchase on the thin plastic-covered mattress that crackled beneath his weight. It was worse than the ones on the tenth floor medical student on-call suite, where he should have been. *Where the fuck am I? What am I wearing?* His eyes, caked with sleep, cracked open and met darkness. A single red LED light on the ceiling twinkled on and off at ten-second intervals. Bits of memory mingled with dream fragments. It was after dinner, he'd been finishing his day's scut work on the oncology floor, which had consisted of checking labs and drawing blood, making sure his patients' IVs hadn't become infiltrated. *Where am I? What's happened? What did I do?* Snippets of memory, Antoine dying in bed. His wife… little Jasper. *What have I done?*

With stiff fingers he touched the bare skin of his legs; his boxers were still on. *Where am I?* He felt a dull pain in the meat of his right bicep. There was a lump there, like he'd been given a shot. Loose fabric hung around his chest. There were snaps over his shoulders. *Why am I wearing a johnny coat? What's happened?* Fear shivered through his thoughts. He'd been dreaming of Amos, the puppy he had as a child, one of his earliest memories. A day he'd never forget. It was a dream he'd had before, filled with the freedom of youth and the cruelty of Grandma Anna. She'd made his parents give Amos away.

God, no. His eyes gathered details. *What have I done?* Images formed in the darkness. He was in a small closed room. If he strained he could hear the muffled sounds of the emergency room. With a sickening clarity, he realized where he was—one of the three locked psychiatric observation rooms in the Emergency Department. *They've given me drugs. What did I do?* He thought of Amos and Grandma Anna. *"They will lock you up and kill everyone you love."*

"What have I done?" He was in Antoine's room. He remembered the tingle in his fingers and Jasper pulling on his hand. *"Make my daddy not sick. Promise me!"*

He startled at the sound of a deadbolt. The door opened, and a female voice called out, "He's awake…. Miles, I'm going to turn on a light. It might hurt your eyes."

Blinding light flooded the room. He blinked his eyes shut, and as he cracked them open, fear blossomed into panic. There in the doorway, in a starched white coat with his name embroidered over the pocket, stood Dr. Gerald Stangl.

Miles pushed back into the bed. His eyes met Stangl's.

A half smile played over the doctor's thin lips. His pale blue eyes, broad forehead, and slicked-back blond-shot-through-with-silver hair had changed little from how Miles remembered him. The first words out of his mouth were "Hello, Miles. No surprise finding you here." He nodded toward the nurse. "You can leave us. I know this patient. I evaluated him many years ago…. We're old friends."

Stangl waited for the slide of the deadbolt. He tilted his head, his gaze fixed on Miles. "I have to say that I was surprised they accepted you here. Then again, your intelligence has never been the issue."

"Why am I in here?"

"You don't remember?" Stangl asked. "Interesting."

"No."

"I wonder if that's true. You assaulted two security officers. One of them is still being assessed. A couple broken fingers, a sprained wrist. You were quite the berserker."

"No. That's not possible. I would never do something like that."

"That, Mr. Fox, is not the part in question. There are witnesses." Stangl pulled his tablet from his lab coat pocket, and swiping his finger across the screen, he read, "Memo to chart 10:15 p.m.: A call bell came from the roommate of patient Antoine Dey. Upon going to check, one of the medical students was in bed with Mr. Dey, hugging him. The student was instructed to cease his activities, to which he did not respond. There appeared to be significant inappropriate physical contact between the medical student and Mr. Dey, who has terminal cancer. A second directive was given to the medical student, which was also ignored, at which time this writer called a security code.

"Two security officers attempted to first verbally instruct the medical student to cease his activities, and after multiple attempts, they began to physically remove him from the patient's bed. The medical student responded by holding the patient in a dangerously violent manner. Additional security officers arrived and proceeded to implement a standard five-point takedown procedure with the medical student. He resisted, became assaultive toward security, but was eventually restrained and removed from Mr. Dey's room."

Stangl looked up from the tablet. "Ring any bells, Mr. Fox?"

Fear stayed Miles's tongue. *Let Stangl talk.* No, he didn't remember any of what was in that note. What he did remember, and would never share with Dr. Gerald Stangl, was the unbearable struggle Miles had faced since starting the oncology rotation a month earlier.

As a fifth-year student at the Lister School of Medicine, in an accelerated six-year program in which he'd receive both his bachelor and doctorate degrees, Miles had cleared all the academic hurdles. He believed he'd put to rest all of Grandma Anna's warnings and threats. She'd been violently opposed to his becoming a doctor. He'd known why, and he'd known that the start of year five would be his testing ground, as that was when the doctors in training began their clinical rotations, most of them on the wards of Mercy Memorial Hospital.

Whatever this thing was inside of him, what Grandma Anna called "the gift" and sometimes "the curse," had been mostly quiet through his six weeks of obstetrics and his month of psychiatry, much of which had been spent interviewing patients in the room where he was now held prisoner. He'd started to wonder if Grandma Anna wasn't overreacting. For God's sake, she took away a six-year-old boy's puppy. *"He was hurt, Grandma. I just wanted to help."*

While he knew his grandma loved him, she'd told him horrible stories of men in dark uniforms and doctors in white who had killed her entire family. Every summer of his childhood and most of third grade was spent at her house on Truro, often just him and her. At night she told her stories, and before he could fall into horrible dreams, she'd extract a promise. *"Promise me you will never use the gift. They will lock you up and kill everyone you love. Promise me!"*

"Not talking." Stangl raked his gaze over Miles. "Let's see what happened next." He tapped the screen. "Here we go. Oh my." His smile broadened. "*Security code 1836: Called to Avery 6 for a reported assault on a patient. Arrived on the scene to find patient Antoine Dey being physically restrained and assaulted by Miles Fox, a medical student assigned to Mr. Dey. Mr. Fox was observed to be in Mr. Dey's bed, holding him and touching him in a bizarre and inappropriate manner.*

"*Mr. Fox was repeatedly redirected to cease physical contact with Mr. Dey. He ignored all attempts at de-escalation, and a full security code and takedown was initiated. In the process Mr. Fox became assaultive toward security staff. Nursing requested and received permission to administer emergency tranquilization, which had no apparent effect. A second injection was administered, and Mr. Fox was able to be removed from Mr. Dey's room and was placed in five-point leather restraints. In the course of the takedown, security officers Hall and Bracket were injured and were subsequently sent to the emergency room for evaluation and treatment.*

"*Based on the erratic behavior of Mr. Fox, the attending physician on Avery 6 directed this writer to have Mr. Fox brought to the psychiatric emergency room to be evaluated.*"

Stangl's voice trailed off, and the muscles in his cheeks twitched. "Do you believe in fate, Mr. Fox?"

Miles remained silent. The notes Stangl just read both fascinated and terrified him. He remembered none of it. What ran through his head were Grandma Anna's warnings about the gift. *"Never use it. Once they know, or think they know, you will have no peace. Everything and everyone you love will die. Promise that you will never use the gift."*

And so he promised when he was six, and seven, and every year since. *"No, Grandma, I will not use the gift. No one will know."*

What the fuck have I done?

Stangl's question hung between them.

Do I believe in fate? This isn't random. He looked at Stangl, and his mind skittered over isolated facts. How was it that Dr. Gerald Stangl, a man who'd evaluated Miles in Brookline, Massachusetts, halfway across the country some fifteen years ago, was now standing in a New Orleans emergency room, once again holding Miles's fate? *Do I believe in fate?*

"I don't believe in coincidence," he said.

"Good," Stangl replied.

Miles sensed Stangl's excitement… his triumph. *Do I believe in fate? What the fuck is that supposed to mean? This is no coincidence.*

"Please, let me out of here," he said. "I haven't done anything wrong."

"The evidence argues against that, Miles. You're at least dangerous to others, possibly dangerous to self."

Miles knew the words, the tick boxes used to involuntarily hospitalize a psych patient—dangerous to self or others, gravely disabled as defined by Louisiana statute. "I'm not crazy."

"Said the eight-year-old boy whose parents brought him to see me because he was hearing the voice of a dead great-grandfather he'd never met. No, not crazy at all. I'll say now what I told your parents then. You have schizophrenia, Miles. You can't differentiate between fantasy and reality. What's more, your delusions make you not just crazy… but dangerous."

Miles felt the walls press in. "Why are you here?"

Everything about this was wrong. *How is this possible?* He knew Stangl was a professor in the department of psychiatry, a fact he'd learned as a first-year medical student when he'd been shocked to see Stangl walk into the lecture hall of his Introduction to Psychiatry course. He'd slipped out, not wanting to risk being recognized by a man who'd attempted to strong-arm his parents into locking him up when he was eight.

It had freaked him out and led him to search the Internet. Stangl had joined the university the same year Miles enrolled. He was the medical director of Lakeshore, a large psychiatric facility outside the city. He was the lead investigator in several NIMH grant-funded projects, and was also associated with Kruft Pharmaceuticals, a German-based multinational corporation. His Internet search had led to feature articles that talked of Stangl's accomplishments, the millions of dollars in grant funding, and big pharma research money he brought into his facility and into the university.

"I'm here to write the commitment paper, Miles. Something I should have done years ago."

"No! Please, don't. You can't."

"They'll lock you up."

Stangl lowered his voice. "It's done, Miles. Resign yourself to it, and if you know what's smart, you'll do as you're told."

"Let me call my family. You've got to let me do that."

"You're too distraught."

"Please, let me call my family." Desperation mingled with the dangerous pull of helplessness. *I have to get out of here.*

Stangl nodded, his expression almost sympathetic. He slipped the tablet back into his lab coat pocket. "You'll be transferred in the morning."

"What? Where? What are you talking about?"

"To Lakeshore." Stangl stood by the door.

"Where you're the medical director."

"Yes. I'll be your doctor, Miles." He swiped his electronic key card against the handle.

"Please, let me call my family. This isn't right. This isn't right!" He rose from the bed. He saw Stangl's hand on the door. *It's open.* He sprang off the bed, but Stangl was fast and beat him through the door.

Miles grabbed the door's edge and dug in with his feet and legs. He pulled back, desperate to not let it lock again.

The older man braced his weight against the door and shouted, "Nurse! Call security! Now! He's trying to go AWOL!"

An aide rushed to Stangl's assistance, and together they shut the door and slid the bolt home.

Shit! Helpless, Miles watched through the tiny window as the male nurse—Bob something, who Miles knew from his rotation last month— drew up a syringe. He knew it contained a combination of a powerful tranquilizer and a sedative. How many times had he been on the opposite side of this situation? He saw how this looked, all of it feeding into Stangl's assertions about Miles's mental state. His pulse raced. *I have to get out of here.* There was more at play than what was on the surface. Grandma Anna had been right all along, and now he'd been stupid, and…. *"They'll lock you up. They'll kill everyone you love."*

Uniformed guards crowded into the ER psych unit, all of them focused on Miles. The nurse nodded, and as a single unit, five security guards, with Stangl watching from behind the Plexiglas nurses' station, entered his room. The leader looked at Miles dead-on, and his tone was firm but kind. "We can do this the easy way or the hard way. Either you let the nurse give you some medication that will help you calm down, or we'll be forced to put you back into restraints. The choice is yours."

"I need to call my family," Miles said, trying to hide his panic. "Please, just let me call my family."

The guard sounded sympathetic. "I'm sorry, but not right now. The doctor said no telephone while you're this upset. Now will you let the nurse give you the shot? Or do we need to put you in restraints?"

Miles saw no escape and no choice. "Go ahead. I won't fight." He knew if he resisted, not only would they tie him down, but they'd also increase the dosage. At least for now, it was best to give in.

He felt the cool swab of alcohol and then the stab and pressure as the nurse injected the knockout shot into his already sore upper arm. "You should get back into bed," Nurse Bob directed. "This will make you fall asleep."

Miles did as he was told. He sank onto the stiff mattress and pulled his knees to his chest. He watched as the guards and Nurse Bob left his tiny room, shutting the door behind them. He heard the bolt and felt despair and the first calming effects of the medication. He struggled to make sense of his situation, of Stangl's presence, and his question: *"Do you believe in fate?"*

But as the drugs pulled him down, other emotions and random memories came into play. *"Amos was hurt, Grandma. I knew I could make him better."*

He could see her eyes, bright and green like his, the hard line of her mouth. His cheek throbbed where she'd struck him as tears spilled down his face. *"You must never use the gift."* Her words were like a whip. *"Promise that you will never use the gift."* Her fingers like talons on his tiny shoulders, her eyes boring into his. *"Promise."*

"I promise, Grandma."

"And when you see the man in your dreams and he asks you to go into the lake?"

"I won't go. I promise. I won't go into the lake."

Sinking back with his bare feet dangling off the bed and his head cradled where the walls formed a corner, he slipped into unconsciousness.

The dream started where he knew it would, at the edge of a forest in front of a deep crystal lake. He stared across its surface. Far in the distance, a volcanic mountain rose from its depths, but his attention was trained on the water. Like seals off the shore of Cape Cod, dark-haired heads bobbed to the surface. The one closest to him had a name—Tomas. He rose from the depths dressed in a loose shirt and britches that tied with a string around his waist. His long black hair hung loose around his shoulders, and he fixed his green eyes on Miles.

"So, my boy. Today you broke a promise to my sweet Anya. Care to make it two? The lake awaits; it always has. Come in—the water is warm, your family is here, and the choice is yours."

Chapter 6

GERALD LEARNED at a young age to school his emotions. The smile on his face was both mask and armor. Like an actor he colored his expression with overtones of compassion as he gave instructions to Nurse Bob and completed the documentation that would ensure an efficient transfer of Miles Fox to Lakeshore.

"I'd evaluated him when he was a child. Youngest case of paranoid schizophrenia I've ever seen." He glanced at the monitor that showed Miles passed out and slumped against the wall. It was a thrill to see his quarry up close, the unmistakable green eyes, and even better—and what made it hard to contain his excitement—actual proof the boy carried the grail gene. There were witnesses and a dying man who was no longer dying. His smile broadened. *At least not from cancer.*

Nurse Bob shook his head. "I did not see that coming. I was working with him just a few weeks ago. He seemed normal. Funny. Smart…."

"That's the thing about paranoid schizophrenia, and it's a shame they left it out of the DSM-5, as the label is both descriptive and prognostic. They can be quite high functioning, but the delusions persist. The smart ones, like Mr. Fox, have some awareness that they need to keep aspects to themselves. It doesn't mean they have insight, just that they've learned others will challenge them and get in their way. So they hide it. Once you get into cases with IQs above one twenty, like Miles Fox, it's best to be worried."

"What do you think he was doing with that patient?" Bob asked.

"No idea, at least not yet. I'm certain it has to do with a deep-set delusion."

"I've been doing this for years," Bob offered, not used to having a bigwig psychiatrist like Dr. Stangl spend time in the emergency room in the early a.m. but glad for the company and this reflective calm after Fox's earlier fireworks. "Sometimes you just never know. So when he was a kid, what brought him in?"

"The same stuff that's going on now," Gerald offered like a fisherman chumming the water. "He heard voices. As I recall, one of them was his dead great-grandfather, whom he'd never met, but it was specific and quite fixed. He'd been referred by his school psychologist. His family was reluctant to have him evaluated, and they didn't like my findings or the recommendation that he be put in a residential facility. They withdrew him from treatment. It went so far that I had to report them to the Department of Children and Families. Denying him treatment was parental neglect. And now here we are. The part I find most alarming is that some moron, or cast of morons, saw fit to admit him to medical school. Miles Fox should be nowhere near patients." *But I was right; I was right all along. The wait, the caution…. It was all worth it.*

"I'm sure you're right," Bob said, clearly not sure at all. "He seemed okay when he was down here."

Gerald nodded. "Good, so hopefully we caught things before anything really bad happened."

"You saying he's dangerous?"

He paused and looked from the monitor to Bob. "When he was a child, the reason I felt so strongly that he needed residential placement had nothing to do with hearing voices. It had everything to do with violent and paranoid delusions. He believed there were conspiracies directed against his family."

"Really? In my experience that doesn't end well."

"Exactly. Because the delusion is real to him, he's faced with one of two choices: run away or turn and fight. And even as an eight-year-old boy, Mr. Fox was a fighter. He was obsessed with ninjas and martial arts, but once you scratched below that, it went deeper. Eight-year-old boys should not have encyclopedic knowledge of semiautomatic weapons and how to make explosives from things obtained at the local hardware store."

"No shit! Excuse me…."

"It's fine, but you can see why we must take this seriously. Whatever happened upstairs with Mr. Fox and that patient is the tip of a large and dangerous iceberg. So…." Gerald pushed up from the chair. He glanced from Bob to the monitor. "Everything should be set for an early-morning transfer. If there are any hitches, Bob, I've left my cell number. Do not hesitate to call."

He paused and grabbed the handset off the table. "Were you here when they admitted Louis Drake?"

"No, he'd already been sent up when I got here. Why?"

Gerald shook his head and dialed the unit. "Some moron admitted him without adequate medical clearance."

"What's wrong with him?"

He put a finger to his lips as the nurse upstairs picked up. "It's Gerald Stangl. I wanted to see if the ID fellow rounded on Louis yet." He listened and nodded. "Good…. And you can manage the IV antibiotics on the unit? … Excellent. Thank you." He hung up and looked at Nurse Bob.

"What's wrong with Louis?"

"Cellulitis on his foot, probably MRSA, and if he hadn't come in today, he'd be on his way to losing his foot… or worse."

"And they didn't catch it?"

"No, and it's the kind of sloppy care that makes me furious."

"Welcome to my world," Bob said. "Just getting the ER docs back here for medical clearance is a huge pain in the butt. They don't want to come, and at best they wave their stethoscope over our guys, pronounce them fit to be admitted, and that's the end of it. Two minutes, tops… and that's including the documentation."

Gerald pulled out his tablet and logged on to Louis Drake's chart. He flipped through the admission work, noting the psychiatric resident—Lauren Flynn—who'd handled the admission, and the ER doc—Christopher Blaise—who'd done the preadmission physical. He clicked on the line drawings of a man's body, front and back, where abnormalities, old scars, wounds, and so forth were supposed to be noted. The obviously lazy and/or incompetent Dr. Blaise had checked the box for WNL—within normal limits. "How do you not examine a seventy-one-year-old homeless man's feet?"

"I know," Bob said. "But what can you do?"

Gerald powered off his tablet and slid it back into his pocket. "Quite a lot, actually. But that can wait for the morning. You have everything you need for Miles?"

"Yup, we're good. If our boy acts up again, we know what to do."

"Excellent. You've been a big help, Bob. Thank you."

It was 1:00 a.m. when Gerald drove his black BMW through the electronic gates that opened onto the grounds of Lakeshore Hospital. Spread over a two-hundred-acre campus and sited on a peninsula that jutted into the now tranquil waters of Lake Pontchartrain, it was a facility with history. Founded in 1878 as the Louisiana Hospital for the Insane, it had been part of the moral treatment, which believed hard work and fresh air were of benefit to those suffering from psychiatric maladies. From there it evolved into one of the state's major lunatic asylums, with a surgical suite for lobotomies and another where ice baths and insulin shock therapy were routinely administered.

By the 1950s it housed over four thousand patients before lawsuits in the '60s, '70s, and '80s kicked in, alleging the residents were deprived of due process and their civil liberties. The phrase "least restrictive setting" became the key that unlocked the doors and emptied the wards. Now homeless, these thousands flooded the streets of New Orleans. Many of them, like Louis Drake, had spent decades at Lakeshore.

By the '90s the population shrank to under two hundred before the state decided it was too expensive to maintain, and in 2000 it transferred the remaining long-term patients to other facilities and closed the doors.

After over a century of chemical dumping on the grounds, and with crumbling buildings riddled with asbestos-wrapped pipes and insulation, the property became a white elephant on the state's ledger. So when Harmony Health Options (HHO), a for-profit chain of psychiatric hospitals and a subsidiary of Kruft Pharmaceuticals, offered to take it off their hands, the state quickly wrote up a hundred-year lease with an in-perpetuity clause.

In 2003 Lakeshore reopened with single-occupancy rooms and specialized chemical dependence and mental health programs for the wealthy and well insured. At two thousand dollars a day, one could enjoy intensive psychotherapy, trauma-informed yoga, Pilates, mindfulness seminars, an invigorating dip in the Olympic-size pool, circuit training, and peaceful strolls along the lake and through the mangrove swamp.

Finally in 2010 Dr. Gerald Stangl, Kruft's preeminent neuropsychiatric researcher, moved from a similar hospital in Boston with his son, Calvin, and became Lakeshore's medical director. In the process Lakeshore became a nationally recognized research facility specializing in cutting-edge neuroimaging and Stangl's particular area of expertise—epigenetic medicine, the study of what caused particular genes to be turned on or off.

"Do you believe in fate, Mr. Fox?" he said aloud as he drove toward his glittering and anomalous steel-and-glass research pavilion. Not one to give in to emotions, Gerald was hard-pressed to contain his excitement. *Finally, it's finally happening. He is the one… and I have proof.*

But time was of the essence, and getting Miles Fox out of Mercy Memorial and into Lakeshore couldn't happen fast enough. Yet to seem overeager could incite suspicion. Too much had gone into this moment. Too much sacrifice.

"Every great endeavor carries risk." It was something Grandpapa Oskar would say, his image and that of his father Frederick never far from mind, like shades that walked beside him. The pain of losing them was still so close… and so horrifying.

Voices of hard-faced guards and wardens echoed in his brain. *"You made them watch. Now your son shall watch."* And he had, for eternity. His father and grandpapa, the moment when they dropped through the trapdoor, the nooses around their neck. Father with his muscular build and extra weight died quickly, his neck broken as the rope snapped taut.

But not Grandpapa, who dangled and swung, dark spots on his striped prison trousers as he lost bladder and bowel control. It was an eternity, Father still and dead, and Grandpapa, who would not die… the stains getting larger, the panic on his face, his eyes bulging as he struggled for life.

The memories were never far, and Gerald pushed them away as he drove around the back of the six-story rhomboidal building. The moon shimmered on its mirrored surface. *What would they have thought of this?*

He pressed the remote, and one of three bay doors rose, revealing a cavernous loading dock and warehouse. The headlights caught his son, Calvin, waiting for his return. The boy, nearly a man, seemed eager and tentative, like a child wanting to see what his father brought home but uncertain if he'd like it.

As Gerald pulled in, Calvin approached.

"Is there proof?" the seventeen-year-old asked.

"Yes," Gerald replied, taking stock of his handsome son: just shy of six feet, with straight blond hair and pale blue eyes like his and the nurse he'd selected to bear him.

"There's no point if we're not sure," Calvin added. "This would all have been for nothing if he doesn't have it. Can you imagine, Father? All these years, all this planning. We're still not certain. We don't have proof."

Gerald felt annoyance. *How dare he question me?* Increasingly Calvin's attitude had changed. Something had happened to the docile child who'd followed his every word, who drank at the font of wisdom that flowed through the millennia. Getting out of the car, he weighed the boy's words. Not blatantly insubordinate, his rebellion was in the tone and the delivery.

"Come," he said, wondering if this was part of being the father of a teenager, one who'd raised Calvin free from the paralyzing nightmares that had haunted his own childhood and still followed him.

"There's no point in taking him if we don't have proof," Calvin said as he trailed his father. "He seems pretty normal."

Gerald wondered at his son's demeanor. Was he deliberately trying to anger him?

He pulled his key card from his breast pocket. Once inside they passed down a long corridor with a honed marble floor. He placed the pads of his fingers onto the scanner, and the door clicked open, revealing a small landing and staircase.

Down they went into a portion of the building that was for their eyes only. Built over the footprint of a prior structure—a home for shell-shocked WWII veterans—the Stangl Research Pavilion had risen like a phoenix from the ashes, or more accurately a bomb-shelter-like two-story foundation sunk into the Louisiana mud and clay. While the state had been eager to unload the toxic site, once done, they'd expressed great concern over the environmental impact of any new construction. The proximity to Lake Pontchartrain and its wetlands had mired Gerald's plans for his research facility in red tape, along with avaricious land inspectors and wetlands commissioners who simply could not sign off on the environmental impact.

End of the day, despite the aggravation and the bribes, Gerald could not have anticipated the serendipity, the unanticipated treasure of his building's original foundation. While the upper floors of the old structure were worthless and beyond salvage, what lay beneath was a marvel of postwar enthusiasm and the ingenuity of the Army Corp of Engineers. The cement was enriched with epoxy to prevent cracks and to seal out the moisture. It had been poured over interlocking steel plates and girders to construct walls thick enough to withstand a nuclear attack. The pavilion's architect had wanted to demolish the foundation and start from scratch. Gerald had seen the folly of such a plan.

"It stays," he'd said. *Our future is built upon our past.*

Gerald looked at Calvin. "Let us find our proof."

Motion-detector lights switched on as they entered the upper basement, which contained an unused high-security two-bed patient ward with walls constructed of a clear, unbreakable polymer, facing an expansive, gleaming-white nurses' station.

Change. Behind the nurses' station, they went into a small room that contained medical supplies and a shelved wall of medications tidily arranged and labeled.

Gerald found a spot halfway up the side of the shelving with his hand and pressed in. The wall shifted. It swung on concealed hinges into the room, revealing the stairs to the subbasement.

In contrast to the stark white and translucent modernism above, the lower level consisted of a long hall with polished steel panels. At the far end was a high-security door that connected the building to a series of tunnels, most of which had long ago crumbled under the weight and wet of the swamp. Off the corridor were four locked steel doors and the elevator.

Gerald placed his fingers into a reader, and a door opened into a dimly lit cement-floored room. The furniture was old and dark, much of it culled from the unused buildings on the hospital grounds.

Calvin walked into the room his father used as an office and booted up the computer. Using his father's Mercy Memorial ID code and password, he logged in to the hospital's medical records. "What's the patient's name?" he asked.

"Antoine Dey."

Calvin pulled up the record of the forty-two-year-old plumber who was admitted two weeks earlier. He glanced at the diagnosis: stage-four hepatocellular carcinoma. He clicked the tab for radiology and imaging. He scrolled to the chest and abdominal X-rays obtained barely an hour ago. He read the indication for the early morning procedures.

Patient reports feeling something strange in his chest and stomach. From there he pulled up the posterior/anterior and lateral images and the flat plates of the abdomen.

Gerald walked behind his son. He fixed his eyes on the screen, his expression tense. *Yes*, he thought, *X-rays are primitive.* As he took in the data, his excitement grew. *And I wasn't wrong.*

"They'll order a CAT scan, or more likely a full-body MRI, in the morning. This is it. This is really it!" His jaw hung slack. *It's real, it's real. Finally.*

There was no denying what glowed in living black and white, or rather, what didn't glow before him in black and white and gray. *It's all real.* Gerald felt euphoric, as if the weight of a lifetime had been lifted from his back. All the doubts he could never quell. What if all the legends and sacrifices had been about chasing a fairy tale? *Papa... Grandpapa*, their bodies forever hanging in his dreams; he didn't want to see the dark spots yet always did. *You did not die in vain. I will finish this. I will fulfill our destiny.*

Silently Calvin tabbed to Antoine Dey's prior chest X-rays and pulled them up for comparison. As the images passed before them, Gerald marveled at the miraculous. *It's real!* The gift that passed in the blood. The thing that had obsessed his grandpapa and father and countless generations before them. Here was scientific proof. The gift was not a myth. Antoine Dey's tumors were gone. Gerald's eyes welled with tears, the first he'd allowed himself in decades. Papa's final words were never far: *"You will not cry. You will show no emotion. You are my son, and you are strong."*

"So it *is* real," Calvin stated.

"Of course." He looked at his son's face reflected in the monitor. "You are surprised?" Gerald asked as annoyance crept over his joy.

Calvin looked from the screen back at his father. He bit the inside of his lip. He sensed Father's temper, never far from the surface. *Don't do it. Keep your mouth shut.* Sometimes it was all he could do to not scream, to not go running from the lunatic asylum they called home. "Father, my entire life I have been fed a diet of fantasy. Yes, I understand we're part of an important lineage that goes back, possibly before the start of the historical record."

Calvin wheeled his chair away from the computer, creating a distance from Father. This was not a discussion to have within arm's reach.

"But with all of that… where's the proof? I mean, this is something, at least, but…." He closed his eyes. *Don't say it, don't say it.* "It's not much. It's a hospital, for God's sake. X-rays get switched all the time. This is not a lot to go on."

Father and son faced off in the darkened room. Calvin tried not to recoil from the slap he knew would land hard and fast across his cheek. It didn't come. *Don't let him see your fear. He hates weakness. He hates your weakness.*

Gerald stared at his son. A tight smile on his lips, he nodded. *You can't blame the boy. You've had doubts your entire life. This is the first real proof.* His excitement resurfaced. "More proof is coming, Calvin. And we'll be ready. Come."

Calvin would rather have stayed put and engaged in an activity that gave him a tiny relief from the prison of his life. Left to his own devices, he'd hack into the hospital's security cameras and pop in on the lives of the doctors, nurses, the aides, the busy people, mostly of color, in the kitchen and laundry.

And he most certainly would spend time spying on the psychiatric emergency room, where the handsome Miles Fox lay huddled in bed. While Father was out, he'd zoomed in on the man's even features, his high brow, Slavic jaw, and his strong cleft chin. He'd pulled back and scanned the bare flesh of his runner's legs dusted in fine black hair that looked soft as silk. He'd felt the stirrings of arousal.

What would Father say if he knew Calvin harbored a crush on the man Father had pursued from Boston to New Orleans? *He's so handsome.* Calvin played treasured memories of being in the anatomy lab around Miles and all his older friends. Father, as a full professor, had made it possible for the then sixteen-year-old homeschooled Calvin to audit classes with the medical students. Each time Miles spoke to Calvin, or even just looked his way and smiled… *with those eyes, those beautiful eyes….*

"Come," Father repeated.

"Coming." Keeping at least an arm's distance away, he trailed Father into an adjacent room. He knew what was coming, and after seventeen years, he still had to brace himself.

"What is it that mankind most desires?" Gerald asked, as if lecturing a group of medical students.

It wasn't what Calvin expected, and he blurted out his answer before he could filter it. "Love."

Gerald, not prone to humor, snorted.

The sound startled Calvin. He stared at Father, wondering when exactly he went from following the man like an eager puppy, to fearing him, to this new and dangerous mix of emotions. *When did you start to hate him? Why is he laughing?* Father's laughter hurt worse than the expected slap. *He's making fun of me.*

"I sometimes forget you're seventeen. So does she have a name?"

A sliver of fear cut through Calvin. This was dangerous; best to say nothing.

"Why, son, you're blushing. But no, love, despite centuries of ridiculous poetry and songs, is not the answer. It never was. Try again."

Calvin despised and dreaded these grillings, which continued until he produced the answer Father wanted or failed so miserably they ended with a backhanded blow across his face. "Power?"

"Are you even trying, son? One last chance."

Calvin felt Father's approach. He steeled himself and thought, *One day this will be over. One day I will be through with this man.*

And then it came to him. What all of this was about. He—Calvin—was at best a dependable servant to the man's obsession. An Igor to his Dr. Frankenstein, a sniveling Renfield to his Dracula, and he was sick of it. He raised his chin and met Father's pale eyes. He tried to read his expression in the dimly lit room, but it was pointless.

"To conquer death," Calvin spat out, and while he felt the impulse to back away from the expected strike, he held steady, his eyes not wavering from Father's. "Immortality."

Gerald gave a half smile. "Good." He stepped into the distance between them.

Calvin flinched. He caught Father lifting his right hand up and tried to keep his head steady. *I'm sick of this. I want him dead. I want him dead. I want him dead.*

The slap never came. Father's open palm landed on Calvin's right shoulder, and he tapped it gently once, twice, and then a third time, which ended with a gentle squeeze before Father removed it. "Excellent! Calvin, we are heading into virgin territory. The thing… the grail… it is within our grasp."

Calvin felt at sea. The compliment and the pat on the shoulder—*what the hell is this?* Something loosened in his chest. Father was smiling, and not with his usual masklike expression. This was different; there was a liveliness in his voice.

"All the pieces have been there, boy. You just needed to string them together. It's not something I could do for you. Come."

Calvin saw the hand as it came for him. He braced for it. And again there was no strike. Father rested his hand on his shoulder. "Come, let's connect the dots and get ready for the new ones."

"Yes, Father," he said, and he let himself be led across the chill room to something far worse than a slap across the face.

Gerald released his hold on Calvin's shoulder and removed a key ring from his pocket. He selected an iron skeleton and unlocked the first section of a floor-to-ceiling oak cabinet. "Give us some light, Calvin."

Calvin smelled the cabinet's contents before seeing them: musk, damp, with traces of menthol and spearmint. He would have nightmares for days to come. It always came after a visit to Father's private museum. He switched on a gooseneck surgical lamp. It flooded the surface of a broad stainless-steel table they had retrieved, along with three others, from what was once a bustling shock-therapy suite.

He glanced up as Father hoisted the first of the large sealed glass specimen jars from the cabinet. Childhood memories assailed him of a similar cabinet in the basement of their Massachusetts home, that one also on the grounds of an old converted asylum owned by the Kruft Corporation. He shut his eyes, not wanting to see what floated inside the jars of spearmint, wintergreen, menthol, and cinnamon-scented embalming fluids.

"Son." Father's tone was encouraging. "It's only flesh. There's nothing to fear. Open your eyes."

Calvin obeyed and met the star of his own after-hours horror show. There, floating since it left the company of its body seventy years ago, was a man's head. Through the thick, slightly yellow glass, the skin was sallow. Its green eyes, like a child's marbles, stared back at him. As a little boy, Calvin named this one Tom. He guessed the man's age to be around thirty to thirty-five. His hair was jet black, and for someone who—according to Father's stories—had been alive and awake when surgeons separated his head from his body, his expression was serene.

"See," Father said, "nothing to be afraid of. Help me with the others."

It was a familiar ritual, and if Calvin had any friends, he would have made a joke about this just being one of the core courses at Hitler High—Heads in a Jar 101. Going to the cabinet, he selected one of the more intact ones, this one a middle-aged woman he'd named Mary, whose dark hair had been shorn to her scalp. The others, those who had been skillfully dissected in an attempt to discern the workings of these supposedly special green-eyed Gypsies, were the worst. When the nightmares came, and they most certainly would, it was the skulls with eyeballs floating free from their sockets, tethered by carefully dissected optic nerves like balloons on strings, that would be the worst. They'd ride on dark horses, chasing him from one hellish dreamscape to the next. He'd awake exhausted, his heart pounding to the rhythm of demon hooves.

Father and he retrieved the six stars of his nightmares from the cabinet, with Tom on the right, Mary next to him, and four others in various stages of dissection, ending with one he'd called Jack, a bare skull with an intact brain and green eyes floating off to the sides. There were other smaller specimens left in the cabinet, mostly eyeballs, brains, and assorted body parts that had been hastily harvested. Most still bore paper seals with swastikas and date stamps from 1943 to 1945. Calvin averted his eyes from Jack and let his gaze rest on Tom, with eyes like those of Miles Fox.

Before he could filter his tongue, Calvin asked, "If they knew they were losing the war, why did they kill them? What was the point?"

Gerald picked up a stainless-steel probe and tapped the glass of Jack's jar to get his son's attention. Using it as a pointer, he traced the length of the bare optic nerve from eyeball to brain. "Tell me what you know about the healing gift."

Calvin swallowed. *Here it comes.* "It doesn't appear in every generation. Or if it does, perhaps it's not expressed."

"Good. Keep going."

"It only goes with the green eyes. So whatever genetic linkages there might be, it's likely coding on the same genes as the ones for eye color. And if that assumption is accurate, it's probably closely linked as well."

"Yes, reasonable, albeit an untested hypotheses. Continue."

Calvin's gut clenched. "It can go to either sex."

"Obviously, but what else, son?"

Calvin thought back to Antoine Dey's X-rays. Father clearly took them at face value; he was less convinced. Still, if in fact the man's cancer had just been cured by the beautiful man locked up in the emergency room, then something outside the realm of known science was at play.

Unbidden he grabbed Father's key ring off the table, walked to the cabinets, and unlocked one that was retrofitted with humidity control. It was filled with parchment and vellum scrolls and leather-bound manuscripts. He selected an ancient oversized volume with a hand-tooled cover and spine and placed it on the table far from the heads in jars.

Gerald chuckled. "So on the one hand, you're my doubting Thomas, and on the other, you're reaching for the most extreme possibility, the Zosimus legend."

Calvin glanced at Father. He was smiling, and it seemed genuine. It was confusing, but something like hope lightened in his gut. He smiled back. "Maybe it is true."

Gerald's smile brightened further. He chuckled. "Love again. My work is finally starting. So yes, let's talk about Zosimus, because if anything in here is a fairy tale, it's got to be that. The man who stole the Gypsy gift and lived for over a thousand years. For that matter, if it were true, he might still be alive."

Emboldened by Father's mood, Calvin opened the text and scanned the tidy Greek letters and carefully drawn diagrams. "This is the only known account of such a thing happening."

"Yes." Gerald came to his son's side. He reached for the lamp and twisted the neck for better illumination.

Entranced by the adventures of its purported author and fascinated by the illustrations, Calvin had spent endless hours with this book. One section in particular at the center of the book outlined the configuration of the ritual he had performed with his beloved Marta. The ritual—part blood magic and part science—was the one he claimed split the gift in two. He did not take the gift from her, as Father and all the endless others before him had attempted, but instead the gift was shared, not stolen… shared.

The final entry was made in 1212, when Zosimus prepared to join a crusade. "I return to the land of my ancestors, to Egypt. I will be separated from Marta, from the other half of my soul. But as earth, air, water, and fire are forever joined, so too we shall come together. We shall go on. Love is the fifth element, the element of human magic." Calvin loved this book, and even if it turned out to be a hoax, it had filled his boyhood with tales of adventure, heroism, and… true love. "I wonder why he left her?"

"His woman?"

"Yes, Marta. If the legend is real, she's the one who gave him the gift." Before he could stop himself, he added, "She did it for love." He recoiled as Father's hand landed on the back of his head. He flinched as Father touched his hair with his strong fingers.

Gerald grunted. "You still think it's about love. Son, that's called being seventeen. Turn to the configuration."

Calvin opened to the book's center page, his absolute favorite, and spread the manuscript flat. Before them lay a carefully rendered drawing surrounded by tidy Coptic and Greek letters and the occasional hieroglyph, as though neither of the other languages had words for what needed to be said. It was the only place in the manuscript where color embellishments and gold and silver leaf had been added. It showed a man with tightly curled hair and a pointed, braided beard lying flat on a table next to a woman with elaborately coiffed black hair and vivid green eyes outlined in kohl. They were dressed in pleated white skirts, both bare breasted. Their hands were joined, and blood spurted from the man's wrists, the droplets landing into five now tarnished silver goblets. These were arranged at the four corners, with the fifth resting on the woman's navel. Beneath the vessels were hieroglyphs for earth, air, water, fire, and love. Green flames shot out of the chalices and created a hovering dome over the central figures.

With a finger Calvin touched the page where the man's and woman's hands were joined. "He loved her."

"It's a trap, my boy. Zosimus was a great scientist. Like us, he sought truth. If there's any of that in this book, it has more to do with his knowledge and skill as a chemist than any fanciful romance. It's what was in those chalices, it's what was in her, and somehow, if this is truth, he's been the only one to get it right." Gerald looked from the book to the row of heads. "You asked why they killed them? I've wondered the same."

Still high on the excitement of Antoine Dey's X-rays, Gerald unlocked a third cabinet, revealing a collection of single-malt Scotch. He poured generous shots and handed one to Calvin, and then pulled out a steel chair and sat.

He raised his glass. "Sit. Drink."

Calvin did as instructed, keeping a distance between him, the heads, and Father. This early a.m. bonding was confusing. He sipped the amber liquid. *He's never given me a drink before.* It burned his tongue and filled his senses with confusing scents, peat and smoke, not unpleasant.

"I was twelve, younger than you, when I lost my father and grandpapa." Gerald swirled the Scotch and sipped. "I know you've had a strange life, and it's not always been easy. When you were little, you always wondered why you had no mommy. Of course you did, but she was merely a means to an end. I needed an heir. I needed you."

The burning liquor caught in Calvin's throat. *What is he doing? Is he going to tell me? Does she exist? Is she alive? Do I have a mother? Who is she?*

"I'm sure you'd like to know who she was. A nurse back in Boston. She was well compensated for the use of her genetics and her womb. As I recall she was eager to pay off her school loans, with enough left for a down payment on a condo and I believe a Volkswagen diesel. A practical woman, and one whom, I've been pleased to note, has never reneged on the agreement. You are mine and only mine."

Calvin could not believe what had just been said. *I have a mother, she's a nurse, and she is probably alive.* His eyes darted across the heads. His gaze landed briefly on Mary. *Had she been a mother?*

"Like you," Gerald continued, "I never knew my mother. It's our way. And like you, I am an only child, an only son." He chuckled. "We need the heir, but not the spare."

That much Calvin knew, but so much about Father's background was clouded and not something to be discussed. Emboldened by Scotch, he found his tongue. "What happened to your father?"

Gerald swigged his drink and gestured across the row of heads. "They did. You asked why they killed them all. I never got a straight answer, and this is what I think. They knew it was over, the camps would be liberated, and they had to escape. But we're talking about a life's work. Grandpapa, your great-grandfather—Oskar Stangl—he was a brilliant man, a doctor who'd written important treatises on genetics.

"He was not a Nazi, although his work appealed to Hitler. We are a part of something much older. Our work stands upon his, as his was built on the generations of Stangl men before him. He was a pioneer, and like us, he was on a quest for the single most important truth. The one thing that mankind has hungered for since the start of time—immortality.

"Can you imagine how it must have felt to be so close to the realization of not just your life's work, but the ambition and the striving of countless generations of your ancestors, to have it within your grasp? And then to see it slip away as the Americans and Russians flooded the borders? I can feel what they must have felt.

"They had the green-eyed Gypsies; they had witnessed what they could do. They had proof. If their journals are to be believed, far more than what we have with Mr. Dey's X-rays. In hindsight it's pathetic and speaks to how inadequate their tools were. I believe they killed them in desperation. They were out of time, and they needed to know. So they opened them up to look inside."

Calvin looked down the row from Tom, to Mary, to eyeball-floating Jack, and then to Father, who had refilled his glass. "Yes, Father. I think you're right…. But they didn't find their answers. All they found was death."

CHAPTER 7

THIS ISN'T a dream; it has to be a dream. Miles felt and heard the unpaved road beneath the wooden wheels of the caravan. Beside him sat Tomas, a man he'd feared and avoided his entire life, and yet outside of dreams, they'd never met. "This isn't possible. You can't be real," Miles said aloud.

"And yet here we are… finally," Tomas, the revenant of Miles's great-grandfather, said. He held a rolled whip, which he never used on the matched pair of powerful black mares. "What made you finally take the plunge?"

Miles turned to study Tomas, having read somewhere if you looked at something directly in a dream, it would go away. He took in the man's green eyes with fine lines at the corners. His hair was raven's-wing black and full, and like Miles's, it grew back from his scalp in a thick widow's peak. But it was the mustache that held his interest. Like the whip in his hand, each side ended in a carefully rolled and waxed scroll. Miles judged his age to be midthirties. His clothes were homemade and simple: a loose linen shirt tucked into dark drawstring pants. His boots looked like Army-Navy surplus, with hard rubber soles and the top three grommets on each side unlaced.

"I don't know," Miles said. "Desperation, fear, realizing that maybe everything Grandma Anna warned me about is real, and that maybe her solution to things isn't working."

Tomas nodded. There was merriment in his eyes and his voice. "So maybe now you don't follow my Anya's advice to the letter… yes?"

"There is that," Miles admitted. "Yes, apparently I used the gift. Though most of it is a blur."

"Who was it?"

"So you can't see?" Miles asked, his scientist's mind scrambling to make sense of the nonsensical.

"I see fine," Tomas quipped. "Why, Great-Grandfather, what big green eyes you have."

"I'm not Red Riding Hood," Miles replied. "Outside of here… you can't see outside of here? That's what I'm wondering. Can you see me in…? How do you even refer to the real world?"

"This is my home, and it is real. How do you know the dimension in which you'll wake isn't the illusion? Or best still, try this on." He pulled on the reins, and the team stopped in a sun-filled clearing. "Both are equally real." He chuckled and snapped the whip above the horses' heads. "And equally false." The caravan lurched forward.

"You're not much for straight answers, are you?"

"True, and we've not much time before you must wake." With his hand he crossed the space between them and found Miles's.

The physical contact was shocking. *If this is a dream, I've never had one like this. Everything is so real.* He felt Tomas squeeze his hand.

"I shouldn't play with you like this, but Anya has kept you away too long. You've no idea how much that hurt. My Anya exists in a world of pain. But you're finally here, and you need answers. I must stop playing games. No, we can't see what happens in your other world, not clearly, anyway. We can sense, and we can divine. But like your other dreams, those provide only shadows."

"Okay, then tell me what I need to know."

"That you're in terrible danger. Anya is both right and wrong. She is wrong in that we are born to use the gift, which goes by other names, and she is right in that you must keep it hidden. I sense you've not been careful with that part."

"And you would be correct."

"The gift can be quite… exuberant, especially when done by someone who's not been trained."

"Right again. From all accounts I put on quite a show. I'm surprised no one pulled out a cell phone and taped it."

Tomas shook his head. "Do not let that happen. To leave a record like that would be like painting an X for the bear on the honey tree. Did Anya teach you anything about the gift?"

Miles snorted. "Are you kidding? Let's see." Using the Eastern European accent his grandma would get when she described her childhood, he recited, "'Do not use the gift. Never use the gift. If the *gadje* see you, if they know you possess it, they will come for you. They will lay waste to everything and everyone you love.' Is that what you mean?"

Stricken by his words, Tomas's smile vanished. He put a hand to his face and sobbed. "No. My sweet little girl. What she saw, what they made her watch…. No child should suffer so. And unlike you, who finally entered the lake, she has never strayed from the shore. I call to her nightly; she will not come." He wiped his eyes with the back of his hand. "And so we start at the beginning." He blew a sigh between his lips, as though gathering his emotions. "There was a fox; let's call him Miles."

"Story time?"

Undeterred, Tomas continued, his words laid over the steady clomp and sway of the horses and the wagon. "A fox came to the door of a childless couple who lived at the edge of the woods. But when the barren woman opened the door, she saw not a fox but a baby boy, naked and alone. She looked outside, wondering and worried about who might have left such a perfect child on her stoop. There was no one. She strained to hear footfalls or wagon wheels, but just heard the birds in the woods and the wind in the trees. She called to her husband to see the baby, whom she now held fast in her arms. It's a funny thing how love takes root, how somewhere between bending to pick up the child and coming back to standing, her heart became entwined with the baby, who was in fact a fox. So too her husband fell in love with the child, whom they adopted and raised as their own."

"Shouldn't Youth Protective Services have gotten involved? Or maybe the ASPCA?" Miles interjected, annoyed at Tomas's ramblings. "What does this have to do with—"

"Hush." Tomas flicked the tip of Miles's nose.

"Ouch!"

"Clearly my Anya did not teach respect for one's elders."

"Trust me. Respect, fear…. Yeah, she got those across. Fine. So… what happened to Foxy Loxy?"

"He grew up," Tomas said as he looked Miles dead-on. "He grew strong, smart, and handsome, and all around the country, word spread of his strength and his accomplishments."

"Really? So they were posting on YouTube?"

Tomas raised an eyebrow and continued, "No one could run faster or shoot a bow straighter." He grinned. "And all the girls who saw him immediately fell in love."

Miles snorted through his nose.

That stopped Tomas. "You are a very rude young man."

"Well, I'm happy to go along with story hour, but those poor girls are going to be sadly disappointed in Mr. Miles the Fox."

"Yes, I was planning to get to that…. Wait a minute, what are you saying?"

"Miles the Fox will not be sniffing after the girls in your story."

"Ah… I see. Nevertheless, the tale still works. Are we done with interruptions and edits?"

"Sure."

Tomas inhaled. "Let's see. So yes, there was YouTube and Facebook and postings on Tumblr and Twitter. Everyone was impressed with the boy who was really a fox. And he came to the notice of the king to the north."

"Please no *Game of Thrones* references."

Tomas continued, "And the king sent his youngest son"—and Tomas grinned at Miles—"who also preferred boys, and told his son to meet this Miles the Fox and to wed him."

"You are clearly taking liberties with this story."

"I have a whip and will use it if you don't shut up."

Miles threw up his hands. "Not a word…. Kinky."

"So the prince went to the old couple's house in the woods, and the moment he laid eyes upon Miles the Fox, he fell in love. But the fox did not feel the same, and he told the king's son that he was handsome and he was kind but that he could not love him and he could not marry him, and he sent him away.

"Time passed, and the king to the south, who also had a son—who also preferred boys—told his son to go meet this Miles, and if he was all that had been reported, to marry this boy. So once again a king's son came knocking at the old couple's door. He too fell completely in love with the boy who was in fact a fox. But again it was unrequited, and he was sent away with a broken heart. Two more times, two more kings sent their sons to marry the boy. And two more times they went home with heavy hearts.

"The old couple, who'd watched all of the suitors come and go, wondered at their son's behavior. 'My boy,' his mother said, 'four great kings have sent their sons with promises of love and a life with every comfort. And four times you have sent them away. Will you never marry? Will you never take a mate?'

"At that moment a scratch came at the door. The farmer answered it, and there in the doorway was a beautiful red fox. Miles took one look, and to the horror of his parents, his human form melted away and he turned into a fox. In this story," Tomas commented, "foxes can talk, and because he loved the farmer and his wife, and he didn't want them to think they'd done anything wrong, he explained, 'I do not need the riches of kings or the love of their sons. I am a fox, and this will be my mate.' Without another word the two foxes rubbed noses, joined their hearts, and scampered off into the woods."

Miles was about to comment, trying to make sense of any message embedded in the tale, when something rocked his right shoulder. He looked at Tomas. His form wavered, and the wagon lurched. Miles's shoulder was rocked back and forth and a voice intruded into the dream.

"Miles! Miles!"

He cracked his eyelids open. "Where am I?" The data poured in. A dark room; his naked legs against a crinkly plastic-covered mattress. His throat was parched, his muscles stiff, and anxiety plowed over him like a train. His eyes were thick with sleep and the weird dream: *I am a fox.* He felt the strong hand on his shoulder and traced it back to a familiar face, barely discernible in the dim light that filtered through the tiny window in the door of his emergency-room cell. "Luke?"

"Yeah, what the hell, Miles?"

"I'm in deep shit." He pushed back against the bed and tried to sit. Something hammered in his head, and his gut twisted as he remembered his last moments of consciousness: Stangl with his creepy smile, the guards who'd crowded the tiny room, Nurse Bob with a loaded syringe.

"What happened?" Luke asked, sitting at the end of the bed. A ray of light caught him across the brow. It lit his deep brown eyes. His sandy hair was clumped in weird angles from his habit of pulling his fingers through it when stressed.

"What time is it?" Miles asked.

"After 3:00 a.m."

As his eyes adjusted, Miles took stock of his situation. He looked at his best friend since starting medical school—Luke Paxton—twenty-three, born and raised in an ultraconservative Charlestown family, oldest of three, wicked sense of humor, and someone who'd apparently break a shitload of rules for a friend in trouble. He wore the short white coat and scrubs that were the unofficial uniform for medical students when on call at Mercy. Hours earlier they'd eaten fried chicken and okra in the hospital's cafeteria with a couple of other friends as they'd braced for the night.

"Luke, I need to get out of here."

Luke hesitated. "They're saying a lot of weird shit."

"I know."

"Is it true?"

Miles glanced to the door and then up at the dome camera with the red LED light that blinked at ten-second intervals. He pictured Nurse Bob outside the door, seated in front of the monitors. Here was a dilemma, as Grandma Anna's threats and even the words of his dead great-grandfather came to mind: *Never tell*. Then again, she wasn't here, and Luke was.

"You remember a couple years back, we were playing some sort of party game? It was at your place, and the question was, how do you know who your true friends are."

Luke's breath caught. "Sure. I remember that night."

Miles immediately regretted his choice, but in this night filled with errors of judgment, what difference would one more make? "You shouldn't be here, Luke, and thank you. I don't know what happened tonight. Not all of it, and if I told you what I do know, or think I know, you'll get up, get out, and think I'm in the right place."

"Shut up, Miles. You're not crazy, but there's a lot of weird shit happening, and people are saying some freaky stuff."

"About me?"

"Yeah, and about what happened up on oncology."

"Crap. Are there videos?"

"I don't think so. So you're not denying you did something to that guy?"

Never tell. "Yeah, I did."

"And?"

"And you're going to think I'm a nutjob."

"Try me."

Grandma Anna's voice screamed in his head. *"Never tell. Never tell. They will hunt you down; they will not rest. Everyone you love will be in danger. Never tell. Promise. Promise."*

He swallowed and looked his good friend, his best friend, in the eye. He tried not to focus on Luke's lips, which had met his a single time the same night as that party game. After their classmates had gone home, a somewhat tipsy Luke had wanted to see what it might be like to kiss his openly gay best friend. As kisses went it was sloppy and fun and never to be forgotten. But it turned uncomfortable when Luke pulled back, his face confused and frightened. It had led to weeks of awkward pauses and a silent agreement that it would never be discussed… or repeated. Luke was straight and dating a great girl, Miles was gay; they were best friends, and they were cool with that.

What the hell, Miles thought. "I can heal people, Luke."

Luke tapped his forefinger nervously on the mattress. "Shit!" He launched his hand into his hair, pulling it back against his scalp. "Like, let me get this…. You're not talking about 'I'm studying to be a doctor, and I want to heal people with the marvels of modern medicine.'"

"No—I mean, yes, that too. But I can lay on hands."

"Shit…. See, here's the deal, Miles. That's crazy, but you're not, and the weird shit that's freaking people out is that maybe you're telling the truth. And maybe there's a guy on Avery 6 who had stage-four cancer, and something happened to his tumors."

"What do you mean? What happened to Antoine?"

"People are talking. They took him for X-rays, and then when those came back, they called the attending, who ordered a full-body MRI. Your man's insides are clean as a whistle. They're attributing it to the last-ditch chemo he's been getting. So you can lay on hands."

Miles nodded, rocking his upper body on the edge of the bed. "Yeah, and I'm not supposed to tell anyone."

"Sure, I could see how that could be an issue." Luke stared at him dead-on. "So why the fuck did you have to do it where you were surrounded by people?"

"You sound like my grandma. It was late. Antoine's dying. He has two little boys, and he wasn't going to make it through the night. Don't ask me how I know this shit. I just do. And I knew, like, in my gut, that I could do it. But here's the part I don't know, because I've been good, or bad, or I've been something. I've only ever done it once. I am in such deep shit. Stangl's planning to ship me to Lakeshore in a few hours. I'm being committed."

"Why Lakeshore? Why not just admit you to the psych ward upstairs?"

Miles imagined how this must sound to Luke. A guy whose life was carefully planned and who accepted the solid road he'd been placed upon by his cardiothoracic surgeon father. "I've met Stangl before."

"So? We all have. He's, like, the ATM for the department of psych."

"No." Miles lowered his voice, even though he knew the rooms weren't miked. "When I was eight, my parents had to bring me to a psychiatrist to be evaluated for school." He felt Luke's questions and barreled ahead. "You see, not only does your weird friend think he can lay on hands, but I've got a couple other quirks you might as well know about." He hazarded a look at Luke.

"Just do it, man. I won't judge." In spite of the tension, Luke cracked a smile. "Well, maybe a little. I've got to hear what other shit you got. 'Cause we're sort of heading into superhero territory. Can you fly? I always wanted to fly."

"Me too, but no…. I hear the voice of my dead great-grandfather, who I've never met. At least, I used to. And stupid boy that I was, I told my teachers about that. So… had to get seen by a shrink, and guess who it was?"

"Stangl."

"Yup. And back then, you want to know what he told my parents?" Miles felt his fear turn to rage. Stangl's question "Do you believe in fate?" pounded in his head.

"I don't."

"He told them I was the youngest case of paranoid schizophrenia he'd ever seen. He wanted to lock me up. He wants to lock me up now. And here's the worst part…." Through the panic, Miles felt connections start to form. "I think he knows. I think he's known all along, or maybe suspected, and I haven't a clue as to how or why. I think that's why he wants me at Lakeshore. It's not about my being crazy. It's about what I did with Antoine."

"Miles the fox," Luke whispered.

"What did you say?"

"That's what the girls call you, and some of the guys too."

Miles wondered at the turn in conversation. In another setting he might have followed it up. Because while Luke had been clearly freaked by their drunken kiss, Miles had to deal with more fallout than just the possible loss of his best friend. It bothered the hell out of him but was something he'd come to accept: a mammoth crush on a straight boy. One of those things that couldn't be helped, and it brought back his dream. *A fox has to be with a fox.*

SEATED ON the edge of the narrow bed, Luke knew all the reasons he shouldn't do this. He could hear his father, the esteemed surgeon Dr. Craig Paxton, like a claxon in his head. *"Eye on the goal, son. Medical school, internship, a top surgical residency. This is a road from which you cannot veer. There will be temptations, and the Lord allows for a bit of oat sowing. But New Orleans lies just left of Babylon. Do not fall into the pit."*

Luke sensed Miles's fear and believed his peril was genuine. He'd also stopped and looked at the X-rays and just completed MRI everyone was buzzing over. Stage-four hepatocellular carcinoma didn't just up and walk away. They'd attributed it to the experimental chemo they were pumping into Miles's patient. It was an explanation. It was the wrong one.

Sure, the shit coming out of Miles's mouth was hard to take. But after five years of studying together, of late-night pizza and two-liter bottles of Diet Coke, a year of making bad jokes as they cut apart a cadaver in the gross anatomy lab, of making up pornographic mnemonics so they could spit back the twelve cranial nerves or each step in the Krebs cycle for the biochemistry final, he knew a few things about his best friend.

He didn't exaggerate. He didn't lie, but he did keep secrets, and not about being gay. Luke knew about Miles's occasional hookups, but there'd never been a boyfriend—a fact that pleased Luke, and he knew it shouldn't. He imagined what his father would make of the drunken kiss, the most intense few seconds Luke had ever known. Like taking a first hit of heroin, Luke realized it was never to be repeated and probably wasn't included in Father's list of wild oats to be sown. He'd told himself—repeatedly—it was the booze and that Jenna Simpson's kisses, although softer and more insistent, were the right fit for him. *She* was the right fit. A suitable Charleston girl from a suitable family, who was fun and pretty, who'd become a pediatrician and provide suitable grandchildren to keep the Paxton name alive.

But this… his best friend in trouble. He could not walk away. This was wrong: Miles locked up and drugged, about to be shipped off to the private domain of Dr. Stangl. It reeked. And while he hadn't come into the ER with this plan, in that moment he knew it was the right thing, and that there would be consequences.

He whispered, "You know the difference between an acquaintance and a true friend?"

Without missing a beat, Miles answered, "Yeah, an acquaintance tells you who your enemies are. A true friend helps you bury the bodies."

Luke pulled his ID badge and hospital key card from around his neck. He grabbed Miles's hand. "Here." He placed them into his palm and wrapped his fingers around them. He felt Miles resist.

"What are you doing? Luke, no!"

Luke gripped tighter and his heart pounded. "Ssh. Just do it, and take my cell. My code's 7878."

He saw the fear in Miles's eyes. For a moment their hands stayed joined. It threw Luke back to the night of the kiss. *Just like heroin.* And if he were being honest, what he craved was another hit.

Miles shook his head. "Luke, no. You got to think. Don't jeopardize everything you've worked…."

"Shut up, Miles…. You don't have schizophrenia. Yeah, you're crazy as batshit, but that's why I love you. You need to get your ass out of here. We'll figure something out after that. I'm going to leave, and I won't shut the door. Wait till I'm gone, and then use the key card to get out of the ED. Call me on my beeper."

"Luke, I can't ask you to do this. It's too much."

"You didn't ask. I offered, so shut up about it."

And before Miles could tell his friend all the reasons this was a stupid idea, Luke pushed off the bed, and like something was chasing him, he was out the door.

Miles strained to hear the click of the lock and slide of the bolt; they didn't come. He clutched the key card and Luke's phone in his palm. He glanced up at the camera. Nurse Bob had probably watched the entire thing. But between the dark and the way their bodies had been turned, Luke's act of bravery had gone unobserved.

Miles's fingers tingled from the physical contact with Luke. *Don't read anything into it.* He realized Luke had needed to conceal what he was doing, the hand-holding necessary to camouflage the transfer of the key card and cell. *Okay, this is just pathetic.*

He rolled onto his side and curled into the wall, clutching his treasure. He thought of bad movie plots where people escaped and left pillows stuffed under sheets to give the illusion of a sleeping body. And he thought about Luke and the night of the party game and the kiss. He revised the answer to what makes a true friend. It wasn't burying the bodies. But breaking into someone's locked psych ward and giving them the key to get out? Yeah, that was a friend. *But just a friend, Miles. Don't mistake it for something else, something more. He has Jenna. She's great and blonde and pretty and has a wicked sense of humor and loves him, and she's your friend and trusts you and probably knows you have a crush on her boyfriend.... A fox has to be with a fox.*

He played his fingers over the smooth surface of the iPhone. Curling his body to conceal the phone's LED glow, he turned it on and tapped in 7878. He took a deep breath and dialed Grandma Anna's number. He knew the hour wouldn't matter; the woman barely slept. True to form, she picked up on the second ring.

"Grandma?"

"Miles, what's wrong?"

There was no point in being indirect. In hushed tones he laid out the broad strokes of his dilemma, including the appearance of Dr. Gerald Stangl.

Anna cursed at the name. "Get out of there," she hissed, her words clipped and terse. "Get somewhere safe. I'll be there as fast as I can. Have you called your parents?"

"No."

"Good. Don't. We'll deal with them later."

Her anger pulsed from over a thousand miles away.

"I'm sorry, Grandma."

"Miles, being sorry is unimportant. Get out of there." Her tone softened. "I have things to tell you. Things I should have said before. I'll get there as soon as I can." She hung up.

CHAPTER 8

AN HOUR later Miles was free, scared, and confused. He gulped the dregs of two-day-old black coffee and took a look around his one-bedroom French Quarter apartment. Outside it was still dark, just after 5:00 a.m. He couldn't tell if it was paranoia, but having just AWOLed from the emergency room, he figured Stangl would send cops. It wasn't safe here, and holing up at the library or student center, he'd need to use his Lister key card to gain access. *They can trace that… but I can't stay here.*

He thought about Luke and the cozy house he rented with a couple of grad students in the Garden District at the end of the Charles Street line. *He's done enough. Too much. And what's it going to cost him?* It wouldn't take a brain surgeon to figure out who'd helped him. "Shit!"

After he made his escape from the ER, he'd paged Luke and met him on the top floor of Mercy, in the deserted lounge outside the on-call rooms. Along the way he swiped a pair of scrubs, a white coat, and a pair of green plastic surgical clogs. As he returned the cell and ID, he was struck by how much Luke had risked. Of everything in this fucked-up night, that was the worst. There was going to be serious fallout for Luke. He thought of their last few moments.

"They're sending your man for a full-body MRI to confirm the results of the first one. People are freaking out," Luke had said, his expression a mix of excitement and something Miles couldn't quite put a name to. Almost manic.

Miles would have loved to share in that, but all he felt was dread. "I have to leave New Orleans. I don't know what Stangl wants. I just know it's not safe."

"You think it has to do with what you told me about? You think he knows?"

In the midst of all that was happening, Luke's acceptance of Miles's secret was unexpected. It felt odd and good. "I don't know. I mean, how could he know? And… yeah."

"How could he be the same psychiatrist who saw you fifteen years ago in Massachusetts? That's one hell of a coincidence, Miles."

Luke's quick appraisal of the improbability of Stangl's appearance tonight rang true.

"I've got to go." Miles had held out his hand.

"No," Luke said, and he'd pulled Miles into a crushing hug.

He'd stiffened and then relaxed. He'd smelled hospital shampoo in Luke's hair and prayed his friend would weather whatever shitstorm was headed his way. "I've got to go." He pulled back.

As he did, Luke resisted. "I'm going to miss you, man."

"Me too." And with their faces inches apart and their hands on each other's shoulders, there was a moment. With all the sharing of truths, Miles wondered what was running through Luke's head. For himself, if he were more courageous, he would have given in to the impulse and stolen a kiss. *Don't do that to him. The last one freaked him out. He's a friend. The best one you've ever had. Don't confuse things.* The moment passed, the connection broke, and Miles went flying down the hospital stairs, not wanting to risk the elevators.

The cool night air helped clear his head of the drugs they'd shot into him. He'd raced from downtown into the narrow streets of the French Quarter. His stolen clogs had rubbed against his skin and raised blisters on his heels.

Now, dressed in jeans, a black tee, and sneakers, he gulped cold coffee. "You can't come back here." His words rang in his ears. It wasn't just the apartment he was leaving. The reality of his situation was crushing. "They're not going to let you return. You're not going to finish medical school."

Ever since he could remember, the one thing he ever truly wanted was to become a doctor. He harbored a dream that maybe it would help him understand this curse of a gift. More than that, he believed it would allow him to discover the science behind the magic. It was something he shared with no one, not even Grandma Anna. *Luke would understand.* What would it be like to finally have a confidante, to not have to hide? *Don't think about that. It's too late. Stay focused.*

He looked at his secondhand furniture, medical school books that cost a small fortune, his laptop, and his darkly varnished Italian violin, a gift from Grandpa Henry, Anna's husband, who'd been a wonderful musician and who'd died when Miles was six. His golden retriever, Amos, had been his parents' attempt to help him get over the loss of his grandpa. Even now he could remember Grandpa Henry's laugh, the feel of his strong hands as he placed Miles's fingers on the fiddle strings. His instructions: "Pull the notes from your heart and through your hands. The fiddle, the music, and you become one."

Grandpa Henry gave him the gift of music and, probably because he started so young, a facility with the violin where he could play both by ear and read music. From grade school through high school, he'd won competitions and could have pursued a career as a violinist. And always when he looked out over an audience or the congregation at Temple Beth Shalom, he imagined Grandpa Henry. *She could have saved him… and she didn't. She loved him, and she didn't use the gift.* Grandpa had died at the house in Truro. Had Miles been there, he had no doubt he would have saved his grandpa. But he'd been with his parents in Brookline. *She chose not to save him. She said she loved him. What is wrong with her?*

He scanned his other possessions, which were few, Grandma Anna's homilies having shaped so much of his life. *"How many pairs of pants can you wear at one time? How many beds can you sleep in?"*

He remembered how furious she'd been when he told her about applying to medical schools. But he'd known what her response would be. *"It's playing with fire, boy."* His parents, on the other hand, had been thrilled. They viewed his music as a worthwhile avocation but too hard and too risky a life. Rachel and Joseph Fox were practical people, his mother a high school math teacher and his father a computer systems analyst who worked long hours and was always on call to his customers. They'd been proud of his choice and excited when multiple medical schools accepted him, and even more excited when he got into Lister's six-year program along with a scholarship that covered everything but his apartment and supplies. In one year he was supposed to graduate. He would have walked across the stage and received two diplomas, a bachelor of science and his medical degree. Now he would get nothing.

He startled at the wail of a distant siren, not unusual for the neighborhood or the time of night. *Is it for me?* He glanced at his laptop and then at the violin on the mantel. Not knowing when, if ever, he'd return, he picked up the instrument and resisted the urge to play or even pluck the strings to hear its voice. He stowed it and his bow in the case. He glanced at his music stand. The lyre was thick with annotated scores, everything from

Schubert to songs he'd play at the High Holidays—the Kol Nidre, "Yigdal," a haunting Ladino version of "Adon 'Olam." There were unbound pages of handwritten Jewish folk songs and prayers that had belonged to Grandpa Henry. He thought of grabbing those, but they were all long ago committed to memory, and even taking the violin was more baggage than was safe.

The siren grew louder, and whether or not it was coming for him, he wasn't taking the chance. With coffee in one hand and his fiddle in the other, he fled out the alley door.

His ears strained for the direction of the siren; it was fading. *Not for you, at least not this one.* He looked up at his apartment window. Where did one go to hide in New Orleans at 5:00 a.m. on a Wednesday? He had no car, thirty dollars in bills, his laundry quarters, and a violin. His cell had been confiscated by hospital security. Grandma Anna was supposedly on her way, which would take care of the cash issue and likely his escape from the city. Problem was, even if she got right on a flight, it would be hours before she arrived. And he needed to find a phone to call her.… *Not the biggest problem right now.*

He took a deep breath and caught the stench of garbage from the nearby dumpster. At the back of the alley, a familiar homeless man slept inside a cardboard box. *Not a bad place to hide, but too close.*

His rational mind raged against the bizarre turn of events. *But what's the worst that Stangl can do? Send a couple of cops looking for me? It's not like the New Orleans Police Department is going to throw much manpower behind an escaped mental patient.*

And with that thought, he headed toward the heart of the Quarter. There were always crowds on Bourbon Street, and a lot of the clubs were open twenty-four hours a day. He'd hide out there, wait for Grandma Anna, get the hell out of Dodge, and try to figure out what to do when the thing he most wanted was taken away.

As he recalled again that he might never graduate from medical school, there was something else, and it hurt far worse. *You're never going to see him again.* While he never meant for it to happen, there it was, a huge crush on his best friend. But it went deeper. *Yeah, a true friend helps you bury the bodies, and springs you from locked psych wards… and lets you kiss him when he's drunk. And you can't ever see him again. And why does that hurt more than anything else?*

CHAPTER 9

GERALD STANGL stormed onto the ER floor. It was 8:00 a.m., and the call from the nurse had come thirty minutes earlier. "Dr. Stangl, we don't know how it happened, but your patient, Miles Fox, the one who was to be transferred to Lakeshore, went AWOL off the unit sometime after 3:00 a.m."

He slammed the steel door onto the psych ward open. He clenched his jaw and wanted to scream, *Who did this? What moron let this happen?* He held his expression tight. *Someone will pay for this.* But right now he needed to track down Fox. It had been a night, and now a morning, filled with powerful emotion. Prior to the discovery of Fox's escape, he'd viewed the full-body MRI of Antoine Dey. Not a tumor to be seen. The oncologists chalked it up to their poisonous chemo cocktail. *Idiots.*

He looked at the gray-haired nurse behind the counter. "Where's the one who was on last night? Bob?"

"He's gone," she said.

A muscle twitched in Gerald's jaw. *How could somebody be so stupid?* "I need to see the security film."

"Here," she said, indicating the seat next to her behind the counter. "I had the head of security pull up the footage once we saw he was gone. He pulled a *Hogan's Heroes.*"

"Excuse me?"

"You know, the pillows under the sheet thing."

Gerald had no tolerance for the woman's prattle. He focused on the screen as she fast-forwarded through his interview with Fox. "Stop!" he ordered as a tall young man in scrubs and the short white lab coat the medical students wore entered the room. The time stamp read 3:08 a.m. "Who's that?"

"I don't know," she said. "I've seen him around. I don't think he's rotated through here, or at least not when I've been on."

"Zoom in."

"Excuse me?" The nurse balked at his tone.

"Please, we have an extremely serious situation here."

"That's no reason to be rude."

Gerald imagined how it might feel to wrap his hands around this annoying woman's throat. He gritted his teeth. "Sorry, I apologize. Now could you please zoom in on the man in the white coat?" *And may you die in your sleep tonight.*

"Thank you."

Bitch. Now do it! Gerald watched as she enlarged the image. It pixilated, and he could just make out the block letters on the man's name tag—Paxton. "Now go forward… please."

With rapt attention he studied the interaction of the two men. They kept their bodies turned from the overhead camera. And when Paxton got up to leave at 3:20 a.m., his ID tag was no longer around his neck. He watched Fox pretend to sleep.

"Stop! Zoom in again…." Gerald felt as though his head might explode. "He's making a call. Is there sound? I need to hear."

"No sound," the nurse said. "It's illegal to have audio."

Who are you calling? Maybe that Paxton. Maybe his parents. The grandmother? That was who he wanted to call. "Advance it…."

Dumbfounded, he watched Fox mold his bedding into what should never have passed for a sleeping person. Twenty minutes later he was out of bed, his body pressed against the door, checking to see if the nurse was at his station. And then he was gone. It sickened him. *Four and a half hours. He could be anywhere. This can't be happening. There will be hell to pay.*

He grabbed the phone and dialed the hospital operator. "This is Dr. Gerald Stangl in psychiatry. I need you to patch together a conference call with the head of hospital security and the New Orleans Police Department. We have a serious situation. A dangerous and psychotic patient has escaped from the emergency room."

He waited, his attention split between the phone and the ludicrous pillows under the sheet that shouldn't have fooled anyone. Disgusted, he entered his pass code into the hospital's electronic medical record and pulled up Fox's chart. He clicked through the recent notes, including the discovery, hours after the fact, that the man had escaped. He berated himself for not having made the transfer last night. It had been a calculated risk, and it had exploded in his face.

The line clicked, and the operator came on. "Dr. Stangl, I have Detective Johnson and Mr. Edmonds, the head of hospital security."

"Thank you. Gentlemen, I'm Dr. Gerald Stangl, and last night I wrote a commitment paper on a dangerous and psychotic young man—Miles Fox. At approximately 3:40 a.m., he went AWOL from the psychiatric emergency room."

The detective spoke. "Dr. Stangl, when you say dangerous, are you talking about to himself or others?"

"Others. Miles Fox has paranoid schizophrenia with fixed delusions that there is a conspiracy directed toward him and his family. Based on these delusions, and voices he's been hearing since he was a child, Mr. Fox told me that he's been stockpiling weapons and explosives and intends to commit an act of violence. He believes the only way to save his family is through the shedding of innocent blood, the more the better. We're talking Columbine. I cannot stress how dire this situation is."

The detective interrupted. "Why are you just calling now? Seems like four hours ago would have been good."

The director of security interjected, "It was just discovered. Apparently the patient disguised his escape. And while I can't speak to what the doctor is telling you, I do know the man is dangerous and injured two security guards during a takedown yesterday."

The detective spoke over him. "Dr. Stangl, what can you tell me about your patient? And the more explicit the better, starting with his home address, contacts for family, close friends, and anyone else who might know of his whereabouts."

"Of course, Detective. Also, you should know that I've written a commitment paper for Mr. Fox based on his level of psychosis and dangerousness to others. When he's found, he is to be taken to Lakeshore Hospital's high-security forensic ward."

"I'll need a copy of the paper."

"Of course, I'll be sure you have that and anything else you might need. But I cannot overstress the seriousness of this situation. People will die if Miles Fox is not apprehended. I pray we're not too late."

CHAPTER 10

WITH AN Angels cap pulled low over his brow and his violin on the booth, Miles cradled his third cup of coffee and glanced anxiously toward the door of the Swamp Witch, a small blues bar on Bourbon Street. It was 10:00 a.m.; he'd been there for over an hour. The place was empty save for Marie Levesque, the owner of the funky club where he and Luke, usually with Jenna and a couple of their classmates, would come, spread their books, and study for hours, taking advantage of the two-buck beers, gooseneck lamps, talented local musicians, and Marie's good nature, which at times extended to free drinks and impromptu and scarifying tarot readings.

He felt her dark eyes on him. *She has to be wondering what I'm doing here…. No books. I should be at the hospital. This was a bad idea.*

Through the bar's open door, he could tell something was happening on the street. There were too many cops. They were looking for someone. He tried to reassure himself. *They don't do manhunts for escaped mental patients. Do they?*

Marie glanced in his direction and then out at the street. She shook her head and tied back her black-and-silver curls. As though making a decision, she headed from behind the bar toward his table.

"So, Mr. Medical Student. You come into my place to hide? You're not the first."

He looked up from under his cap. Their eyes met. He knew she could yell for the cops, that at any moment she would. "I have nowhere to go."

"You kill someone?" she asked.

"No."

"Rape?"

"No."

"Child molester?"

"No."

"Mug someone and steal their fiddle?"

And whether it was the weirdness of his plight or the lingering effects of the drugs, Miles blurted out the truth. "I healed a man."

"Well, that's a new one." With her dark eyes fixed on his, she reached out a hand and pulled off his cap. She glanced toward the open door as a pair of uniformed officers headed their way. "Violin boy, go in the back. There, through the curtain."

As she grabbed his cup and saucer and swept them onto a nearby bus tray, he slid out of the booth.

"Thanks." He darted behind the black curtain, which had a sign over the frame—EMPLOYEES ONLY. His heart raced as he took stock of the dimly lit room packed with papier-mâché masks and racks hung with spangled Mardi Gras costumes. There was a single door beneath a neon exit sign and no windows. A lever across the door read EMERGENCY EXIT ONLY. ALARM SOUNDS WHEN OPENED. That would not be an option, at least not a good one.

He pressed his ear to the curtain and listened to Marie and the cops.

"Is he dangerous?" she asked.

"Yeah, an escaped psycho. His name's Miles Fox," a male voice replied.

"Are we talking something Mr. Fox has done or something he might do?"

"We can't really say, ma'am. You're sure you haven't seen him?"

"Let me take another look."

Miles's heart pounded in his ears. *Why is she helping me? Is she helping me?* He glanced back at the alarmed exit. He'd have to leave the violin, but maybe if he made a run for it....

"No." Her voice came clearly through the curtain. "A fine-looking boy—what pretty eyes. I would have remembered that one." Her tone turned flirtatious. "I always remember the handsome ones."

The officer cleared his throat. He chuckled, "I'll take that as a compliment."

"Well, I do appreciate the efforts of our boys in blue. Perhaps you men would care for a small libation before continuing your fox hunt."

"Another time, but thanks."

Miles sensed the officers were about to leave. He took a careful breath. *Why is she helping me?*

"So he really is dangerous, this Mr. Fox?" she asked.

Miles braced. She was going to turn him in. He put down the violin, his eyes trained on the exit.

"That's what we've been told, and we're not at liberty to give the details."

"Of course, you don't want to create a panic. It seems I should probably lock the doors, at least until the danger has passed. Not like I get much business at this time anyway."

"Not a bad idea," the officer responded.

Miles strained to hear their conversation as they walked away. There were sounds of street noise, and then the firm thud of the door shutting and the scrape of the geared mechanism that set the security bar in place.

"So." Marie pulled back the curtain.

"Thank you," Miles said, still feeling the race of his pulse. *Why is she helping me?* He looked behind her at the now barred door. "Why did you do that? I mean, I'm grateful…." He told himself to shut up, to not look a gift horse in the mouth. *Why isn't she saying anything?*

She stared at him as though making some decision. "Mr. Fox, you say you healed a man. They say you're crazy. Could both be true?" She let the curtain drop and headed toward the bar. He followed as she pulled down a bottle of top-shelf bourbon and poured two doubles. "Mr. Fox, since I've done you the courtesy of saving your ass, I would like the truth, the whole truth, and nothing but the truth, so help you Goddess. Can you do that?"

"Sure." With violin in hand, he looked around the deserted room. The only light was from tiny red and blue LEDs along the back bar. The front windows were heavily curtained to protect the daytime drinkers from gawkers, spouses, and debt collectors. "Why are you helping me?"

"Because I believe you healed a man, and that indeed makes you dangerous, but you already know that."

"I don't know anything," he admitted.

"That is unfortunate, as clearly the streets are not safe for foxes." She slid the tumbler of bourbon across the counter and produced her well-worn tarot cards from under the bar. "Now throw this back and shuffle these. I need to read your story."

CHAPTER 11

Luke knew his actions would have consequences. So when he was summoned to Dean Beverly Strachey's office on the top floor of the medical school's administration building, he wasn't surprised. What he didn't expect was to find two New Orleans police detectives.

It was 10:00 a.m. He was in his scrubs from the night before. He'd hoped to go home after morning rounds, crash for a few hours, and then make it back to the hospital for his Wednesday afternoon clinic. He felt anxious as he faced the detectives and the short, silver-haired dean.

Dean Strachey made the introductions. "Mr. Paxton, these are Detectives Johnson and LeClerc. They have some questions they need to ask you about last night. Please sit." He did. They didn't. Luke felt his gut tighten as he looked up and tried to read the blank facial expressions of the two dark-suited detectives. The dean smiled at him as if all were right as rain. She gripped the edge of her desk with her small hands. "But first," she said, "I have one. What happened last night?"

No, this is not going to go well. Her tone and expression were pleasant, but the question was an open-ended landmine. He reviewed his actions of last night. He knew they'd have reviewed the security tapes from the ER. What he didn't know was what they actually saw. Then again, they weren't stupid. Everyone knew he and Miles were friends.

"It was wrong," he said.

"What was wrong?" the taller of the two detectives asked, the expression on his face now interested and friendly.

Luke looked at the man's ID badge clipped to his breast pocket—Detective Layton Johnson. He'd smiled for the picture. His light brown eyes and even features were a tribute to his New Orleans lineage.

"Just to be clear, we're talking about Miles, right?"

"Yes," Detective Johnson answered. "Miles Fox, who you visited at 3:00 a.m. in the emergency room last night. So what was wrong?"

"Miles isn't crazy."

Dean Strachey, still smiling, spoke through tight lips. "And you, a medical student, are equipped to make that clinical decision? Which, having just reviewed your transcripts, you haven't gone through a single psychiatric rotation. So please, tell me what you're basing your conclusion on. I'm eager to know how your psychiatric acumen is greater than that of a full professor who wrote a legally binding document to commit Mr. Fox for needed treatment. Please educate us."

Luke was struck by the dean's sarcasm and barely restrained fury. His few interactions with the woman had been nothing more than the standard meet-and-greet at the medical school functions they were expected to attend, including the annual Halloween blowout at Stangl's Lakeshore Hospital. *And what was that about a legal document?* He looked from the dean back to Detective Johnson. His tall partner hung back, his eyes trained on Luke.

"Do I need a lawyer?"

"Your call," Detective Johnson stated. "Right now we're just asking questions. We have an escaped mental patient and a doctor telling us he's dangerous. It's clear you helped him get away. What we need to know now… is where is he? This is a chance for you to undo some damage. Where is he, Luke?"

"I don't know." It was the truth, and it kicked off jumbled memories of last night. Of Miles curled up in the emergency room. The fear on his face. *What if it wasn't fear?* He replayed the interaction. *What if I missed something? What if they're right? What if he is crazy? Or dangerous?* Without intending to, he laughed.

"Something's amusing, Mr. Paxton?" Dean Strachey asked. "Because we could all use a bit of humor right now. Please do tell what you find so funny?"

Luke looked across at the stocky dean in her boxy silver-gray suit. "Miles isn't crazy," he repeated. "That's what's funny, or maybe messed up. How anyone could make that conclusion."

"I see," the dean said. "And you're aware that he assaulted one of his patients on the oncology ward, that it was witnessed, and that he subsequently went berserk. I imagine you also knew that in the process of taking him down, because he was completely out of control, he injured two security officers."

"That's not what happened," Luke said, and the moment the words were out, he regretted them.

"No?" Detective Johnson asked. "What did happen?"

Suddenly Luke faced the secret Miles had kept his entire life. He rolled it around in his head like pebbles in a tumbler. *What would they think if I let it out?* He played the words in his head: *Miles didn't assault that patient, the one they did a full-body MRI on this morning, the one who no longer has tumors anywhere in his body. Miles healed him. Yeah, that will go over well.* "He didn't assault his patient."

Detective LeClerc finally spoke. "He's not telling us something. Why are you lying to us, Dr. Paxton? I understand that Miles Fox is your friend, and we all do things to help our friends. But yours is sick and needs help. That's all we want to do here, get your friend the help he needs. Where is he, Dr. Paxton?"

Dean Strachey interjected, "He's not a doctor, he's a medical student. And after this… it's unlikely he'll ever be a doctor."

Her words stung but didn't surprise him. He knew. Even last night he'd known.

The dean seemed determined to make her point, and Luke couldn't tell if it was for his sake or the detectives'. "Starting with gross insubordination. He countermanded the orders of an attending physician, who happens to be a brilliant psychiatrist and renowned researcher. Not to mention breaking multiple hospital and medical school policies about not sharing ID badges…." She was on a roll; her words pounded down on him.

Luke tried to remember that last meeting with Miles after he got free of the emergency room. He'd called Luke, and they'd met in the lounge outside the on-call rooms. Miles had been freaking out—*but he wasn't crazy, just scared.*

He'd given Luke back his phone and key card. "They'll never let me back in," he'd said.

"You don't know that."

Emboldened, he'd put his hand on Miles's shoulder. He'd hugged him. He was just comforting a friend, nothing wrong with that. When Miles pulled back, Luke stared into the green of his eyes. In that moment all he could think about was what it might be like to kiss him. *Just one more taste of heroin, I can handle it, I can stop anytime I want.* It caused him to recoil.

"You need to get away from here," he'd said. And what had run through his mind was, *You need to get away from me. I need to get away from you.*

"Tell us about his weapons," Detective Johnson prompted. "Where does he keep them?"

The question jolted Luke back to the present. The dean glared at him, and the two detectives were getting impatient. "He doesn't have weapons," Luke said.

"How can you know that?" LeClerc asked.

"We've been study partners since first year. I've been in his apartment more times than I can count. Other than some crap kitchen knives, Miles doesn't have weapons. He's antigun, plus even if he wanted one, he has barely enough money to make his rent."

"What about a storage facility?" Detective Johnson asked.

"I doubt it. And considering how he lives on ramen and mac and cheese, I can't see him forking over the rent for that. Why would you think he has weapons? That's crazy." Luke realized there were things he didn't know. Someone had painted a picture of Miles that was far from the truth. *At least the truth you think you know. What if* this *is the truth?*

"Where is he, Luke?" Detective Johnson repeated.

"Home, I guess."

"His apartment on Grinwald?"

"Yes."

"We've been. Where else?"

Luke wondered where Miles would run. He suddenly hoped… and feared he'd turn up on his doorstep. "I don't know." He thought through their usual hangouts, the bars both on and off the Bourbon Street strip, one in particular where they'd study until the two-buck beers made it impossible. The cheap Indian buffet on Canal, the diner down the street from Luke's house where they let you sit for hours with your books spread over the table, drinking chicory coffee till your insides buzzed and your hands shook.

"Think, Luke. Friends he'd go to… other than you."

Right, he thought, *they've already been to my place. Probably have it staked out if they think he's this dangerous. Shit! At least they haven't found him.* The thought brought a strange feeling. *Just run, Miles. Get away from here.* Tears formed, and he held them back. He would not show weakness in front of the dean, who was out for blood, or these two detectives, who were someone's puppets—but who was pulling the strings?

Detective LeClerc spoke. "I think we've gotten all we're getting."

"And it's not much," Johnson replied, his gaze never leaving Luke. He pulled a plastic case from his breast pocket and handed a card to the dean. He pulled out a second and gave it to Luke. Before pulling his hand back, he said, "If you remember something, you need to call." His eyes didn't break contact as the two men held the card between them. "You asked if you needed a lawyer, Mr. Paxton. It's going to depend. At the moment, you abetted a committed mental patient escaping the hospital. Depending on what Mr. Fox does, that can quickly go from a misdemeanor to a felony. If you're not telling us something, you need to do it now. Later won't look good."

Luke didn't flinch. "I don't know anything more." *And I'm certainly not going to tell you that Miles healed a man of stage-four cancer and that someone is deliberately spreading lies about him.*

Johnson released his grip on the card. "If he tries to make contact, you need to call us. This is serious, Mr. Paxton. It's not just getting into trouble with your dean. Do you understand?"

"Yes, sir."

"Good." He looked at Dean Strachey. "Doctor Strachey, you have our number. If Mr. Fox attempts to contact anyone at the hospital or the school, please give us a call."

"Of course, Detective." She shook their hands and escorted them to the door.

Luke saw the opening and started to get out of his chair.

"Where do you think you're going?" she asked. "We have business to complete here, Mr. Paxton. I need your ID and key card. You are currently suspended, and a recommendation is going to the board for summary expulsion. You do, of course, have the right to appeal, but based on the number and severity of hospital, medical school, and criminal infractions, you don't have a leg to stand on. I've contacted your parents and suggest you do the same. I don't know what you were thinking or what you hoped to accomplish, but your juvenile actions have cost you your career. You will not continue with us, and with all of this in your file, it is unlikely you will find another medical school willing to take you."

Luke felt numb. He pulled apart the Velcro closure on the lanyard around his neck. He placed his ID on the dean's desk. He looked at the key card that, hours earlier, he'd pressed into Miles's palm. He realized Miles never once asked for his help. *This is all my doing.*

"Now you can leave," she said.

After thirty hours without sleep, the events of last night, and now this, his body felt leaden. He stood and imagined the conversation that had occurred between the dean and his father. As he made his way to the door with his back to the dean, the tears came. They weren't for himself, or at least not mostly.

I hope you get away. Get far, far away. Don't come back. And that's the part that hurt worst, that opened something hollow in his chest. The realization that *I'm never going to see him again. Oh God, why does that hurt so bad?*

CHAPTER 12

ANTOINE DEY did not want to overthink things as he retrieved his meager possessions from the narrow patient's locker and packed them into his suitcase. Less than two weeks ago he'd been admitted to Mercy Memorial for what would have been the last time. He'd come to die, and now he'd never felt more alive.

He grabbed his one suit, a dark navy one he'd worn at his father's funeral. It was in a dry-cleaner's bag along with a white shirt and tie. It was what they were to bury him in. *Kind of a pity, as I only wore it the once.*

Two months earlier his oncologist, Dr. Rayburn, offered him the final choice: hospice where he could die high on pain pills at home with his wife—Lila—and two little boys—Jasper and Moses—or undergo a final round of aggressive experimental chemotherapy. He'd opted for the latter, although it came with little hope.

"I can't promise much," Dr. Rayburn admitted. "A month, maybe more. We have to be realistic. It's gone too far, Antoine." And as the good doctor often did, he apologized. "I'm so sorry."

Antoine wondered how often his poor doctor apologized to patients for illnesses he hadn't created. "It's not your fault," he'd said.

"True, but for all the advances that have been made in fighting cancer, it's a war that's still being lost."

"Nah," Antoine had offered, "just this battle, Doc."

But that was then. Now, dressed in a favorite pair of olive-drab work pants and a short-sleeve button-down monogrammed shirt—A Good Dey's Plumbing—embroidered over the pocket, it was time to leave the death house.

As he hoisted his case off the metal-framed bed, Dr. Rayburn, with his flock of white-coated residents and medical students, crowded into the doorway.

"I can't talk you into staying?" the doctor asked.

"Nah," Antoine said, feeling a twinge of anxiety that perhaps they wouldn't let him leave. But then something intruded in his thoughts, a niggling fear. "You said there's no trace. It's all gone, right?"

"There's nothing on the MRI, Antoine. But cancer's a tricky thing. It hides. It can be in the blood, the bones."

Antoine nodded as he gripped the suitcase handle. "Do you want to take more blood? I gave enough to feed a family of vampires this morning. But if you need more…."

"It's not that." Doctor Rayburn seemed perplexed. He shook his head. "You look well, Antoine."

"I feel well. No, wait a minute." He paused and took stock of his body. There was no pain, not even the catch in his side he should have listened to years earlier. The catch that signaled something was wrong. 'Course he'd had no idea how wrong. But now not even that, and certainly not the crushing agony as the cancer invaded his organs and then dove into the marrow of his bones. "I have no pain, and I told them I didn't want any more of those shots or the pills."

"Be careful with that, Antoine. There can be a pretty bad withdrawal if you just stop cold turkey. Morphine is potent stuff."

"Right." Antoine saw the bevy of young doctors nod their heads in unison. "I took the last shot of it last night. How long till the withdrawals start?"

Rayburn inhaled, sweat beaded across his deeply receding hairline. "With the doses we've been giving you… hours ago. So nothing? No cramping? Nausea? Gooseflesh? Chills?"

"Not a bit."

Dr. Rayburn pulled a tiny LED flashlight from his breast pocket. "May I?"

"Knock yourself out."

He shone the light into Antoine's eyes. He seemed perplexed. "How much morphine was he on?"

The chief resident pulled up Antoine's medication records on his tablet. "Between the long-acting and the immediate release, about a hundred and sixty milligrams a day."

"It doesn't make sense. You've been opioid dependent for the last three months."

Antoine didn't know what to say. He figured his lack of withdrawal, just like the miracle of his cancer, had everything to do with Miles, the dark-haired young doctor who'd come into his room last night. The one who'd promised his little boy to make him well. He'd heard Jasper's pleas from his bed and wondered how the earnest young doctor would handle them. What then transpired a few hours later was still beyond his comprehension.

He'd been filled with so much pain, and all that morphine did was make him feel like he was wrapped in cotton batting, hurting and numb at the same time, the last weeks and months like an opium dream. *And if this is a dream, I pray that I don't wake up.*

"You know, that's the other thing, Doc. It's not just the pain that's gone. My head is clear, and my wife and boys are waiting on me downstairs. I have to get going. Dr. Rayburn, you told me once that sometimes the cancer just up and goes away. That sometimes miracles happen. I don't know if you were just saying that to give me hope, but that's what happened. You got to believe that."

He looked toward the wall of white coats, hoisted his suitcase with a firm grip, and headed through them. He looked at each of their faces, searching for one. Those green eyes weren't something you forgot. *He's not here. But didn't something happen?* It was hard to remember. *Some kind of commotion.* People had flooded his room, but that wasn't the part he most remembered. It was that young man's voice, soothing him as he held him, like he'd hold his boys, and then something happened, like electricity flowing from that Miles into him. His fingers moving fast as lightning.

On the other side of the band of doctors, he paused. *Something's not right.* "Where's Miles? You know, the tall one of you with the green eyes."

Dr. Rayburn stiffened, and his followers grew silent. "I was hoping you'd let that pass, Antoine. Rest assured that Miles Fox will never again be anywhere near a patient at Mercy Memorial, or anywhere else, for that matter."

"Huh?" Antoine wished he could remember. At some point he'd passed out, probably from that damn morphine. When he'd woken his room was in chaos: guards and nurses, a man cradling an obviously broken hand or wrist. But no Miles.

Rayburn pushed through his retinue and stood a couple feet from Antoine. "We understand if you want to file a complaint. Things like that should never happen."

Antoine cracked a smile. "I don't know what you're talking about. I just wanted to find the man and shake his hand. That's all. He made a promise to my son, and it looks like he kept it. Now I got to go. I'll keep all the clinic appointments, and you can take as much blood as you want, but I got to go."

That's just weird, he thought as he passed through the ward to the bank of elevators. While he'd like to know what the hell they were talking about, getting the hell out of the hospital and back to his family was all he wanted. He bit his lip and tapped his fingers against the handle of his suitcase as the elevator brought him down to the lobby, with its bronze fountain of Jesus healing the leper. He told himself that he'd track down that Miles—and now he had a last name, Fox—but that would have to wait.

"Oh sweet Lord!" There they were, Lila holding Baby Moses, and his ma with Jasper in his blue-jean overalls with the penguin on the bib. Tears flowed as he raced across the lobby, not caring how he looked. He wrapped his beautiful wife and sweet babe in a tight embrace as Jasper threw his arms around his leg.

His ma's voice whispered in his ear, "Sometimes he answers our prayers." His mouth found Lila's. Her tears mingled with his as he tasted the sweetness of the woman he'd loved since high school. There was electricity here too. *There's magic in the world. I love you so much. So much.* He clutched her tight with his free hand, the baby cradled between them.

Jasper squealed, "Daddy's coming home!"

Yeah, I am. Standing there, holding his family tight, he realized how close they'd come to disaster. He pulled back from Lila. Like him, she was forty-two, still beautiful with full lips and dark liquid eyes. He wiped a hand down the side of her cheek. *How many tears has she cried for me? I have got to be a better man for her, for them.* He shrank from the enormity of what almost happened. *I have no life insurance. She has no job. She's got the boys to raise. How could I have been so selfish, so stupid?* His lips gently touched down on hers. *Just a taste.* "Lila, I want to stop at the office and take care of some stuff. That okay?"

"Sure, babe. But I got to warn you, there's going to be a lot of people. Kind of a homecoming thing."

"Got it. But we'll kick 'em out when we want. You know what I mean?" *Sweet Lord, she is so beautiful.*

"Oh yeah." And with the baby strapped across her chest, she took his hand as his ma pried Jasper from his leg.

"The little one's getting strong," Ma remarked as they moved en masse through the revolving doors.

Outside the late-morning sun beat down on their heads. Even this late in October, the mercury was kissing ninety. Antoine breathed deep. "I'm going to be a better man for you and the boys, Lila."

She gripped his hand tighter as Uncle Roy pulled up in his Prius. "I don't know what you're talking about, Antoine. I've got the man I want."

"I can be better, Lila. I've been given a second chance, and I'm not wasting it."

Roy popped the hatch, and Antoine stowed his suitcase as Lila and his ma strapped the children into their car seats.

Antoine looked down the avenue toward Canal Street, the sun on his back, his thoughts clear for the first time in months. *Nope, no withdrawal here.* He watched as his precious family got settled in. *Be a better man, Antoine.*

"I'm going to check in at the office and then be right home."

Uncle Roy looked back from the driver's seat. "You don't want us to drop you there?"

"Nah, I need the walk. I feel weak as a kitten."

"Good enough."

Antoine tapped on the passenger-side window.

Lila pressed the down button.

"Just one more."

They locked lips as Jasper squealed "Wheee!" from the backseat.

"So good." Antoine let her taste, smell, and feel linger.

"Don't be long," Lila said.

"I won't."

And Roy put the car into gear and they drove off.

FROM THE air-conditioned comfort of a black 5-Series BMW, Calvin Stangl observed the family pile into the blue Prius. With earbuds embedded, he pointed the antenna of the listening device toward the Deys. It was like watching a different species. It ran deeper. *This is what families are supposed to be,* he thought. He looked at Lila Dey and how her gestures and words emanated love toward her children and her husband. He wondered what it might be like to be a part of Antoine's coming-home celebration. To be part of a real family.

Like a river rock worn smooth by the passage of time and water, Calvin's mind wandered a familiar path. *Where is my mother? Who is my mother? Is she even alive?* And always the uncertainty: *Did Father kill her? He says he didn't, that it was a business arrangement, an egg and a womb in exchange for a car and some cash.*

When he was little, before Father's displeasure turned to a slap across the face or a punch to the back, he'd asked, "Father, where's my mommy?"

Father's reply was "You don't have one, son. You're mine and mine alone."

When he was thirteen and used to Father's mercurial shifts in temper and lightning-fast strikes, he mustered courage and asked again. "Who is my mother? Where does she live? Is she alive?"

The answers, then, were worse than the anticipated beating. "She never wanted you, son. She had you for money, and I have no idea where she is now, or if she's alive."

As Lila Dey buckled her infant into his seat, Calvin listened to her nonsensical cooing and the baby's giggles. He imagined Father's comments. He would most certainly disparage their skin tones and make harsh comments about the mingling of blood. It would be for Calvin's ears only. At times trying to keep the man's personas separate was dizzying. As a young boy, he was confused by how the father who commanded respect in the psychiatric hospitals and research settings where he ruled supreme could be the same man who drank whisky and ranted without pause about racial superiority. For Gerald Stangl, the outcome of the Second World War had doomed humanity to mediocrity and a devolutionary process that, if not stopped, would leave the human race as a pack of slobbering imbeciles.

Calvin aimed the antenna toward Antoine. He was speaking. "I'm going to check in at the office and then be right home." The couple kissed and exchanged endearments.

He's not going with them. That's too bad. Disappointment washed through him as Antoine waved and the Prius drove off.

With the motor idling, Calvin watched Antoine Dey head toward Canal Street. He pulled up the address for A Good Dey's Plumbing and entered it into the GPS. He mentally calculated the time it would take Dey to arrive. He thought of what he'd need to complete this task. But the hardest part was already done. Like Father, he too could change, and like throwing a switch over all the soft emotions Father despised, Calvin turned off his humanity. He was here to do a job. Antoine Dey, with his lovely family, was a means to an end, and the ends always justified the means.

CHAPTER 13

Miles's hands trembled as he shuffled the tarot cards.

Marie, who'd just saved his ass, lit a candle in the darkened bar. "You are part Gypsy," she said, and she instructed him to cut the deck.

"No, I'm Jewish."

"You are part Gypsy," she repeated. "Romany, like me, and of an ancient line. Children of the wind… of the dark blood." She selected a first card. "The Queen of Cups. It travels in your grandmother, and she is frightened. She is a woman with two faces. One she shows to you, and the other to the rest of the world. Not even her own child, who she did not want to bring into this world, knows who and what she really is. A woman of secrets. She is interesting."

She drew a second card. "Ace of Wands. She is traveling…. As we speak she is in the air. Because one does not believe in witches"—she winked at Miles—"I'd say she is on an airplane. She will arrive soon."

She placed a third card across the first two. She inhaled sharply. "The Magician inverted. Well, those handsome officers told me you were in danger, or rather, you were danger. But that is just the tip. Something bigger and darker lies below." Marie stared at the cards and then at Miles. "It's in your eyes." Her voice grew breathy. "Your eyes, your eyes, your eyes." She chanted and gently rolled her upper body back and forth. "Your eyes, your eyes, your eyes…."

Miles watched the usually jovial and flirtatious woman as she entered a trance. He wondered at her pronouncements. She was spot on the money, but with a few good guesses…. *But how did she know Grandma Anna is coming?* His rational mind answered, *You must have said…. No, you didn't.* He stared at Marie. The shadows from the candle cut deep lines in her face. *Why is she helping me? Is she helping me? You need to get out of here.*

"No." Marie spoke, her voice now deep and masculine, with a thick Eastern European accent. "You are safe here. For now. I must speak to you."

That voice. I know that voice.

"Of course you do."

"You're reading my thoughts." *This is not happening… not possible.*

"Yes, it is. I am Tomas. I believe we've met." Marie started to laugh, only it wasn't her voice. "A fox must be with a fox, a modern retelling of an ancient tale." Her eyes widened, and she reached for her whisky and drained it. "This is delightful! I miss spirits. And now I am one." She doubled over with laughter.

Miles struggled to make sense of her bizarre display. Yes, maybe he'd said something about Grandma Anna—*No, you didn't*. But this, how could she know about Tomas, about the dream he'd had in the emergency room? "Prove it. Prove you are who you say."

"I'll do far more than that. Gaze into the candle, boy."

Miles did as instructed, at first feeling foolish, and then something shifted at the periphery of his vision.

"Don't fight it. Let it come."

A man's green eyes formed in the flame, and below them a handlebar moustache. There was no mistaking him. Tomas, the man from the lake, the man from his dream. The image broadened like a movie opening onto a scene. Tomas embraced a naked and emaciated old woman; she was dying, and they were in some kind of 1940s operating room. The two were fused. *Gift. He's using the gift.* Fascinated, he focused on Tomas's hands as they fluttered over the woman's body. His fingers blurred. The vision broadened, and he saw others. Some in black uniforms with Nazi insignia, men in long white coats, and a nurse in blue and white.

"Why are you showing me this?"

"Ssh, watch."

Miles let his focus widen. There was a little girl being restrained by the nurse and a soldier. The child was frantic. Tears flowed from her green eyes. *That's Grandma Anna.* He struggled to hear what was being said. Her lips formed a plea for her papa as the nurse dug her fingers into her shoulders and the soldier gripped her tight around the middle. They were forcing her to watch.

Tomas completed the healing. He released the woman. His eyes met his daughter's. There was resignation in his expression. He shook his head as though willing her to be silent.

The doctors examined the woman Tomas had healed. They drew vials of blood from her arm.

One of them nodded to a pair of guards. They grabbed Tomas by his arms and strapped him to a surgical table.

The little girl screamed. Miles realized she was speaking in a foreign language, but he could understand it. "He did what you want. Let him go. Let my papa go."

What followed was brutality unlike anything Miles could have imagined. And through it all, they forced the little girl to watch.

A nurse wheeled a metal tray to the table where Tomas was strapped. She pulled back a linen cover to reveal an assortment of gleaming scalpels and a surgical saw. A surgical lamp was adjusted over Tomas, and a pair of doctors set to work decapitating him while he was awake.

He gasped his final words out to his daughter in a language Miles should not have understood. "I will never leave you. I am in the lake. Find me in the lake."

Marie blinked and shook her head. She looked from Miles to the cards in front of her. Her eyes found the bottle of whisky. She grabbed it and took a long swig. "Well, that was… awful… and interesting," she said.

Stunned by what he'd just witnessed, Miles wondered what other horrors were to be revealed. "What?"

"Wait." She held up a hand as though listening to something. "I've a message for you." She appeared confused. "Right…. Oh, that is good. Yes, I can see how that might work. And the fiddle should help."

To Miles she appeared to be holding a conversation, only it wasn't with him.

"You'll find your answers in the lake, Mr. Fox." She drew a final card and placed it crosswise atop the others. The Fool. She smiled, and still chatting with someone not in the room, she nodded. "Are you certain this is not revenge for messing with your tale? Yes." She smiled and focused on Miles. "It is not safe for you here. I must send you on your way." She retrieved his Angels cap from off the counter. She stared at the logo. "Magic does exist. You more than anyone should know that. The trick is to not ignore its subtlety. It whispers." She laid the cap down on the bar. "And now… I need you to strip."

FORTY-FIVE MINUTES later, Marie put down the airbrush gun and stepped back from Miles. They were in the back room behind the curtain, interrupted by incoming wait- and kitchen staff who thought nothing of the duo's activities, other than one who asked, "We turning into a strip club?" and Marie's pretty niece, who looked him up and down and asked, "Gay or straight?"

"Gay."

"Damn!"

Marie chuckled at her handiwork as he stared in the full-length mirror. He was naked save for a pair of gossamer wings, the skimpiest of silver Mylar briefs, and a pair of silver sandals that laced up his calves. His entire body, including his hair, had been airbrushed silver and then doused in glitter. Even his violin hadn't escaped, the bow wrapped in silver ribbon and the fiddle dusted with the same paint she'd used on his skin.

"It all washes off," she'd assured him as she sprinkled glitter down his back.

Despite the peril and the terror of what they'd witnessed, he observed how much fun she was having. "You're taking far too much pleasure in this."

"Don't be silly. Painting hot naked men is part of a New Orleans woman's civic duty. Now you must go. But wait…." She reached into her blouse and removed two twenties from her bra. "Hmm. You'll need this." And like tipping a stripper, she grabbed the edge of his briefs and tucked the bills inside.

She whispered, "Now I'm serious, it's not safe here." She led him to the front of the house and pulled back the security bar.

"Shouldn't I go out the back?" Miles asked, looking toward the door where the staff had come in, which, despite the sign, was not alarmed.

"No. You are dressed for Bourbon Street, not for the alley."

He hesitated in the doorway. It was early afternoon, and the street was alive with tourists and barkers trying to lure customers into the clubs. There were also cops. He reminded himself they were always in force for crowd control and to redirect the drunk and the homeless. *But not this many. They're here for you. This can't possibly work.*

"Cher, your dead great-grandpappy assured me this will work. You have him to blame if it doesn't. You must go."

He looked back at the mostly empty bar, dark and safe. But it wasn't. This was only a resting place. Even now the afternoon employees were prepping tables for the lunch crowd.

So with violin in hand and forty dollars wedged in his briefs, he ventured out. He was immediately spotted by a group of tourists, their smartphones raised as they took his picture. If not for his nakedness and the fact a good portion of the NOPD was hunting for him, this wasn't so different from Sunday afternoons as a teenager when he'd take his violin, open up the case on the broad sidewalks of Harvard Square, and play. The first time he did it, his parents had freaked, but when he came home with over two hundred dollars in cash—far more than he could have made at the minimum-wage fast-food jobs his peers were taking—they'd relented. Of course, back then he had the advantage of being fully clothed.

"Play something," a little boy out with his parents shouted.

Yes, I suppose I should. He focused on the tourists and let the muscles of his face go blank. The silver people were a New Orleans standard; like living sculptures, they wandered the streets. He'd seen them but never really paid much attention to their subtle pantomime.

With efficiency of movement, he brought the fiddle to his chin. *I'm an angel*, he thought, and he brought the bow to string and pulled out the first notes of Schubert's "Ave Maria."

It was years since he'd played on the streets, and he was struck by the power of the instrument as it rose above the clamor of Bourbon Street. Tourists and locals stopped. They encircled him, first one, and then two and three deep. He caught glances from cops, but they weren't hunting a silver-painted violin-playing angel, and so they passed him by. Still. *It's just a matter of time. Someone will recognize me.*

With no expression on his face, he gazed out at the thickening crowd as his fingers found the familiar notes. *They've boxed me in.* Without dropping a note, he started to walk. He came to the crowd's edge, and with fiddle in motion, he made a sweeping bow. He turned his head as though on a pivot and made eye contact with a young woman. She giggled and stepped back, and the crowd parted. He dodged both male and female hands holding bills, which, like Marie, wanted to cop a feel as they tipped the player.

He shook his head no and kept walking. *So one crisis averted. Where do I go?* A few tourists followed, but mostly he gathered stares as he made his way to the intersection of Bourbon and Canal.

The "Ave Maria" gave way to one of Grandpa Henry's favorite Hebrew prayers, "Yigdal." Its haunting minor key brought memories of standing in front of the congregation at the High Holidays and playing for the packed synagogue, his parents and sister, Maya, seated in the front with looks of pride on their faces. Keeping his expression blank, he could only imagine what they'd make of this. *How the hell did you get yourself into this? Don't think, just play.*

A couple of hundred feet ahead, he spotted the St. Charles Streetcar as it headed toward a nearby stop. He knew he shouldn't…. *Luke's done too much.* As he thought of all the reasons why it was wrong to go to Luke, he quickened his pace, and not missing a note, he arrived at the stop as the trolley pulled in.

The female conductor gave him a slow up-and-down. "If you play something churchy, the ride's free."

He nodded, and reaching deep into the violin's lower register, drew out "Amazing Grace."

"That is lovely," she said. "I always said I've got an angel on my shoulder…. 'Course there's a devil on the other one. And now I've got one on my streetcar. This one's on the house." She winked and gestured him in.

Still playing, he climbed up and looked back over the rows of varnished wood benches. It was half-full and all eyes were on him. A few had started to mouth the words, and one woman with a lovely alto was humming harmonies. *Just keep playing.* The benches were too tight for him to get adequate bow room, and so he widened his stance and pressed his painted back against one of the metal pipes that ran from floor to ceiling. The trolley rumbled off, and he found that by keeping his knees and ankles loose, he was able to play and keep his balance. The conductor, her head bobbing to the music, eased extra smooth into the stops.

"Amazing Grace" gave way to "His Eye Is on the Sparrow," which gave way to Beethoven's "Ode to Joy." He even snuck in the ancient Hebrew tune "Eli Eli."

"I don't know that one," said the woman with the alto, who'd changed her seat to be next to him, "but it's lovely." She raised her voice, easily finding the song's soulful sweet spots, as did several others.

As the trolley passed from the French Quarter through the claustrophobic buildings of the industrial section and finally into the gracious homes of the Garden District, Miles played on.

A few stops from the end, the woman with the alto got up. "That was certainly a treat, young man. May God be with you, and may he keep you and all that you love safe."

Miles let the smallest of smiles cross his lips. As she got up to leave, he pulled the opening strains of "Swing Low, Sweet Chariot."

She stopped. "You did not just do that." She belted out the refrain, and with obvious reluctance stepped off the trolley, then continued to sing in full voice as it rolled away.

The car thinned out, and the Norman turrets of Loyola University came into sight. *Don't do this to him, Miles. Think of something else. Somewhere else. The cops are after you. You don't know what lies Stangl spread. Don't do this to Luke. He's done too much already.*

Without thought the melody shifted again. It was the Kol Nidre, a sacred piece reserved for Yom Kippur, the day of atonement.

The streetcar came to its final stop. The conductor called back to him, "You're more than welcome to stay on board. I turn around here."

He shook his head no, and with a courtly bow and flourish of harmonic chords, he stepped off the trolley. There were far fewer people on the streets here, mostly students heading between classes. And unlike the French Quarter, he was the only one in costume. *You can't stay out here.*

He glanced from the stately live oaks across from Loyola that had weathered Katrina to the tidy tree-lined streets where he, Luke, and Jenna would wander, quizzing one another for upcoming histology and microbiology exams. He let the violin hang at his side. The time to draw attention to himself was over. Of course, being mostly naked and silver made that impossible. *Just stay in the role. This is New Orleans. Halloween is a week away. They'll think I'm going to a party.*

The silver angel had gotten him this far, but with little money, no clothes, and a manhunt trying to track him down, he was out of options. *And that's not all, is it?* He scanned the broad street for cops. There were no cruisers, no officers handing out his picture. *Have they stopped looking?*

He walked quickly over the familiar blocks that led to the two-story clapboard house Luke rented with the two "Js"—Joel and Justin. *They should both be in class. Shit! It's Wednesday, Luke's primary-care clinic day.* It didn't matter whether he was post-call or not. *He's going to be in clinic. Maybe I can hide in the toolshed, but then what?*

He rounded the corner and imagined dozens of eyes watching him. Rather than go to the front of the tidy house, with its pretentious white columns and broad porches on the first and second floors, he ducked through the side gate and headed around back to the kitchen door. He looked at the toolshed and at the yew hedges that obscured the yard from the neighbors.

You shouldn't be here. This isn't fair to him. He thought of what Luke had said in the emergency room. "You didn't ask. I offered, so shut up about it."

Maybe that was true… but he was just being a stand-up guy. This is different, Miles, and you know it. Torn between knocking and hiding out in the shed, he startled at the sound of the kitchen door opening.

Luke peered through the screen. He looked dazed and wired, having not slept in two days. "Miles?" He took in the full effect, from the silver violin to the Mylar Speedo. "Wow. Quite the look you got there."

"I couldn't think of anyplace to go. You don't have to let me in." *I shouldn't be here. He's going to help because he's a good guy. Don't do this to him.*

"Don't be an idiot." Luke opened the screen. He tried not to stare.

"I know," Miles said. "Can I use your shower, and maybe borrow some clothes? All I can think is that when they catch me, I'll be in a downtown lockup dressed like Tinker Bell. Is anyone else home?"

"No. They're both at class."

"Okay, I'll just shower this crap off and get out of here."

NOT FOR the first time that day, Luke wondered if he was losing his effing mind. Everything seemed unreal, between no sleep, Miles's bizarre revelations, his meeting with the dean, and the two detectives. But no, Miles just showed up at his door looking like a silver god complete with wings and a violin. In any other circumstance, this would have provided weeks of ribbing, postings on Facebook, Instagram, and Twitter, all the fun crap Halloween and Mardi Gras always generated.

He heard the shower and tried to block images of his handsome best friend upstairs and naked. He imagined the drain flowing with sweat and silver paint. *Don't,* he warned himself. *The cops are looking for him, you've just been expelled, and you have to deal with your father. Don't think about him. He's your friend. Your hot friend. Your guy friend. You don't let yourself think about guys, Luke. Not like that. You don't…. Yeah?*

He headed to his bedroom and grabbed a pair of jeans, a faded black tee, and a pair of not-too-beat-up running shoes. He tried to shut down the chatter in his head as he opened his underwear drawer and selected a pair of blue-and-white striped boxers. *Just open the door and hand them in. Jesus, stop being so lame; it's not like you haven't seen him naked.* And he flashed on the silver man outside his kitchen door, who was now in the shower down the hall. *Yeah, and it's not like you haven't had these thoughts before either.*

"Crap." Struggling to get his emotions under control and feeling like he might have a panic attack, he thought about those detectives and the meeting with Dean Strachey. "Let's recap, Luke." The sound of his voice helped him to calm. "You've been kicked out of medical school, the cops are probably outside your door right now, and you're suddenly deciding your best friend is kind of hot." *No, moron, it's not sudden, and you know it. Just don't go there, please don't go there. Think of Jenna. She loves you. You love her….*

Holding the stack of folded clothes with the shoes on top, he stopped outside the bathroom. He stood and listened to the water. He pictured Miles on the other side of the door. How many times had they showered at the gym after racquetball, or circuit training, or pummeling one another at Krav Maga class?

"They released your patient, Mr. Dey," Luke said.

"What?" Miles shouted back. "I can't hear you."

Luke cracked the door. The room was filled with steam, and he averted his eyes from the spectacle of Miles's tall silhouette through the fogged glass shower door. "Your patient, Mr. Dey. He signed himself out. Before I got off my shift, I pulled up his files. They did two full-body MRIs…. They thought there was a mistake."

Luke swallowed as Miles turned off the shower.

"The tumors were gone. I went and compared the films. He was filled with cancer, Miles. Everything you said was true." Luke felt as though his head would explode. "He was stage four."

Miles slid the shower door back and grabbed a towel from the wall rack.

Luke stared at the floor as Miles wrapped the towel around his hips and stepped out.

MILES LOOKED at Luke. *He's exhausted,* he thought, but something else, and the word that came was "tormented." *Something's wrong here. It's Wednesday. He shouldn't be here.* "Why are you home, Luke? What's happened?"

Luke grimaced. He wouldn't make eye contact. "Apparently I abetted a dangerous mental patient. I'm suspended…. Probably expelled."

"No! Luke, I'm so sorry. You shouldn't have helped me."

Luke looked up. "What the fuck, Miles! You're my friend, and you didn't ask for help; I gave it to you! I gave you my cell phone. You didn't ask for it, and I fucking put my key card in your hand."

Luke lunged for Miles; he smashed his mouth against his friend's. It was more violence than kiss, teeth against teeth.

Just as suddenly he recoiled. "Fuck! No! Miles, I'm so sorry. I'm not gay, I don't know… I'm sorry." He turned to flee the bathroom.

"Luke!" Miles grabbed him by his shoulders. "It's okay. What's going on?" His hands rested on Luke's shoulders. "Please calm down." He felt his friend's fear and confusion, but there was more, and their proximity and wearing only a towel made things problematic. "I know you're not gay. I am…. And I've not been honest with you about my feelings. I feel shitty about that. And if you still want to be my friend, and I'll understand if you don't, I'll tell you the truth, about that, about everything." He felt Luke relax and his panic recede. "Can you look at me?"

He released his grip, and Luke turned to face him.

Luke winced. There was blood on Miles's upper lip. "I didn't mean to do that. What's wrong with me?" He looked down and saw the front of Miles's towel tenting up. *He's not the only one who's been hiding shit.* "I'm lying too," he said.

"About what?" Miles asked.

Luke's chest tightened. It was like he was falling, his senses pounded by the steam, the sweet smells of grease paint, soap, and Miles. It was too much, the water beading down his chest. The green of his eyes, the shape of his mouth. *This is a drug.* "My feelings for you." Without thought he touched Miles's cheek. There were still traces of silver. His fingers tracked down the dark, moist stubble to his lips. "I want to try again." *Just one taste,* he thought.

Miles held his gaze and didn't move, as if giving Luke a last out.

Please, Luke thought, *don't make me beg.*

Miles closed the inches between them, and their lips met. The connection was immediate and unexpected.

Luke gripped Miles's sopping hair, pulling him close. Lips and tongues fused, violence and sweetness and ache and need. Luke knew there was no turning back. This was heroin, and he was hooked.

Chapter 14

Anna Warren glanced at the arrivals board at New Orleans's Louis Armstrong International Airport. It was one thirty in the afternoon. She'd wasted no time following Miles's early-morning call. She'd stuffed a change of clothes, her cell, and an iPad into an oversized leather shoulder bag and pushed eighty miles per hour on the drive from Truro to Logan Airport.

While nothing about this nightmare was lucky, that she was able to get on standby for the JetBlue commuter flight to New Orleans was a godsend. *This is all my fault*, she thought, a theme that had plagued her since the phone call with her grandson. It wasn't just that she hadn't prepared him; her regrets ran deeper. *I should never have had a child. This should have ended with me.* At eighty years old, Anna knew the dangers facing Miles were real, and the stakes were high.

She checked her cell, expecting to see messages from Miles. There was nothing from him, several from her daughter Rachel, and three from a number she didn't recognize. She dialed her daughter.

"Mother, where are you?"

"At home, dear," Anna lied.

"Have you seen the news? I can't believe it. What's happening? He can't have done the things they say."

"What are you talking about?" Anna found a seat in the terminal and pulled out her iPad. She clicked onto the *Huffington Post* and tapped in the words Miles Fox, New Orleans.

She listened to Rachel as she read the news about Miles. It was horrible. She'd come to New Orleans expecting to comfort Miles, to tell him—in a kind way—that she'd been right all along about medical school, that it could never be for him, and she'd bring him back to Cape Cod to lick his wounds and regroup. In her fantasy she would extract a promise that he would never again use the gift. A promise she'd made him make every year since the nightmare with that dog. It was simple in her head, but not this. And yet a part of her knew this was coming. It had always been coming. *This is fate, and you can't run from it.*

"Mother, are you listening?"

"Yes, dear." Anna concealed her mounting dread. The news stories didn't make sense. And in her experience, when things didn't make sense and a green-eyed child with the gift was anywhere in the mix, something horrible was about to happen. She shuddered. *Or might already have happened.*

Rachel's confusion and worry came through clear. "Joseph called the dean of the medical school. She wouldn't say much. Miles isn't dangerous. How can they say those things? Joseph and I have to go to New Orleans. He's going to need us. Mother, I'm so frightened. All those guns.... What if they think he's armed? What if…?"

Anna needed to end the call. Her daughter's panic made it hard to think. Never far from paralyzing flashbacks of her childhood, Anna struggled to stay grounded.

"Mother, Maya isn't taking this well. We were hoping you could stay with her for a few days."

"I'm sorry, dear, I can't. I did something stupid and sprained my ankle. I'm not terribly mobile right now. And rather than going to New Orleans, it might be better to stay put. Miles will need to know where you are. You'll be able to help him better from Brookline. Yes, that would be best. I'm sure everything will work out fine. Dear, there's someone at the door. Call me later."

Before Anna could hang up, her daughter asked, "Why didn't you pick up earlier?"

"I didn't hear the ring. I must have put it on mute."

"And the house phone? I tried that several times."

"Dear, enough with the questions."

"Mother, where are you?"

Anna thought of several easy lies. But for once the truth seemed easier. "New Orleans, dear. I've come to find Miles. I will bring him home." Before her daughter could say another word, Anna hung up and put the phone on mute.

With a hand to her mouth, she read the reports on the iPad. They portrayed Miles as a potential mass killer, stockpiling weapons with paranoid fantasies of taking vengeance on a world out to get him.

She tried his cell. Again, no answer. She wasn't surprised, knowing how easily those could be traced. He said he'd call her. She checked the history on her phone: more than a dozen calls from her daughter and three from a strange number. She did a quick web search on the mystery number. It had a New Orleans area code. *It has to be him.* She hit Redial.

A woman picked up. "Swamp Witch."

Anna paused.

The woman on the phone spoke. "Don't hang up. You're looking for someone."

"Yes," Anna said.

"A fox, perhaps?"

"Is he there?"

"Left over an hour ago. It wasn't safe here. Sadly, it's not safe for him anywhere, but you know that, don't you?"

"Where did he go?" Anna asked.

"To a friend, possibly a boyfriend. I couldn't see that clear."

"What? My grandson is gay?"

"Not the most pressing of his concerns."

"True," Anna said.

"He's in terrible danger, as are you. For someone so filled with life, he's surrounded by death. But again, you know this. Is there anything I can do to help?"

"I have to find him."

"Wait," the woman said.

Over the line Anna heard the woman step away from the phone. And then she came back. "I see a cemetery, I can't tell which one, and a white house, not a big one, with pillars and wisteria. It needs paint, and the grass is long. Wait…. He's on the St. Charles Streetcar. He's mortified, and people are staring at him. Tourists are taking his picture."

"I'm too late."

"No," the woman chuckled, "but you should head to the Garden District, toward the end of the trolley line. If I see more, I'll call you, but go quick. The danger is near. Death, horrible death, is near."

Chapter 15

Antoine Dey lay on a cold metal table in a room that smelled of pine disinfectant. *It must have been a dream.* His disappointment was devastating. *I never left the hospital. There was no miracle, but why can't I move?*

He tried to remember Lila and the boys picking him up at the hospital. The bronze Jesus healing the lepers, Uncle Roy at the wheel, the sun on his face. It had seemed so real. But now… he took in his surroundings. He couldn't move his neck, but he could hear and feel. The table was so cold beneath his bare skin. *Why am I naked?*

He heard two men's voices and caught glimpses of a young blond man. *This isn't a dream. What's happening?* He'd gone to his office, and the young man had come in looking for a plumber. Antoine had been skeptical, but through the window he'd seen the boy's black BMW. He'd said his father was putting an addition on their home, and they needed a plumber. *Either that was a dream, or this is.*

He tried to move. *What's happening?* Tears of fear and frustration slid down his face.

"No, Mr. Dey," the older man's voice said. "The only muscle that works is your diaphragm, and if we're not careful with your dose of tetrodotoxin, that will be paralyzed as well. Interesting fact about that drug: it's derived from toadfish venom. But please, calm yourself. I'm certain that this must all be confusing and scary. It is however, necessary. I'm Dr. Gerald Stangl and you've met my son, Calvin."

Antoine relaxed. *He's a doctor. I am in the hospital. Do I still have cancer? I'll ask when the medication wears off.* But then came a different doubt. *Why would a doctor send his son to my office? But maybe part of this is a dream, and things are jumbled. It's the drugs. His son looks too young to be working in the hospital.*

That started him thinking of his own boys. Would Jasper or Moses join him in the family business? He could imagine the day they'd change the signs, find a new play on words to replace A Good Dey's Plumbing. Dey and Sons Plumbing; too boring. Maybe Sonny Dey's Plumbing, or A Sonny Dey's Plumbing. He'd buy a second red truck and put the white letters on

93

the side. They could do their apprenticeships with him, or if they wanted, he'd ask one of his friends at the trade guild to take them on....

"We're going to run a series of tests," Dr. Stangl explained. "You've been through something extraordinary, and we've limited opportunity to study the effects. The test we're doing now is a functional MRI. It's similar to the MRIs you've had, but it's the difference between taking a snapshot and a motion picture of the brain and the body. Calvin, start the infusion. It's a fascinating bit of machinery. Over five million dollars and the type of thing that was completely beyond the science of my father, my grandpapa, and all the many before them. This is a new age and an exciting time. And you, Mr. Dey, are part of history."

While still confused, the fear was gone as the doctor explained the procedure. This felt familiar. Doctors explaining tests, him nodding his head as though he understood while all the time just wanting them to keep him alive for his family. *I was an idiot. I didn't make plans.*

And then he remembered that's why he left Lila and the boys and the celebration. He'd gone to the office with the single intent of tracking down the biggest life insurance policy he could buy and signing on the dotted line. *But that was real.* He'd gone online and quickly found his having had cancer limited the policies he could find, even the ones through the trade guild. His thoughts drifted to that last kiss with Lila. He wondered what day it was. *Did they have the party? Was I there and forgot the entire thing?*

Antoine felt a burning in his arm. It spread a tingly warmth through his body. Beneath him the table started to move, and he was slid into a metal chamber. *Didn't they just do this one? Right, the doctor said this is different, like a movie.* He listened for the doctor's voice as the machine began its rhythmic clanging.

CALVIN WATCHED the LED monitor as the radio-labeled glucose they'd infused into Antoine Dey lit up in the colors of the rainbow. Red and yellow for areas of increased metabolism, blue and violet for regions with lower glucose utilization and presumably less activity.

"Can you identify the regions where the tumors were?" Father asked.

"Yes, the compression on the surrounding tissues and organs is like a negative impression." *And so start the questions. I will not flinch. I will hold my ground.* And just as he did when jabbing the needle into the back of Antoine Dey's neck, he flipped the imaginary switch that allowed himself to feel nothing. *I am a machine, and he cannot hurt me.*

Slice by slice he watched as they scanned Mr. Dey's body for traces of cancer and observed the extent to which the metastases had gone.

"I doubt he'd have lasted the week. Possibly even the night," Father stated.

"Yes, you were right," Calvin said. "All these years, all this waiting, you were right. Miles Fox has the healing gift." *And what do you intend to do with him, Father?* He stared at the monitor. He wanted to ask why this series of experiments was necessary. They'd seen the MRIs that had been done at the hospital. No, they weren't this fancy, but they provided the answer. Antoine Dey was tumor-free, and Miles Fox had healed him. *This isn't necessary. I want this to stop.*

"Yes. I was right."

"But he got away," Calvin said. *You thought you had him and you didn't. Does that hurt, Father?*

"He's close. Yes, he slipped away, but the fox can only run so fast or so far. You have to understand the workings of destiny, son. We spend our lives focused on the science, but there's more in the world than what we can see on a scanner or under the electron microscope. Other forces are at play."

It wasn't the response Calvin expected. Where was Father's rage, his fist? *Something's different.*

"It was no coincidence that Joseph and Rachel Fox brought their precocious eight-year-old to see me. If we've learned anything from the past, Calvin, it's the importance of waiting for the right moment. I'd wanted to start this work all those years ago and was thwarted in my efforts. To have pressed would have created unnecessary risk. But that's not why I didn't move forward."

"You didn't have the technology," Calvin added.

"Exactly, and while we now know with absolute certainty that the bloodline continued, Miles Fox is perhaps the only phenotypic example on the face of the planet. Although I wonder about the grandmother; she too has the green eyes. He—possibly they—are a precious resource not to be squandered."

Calvin thought of the cupboard with six heads in jars. "They should have left one alive."

"They should have done lots of things. And if the grandmother is the carrier, as she must be, it's possible they did. My father was about your age when they left Germany; he and Grandpapa would tell me stories of the final days. Of the desperation in the camps as they tried to complete their experiments, knowing time was running out. They made mistakes, and as you're well aware from their journals, the final experiments were sloppy and wasteful."

"They remind me of a child who breaks a toy to try and see what makes it work and then is upset when he realizes the toy no longer works."

Father nodded. "An apt metaphor. I see no trace of tumor, do you?"

"No." And unbidden, Calvin pressed the button that stopped the test and retracted Antoine Dey from the chamber. Something swelled in his chest. *Why is Father treating me like this… like a colleague?* "We'll use the labeled staphylococcus first?"

"Yes."

ANTOINE'S EYES adjusted to the fluorescents. The young man was by his side. "It's remarkable, Mister Dey. There's no trace of cancer. You are in complete remission."

Antoine felt something ease inside. *Remission.* Could there be a sweeter word? He just wished he could remember how he came back to the hospital. *It wasn't a dream… and it doesn't make sense. And why is a teenager giving me the test? This isn't right.*

"What you're now receiving," the young man explained, "is a highly virulent and resistant form of bacteria. They call it flesh-eating. What we need to find out is whether or not the healing you underwent less than twenty-four hours ago has residual effects. If it does, the bacteria will be rendered harmless. If it doesn't…. Well, then we've learned something important."

He felt sick as the boy's words sank in. He wanted to scream, to rip the IV tube from his arm, but he was paralyzed with toadfish poison, and none of that was possible. Tears squeezed from his eyes. This can't be happening. *I'm in remission. Please don't. How could someone do something like this?* He felt the cold liquid enter his vein and creep up his arm and toward his heart.

"I'm afraid we're going to have to keep you awake for this," the boy said. "Too many variables if we give you drugs. Maybe you should try to think about your family. They seemed real nice."

CHAPTER 16

STILL IN her blue scrubs and short white coat, Jenna Simpson, blonde, twenty-two, a one-time first runner-up of Miss Teen Charleston, couldn't get her mind to shut up as she jogged the three blocks from the trolley stop to Luke's house. He hadn't shown up for his Wednesday clinic, and rumors about him swirled among her classmates.

She sprinted the last few yards and, barely winded, grabbed her key ring from the outer pocket of her backpack. She opened the front door. The stuff they were saying couldn't be true. *Expelled? Luke? Not possible. Or some kind of mistake. This has to get fixed... if it's even true.* And they were saying stuff about Miles. Yes, she loved Luke, but Miles too, in a way. He was unlike anyone she'd ever met: funny, smart, someone to confide in, and if he weren't gay.... They'd gravitated together almost from the first week of medical school. Even now, when they were mired in the rigors of the clinical rotations and brutal on-call schedules, they all found the time to get together, to study, to check out the local clubs. *This stuff can't be true. Luke expelled.... Miles assaulted a patient. Not possible.*

Standing in the front hall, she called out, "Luke? Luke?"

Is he even home? There's got to be an explanation for this. And what if there isn't? She heard sounds from one of the upstairs bedrooms. "Luke?" With her runner's legs she took the stairs two at a time.

"Luke?"

She flung open the door, and was halfway through when her brain caught up with her eyes. Luke in bed, buck naked with an equally naked second body. A very male body.... Two pairs of shocked eyes. Luke's and Miles's. Random thoughts tumbled through her head. *What the—? Why is Luke in bed with...? He's got such beautiful eyes. They've been having sex. It smells like sex.* The bedding was mostly on the floor. Luke and Miles glistened with sweat. The sun through the slatted blinds caught sparks of silver glitter on their flushed skin. *Luke, my boyfriend, is having sex with Miles, my friend, my good friend.* Time froze as she took in the details, from the blood on Miles's lips to his ripped abs to Luke's shocked expression as he simultaneously tried to cover himself and go to her.

"No." She whipped her hand up to her lips. "No." She backed away. *This isn't possible.* The blood drained from her head and her knees weakened. "Oh my God." She stared at Miles. "How could you?"

"Jenna!"

Grabbing the sheet, Luke tried to get out of bed, but the material tangled around his legs, and he nearly toppled off the side.

Time went from standstill to rapid motion as he flailed his arm for purchase.

Miles grabbed him by the wrist and steadied him.

Still frozen in time, Jenna's head swam. *I have to get out of here. They're both so beautiful. How could they?* And stranger thoughts, which she shut right down. *What would happen if I stripped naked and joined them?*

"You!" She glared at Miles, with his beautiful eyes and perfect body. "I thought we were friends."

Whispered comments batted her thoughts, discussions among her girlfriends about what close friends Luke and Miles were. How it was such a waste Fox was gay. And the thing her friends wouldn't say, at least not with her present: *Are they too close?*

Her rage surfaced. "How could you? You know the cops are looking for you. I hope they catch you. I hope they lock you up. I hope…." She wanted to scream, to plunge her fingers into his pretty green eyes—*prettier than mine.* Luke was hers. Miles was her friend; she told him everything. "How long has this been…? Oh God." Something lurched in her stomach. "I'm going to be sick."

She backed away, needing to get away from them. But the images wouldn't stop. The way Miles kept Luke from falling, the way Luke, *my Luke*, looked back at him. "Oh God." *This is all going to get out. Everyone will know.* Her cheeks burned. *How long have they been together? How long have they been lying to me?* And with that thought, her scream finally came.

STRICKEN, LUKE looked from Jenna to Miles's firm grip around his wrist. He wondered how this day could get worse. *But no, parts of it weren't bad at all.* His body hummed as though awakened from a sleep.

He shook his head and looked back to Jenna, whom he'd dated for the past two years, her hair in a ponytail, her blue eyes close to the color of her scrubs and about to bug out of her head.

"Jenna." He wanted to go to her, to tell her none of this was her fault. To hold her and explain he hadn't intended for this to happen. The words stuck as he took in her panicked expression. "Shit." He regained his balance, let go of Miles, and made an awkward grab for his shorts on the floor as she fled the room and slammed the door.

From the hall came her strangled scream, as though something was tearing inside of her. He looked to Miles. "I've got to go to her."

"Of course. Luke, I'm so sorry."

He shook his head. "Don't be."

His long legs landed on the floor, and he moved cautiously toward the sound of Jenna's sobs.

He opened the door. "Jenna."

She was by the stairs, her hand clenched around the banister, a strand of hair caught in her mouth. Her makeup was smudged, and she batted at her eyes and nose with the back of her lab coat. "Get away from me, Luke. I don't want to talk…." She stared down at the hall below and then back at him. She twisted her mouth, her jaw tight, and her breath was high in her chest. "So you're gay now, is that it?"

He said nothing, hoping she'd calm, knowing nothing he might say would make this right.

"What's the matter? Cat got your tongue, or maybe a fox? Oh God, what am I going to do?" She seemed confused and furious. "How could you? How could he?"

He took a step in her direction.

"Stay back!" she warned, her hand tight on the railing. She started to bounce on the balls of her feet as if ready to launch down the stairs. "Tell me this," she said, unable to look at him. "How long? How long have you two been… fucking!"

"Just now," he stated.

She nodded, still bobbing on her feet. "Was it good?"

"Jenna, don't do this. Let's go downstairs, I'll make tea, we'll…."

"*Was it good?*" she screamed.

"Yes." And that was the truth, and while he hated the pain she was going through, pain he and Miles had caused, there was no turning back. Maybe he was bi… maybe gay, maybe it was just Miles. There was no comparison, and he shrank from the inevitability of her next accusation.

Her voice softened as she gazed at the front door. "It was better than with me, wasn't it?"

"Don't do this, Jenna."

Her head swiveled and she looked at him dead-on. "Just answer the fucking question, Luke. Did you like fucking him better than me?"

Her words hung in the air. Jenna rarely swore. "Jenna…."

"Right, good answer, Luke." She ran down the stairs and then stopped. She looked back at him and pulled out her cell.

"What are you doing?"

She pressed the emergency function and the operator picked up. "Nine-one-one, what is your emergency?"

"My name is Jenna Simpson. I know where Miles Fox is."

MILES BOLTED from bed and grabbed jeans and a tee from Luke's closet. He tried to cram his feet into a pair of sneakers, but his twelves wouldn't make it into Luke's tens. As he fumbled into clothes, he heard Jenna's anguished accusations. *What the hell have I done?* He hadn't intended for any of this to happen. *Yeah, and you're the one who showed up on his doorstep dressed like a stripper. What have I done?*

He knew he couldn't go out into the hall, that showing his face would be more salt in Jenna's wound. He looked to the window.

Luke reappeared in the door. "Miles, she called the cops. You got to get out of here."

"Shit!"

Miles threw open the bedroom window and stepped onto the porch roof. His bare feet sizzled on the tar shingles as he half slid to the edge. He crouched and grabbed for the copper gutter. He dropped over the side, trying to keep his joints loose. He heard Jenna's sobs from inside as he assessed his options. The tall hedges in the back, while providing blockage from the neighbors, gave him only a single point of escape—the side gate, which would take him right by Jenna and the cops who were probably seconds away…. *If they're not already here.*

He reappraised the ten-foot hedge and glimpsed wood-slat fencing behind the evergreens. It was impassable.

He grabbed the gate handle, threw it open, and tore across the lawn and toward the street. Not slowing, he tried to think of any place to hide. Maybe Audubon Park across from Loyola. As he sprinted past stately homes, he glimpsed garages and toolsheds, but if the cops were hunting for him, they'd check those. He was out of options, and for the first time since he escaped from the emergency room, he thought about turning himself in.

You haven't done anything wrong. Aside from destroying your best friend's life, really hurting Jenna, and trying to heal a man with end-stage cancer. What's the worst they could do to you? The thought had merit, and he was about to slow, to just throw up his hands, when he pictured Gerald Stangl. *No, you have to keep running. You can't let him lock you up. He knows about you, about what you did.*

His attention was pulled by a silver sedan as it screeched to a halt, having just made the right onto Luke's street. The driver threw it into reverse, hung a J-turn, and headed toward him.

Miles stopped. He glanced back at the direction he'd come as the silver car bore down on him. *Undercover cops.* He zagged across the street and headed toward St. Charles, Audubon Park now seeming his best bet, when he heard a woman shout his name.

"Miles, stop!"

He did. He pivoted, fixing his eyes on the slowing silver car. He peered into the driver's side. "Grandma?"

"Get in the back!"

He yanked open the door, taking a last look at Luke's house, unable to see either Luke or Jenna.

"Hurry!" Grandma Anna urged. "Get in and stay low. We have to get you out of here."

"No shit!" He dove into the backseat, then pulled the door shut.

"Young man, there's no reason to swear." And taking the first left, she drove toward the interstate.

Chapter 17

M**iles tried** to catch his breath, his head wedged behind the passenger seat. The carpet scratched his face, and he played his tongue across the sore spot on his lip. He could still taste Luke and smell him on his borrowed clothes. "How did you find me?" he asked.

"Swamp Witch, woman named Marie," Anna said, her voice terse as she kept to the speed limit and aimed for the highway. "You tried to call me from there."

"I did…. I was hoping you'd see the New Orleans number and figure it was from me. They took my cell in the emergency room. Even if they hadn't, I'd have had to ditch it."

"Yes, those can be traced," Anna said.

"No flies on you."

"You thought otherwise? Marie is an interesting woman."

"She helped me. She hid me."

"She also said something about a boyfriend."

While Miles had come out to his parents before going off to college, it wasn't a discussion he'd had with Grandma Anna. Huddled in the back of her rented Ford Focus, with much of the NOPD looking for him, seemed as good a time as any. "I'm gay, Grandma." He stared at the painted black metal mechanisms under the passenger seat and held his breath. He knew he hadn't told her when he told his parents because he was more concerned about her reaction than theirs. It was a basic fact of his life. While he loved his parents and his little sister, it was Grandma Anna and her opinion that mattered.

"Good. It's for the best."

"What?" He braced against the seat as she took the left onto Tulane Avenue.

"Good. I said it's for the best…. Stay down, there's cops on the ramp for the I-10."

"Are they stopping cars? Do I need to run?"

"Stay low."

The car slowed. He heard the blinker for the ramp and felt the acceleration as she merged onto the highway.

"Stay down till we're out of state."

"Not a problem…. So why is it for the best if I'm gay?"

"No children, of course."

"What?" Not for the first time, Miles was puzzled by Anna's reaction. After twenty-three years, much of them living in her house on the Cape, it was a rare event when he could predict what would come out of her mouth. "I thought grandmothers were supposed to want great-grandbabies."

"We have much to discuss, boy. I never wanted to have your mother, and I prayed that she'd never have children."

"Awesome. So you're saying you wished I was never born?"

"If you want to put it that way, and don't get all soft, boy. You know that I love you, and I love my daughter and your sister. It would have been best if none of you had been born."

Despite the fact she'd flown halfway across the country to save his ass from a deranged and possibly dangerous psychiatrist, it felt like he'd been kicked in the gut. "Then why did you have Mom?"

"Watch your attitude, boy. Yes, my words are harsh, but would you rather hear lies for the next twenty-four hours?"

Apparently you've been feeding them to me for the past twenty-three years, so what's another day? He kept those thoughts himself. "So why did you have a child?"

A wistfulness entered her voice. "It was your grandfather. Henry could charm the scales off a snake. He so wanted children, and for years he accepted my reluctance. I loved that man so much, Miles. I see a lot of him in you. Do you even remember him? You were so young when he passed."

"I was six. Yeah, I remember some. Mostly with the violin." With regret he thought of Grandpa Henry's fiddle, the bow wrapped in ribbon, the instrument sprayed silver. He'd left it on Luke's kitchen table. *I left Luke. I betrayed Jenna.*

"He wooed and he won me with that fiddle. He played at my parents' *shul*. I'd watch him from the women's galley: young, tall, and so handsome. And don't think he didn't know it. He was a sight, and the way he played…." She chuckled. "He was a rock star."

"He kind of was," Miles said, having treasured memories of watching Grandpa play, even as a little boy wondering if he'd ever be that good, if anyone could be that good. It had driven him to practice daily, to soak up every lesson, never knowing how few there would be. And before he could stop himself, he blurted out the question he'd always wanted to ask her. "Why didn't you save him? Why didn't you use the gift to save him?"

There was silence. He knew she'd heard him, and was tempted to sit up.

After more than a minute, she spoke. "From him you learned the violin, and I see those lessons took. From me you've learned nothing. Don't you see, boy? As you hide in the back of a car and we try to figure out where to go? What to do? The *gift* is a curse. Yes, I could have healed my Henry. I could have held back death for years. You would have grown up with your grandfather; he would have been so proud of you. He would have argued with me and told you to go to medical school, or go be a famous violinist, or play the damn thing on the street for money. He would have loved that…. probably want to join in."

"So why didn't you?"

"I was afraid."

"Of what?"

"Of seeing the love go out in his eyes. Of having him look at me with fear or disgust, of having him see me as something other than the woman he loved."

"You never told him."

"Correct, and that's the reason I never wanted children. I wanted this thing to end with me, and I was never able to tell him. I'd always known I'd not wanted children. It was wrong for me to marry him when there were so many girls throwing themselves at him. I don't think he believed me when I said I didn't want children, or if he did, he thought he'd change my mind."

"Which he did."

"Eventually, yes…. I had two abortions, Miles."

"What?"

"Yes, I couldn't bear the thought of bringing a child into the world, of keeping this thing alive."

"Did Grandpa know?"

"Of course not. When I became pregnant with your mother, I had already made the appointment to terminate."

This is crazy, he thought, realizing how close he and his entire family had come to nonexistence. Keeping his anger back, he asked, "So why did you have her?"

"Henry discovered I was pregnant. I let it go too long, and his mother, may she rest somewhere, whispered in his ear that I looked as though I were with child. He asked if it was true. The idiot. The beautiful idiot. He was so happy. To him the thought of a child was the most wonderful miracle. To me… I was terrified."

"Of giving birth?"

"Boy, pay attention. We have a long drive. I plan to tell you things, and I don't want to repeat any of it. Things I held back when you were a child. I now see the error in that. So keep up. Not of giving birth. Women have been doing that since the start of time, and if the baby and I had died in childbirth, that would have been a sad blessing. Henry would have grieved, and any one of a dozen young women would have gladly shared his bed and given him a houseful of children…. When your mother was born, the first thing I asked the doctor was 'What color are her eyes?' And I held my breath as he brought her to me. They were dark blue but not green, and I remember Doctor Roth telling me they would eventually turn brown like her father's. Such relief, all I could think… she doesn't have it. Maybe this will be okay. I've given him a child, and there will be no more. Maybe, and I prayed, please God, let me be the end of this."

"So the gift always comes with green eyes?"

"Yes."

"I'd wondered. So you and I, and no one else?"

"No one alive, at least as far as I know, and I would know better than any."

Wedged in the back, Miles weighed her words. He balanced them against all the things she'd told him in the past. The dire threats should he ever use the gift, that horrible things would happen to him and everyone he loved. He thought of the horrific vision he'd seen at the Swamp Witch. "They killed them all, didn't they?"

"Yes…. How do you know that?"

"I saw it."

"How?"

"Marie, the woman at the bar. She showed me a vision, maybe my mind playing tricks. But there were Nazis and doctors, and the man from my dreams—Tomas. They killed him, and I think you were there. You were really young…. They made you watch."

The car swerved, and a horn blared as Anna struggled to get back in her lane. "Quiet, boy. I don't think about those things."

Anna's pulse quickened, and her nostrils filled with the scents of blood and human waste. She bit the inside of her mouth, having discovered pain could sometimes derail the flashbacks. "I will not think about that." She tasted the salt of her blood and focused on the car in front of her. "How much have you disobeyed my instructions?"

"Until the past twenty-four hours, not at all. But right now it seems I'm doing absolutely everything you told me not to."

"You followed my father into the lake?"

"I did."

"Why, Miles? Have you heard nothing I've told you?"

"I've listened my entire life, Grandma. The problem is you've not been telling me the truth. Have you never followed him? He calls for you every night."

"No. I will not go with him. And yes, he calls." Her voice softened. "So what did he show you? What's in the lake other than my dead relatives bobbing like apples in a barrel?"

"It's a door." He tried to remember the dream in the emergency room. "You dive in and come out on dry land." Another piece clicked into place. "We were on a caravan, him and I, like you see in documentaries about the Gypsies." He listened close as he dropped the word, and he heard a catch in Grandma's breath. *Got you.* "So it is true. You're a Gypsy. You're not Jewish."

"I am Jewish."

Like pulling teeth. "And you were born Gypsy. Your parents were Gypsies; they were Rom. Tell me the truth, Grandma."

"Fine. Yes, I was born Gypsy, and my parents were Tomas and Magda."

Since the day Miles was born and his green eyes looked into hers, Anna had braced for this moment, the events of the last day having confirmed everything she believed to be true about this wretched thing that flowed in their veins.

"So who?" he asked from his hiding place, struggling to piece the story together. "So who are Sadie and Max? If your parents were Tomas and Magda, how…?"

With blood in her mouth, Anna wondered how much of the story she could tell without losing her mind. "I was in Hitler's camps, Miles. The vision the witch gave you was a true one. Apparently we aren't the only ones with gifts." *Don't let yourself see it. Say the words, tell the boy what he needs, don't look in your father's eyes or hear the sound of the knife cutting into his throat, the saw back and forth across the bones in his neck. The one who grabbed him by the hair and…. Look away. You're in a car. You have to keep Miles safe. Watch the road.* "They killed my father, and my uncle, and my grandmother, who all had the gift. There were three others as well.

"I was little. They burned numbers into my wrists. I try not to remember these things, Miles. But you would know, and yes, it's important that I tell you. Maybe the truth will help you see that the gift is not something to be used, not ever. It was soon after they'd killed my father"—*just get the words out, don't look at them, don't hear the screams*—"maybe a day, maybe two, and different soldiers had entered the camp, and they put us into groups, and my mother, my real mother—Magda—told me to go with a Jewish couple she'd befriended, Sadie and Max Rothstein. Their children had been murdered by the Nazis. She told me I was to go with them. I was to be their daughter. She told me to be a good girl, and she told me that no matter what, I was never to tell them about the gift. Never tell the gadje."

"So that's where it's from? Gadje? I thought it was Yiddish."

"No. It's Romany. It means 'stranger.' Never tell the stranger who you are or about the gift. That was the last time I saw my mother."

"Why would she give you up like that?"

Will he leave nothing alone? "I was seven, Miles. I was surrounded by blood and death and soldiers. All I remember is the chaos and wanting my papa… and now my mother was throwing me away. Giving me to a couple who were like matchsticks about to break. I had no idea why she would do such a thing. And at night, in between the most horrible dreams you can imagine, Papa would come. He wanted me to go into the lake, and I would see all the green-eyed heads bobbing in the water, like the heads…." *Stop, don't. Don't think about this. Breathe.*

"Grandma, are you okay? You don't have to do this all at once. I really want to know, but this is heavy. Maybe take a break."

"No. You need to know. And it's best with you hidden, like talking to myself. Although isn't that a sign of madness, and might that be better? If we were both mad and none of this had happened… was happening.

"It wasn't until I turned thirteen that Mother Sadie told me, or at least the part she knew. She said that my mother feared for my safety if I stayed with the Gypsies, that I would be hunted and killed like Papa and the others. Sadie told me that she had tried to talk my mother out of it, but she didn't understand because my mother never told her of the gift."

"Sadie never knew?"

Anna stared at her hands. A trickle of blood oozed from her right palm from having gripped the wheel too tight. "Not then, no. But I finally understood. The numbers on my wrist… being Gypsy. My real mother, Magda, knew they'd come looking for me. That it wasn't going to end with the camps and with Hitler. It runs deeper. They'd come looking for a Gypsy girl with green eyes, not a Jewish girl."

"The scars on your wrists…. Everyone thinks you tried to kill yourself."

She glanced at her buttoned sleeves. Just that caused the ancient scars to itch. "When I was thirteen, I took my father's razor and I cut off the tattoos. I understood my mother's sacrifice. They could still identify me by the numbers, but only if they were there."

Miles started to rise up from the back. "Grandma, I'm so sorry, I…."

"Boy, stay down! It was a long time ago. I told Sadie and Max that I did it to be free from the camps, that I didn't want to go through life marked by Hitler. I cut deep, and I made a mess of it, but you want to know something?"

"What?"

"It didn't hurt. I mean, at first, yes, but then there was something peaceful about it. I watch these TV shows where teenagers cut themselves, how it makes their pain go away for a bit. I think that's true. I felt peace as I cut them off. I found calm in the pain and the blood."

"You said Sadie didn't know about the gift then. But she found out, didn't she?"

"Yes." Anna's scars tingled. She glanced at the GPS. They were near the Mississippi border. She scanned for cops and checked the cruise control against the speed-limit signs. *He would know all of it. All the secrets, my lifetime of lies.* "She found out. I suppose you want to hear about that…. There's the Welcome to Mississippi sign. Still best you stay down awhile."

She didn't want to meet his eyes, to feel the weight of his stare, his accusations, his pity, his love.

"Sure…. So how did Sadie find out?"

"I've used the gift only once in my life… on her." Anna could hear the questions queue in her grandson's head. "Give me a couple seconds, and I'll tell you the story. It's all connected. Everything leads to everything else, to us driving like escaped prisoners. It goes back to the camps and to the ones who came before us. It wasn't long after I cut off my tattoos, and you can imagine the things they said about that. This was Brookline in the 1950s. Girls in good homes didn't do strange things like that. But I wasn't the only one from the camps. I wore longs sleeves to hide the numbers, and nothing changed when I had to hide the bandages and then the scars. It wasn't long after when I first smelled the rot on Sadie. The cancer smell. You know what I'm talking about?"

"Yes, like bad meat in the sun."

"Exactly." *Interesting, all these years to not have shared these things.* "It was inside of her… in her womb. But the worst part was she thought the swelling in her belly was a baby. She was so happy, that after losing her two little boys in the war, she was going to have a child. But that's not what it was. And every day I smelled it growing. When she finally went to the doctor, he told her that it was not a baby, but death. He told her she had let it go too far, and there was nothing to be done."

Anna pictured Sadie as she sat her down to tell her the awful truth. *"You need to take care of Max. He's been through more than anyone should have to endure. We all have. Help him, Anna."*

"I want to say I couldn't stop myself… because I could have. But the urge to use the gift was unbearable."

"I know," he whispered.

"Yes, I suppose you're the only one who does. I didn't know what I was supposed to do. If I'd ever followed Papa into the lake, I might have had some idea, so I just let it happen. I lost consciousness, and when I woke up, I was on the floor, and Sadie was in the bathroom. She was sobbing, and when I went to help her, she screamed at me. 'What are you? What have you done?' She called me witch and worse. There was blood down her legs, and in the toilet I saw clumps of pink flesh. I tried to go to her, but she wouldn't let me near."

"I'm so sorry, Grandma."

She saw him raise his head in the mirror. His green eyes met hers, and yes, she saw sorrow, but mostly love… for her. "There's no unmaking the past, boy. Sadie cleaned herself up, and she never spoke of it. But everything changed. She never looked at me the same. I frightened her. I had no idea what she saw. At least I didn't until that horrible day with you and the dog. You see, the few times I'd seen my father use the gift, it was subtle, everything except his hands, and even those he kept hidden, as though knowing the strangeness would frighten people. No wonder she called me those names."

"What does it look like?"

"Like the miracle it is. Your hands were like two birds, and you could see something thick in the air passing between you and the dog. At least I could see it. I wonder what that awful man saw."

"The one who hit Amos?"

"Yes."

"You made my parents give him away."

"I did."

"I hated you for that. I cried for weeks. First Grandpa Henry, and then Amos."

"I had to make you understand. It was not the time to be gentle."

"Yeah, you made your point. But did you ever think that maybe the reason your father could keep it subtle has something to do with the lake? What if you've been wrong this entire time, Grandma? Maybe the point is that we have to go with him…. Do you want me to drive for a while?"

"No… and if you want, maybe you should try to get some sleep. We can take turns, but I'd like to put a couple hundred miles between us and New Orleans before we stop."

"You think they'll come after us?"

"I do, and between this rental, which has GPS, and everything being traceable, we need to prepare for the worst. But at least we'll have you in a different state, and I'll call Morris Brock. He'll represent you. Dr. Stangl is not going to get his hands on you. I will not let that happen. Now, if you're not going to sleep, I've a question or two for you," she said.

"Okay." And he sank back against the seat.

"Tell me about your boyfriend."

CHAPTER 18

CALVIN STANGL, dressed in black, his blond hair hidden under a knit ski cap, and wearing night-vision goggles, popped the lock on the back door of Miles Fox's Grinwald Street apartment. Entering, he checked the stove clock: 10:38 p.m.…. His night's mission was an easy in and easy out, but as he placed a gloved finger on the edge of a half-filled coffee mug, something tugged at him. *Just do what you came for. Don't take risks.* He nudged the mug, looking at its dark, oily surface. *His lips were on that.* The man who'd populated his nightly fantasies for over a year. A man whose lips he'd imagined kissing hundreds… thousands of times as he'd hug and grind into his pillow.

There were no dishes in the sink, and there was tidiness to the mismatched dishes in the glass-fronted cabinets. *He came back here after leaving the emergency room. What did he take? What does someone take when they're on the run? What would I take? What did he take… who did he take?*

His thoughts were pulled back to the Zosimus manuscript and its implications—life immortal with one's true love. Father did not believe in it. *How can he not see it?* If the fantastic tale of the man who lived over a millennium could be believed, then the answer was in fact… love. What else could it be? Zosimus fell in love with the Gypsy woman; he performed the ritual that separated the gift from the healer, like an egg yolk from the white, and somehow both he and she were transformed. Or was it just a fairy tale dreamed up by a bored twelfth-century scholar? It was a dizzying and terrifying thought. *Father would kill me if he knew, if he even suspected. Just do what you came for.*

After going through the kitchen, he entered a cozy living room with a sofa, TV, and laptop computer set up on a table comprised of a door placed across stacked cinder blocks. *This is how he lives. He's not rich. I could give him things.* Knowing Father would object, he pulled off his goggles and pulled out an LED flashlight, wanting to see the true colors.

There was a small fireplace and in front of it a chrome music stand thick with opened books of violin concertos and sonatas. Around that were mounds of music, as though he'd finish playing something and then toss the piece to the floor to get at the one behind it. He looked around for the instrument. *So that's what you take. Your grandfather's violin.*

His mind flashed on Antoine Dey's beautiful family, a family Mr. Dey would never see. *Do what you came for and get out. Father's timing this. He'll want to know why you took so long.*

He spotted the flashing light on the answering machine. There were eight unplayed messages. *You don't have time. The neighbors might hear.* He found the volume with his gloved fingers, turned it down, and pressed Play.

An electronic voice announced, "You have eight new messages. Message one, Monday, October nineteenth, 7:20 a.m." A woman's voice. "Hi dear, it's your mother. I know you're on call today, and I wanted to try to get you before you left…. Guess I didn't, or you're screening your calls. When you get this, call me. I'm trying to make plans for Thanksgiving and was hoping you'd be able to make it this year. I know it's tough getting away, but we'll spring for the ticket, so don't worry about that…. Love you. Bye."

The next message was a robocall from the power company, followed by a physician recruiting agency announcing a free dinner for medical students and residents. Calvin clicked through those. "Message four, Wednesday, October twenty-first, 9:00 a.m." Rachel Fox's voice. "Miles, what's going on? I got a call from your dean. What's happening? Please, if you get this, give us a call. I tried to get you on your cell. I don't understand. What's happened…?" There was a pause as though Rachel Fox was waiting for her son to decide whether or not to answer. "Honey, I don't care what's happened, please call. We're worried sick. We love you, dear. No matter what, we're here for you."

Calvin listened to the woman's distress as he scanned framed family-and-friends portraits that covered an entire wall. Miles at his high school graduation, his mother and father hugging him, his sister Maya nestled in the folds of his gown. A color picture of Miles and his grandmother: he couldn't have been more than eight, their green eyes practically glowing from behind the glass. There was a vintage sepia photo of a thin dark-haired man with a violin in front of an imposing white marble synagogue, and one of the same man with a full head of bright silver hair, leaning over a very young Miles, who was holding a violin that was too big for him.

Calvin stared at the intensity in the boy's expression, his chubby fingers on the strings, his grandfather's amusement, and something else… love.

Next to that hung a more recent photo of Miles cross-legged on the floor with another man. Calvin instantly made the connections. *That's the one who helped him escape—Luke Paxton. Why would he do that?* He brought his face and the flashlight closer to the image. There was an empty pizza box, large bottles of soda, and a human skeleton scattered on the floor. The two young men were grinning and holding surgical probes, obviously caught up in some late-night study session. *They seem so happy.*

It was from last year's anatomy class, one Calvin had audited. Only for him there had been no invitations to late-night study sessions. All the medical students knew he was Gerald Stangl's teenage son. They'd smile and joke with him; a few of the girls would even flirt and call him cute. Even so, the memories were crisp: long hours dissecting his cadaver with his partner, Greg, with his scraggly ginger beard and an annoying habit of destroying nerves and blood vessels that needed to be protected and labeled. But always, two tables down, was Miles… with this Luke. When the course started, Calvin had thought his fixation on Miles was due to Father's obsession with the gift and the firm belief that Miles possessed it. As the weeks and months passed and the green-eyed man crept into his fantasies, he knew the truth was something else, something Father would never accept. It had been a delicious agony, stealing glances two bodies down. Sometimes Miles would meet his gaze… and smile.

He studied the faces in the picture, Miles's so familiar and burned into his mind, but the other one…. *Luke Paxton.* He tried to find the obvious flaw in the handsome man's even features and disheveled hair. But no, just long-limbed ease, the all-American man, drinking Coke and eating pizza, with… *his friend? Boyfriend? No, he was with the blonde girl; she's probably the one who took the picture…. Why are they so happy?*

The answering machine continued as he passed the light's beam from photo to photo. The next two calls were from Miles's mother and then his father, their tones increasingly desperate. "Call us, please… just call. We'll figure this out. We love you."

The mechanical voice came on again. "Wednesday, October twenty-first, 8:12 p.m." Calvin stared at the caller ID. It was a New Orleans number. "Miles, it's Luke. I don't know where you are or if you'll even get this. I don't know what to say."

Calvin tried to tease out the man's subtext. He sounded as if he were in pain. *So he's not with you… unless this is some kind of trick.* It also sounded as if he might have been drinking.

"If you get this, I want you to know that I don't regret it, none of it. Everything I did… I wanted to do…. Things are bad. My parents are coming to get me. I can't stay here. I'm pretty sure I'm going to be expelled. There's going to be some kind of hearing. I don't regret a thing, not a thing. I… I don't know what's going to happen. I just want you to know… I really care for you. Please be safe. I…. Oh shit! My parents just pulled up. I don't know where you are or… I miss you. Please be safe. I… I've got to go." Luke Paxton lowered his voice to a whisper. "I love you." The line went dead.

What the hell is that? "I love you"? What the hell? The machine clicked onto the final message: Thursday, October twenty-second, 10:00 a.m.…. It was the recruiter asking if Miles was attending the dinner tonight. Calvin glanced at his watch. It was nearly 11:00 p.m. He'd stayed longer than he should have.

Confused by Luke's message and the visceral response it triggered, he went into the bathroom. He tucked away his flashlight, pulled the goggles over his eyes, and retrieved a curved surgical probe from his backpack and fished it down the tub drain. *What kind of man tells another man he loves him? Especially when one of the men is a known homosexual?* Father had revealed this fact during last night's drunken rant. *"Gypsy, Jew, and fairy! It's the mongrel trifecta!"*

Calvin's probe caught on something soft. He twirled the instrument between his fingers and pulled back. Through the goggles he examined the clump of congealed soap and black hair. *I love you.* Was that something friends told each other, or was that reserved for boyfriends? Was Luke Paxton Miles's boyfriend?

Calvin stared at the tangled-hair-and-goo ball, his emotions unexpected and strong. His rational mind tried to process the information. *If Paxton were a boyfriend, that would explain everything, wouldn't it? Who else would risk so much for Fox? Would I?* He bagged the hairball and tucked it in his backpack. *Father will wonder what's taking so long…. Fuck Father!*

He left the bathroom and opened the door to Miles's bedroom. He couldn't stop himself, opening the drawers of Miles's secondhand bureau. His breath quickened as he stared at the folded boxers and briefs. *Don't touch anything. What would Father say?* His gloved finger caught on the fabric of a jockstrap. He pulled it up and stared at it, mesmerized by the ribbed fabric over the pouch. His mind skittered over images of Fox wearing just that.

"Shit!" He dropped it into the drawer, not wanting to acknowledge the force of the erection straining against his zipper. He shut the underwear drawer and looked around as though expecting Father to appear.

If he finds out… shit. He had the thought to put a hand down his pants and jack off. *Don't be an idiot. You want to leave DNA? Focus. You did what you came for.* His trapped erection bordered on pain. *Think of something else. Heads in jars.* And just like that, crisp images of Tom, Marie, and floating-eyed Jack did the trick.

Still, he couldn't make himself leave. He checked the closet, noting the single dark navy suit and half a dozen ironed shirts on hangers. *Aren't gay men supposed to have a lot of clothes?* On the single closet shelf were two pairs of folded jeans. *You need to get out.*

He bit his lip and turned. By the bed he spotted a stack of textbooks interspersed with paperback novels. He scanned the titles—an assortment of classic sci-fi with lurid covers showing mostly naked men and women on ethereal planets, a photo book on the Israeli martial art Krav Maga, and two well-highlighted oncology texts with torn pieces of notepaper serving as bookmarks. He flipped one open, and then the other. The bits of paper and most detailed highlighted sections related to hepatocellular carcinoma. *Dey wasn't random. Father might want to know that. Now get out. You have to get out.*

His gaze returned to the scarred bureau. *What would be the harm?* Before he could stop himself, he opened the top drawer, grabbed the jockstrap, and stuffed it into his back pocket. *If Father finds that, what will you say?*

Heart pounding, he exited the bedroom and headed toward the kitchen. *His laptop, he left that. Father would want you to check that.* He crossed the room and booted up the ThinkPad, clearly the most expensive thing in the apartment. At the bottom he noted Fox's browser choices, expecting to find the usual ones like Internet Explorer and Firefox. *That is interesting—he surfs on the dark web. Why?*

No stranger to the workings of the hidden web, Calvin pulled up his favorite search engine. He smiled and felt something shared with Miles. His computer history, like Calvin's own, was untraceable. For Calvin, concealing his activities on the web was necessary. If Father ever learned the sites he visited…. *Would he actually kill me?* It was a question Calvin had pondered since he first realized at age thirteen what made his penis erect and what didn't, his entire sex education provided via a cornucopia of Internet porn. Women did nothing for him. He would stare for hours at their naked images, explicit pictures in all manner of sex acts, but his attention would be drawn to their male partners, with lean limbs, ripped abs, and hard cocks. *Is that why Fox uses the dark web? Is there another reason? What is he hiding?*

Even more than the purloined jockstrap, the urge to take the laptop was intense. With enough time he'd unlock its secrets… Fox's secrets… but Father would find out. *It's too dangerous.* What he did do was type an e-mail to one of the NOPD detectives involved in the investigation. He left it with an eight-hour delay before it would be sent. *That should be more than enough.*

Standing in the middle of the living room, he took a final look. *I've left nothing, I've changed nothing.*

"Shit!" With a start he realized that wasn't true. The blinking light on the answering machine was now solid red. By replaying the messages, he'd reset it. *That was a mistake. But how big a mistake? Shit. Not good.* His cell vibrated in his pocket. He didn't pull it out, knowing it was Father. He looked at the machine. *No one will notice. When it all starts, they won't bother to check. Don't think about it.* And silently opening the kitchen door, he left.

CHAPTER 19

IT WAS nearly 7:00 p.m. Thursday when Anna and Miles pulled into the gravel drive of her Truro house. They'd driven over twenty-four hours from New Orleans, stopping only for gas, coffee, shots of energy drinks, and bathroom breaks. Neither one had slept more than an hour.

"I'll put on coffee," Anna said as she entered the alarm code into the keypad.

"Mom knows none of this." Miles followed her in, his senses comforted by the familiar salt air and residual scents of his grandma's cooking.

"No. These things are for your ears only."

"And this is the truth? After all these years…." He felt wired on caffeine and Grandma Anna's revelations. "Why now?"

"Because I don't know what else to do, Miles." She sounded defeated. "When you were eight, they came for you. I knew they would. They always do."

"Right there… *they*. Care to define who exactly *they* are?"

"I don't know. Not exactly." She poured water into the coffeemaker and pressed Brew. "When I was a child, they were the doctors in the camp. They knew who we were, what we were. It was no accident, that camp and those doctors. And forgive me for not having written it all down, but I was so young. Some things are burned in my brain, and a lot I can't remember. But the night the soldiers came to our camp, they lined us up and shone lights in our eyes. All of us with the green eyes were separated out, as were our close kin, mother, father, sister, and brother. The rest they lined up in a row and shot. In the morning they made us dig a trench. We buried them in a field. It was spring, and there were purple flowers. And then we marched. It seemed forever. It must have been two or three days, maybe longer. The soldiers rode in trucks and the doctors in their shiny black cars. Occasionally they'd pull one of us from the march and we'd be examined. They were all quite excited. I was too young, and my German was poor."

"They knew about the gift?"

"Yes, they came for us. There is no other explanation."

Like dots in a child's puzzle, Miles made the connections. "These things aren't normal, Grandma. We both hear the voice of your father. We have the same dreams."

He watched her pour the coffee. For the first time, he realized how old she'd gotten. Her hair was pure white, still in the bun she always wore. *She's lost weight. Maybe it's just the stress.*

"You think Stangl is connected to the Nazi doctors."

She handed him a mug of strong black coffee and stirred sugar into her own. She settled across from him. "There is no other explanation. I don't know how Stangl knew, how he found us… found you. Like the Nazis did with us, he's followed us. It doesn't seem possible, and yet it is. And just like them, he's surrounded himself with respectability. Perhaps they were never really Nazis—those doctors—but just saw the opportunity. They say that Hitler was obsessed with anything occult. Who knows what miracles the doctors whispered in his ear? I'd not thought of this. But I remember, not long after they killed Papa and the others… maybe a few hours… their shiny black cars left the camp. I never saw the doctors again… and now we have Stangl. Like them he's an important doctor, doing important research. He has money and influence, and he knows who you are, what you are." She shook her head. "How can this be happening? How is this possible? And yet I knew… I always knew."

Miles sipped the hot, bitter coffee. "Stangl said something in the emergency room. 'Do you believe in fate?' Maybe we have to step away from trying to make sense, at least the sense of what we think is real. Let's face it. I did something to a man with terminal cancer, and he's now tumor-free. That's not normal. Or what I did with Amos, or what you did when you saved Sadie."

He pushed back from the table. *Do you believe in fate?* He looked at Anna. "I love you so much, Grandma, and after all this time, you can still scare the shit out of me."

She cast a disapproving look at the use of profanity but was too exhausted to comment.

"But here's the thing, Grandma… how do you know you're right?"

"About what?"

"All of it. You were seven when the camps were liberated. You experienced horrible things. I can't imagine how such evil can exist. And it does, and I know that's why you've done the things you have. The stories you frightened me with when I was little, telling me people would hurt my family if they knew I could heal. Giving Amos away…. Those were some pretty screwed-up things to do to a little kid."

"I—"

"Yes," he interrupted, not letting her speak, "you thought it was in my best interest."

"Cruelty to save someone you love is not evil. It is necessary. I did what needed to be done."

"And what if you got it wrong? Knowledge is power, Grandma. You say that since he was murdered, your father calls to you in your dreams. And since you were a little girl, you've blocked him out."

"I didn't want the gift." She stared into her mug. "I never wanted it."

"You were seven. You'd survived untold horrors, and those you loved hadn't. Maybe it was the wrong decision to block him out. And then I came along, and you're sticking to the choices you made when you were a traumatized little girl. Don't you see? You're the strongest person I know, and yet everything you've ever told me comes from fear. I'm tired of the running, Grandma…." He paused, regretting what he needed to say.

"All of this running, this not hearing out your father, seeing what he has to tell us, show us…. If we went into the lake, maybe we'd get answers." *Don't say it*, he thought, but her own words argued against holding his tongue. *Cruelty to save someone you love is not evil.* "You got this wrong, Grandma. And if Stangl is somehow connected to us, he has a huge advantage. I agree that a lot of this makes no sense. But that has to be because we're missing information. Of all possible psychiatrists in the country, how is it that my parents brought me to him when I was eight? And it makes no sense that he's a bigwig doctor at the medical school where I get accepted… or that he's the one who just happens to walk into the emergency room after I heal a patient and apparently lose my shit in the process. None of it makes sense, and yet we live in a world where everything is caused. So it has to make sense. There is an explanation." *And you've done all you can to keep it from me.* Anger surged as he realized the truth of his words. "I have to take a walk."

She didn't argue as he grabbed a fleece-lined hoodie from the closet and headed out into the cool fall night. He inhaled deep, and without thought, headed down the lawn toward the hedge. He found the same hole, now thick with wild rose, where Amos had bolted all those years back. Retracting his hands into the sleeves, he pushed through to the street on the other side. There were no cars, and the sound of the waves beyond the dunes called to him. He thought about Grandma Anna and wondered at the depth of his anger. *Not only has she lied to me all these years, it's all been from fear. Cut her a break, Miles.* The images in Marie Levesque's candle returned. *So what you saw, or thought you saw, happened. It wasn't a hallucination or residual from all those drugs they jammed into you.*

To Miles, all of this new information was like running an experiment. You never wanted to trust a single test result, but rather, you waited to draw conclusions until all the results came in and you'd run the test at least twice. *And now you have, even a third if you're going to believe a man in your dreams. So let's review the facts, even if they come from a traumatized seven-year-old girl, creepy doctor, dead great-grandfather, and Gypsy fortune-teller who got far too much pleasure from having me strip naked and painting me silver.* He snorted and laughed at the memory. It felt good, and the sound of the surf and the breeze off the water were like a tonic.

And then he thought of Luke. "Crap." He'd tried to call him from a gas station in Virginia. Joel, one of the Luke's roommates, picked up. "He's gone, man. His folks came for him. It was ugly."

"Did he leave any message for me?"

"Yeah, don't try to get in touch with him. It's bad, man, totally messed up. He's going to get expelled. You're all over the news, and this call is probably being tapped. And Jenna is freaking. I don't know what you guys did, but she's taking it hard.... So where are you?"

"Gone," Miles said, and not knowing what else to do, he hung up. Everything about the call made him ache—destroying Luke's career, betraying Jenna's trust.

In the big picture, Miles knew whatever happened with Luke mattered. *He put everything on the line for me... and more.* Miles always subscribed to the philosophy that words were cheap. It was a person's actions that mattered. Luke had not only jeopardized his medical career, but late-night conversations, often after several beers, had given Miles more than a glimpse into the hell facing his friend.

"My dad can't stand anyone who's different or even anyone who disagrees with him. You should see his office staff, like a bunch of scared rabbits. 'Yes, Dr. Paxton. Right away, Dr. Paxton. Is your coffee hot enough, Dr. Paxton?' It's the same at home. I don't think I've ever once heard my mom disagree with him. And while he won't say this around people who aren't exactly like him, he's a big old bigot. Blacks, Jews, Hispanics… gays."

"Luke…." Miles stared out at the ocean, the waves tipped silver by the moon. "What the hell did we do?"

In the chaos of the last two days, there was that island of unbearable joy. That first kiss. He put his hand to his lip and felt the twinge of exposed nerve where Luke's teeth had broken the flesh. *What were you thinking?* And then what they'd done in bed. Miles knew Luke had never been with another man, and yet there'd been no holding back on either of their parts. *So what was that?* He'd never had that intensity with another person, not even close.

Staring at the ocean, he pictured Luke. *What are you doing now? Are you okay?*

Do you know that I love you? The truth of that brought him to a stop. He spoke into the wind and the surf. "You love Luke. And not just like a friend. You are in love with your best friend. I love Luke."

He bent to pick up a flat gray rock and collected a second and a third. He skipped one across the water, and the others followed. He looked for fresh ammo when a man's voice called out.

"Miles."

He spun around. "Who's there?"

It came again. "Miles."

"Who's there?" But he already knew: the accent, the suppressed humor. "But I'm awake."

"So you say." Tomas emerged from the waves. The water beaded off his clothes, and his boots left no prints as he crossed the sand.

Miles stared. He thought of Anna and the last twenty-four hours of revelations on the road and in her kitchen. He had no doubt she'd gotten almost everything wrong, and now it was time to test that hypothesis.

"I need you to tell me things," he said to his long-dead great-grandfather, who grinned as he twirled the tips of his mustache into vertical peaks.

"Yes, of course," Tomas said, and he extended his hand.

Miles looked at his own pale fingers against the hoodie's dark fabric. He nodded and took Tomas's hand. The touch thrummed like low-voltage electricity.

"Come," Tomas said, and he stepped into the surf.

"You're kidding, right? Is this where I walk into the Atlantic after two days without sleep and drown myself?"

"Not the story I'd planned to tell. I prefer ones with happy endings, don't you? Now come. You want answers."

"It's not the lake," Miles said, realizing this was beyond madness. He was fully clothed, and the water was ice cold.

"Of course it is," Tomas replied. "It's all the lake. Now come with me… or don't. You have a choice. You always have a choice. Now choose."

Miles stared at the breaking surf and then at Tomas's boots as ripples crested over them. His rational mind made a last stab—*this is madness. Yes, madness.* But in reviewing the events of the last two days… of much of his life… it was madness that made sense. He gripped his great-grandfather's hand. *It tingles.* And he followed him into the ocean.

UNLIKE THE dream in the emergency room, where he'd been drugged, Miles felt wide-eyed and alert. He wanted to observe everything, starting with the way the water wasn't wet against his ankles and shins. His feet stayed dry. *The water is repelled by us.* He thought of the old *Superman* movie when the hero took Lois Lane for her first flight, and it was only when he was holding her hand that she stayed in the air. *What happens if I let go of him?*

He fought the urge to shut his eyes as they waded up to their chests, their necks, their chins. *Keep them open.* Then they were below the surface, and like leaving one room and entering another, they were no longer underwater, but seated on a brightly painted wagon drawn by the same impressive black mares. Along the caravan's sides hung shiny copper pots and pans that jangled in rhythm to the rolling wheels and the clomp of hooves.

"You can let go of my hand if you like… or not, if you don't. After our last conversation, I've given much thought to today's story selection," Tomas said.

Miles smiled and looked out on sun-dappled woods. There were wildflowers in a clearing, chicory, purple strife, and tiny daisy-like hen's bane. And others he didn't recognize—delicate white flowers on graceful stalks, vivid fuchsia blooms that grew in tight clumps. He thought of Tomas's first story. "The fox ended up with a fox."

"It's best."

"Since last we spoke, I might have found a boyfriend."

"A fox?"

Miles chuckled. "Absolutely."

"That's not what I meant. And just because I'm dead doesn't mean I don't keep up. Is he a fox?"

"He's neither Jew nor Gypsy, if that's what you mean?"

Tomas sighed. "So you take *that* to be the story's meaning? That it's about marrying within our tribe? You realize that eventually leads to cross-eyed children with funny-shaped heads."

"So what does it mean?" Miles asked, feeling miffed at having given the wrong answer.

"No, no, no," Tomas said, and he pulled a leather-cased flask from beneath the bench. He uncapped it and took a swig. He passed it to Miles.

"What is this?"

"Try it and find out."

"But what is it?"

"Try it and find out."

"But what…." Miles took in Tomas's amused grin. "Fine," he said, and he drank. It was sweet and not the alcoholic draught he'd anticipated, but a mixture of honey and herbs, like a cool tea. "It's good." He took a second sip and thought of the story, the changeling child adopted by a poor couple, who was wooed by wealthy and attractive suitors, but in the end went with the fox at the door. *Clearly I'm missing the point.*

"You try too hard. These are not nuts to be cracked, with their insides gobbled down. Let's try another…. That is, if you'd like," Tomas said.

"Of course, but before, you said something about the ocean, that it was all the lake. What did you mean by that?"

"Good question, much better than your answer to the story of the two foxes. The answer is water. It's all connected. If you look at a drop, you look at the entire planet; it's been a part of a lake, a stream, the ocean, a child. It's the blood in your veins and the rain washing the street, to the gutter, to the stream, to the river, to the lake, to the ocean, around and around."

"And it's a door?"

"Very, very good. That more than makes up for things. You're not nearly as dim as people say. Yes, it's a door."

"But I needed your hand to pass through it."

"Also correct. Now are you ready for your story?"

He wasn't, really, wanting to pursue this line of inquiry. But Tomas's gaze was on a distant point. A story was coming, and best to pay attention.

"You may know this one," Tomas began, "or at least think you do. It's about a magic trout and a lowly fisherman."

"And his wife?"

"Of course…. Unless I need to change *all* my stories."

"Were you this sarcastic in life?" Miles asked.

"Hush… and attend. This tale, which is entirely true, took place many, many years ago, when the lake was one massive body of water that covered all the earth that was not land. It was the time of the one great continent….

"Now, out on his sad little boat, which could barely hold water, a lowly fisherman landed a magnificent trout. He immediately realized this was no ordinary catch, an observation that was verified when the trout opened its mouth.

"'Oh please, noble fisherman, do not chop off my head and fry me in a pan, but spare me my life.' While this was a time of miracles, a talking fish was not to be taken lightly. But the fisherman was poor, he had a wife to support, and a fish—talking or otherwise—would either put coin in his purse or food in their bellies.

"'Dear fish, I have caught you fairly in my net. It is your fate to be eaten.' And he hauled the net from the water and onto his boat.

"'Wait!' the trout exclaimed. 'I do more than talk. Observe the silver of my scales and the rainbows that dance across my flesh. I am made of light and magic. If you set me free, I shall grant you your heart's greatest desire.'

"This caused the man to pause. He thought, and rightfully so, *If I were a fish and I were caught in a net, wouldn't I say anything to get myself free? And what is my heart's desire? I have a boat, and I have my health.*

I have my wife who loves me and is true. Do I not already have all a man could want?

"But the fish was indeed magical. He heard the man's thoughts as if spoken aloud, and he most certainly did not want to end up on a steaming bed of cabbage. 'You must think of your lovely wife in your humble cottage. What would she say if she knew that you'd caught a magic trout, a magnificent fish that, in exchange for his life, offered your heart's greatest desire? What would she say if she knew you'd killed such a creature?'

"The fisherman was unnerved at how the trout read his mind. There was wisdom in the desperate creature's words. 'She would not be pleased.'

"'Just so,' said the trout. 'If your heart is fully content, then give my wish to your lovely wife. Go home to her and tell her what has transpired. Ask her what she would have of me, and then return to this spot tomorrow, cast your net, and I shall grant whatever she requests.'

"The fisherman was torn and did not want to be taken for a fool. Who's to say that once he released the trout, he would go home empty-handed with no fish, no coin, and no wish?

"As before, the fish heard his thoughts, clear as you hear mine."

"Wait a minute." Miles interrupted Tomas. "You're speaking aloud, aren't you?"

"Let me finish my tale, oh impatient one. But what if I told you that I move my mouth simply to make you feel comfortable?"

"And if you don't?" Miles asked.

Tomas waggled his brows, and keeping his lips still, continued the tale. "So 'I give you my promise,' the trout told the fisherman, 'and you will not be taken for a fool. But give this gift to your faithful wife. I will wait at this very spot and throw myself once again into your net.'

"It was a compelling argument, and the fisherman knew that if his wife ever learned he'd had the chance at a wish from a magic trout and they'd eaten said fish, she would not be happy.

"'I can see,' said the trout, 'you have made up your mind. Free me from this net, speak with your wife, and return tomorrow so I may once again be caught and grant her wish.

"So the fisherman loosed the magic trout and returned with an empty creel to his home and to his wife. 'Wife,' said he, 'I've a tale to tell.' And feeling a bit the fool, he explained all that had transpired.

"She listened, and because theirs was a world where magic did indeed happen, and she loved and respected her husband, she believed the tale… or at least most of it. 'Magical creatures are not known for making good on promises. When caught in a net, wouldn't such a pretty fish say anything to avoid my skillet? My beloved husband, we have nothing to eat tonight, but the tale you bring is better than the richest meal I could prepare. I will find something in the pantry and pull roots from the garden for our dinner. We won't go hungry because your words, and your love, they nourish me. We will do as your fish said, and tomorrow you shall return. But in truth I have you, who I love beyond rubies and diamonds, a roof above our heads, and on most days, enough food to fill my belly. Still, a wish from a fish is a fine thing.'

"And she thought of others in their town, the mayor's wife, with her fine home and beautiful jewels, the furrier's wife and her sable coats and ermine collars. 'I suppose,' she said, 'a bigger house would be nice, with enough land to plant a proper garden. That will be our wish.'

"And so they found onions and flavorful mushrooms, and pulled carrots and radishes from the garden. She stirred in cumin and turmeric and their last pitiful handful of rice, and they enjoyed a delicious stew, which, yes, had there been bread to soak up the gravy, and fish, would have been better.

"Come dawn the fisherman launched his boat. He rowed to the same spot and cast his net. He waited and wondered and regretted his decision of the day before. But within moments the fish appeared, and with its scales glistening in the sun, it leapt into the net.

"'As promised, I have returned. I can tell that you've spoken with your lovely wife and that she has made a wish. Speak it aloud, and it will be done.'

"The fisherman looked at the glorious creature, with its plump body and expressive eyes. He licked his lips and thought how well such a fish might taste married to his wife's stew. *But no.* And he spoke. 'A bigger house would be good, with enough land for a proper garden.'

"The trout clapped his fins three times. 'It is done, go home and see. Now set me free so that I may swim and travel the world.'

"The fisherman started to do did as he asked and then stopped.

"The trout's soulful eyes filled with fear, for he could read the man's thoughts, just as you can read mine. 'What are you doing?' the fish screamed. 'I have granted your wife's wish. You mustn't do this.'

"But the fisherman had made up his mind. He coshed the chatty fish with a single blow of his club, killing him instantly."

"Wait a minute," Miles said. "That's not how the story of the fisherman and his wife goes."

"Ssh," Tomas said without moving his lips. "I'm the one telling the tale, and you'd best pay attention, as there will be a test. Now where was I? Oh yes, a dead fish, which, for good measure, the fisherman cut the head off with his knife. Because he knew magical creatures could sometimes come back from death. He looked at his delicious catch, all shimmery and fat in the bottom of his boat. He pulled up anchor and rowed toward home.

"When he arrived he did not know what to expect. He found his wife waiting for him in the front yard. They looked at one another, and she rose and greeted him with a kiss.

"'Oh, husband dear, I see you have brought us a fat and delicious trout. I hoped that you would. You see, this morning the oddest thing happened. Our house grew into a mansion with more than a dozen rooms, and with it came a magnificent garden unlike anything I would ever be able to manage. Rows and rows of ripening vegetables, fruit trees in bloom as far as the eyes could see. All I could think was it would be far more than either of us could manage. We'd need servants and workers lest the fruit rot on the trees and fall to the ground. Then the rats would come and eat us in our sleep.'

"She loosed his wicker creel, felt its weight, and looked in at the headless trout. Her mouth watered. She kissed her husband again.

"'Come, we will sell fillets from this magnificent beauty and keep some for ourselves. With the money we will buy fresh bread and butter, I shall cook us a feast, and then we will make love. How did you know,' she asked, 'that this is my heart's desire?'

"Overjoyed by her response, the fisherman replied, 'Because in truth, my love, I have all that a man can need or want. I have your love, and we have a home and a life together. I want for nothing, and my greatest wish is for you to feel the same.'

"And that," Tomas said, "is how it really happened."

"I wasn't expecting that ending. The version I know, the wife keeps asking for bigger and bigger things until she goes too far and loses everything."

"I know that one as well, but it's not the tale for you. They both happened, different trout and different fishermen, similar stories that wandered down different paths."

"The part where he chopped off the fish's head. Something about magical creatures coming back to life."

"Good for you," Tomas said.

"Grandma says they cut off your head and they made her watch."

He nodded. "Yes, and for the last seventy years, they've kept it swimming in a jar."

"Like a fish."

"Yes, like the magic trout."

"You're serious. Your head is in a jar someplace?"

"Perfectly serious, and not just mine. It's merely flesh, but it does present some concerns in the modern age."

"Such as?"

"You are pursued by those who hunted me down. But unlike the fisherman, they mean to extract our magic, to pull it from our flesh, and to make it their own. It's been this way since before the continents drifted and the lake was a single body of water. You live in an age where science tugs at the strings of magic. You peer into microscopes and tease apart the gears and wheels that make things run. It is man's nature to want to understand. It is man's nature to want more."

"But she didn't."

"No, this fisherman's wife did not."

"She was content with what she already had. The possibility for more made her see that."

"Correct."

Miles looked out at the wooded glen, the leaves unfurling with the greens of spring. Rays of sun filtered to the forest floor, touching the flowers and making them bloom. "Here's something I don't understand…. If the gift can heal just about anything, why don't we just continually heal ourselves and live forever?"

Tomas snorted. "Why would we do that? We have this… and we know it." With a gentle nudge, the mares pulled the wagon to a sloping crest that looked out on a vista of the lake, and the distant island with its fairy-tale castle on top.

"But…."

"But nothing. This is our compensation. Make no doubt that carrying the gift comes at a great cost. But unlike the rest of humanity, we know this exists. The afterlife is not a question mark; it's a continent. We are immortal, Miles. As long as the gift exists on the mortal plane, we exist."

Having finally gotten a straight answer, Miles pressed on, pulling one from the dozens he needed to ask. "Tell me about our pursuers. You know about them, don't you?"

"I do. Not the exact one who comes after you, but it was this one's grandfather who took off my head." Tomas laughed. "I don't know what he expected to see inside of it."

"So you're the magic trout?"

"Better." Tomas grinned.

"Do I have to guess? I mean, we have this freakish ability to heal people. From what I can piece together, it travels in our genes. And that since the beginning of time, there have been people wanting what we have. And why wouldn't they? So what am I missing?"

"The point of the story, of course. The moral of mankind's story."

"You weren't kidding about the test, were you?"

"What is mankind's greatest desire, Miles? What is mankind's greatest fear? If you answer the one, you can answer the other."

"That's easy…. People fear death."

Tomas clapped his hands. "Yes, you get the gold star. Now answer the first question."

"If we fear death, our greatest wish is to never die."

"A thousand gold stars! We have this. We know that after human death comes paradise…. They have uncertainty and doubt." Tomas grabbed Miles by his wrists.

Miles looked into his great-grandfather's eyes. "And that's why they pursue us, why they cut off your head. They think we hold the key to immortality." He briefly wondered if he too should grow a ridiculous handlebar mustache, as its curlicues were growing on him. Then another thought hit with the force of a train. "No… that's not what you're saying. You've got to be kidding."

Tomas's gaze softened. "Speak it aloud or just think the thought. Either way it is truth. My little Anya hides from it, and we've learned that is of no use, for they still come. Just as they always have. Wars have been fought to possess this thing that travels in our blood."

"No, no, no. This is too much. You're saying we're like the grail. That's ridiculous."

"No, my boy, at this point in human history, I'm saying that you and your grandmother *are* the grail. Within you lies a flame, a spark of magic, a force that can push back death. For that you will be pursued. For that I lost my head. You are Miles the Fox, and you are the grail. You are the holy grail."

CHAPTER 20

NEITHER DETECTIVE Beau LeClerc or his more senior partner, Detective Layton Johnson, had ever seen such a simultaneously tidy and gruesome murder. Antoine Dey's head and body had been separated. The former sat like a paperweight on his desk, with the eyes open, staring at the door. His decapitated, bruise-covered naked body sat upright in the chair as though waiting for the next call to A Good Dey's Plumbing, LLC.

The e-mail to Detective LeClerc had come from a Russian ISP address. The forensic IT guys would go after it, but he knew it was untraceable. All part of the new face of crime in 2015, the so-called dark web, a creation of the US military to keep classified documents untraceable. Its usefulness had spread to unintended purposes, from Eastern European credit card scams and terrorist cells to cheating spouses and teens wanting to conceal their Internet activities from prying parents.

Both men knew to touch nothing, to change nothing as they babysat Dey's office and waited for the crime scene team. They also knew this murder, if they couldn't wrap it up with a bow in the next several minutes, would go to the Major Crimes squad.

"This was Fox's patient," Johnson said to his partner, unable to take his eyes off the two-part corpse.

"Yeah, so maybe that psychiatrist was right."

"Why cut off someone's head?"

"No clue. Look at how clean those cuts are. And check out his arms and legs. Those bruises…. Like a piece of fruit gone bad. He can't have been dead long, judging by the lividity, but his skin looks like it was peeling off, like something was really wrong."

"Whoever did this knew their way around surgical instruments—like a medical student. It's too neat, and why isn't there more blood?" Johnson stared at the purple marks that covered Dey's arms and torso and at the exposed flesh where patches of his skin had sloughed off.

"I know. There's no splatter. Not a drop," LeClerc observed, both fascinated and creeped out by Dey's staring eyes.

"My guess," Johnson said, "he was killed somewhere else, tidied up, and then brought here. Those bruises are new. Purple means fresh. And no

131

clue what's going on with his skin. Like an overripe peach. What would do that to somebody?"

"I'll tell you how my nana gets the skin off peaches when she does her canning…. She parboils them. Not to be gross, but if someone goes to the trouble of chopping off somebody's head, what would stop them from a quick parboil?"

"Hell of a big pot."

"Yeah, and this is New Orleans, where people are always cooking for crowds."

"You don't think…." Johnson stared at the body.

"I don't know what to think…. The warrant for Fox's apartment is still good," LeClerc offered.

"It's not going to be our case."

LeClerc repeated, "The warrant is still good. We're a few blocks away."

Johnson glanced at his partner. "Okay, but let's not do anything stupid. We're merely following the leads."

"Of course. But I've got a strange feeling," LeClerc said.

"So what else is new?" Johnson answered, used to his partner's "my-nana-was-a-voudoun–priestess" mystical insights.

The two men looked through the blinds as the CSI team parked their van, suited up, and swarmed in. Detective Johnson gave their report. "No, we haven't touched a thing. The door was unlocked. Everything is just the way we found it."

LeClerc looked at the headless body as a team of uniformed officers relieved them of scene security. "If this was Fox, and with this kind of deliberate staging…. You don't set up a show without staying to watch. Whoever did this is close. I can feel it."

"It's a stretch." But something about this bizarro murder, and that psychiatrist's insistence that Fox was dangerous and psychotic, clicked. "Okay, Beau, we check out his apartment… and maybe have a chat with Dr. Stangl. I thought he was stretching the point about Fox. Now… shit! What if everything he said was right, and this is just the start? We didn't find any weapons, but there could be a storage unit. Someone who's willing to drain the blood from their patient, chop off their head, maybe give them a quick parboil…. What kind of person does that?"

Chapter 21

Gerald scrutinized his son's hammer blows on the unfinished silver chalice, watching the familiar shape take form. "Stop. Good."

Pride surged as Calvin, dressed like himself with a protective leather apron, annealed the graceful goblet under the laser. *Times change*, he thought, remembering his own father and grandpapa teaching him how to smith the sacred vessels. Each step in the process, from refining the metal to absolute purity to creating a smooth and symmetrical goblet that, when struck, rang like a bell.

Grandpapa would say, *"The shape, it matters."* And when discussing the bells, *"As above, so below."* He would listen in the background as his father and Grandpapa Oskar would discuss the ancient manuscripts and where and how the experiments in the camps had succeeded, and ultimately failed.

Now Calvin's tidy strikes were hypnotic. But just touching on memories of his father, Frederick Stangl, and Grandpapa Oskar brought him too close to that awful day. The stains spreading on Grandpapa's pants. He snapped back to the present.

"The stem, it's not in true round." *Focus on the boy. He is the future. As they focused on you; you were their future. I do this for you and for all the Knights of the Grail who have come before.*

"I know, Father." Calvin removed the chalice from the heating laser and placed it over the wooden form. He resumed his careful hammer blows.

"Grandpapa Oskar said these forms date back to the Crusades," Gerald remarked as the heat and the smells of silver, flux, and sulfur bathed him in nostalgia. How many workrooms like these had he been in? He replayed cherished memories of Grandpapa's steady hand covering his own, teaching the difference between the hammers, how to remove silver scale with acid, how to sense the point at which the metal could be stretched no further.

Gerald's cell rang.

He pulled it from his pocket, saw it was a number from Mercy, and answered. "Dr. Stangl here."

A woman's voice. "Dr. Stangl, this is Moira Divine. I'm working with your patient Louis Drake. I hate to bother you, but he's insisting you said

133

he could call. He says it's, and I quote, 'cataclysmically important.' What should I tell him?"

Gerald smiled, wondering what crazy thought had popped into Drake's head, not even caring how the nurse had mistakenly referred to him as his patient. Then again Louis had figured out his on-call schedule, and for the past couple of years had been a frequent flyer, but only on the Tuesday nights he was there. "Put him on."

"Doc, I got the answer."

"Which is?"

"A dollar told me."

"I assumed as much. Now, Louis, what is of cataclysmic importance?"

"The message on the dollar. They tried to take it from me, but I'm good at hiding. Are you ready?"

Gerald braced as Louis's excited words spilled over the air. "Go ahead," he said, keeping an eye on Calvin's progress.

"It's an F. It wants me to fly and be free. You said I could live at Lakeshore in a house and come and go. I want to do that, but it's an F, so that means I'll be free." There was a pause. "Doc? Did you change your mind?"

"No, Louis, you can stay in one of the cottages."

"For good?"

"Yes. Is that what is so cataclysmic?"

"No, but I didn't want to spill all my secrets to someone who wasn't true and faithful… another F. The answer is in the numbers…. Doc, they've been reset, all but one. All the numbers have been reset except the last one. It's the end and it's the beginning. It's the alpha and omega. The big thing is coming."

"A prophecy?" Gerald asked, having long ago learned how to decipher Louis's rambles based on the serial numbers and hidden messages he divined in currency. The clinical term was "thoughts of reference," that there were special meanings, just for Louis, embedded in dollar bills.

"Oh yes, but here's why I had to call. I needed to know that you weren't lying. That you are fully faithful, not a fool, because the prophecy is for you. All zeros that end in a one. It's an anomaly, an abomination, an end of one era and a start of something new."

Gerald stared at the back of Calvin's head, observing his progress on the chalice. "How do you know the prophecy is for me?"

"I took it from your pocket."

Gerald grunted. It was not uncommon for him to stuff the change from the hospital cafeteria into one of the patch pockets of his lab coat. If Louis saw even the hint of green, the temptation would have been too great. "So because it's my dollar, the message is for me?"

And then Louis said something that caused Gerald to freeze.

"It's the F, Doc. It's fate. Do you believe in fate?"

The call left him unsettled. He got Louis off the line, spoke to the nurse, and gave her the name and number of the admissions coordinator at Lakeshore. "Tell her you spoke with me directly and that Louis can be transferred to one of the cottages. Tell her it's all pro bono. We'll write it off at the end of the year as uncompensated care." *Do I believe in fate? The end of one era and the start of another, the alpha and the omega.*

Calvin looked up. "What was that about?"

"A psychotic patient, a schizophrenic. It's easy to see how in early times they could have been taken as prophets." *Do I believe in fate?*

"They remind me of radios tuned to stations no one else can hear," Calvin said as he picked up a finishing hammer.

"An apt metaphor."

Without a pause in his work, Calvin asked, "How did they manage to get all of the things out of Germany? The books? These molds?"

"We have friends, Cal. Powerful friends. They have been there for us in the past, and they are with us now."

Calvin nodded, never taking his eyes from his work. "I'd sort of gathered that… this place, your being able to move from Boston to here. It's Kruft."

"Yes." He stared at the back of Calvin's head, admiring the regimented *tap-tap-tap* of his hammer blows, like soldiers marching in step. "Soon I'll tell you all about them."

"They used to make cannons and artillery."

"Correct. You've done some research."

Calvin nodded as a bead of sweat dripped from his nose onto the silver bowl. He grabbed a felt and quickly dried the surface before the salt and water could mar the metal. "Everything is on the Internet. The Kruft family is ancient. On familytree.com someone's put in names going back to the tenth century." Calvin looked up from his labors and met his father's gaze. He chewed at his lower lip as if unsure he should say more. "Ours goes back further. At least the men do."

"Correct. So you've researched us as well."

Gerald's phone rang again. He picked it up. "Yes, Daria."

"Dr. Stangl, there are two police detectives who want to speak with you."

"Of course, I'll be right up."

"What's happening?" Calvin asked.

Gerald stifled the chill fear he felt when near police. *This needs to happen.* "I suspect it's about our Fox." *What if it's not?* And with Louis's rant fresh in his head…. *Another F.*

"Should I come?"

"No! Finish the vessel." He walked to Calvin and stared at the nearly completed chalice. Its lines fluid, its upper and lower bowls in perfect symmetry. "What's that?" His attention riveted on a tiny patch of discoloration on the surface. Without warning he backhanded Calvin across the cheek. The sound reverberated, and the teen stumbled. He grabbed the edge of the workbench to keep from falling and stared at his father.

"You left impurity in the metal." Gerald's hand tingled from the contact. It helped clear his thoughts. He grabbed the lustrous vessel, picked up a ball peen hammer, and with three vicious blows, destroyed it. "Melt it down. Start again. Stupid boy! I thought you knew not to take shortcuts. We will have a single shot at this, Calvin."

Gerald's fear resurfaced. *If he makes a mistake like that, what other errors has he made? What's facing me upstairs?* Like falling through time, his mind replayed horrible scenes, the stifling-hot day the Cairo police, accompanied by Interpol, came for Father and Grandpapa. All that followed. Their bodies dangling against a gray stone wall. The guards who laughed and taunted him, who pointed at the stains and made obscene comments.

"This is not a game, Calvin. Melt it down. Do it right."

Shaken, he yanked off his leather apron and replaced it with the starched white coat. He glanced at Calvin, the imprint of his hand a vivid red on his cheek. *The boy has to learn. Why does he glare at me? He must learn life is pain… and he is the last.*

Awash in emotion, Gerald pulled a card from his pocket. He flipped it over and scribbled a number. "If I'm not back in an hour, you are to hide and call this number. Someone will come for you. Now get back to work, and do it right."

On the elevator to his fourth-floor suite, Gerald calmed himself with a Zen technique Grandpapa had shown him, every breath like a whiff of Valium as he focused on the tension in his body, letting it waft away. A mantra repeated in his mind with every inhalation—*life*—and every exhalation—*eternal*. The doors parted and he strode toward his secretary, an attractive and wonderfully efficient Latina.

Life—eternal. *Do you believe in fate?*

In the waiting area in front of her, seated in leather club chairs, were the two plainclothes detectives who'd taken his statement on Wednesday.

Life—eternal.

"Detectives Johnson and LeClerc, please come into my office." He opened the door, affording them panoramic views of the mangrove swamps and the sky-reflecting surface of Lake Pontchartrain. "So how can I help?"

"Thank you for seeing us without notice," Detective LeClerc began. "It seems your warnings about Miles Fox were well-founded."

A knot loosed inside Gerald. "Something happened?"

LeClerc nodded. "There's been a murder, and we've reason to think Fox is the perpetrator."

Gerald tread carefully. A single wrong word…. *Life—eternal.* "I wish I could say I was surprised. It's what I feared. Who was it?"

"One of Fox's patients," Johnson said. "The one involved in the initial incident at the hospital. A Mr. Antoine Dey."

Gerald's fear turned to elation. He wondered which of the breadcrumbs Calvin sprinkled had been discovered. *Too soon for them to know about Fox's DNA under Dey's fingernails. Life… eternal.* "Can I ask if there's more?" *And this is how we bring home the fox.*

Johnson nodded at his partner. "No harm in it. And the more you know, maybe you can give us some insight into what he might do next. Or where he's holed up."

"Of course," Gerald said.

LeClerc spoke. "I received an e-mail from a presumably untraceable ISP address keying us to the location of Dey's body." He shot a look at his partner as though waiting for approval to continue.

"Go ahead," Johnson said.

"Dey had been mutilated. No clue what the autopsy will show, but as a final flourish, our killer took off his head… and neatly, someone who knew their way around a scalpel. It's clear that he was killed in one place and then brought back to his office. But the clincher for Mr. Fox is it appears the e-mail to my office came from his laptop."

"I thought you said it was untraceable."

LeClerc smiled. "It is, but he didn't clear the history on his computer. It's a rookie mistake. So… you were spot-on about him. What else can you tell us?"

Gerald's hand still tingled from striking Cal. *Perhaps I'm too hard on the boy.* Pride in his son's efforts surged; it was Calvin's idea to send the e-mail, and that combined with the DNA evidence under Dey's fingernails would spring the trap on the Fox. All that was needed was to lead the proper authorities to the prey. *Just like ordering takeout.*

"It's what I feared. He's had a psychotic break with paranoid delusions—a world out to get him and his family. He's unstable and dangerous, more so than I had thought. I'll tell you this with medical certainty. If he's not apprehended, Mr. Dey will not be the only victim." Gerald modulated his tone to that of a compassionate doctor. "The tragedy is this. Miles Fox is not a criminal. He's sick, and he needs treatment."

"When he's apprehended, that will be for the judge to determine," Johnson said. "But based on what he's done… and how he's done it… you're right. He'll go to the forensic hospital in Jackson."

"Or here," Gerald offered. "We have a contract with the Office of Behavioral Health to provide forensic services. It's something we do as a specialty. We have a two-inmate high-security suite."

"Good to know," LeClerc said. "Now, Dr. Stangl, seeing as you've been dead-on about Mr. Fox, what are we missing, and more importantly, where do you think he is?"

It took all he had to not grin. "Your first question is partially answered by poor Mr. Dey's murder, but to be honest, I've not yet fathomed the depth of his psychosis. He has an elaborate belief system in which he has mystical powers. I suspect that Mr. Dey figured into these fantasies. It would be speculation on my part as to what tipped the fantasy… this delusion… into murder."

"Like a sacrifice? Is he into Santeria or voudoun?" LeClerc offered.

"Possibly. As to his whereabouts, he has family in Massachusetts. I believe he's close to his grandmother on Cape Cod." He paused, too much could be too much, then again with so much at stake. "She lives in Truro."

CHAPTER 22

"WE'VE TIME for a final story," Tomas said as the wagon cleared the forest edge and they came upon the lake ringed by snow-capped mountains. From the center of the water arose a volcanic island, its distant peak capped by an improbable castle.

"It's beautiful," Miles said as he drank in the warmth of the sun and the rich fragrance of the pines. "Is this real or just in my imagination?"

"It's both," Tomas said. "Others will never see this; we always will."

"That's just annoying. Are you capable of giving a straight answer?"

"It's the truth, boy. For me… for you, this place is real. For the rest of mankind, this is a place of legend. It was Avalon and before that, other names, and they cannot visit."

"Never?"

"How does that saying go? There's an exception to every rule. But that story, while important, is not for today. I've a different one. It's the story of seven brothers and their little sister. They were the children of a powerful king, a man so in love with his wife… their mother… that when she succumbed to a witch's curse, sickened, and perished in a night, he grew blind with grief.

"Now the witch, as dark witches do, lusted after power, and after the king's land and his wealth. She transformed her withered body into that of a nubile young maiden with breasts like buds and a figure as supple as a rose." Tomas chuckled. "I simply refuse to change this one for you."

"Give it a rest already. I don't need the gay-friendly Brothers Grimm."

Tomas winced. "A pair of thieves, if you ask me. But let me continue. She came to the king and comforted him in his grief. She sprinkled his food and his ale with potions, and all thoughts of his beloved wife vanished, replaced by a burning love for the maiden who was a witch."

"This is kind of like *Snow White*. Only instead of the seven dwarves, you're giving her seven brothers. I bet at least one of them's gay."

"Excuse me," Tomas said. "Am I telling the tale, or would you like to take over?"

"No, I'm good," Miles replied. "This is nice, being here with you. It seems a shame it took me so long to figure this out."

"Yes, my Anya worked hard to keep you away. And as we know, she had her reasons. But you need this story, and we don't have much time. The danger that pursues you grows close….

"So the witch married the king. But as one can imagine, she had no interest in playing nanny to another woman's children. More than that, she had plans of bringing forth her own brood, a marriage of magic and mortal. So she devised a plan to rid herself of the bothersome eight.

"On a spring morning, she sent them into the fields to gather berries. There was to be a feast that would include delicious pies and spits of roasted swan.

"Off with their baskets the seven strapping brothers and their little sister went. It was a merry outing, and when they came to the berry fields, they found bushes laden with luscious fruit. Fruit so tempting that before a single berry landed in their baskets, each of the brothers had greedily sampled handfuls of the dark fruit.

"As soon as the bloody juice hit their throats, a terrible change overcame them. Horrified, their sister watched as her brothers were transformed into magnificent white swans. There was nothing she could do to save them as they flapped their massive wings and squawked in panic. She started to run back to her father's castle for help when a squadron of hunters emerged from the forest. They'd been sent to shoot swans and skewer and roast them for the evening's feast.

"Terrified, the little girl turned and raced after her brothers. She clawed at the ground and threw dirt and stones at them to make them take flight. Startled, they took to the skies, leaving their sister alone with the hunters, whose arrows fell short of their marks.

"In despair the little princess turned to the head of the squadron to plead for them to stop, but she did not recognize him. As she stared at him, the flesh of his human face melted to reveal a vicious goblin. Before she could verify the truth of this, the hunters—who were the queen's henchmen—notched their arrows and took aim at her.

"There was no escape, and while she was quite young, her stepmother's evil plan became clear. There would be no way to warn her father, her brothers were gone, and now she would die.

"At that moment, the instant when the first arrow was set to pierce her heart, there came a terrible commotion as seven great swans dove from the skies and plucked the arrow in midflight. They swarmed the hunters, and with their hard beaks and sharp talons, ripped out their eyes. The girl, frightened beyond words, fled into the distant woods. She ran through the day and into the night. Her ears tuned to the sounds of pursuers. But there were no hooves or the clamor of armor. Guided by moonlight, she found her way to a river's edge and to a sturdy tree, and there, in its sheltering arms, she rested. Despite her grief she fell asleep, and she had a dream."

"Of course she did," Miles remarked, thinking how this tale was similar to one Grandma Anna had read to him as a child.

"Okay, Mr. Know-It-All. So what happens in the dream? And if you're going to be a storyteller, you'd better make it sing."

"The dream brings her the answer to her dilemma. Correct?"

"You have no joie de vivre," Tomas replied. "That's your attempt at poetic storytelling? It's not just advancing the plot that matters. It's the content, the subtext. This is where you find the meaning beneath the surface. So do it right, or leave it to me. Otherwise you will miss the point entirely."

"Fine. But I'm right, aren't I?"

"You're not wrong," Tomas admitted. "In the dream the girl's mother comes to her. And here, my boy, I'll give you some clear advice. When someone who loves you visits in a dream, pay attention. For if they are dead, they have taken great efforts. What they have to say is both important and true."

"Like you."

"Yes, well, I've gotten used to being ignored by you and my Anya. But the girl, the little princess, was comforted in the dream, even though what her mother had to say was not easy to hear. She spoke the truth of how the current queen had murdered her and how her sons had been enchanted. But every spell that does not end in death can be undone. And even from beyond the grave, the dead queen was able to lessen the magic.

"'Listen, my daughter. I shall tell you what must be done to save your brothers. For each of them, you must knit a shirt made from the reeds you will gather along this shore. Only when you have completed all seven and have placed them on your brothers will the spell be broken. But while you knit, you must utter not a single word, for to do so will condemn your brothers to remain as swans for the rest of their lives. The one thing I am able to do is that each night at midnight, for one hour's time, your brothers shall return to their human form. As you love them, they love you dearly and will always be near.'

"In the morning when the girl awoke, she did not question her mother's words." At this point Tomas gave Miles a sharp look.

"Yes, well, her mother's instructions were a hell of a lot more straightforward than anything you've been dishing out."

"I thought medical students were supposed to be clever," Tomas replied. "You need to stop thinking in straight lines, boy. Now where was I? And best to not interrupt, as our time is short." Without waiting for a response, Tomas stared out at the island. His words came fast. "So the girl shut her mouth and went into the river and cut reeds. She hauled them up into her sheltering pine, and as her fingers bled and splinters pierced beneath her nails, she knit.

"And that night as her mother had foretold, when the moon was high in the sky, the seven swans descended and turned back into her brothers. They took to the water's edge and gathered reeds that they brought to their beloved sister. But as you can imagine, knitting shirts from reeds is no easy task. It was a full year before she'd completed a single garment, and in that time she uttered not one word. She set to work on the second shirt; another year passed, and then a third and a fourth. By the time she was on the final shirt, she was seven years older and had grown into a lovely maiden. Her beauty was without compare as she sat in her pine and knit stiff reeds.

"Just so was she discovered by a neighboring prince out on his hunt. As if Cupid had let loose his bow, he spied the graceful maiden in her tree and fell in love.

"While she found the prince handsome and kind, she needed to remain in her perch with her finished shirts and the one just begun. Undaunted, the prince cajoled her to join him. Without words she indicated that she could not.

"He declared his love and could see how devoted she was to her labors. He assured her, 'My lady, my truest love, I see and I respect your devotion to your craft. Your fingers are red and they bleed, and yet you continue to work the stiffest of yarn into the most supple of garments. Come with me. Be my bride. I shall ensure that your work continues, and that which you've completed is kept safe.'

"Because Cupid's arrow had struck her as well, she climbed down from her perch. The prince's men carefully gathered the six completed shirts and the one that was little more than a waistband, and triumphant, the prince returned with his bride-to-be to the castle."

Miles interjected, "I always hated that love at first sight stuff. It's not realistic. It's chemical attraction."

"And your boyfriend?" Tomas asked.

"I'm not certain that's what he is… was. I just hope he's okay, and I don't think he is. But continue the story. You said there's danger, and part of me wants to stay here where everything is so beautiful. But that's just running away."

"You can't stay," Tomas said, all humor gone from his face.

"What is it?" Miles asked. "What's wrong?"

"I need to remind myself that the past cannot be undone. We have only minutes before you must leave this place, and there's just so much I can teach in that time. But you need to know this one thing…. If you and your grandmother leave the mortal world and the grail is truly extinguished, then this place and everyone in it ceases to exist. The grail is the flame that keeps us alive."

Miles pondered, "But my mother doesn't have the gift, and she gave birth to me."

"Yes, it can work that way, but there's always at least one of us who walks the earth. Your mother is unlikely to bear another child; certainly my Anya has long passed her time of the moon. Gay or not, it will be up to you. You need to know that. If you perish before you pass the cup, all who have gone before will also die. It's what my Anya had attempted, her reason blinded by the horrors of her childhood. So… let me finish my story."

Miles looked from Tomas to the shimmering stones at the water's edge. This latest revelation made his thoughts spin. *This is too much.* He looked across at the island and saw dozens of men, women, and children, all presumably his ancestors, some on the shore but most in the water. *This is just a dream, isn't it? They're not really alive. This is in my head. A child… I have to have a child, maybe children.* Tomas's words couldn't have been clearer. *If I die, they die. If I don't have a child and pass this on, they die.*

With urgency Tomas resumed his tale. "All was not honey and roses for the prince and his bride-to-be. When he brought her into the castle, the courtiers and his mother and father were struck by her beauty. But his mother the queen had other plans for her son. A simple girl, and a mute one at that, was not a suitable match. Princes were meant to marry princesses of neighboring kingdoms. It's what cemented truces and brought wealth. Whispered rumors swirled about the lovely girl as she shut herself in her chambers and knit.

"'Why does she make such strange garments?'

"'Who would want to wear a shirt made of reeds?' Tongues wagged, ever more vicious.

"'Is this witchcraft?'

"'This much be witchcraft'

"'The girl is a witch.'

"'Our prince has been enchanted.'

"And through this all, the girl never spoke and continued to work the reeds. Each night under the cover of dark at the stroke of midnight, her swans, carrying fresh reeds, flocked into her chambers and turned back into her brothers. They had heard the rumors, and they begged their sister to flee the palace.

"'It is not safe.'

"'They mean you harm.'

"'Come with us.'

"And she'd shake her head no and smile as her fingers never ceased working on the final shirt.

"But as one can imagine, seven swans flying nightly into the window of the prince's betrothed was discovered by a servant, who immediately told the queen. The following night the swans turning into men was observed from a secret hiding hole in the girl's chambers.

"It was all the proof that was needed. Not only was the girl a powerful sorceress, she had invited seven men into her chambers. She was confronted and charged with witchcraft and treason.

"The prince pleaded with her, 'You must speak, my love. You must defend yourself.'

"She would not. With tears streaming down her face, she heard the horrible accusations. The worst of all was that she had been unfaithful to the prince, whom she truly loved.

"The verdict came fast and without question. She was to burn at the stake. And because the queen saw the fierce love in her son's eyes, she feared he would rescue the girl and they'd elope. 'It shall happen today,' she decreed. 'Bind the girl tight and gather the wood.'

"The petrified maiden clutched the bundle of completed shirts, which never left her side. Her eyes landed on those of her beloved prince, who was unable to intercede.

"'Please, Mother, let her continue her work. If I cannot save her, let her have this small comfort as you condemn the love of my life to death.'

"Reluctantly the queen relented, but only because the girl was so beautiful, and already she heard whispers of sympathy echo around the court. *The sooner she is dead*, she thought, *the sooner we can find a suitable bride*.

"So out into the town square they drove the girl in a cart. Her eyes were filled with tears as her fingers never once stopped their work on the final shirt. They marched her from the cart and up to the stake. They bound her waist and chest, but as instructed, left her hands free so that she could find some solace in her work.

"A priest approached and asked if she wanted a final prayer. She shook her head no, convincing the villagers and the courtiers of her guilt. The girl was not of God; she would not even pray for her soul.

"The priest stepped down, and soldiers brought lit torches to the bundles of tinder-dry wood and lit them. The fire spread fast and in seconds licked at her feet and her bundle of reed shirts.

"Just then a horrible commotion came from the sky. Seven fierce swans descended on the square. Six of them beat down the flames with their mighty wings while a seventh freed the girl. She dropped to her knees and loosed the twine on her bundled shirts. She threw the first over the swan that had freed her, and it immediately turned into a strapping young man, brandishing a Damascene sword.

"The villagers and the courtiers, the king and the queen, and of course the prince were stunned by what they saw. One by one the great white swans approached the girl, and they bowed their graceful necks as she placed a shirt of knitted reeds over them. And one by one her brothers took human form. They created an armed circle around the girl, and when she came to the final swan, she took the unfinished shirt that had no sleeves, not knowing what would happen, and placed it over her youngest brother's long neck. Because it was incomplete, so too was his transformation. He became a man, but where there should be arms were two spectacular white wings.

"'I'm sorry,' the girl whispered, her first words in nearly seven years. 'I could not finish.'

"Her brother wiped her tears with the tip of a downy wing, and he took to flight. Spreading his glorious plumage, he hovered above the crowd. 'Good people,' he declared, 'my sister is no witch!'"

Miles snorted. "Seriously? They just watched her turn seven swans into men."

"Hush!" Tomas replied. "Let me—"

Miles looked at Tomas. His expression had changed to one of surprise and fear. "What's happening?" A loud noise like the whirring of a great beast shattered the fabric of the dream.

MILES AWOKE in a violent windstorm. The noise was deafening, and it felt like a thousand stinging gnats on his face and his hands.

A man's voice barked, "FBI. On your stomach, now! *Do it!*"

He tried to open his eyes but was blinded by wind-whipped sand.

The voice shouted again. "Now! On your stomach. Do it now!"

Adrenaline surged as he obeyed the command. He managed to crack his eyelids open and saw black boots and a glimpse of dark uniforms.

Hands roughly grabbed his arms and twisted them behind his back. Instinctively he resisted as many hands pinned him to the ground; a knee pressed hard into his back.

"Miles Fox, you are under arrest for the murder of Antoine Dey. You have the right to—"

CHAPTER 23

CALVIN FELT giddy as he motored down the moonlit stretch of Highway 6 from Eastham to Truro. He played through what needed to be done—grab the old lady, drug her, and haul her back to New Orleans.

It was a struggle to stay focused as he thought back to yesterday afternoon and the news that Miles Fox had been apprehended by the FBI. He'd played and replayed the videos on the Internet news channels. He hadn't bothered to hide it from Father, who had looked over his shoulder, clearly triumphant.

It annoyed him. "How do you know they'll be able to extradite him?" he'd tossed at Father, never knowing—and increasingly not caring—what comment would end in a slap or punch.

"They're FBI. They don't need to extradite. It's a federal case," Father replied, his voice free of emotion.

The intricacies of police procedures were not something Calvin had ever explored. "How did the FBI get involved?" he asked as Father's smug smile reflected back at him in the monitor.

"I might have mentioned something about Fox confessing to similar atrocities in Massachusetts. I told them I thought it was all delusional. But in light of recent events, I was no longer sure. Even I can make a mistake, apparently."

"And that would do it?"

"It seems so."

Calvin had been riveted on the desperate expression on Fox's face as he was hustled into the helicopter. His arrest had been captured by early-morning joggers and beachcombers. One in particular had zoomed in on his beautiful face. If Father hadn't been behind him in full gloat, he would have frozen the image and stared into those eyes. Instead he'd saved that clip, and with his phone connected to the car's monitor, replayed it now. If Father only knew…. *What would he do?*

He hadn't let Father's obvious satisfaction go unchallenged, and he'd pushed. "You really think they'll send him here for a forensic evaluation?"

"I do," Father answered without hesitation.

"Why? Even if they do, it seems they'd send him to the state forensic hospital."

"They'll do what I say. It will make sense to them."

"Why?"

"What is with you? Because I know the man, because we're closer to the court, and because people… important people who whisper into important ears… will tell those in charge that Miles Fox, and the interests of the case, will be best served by having him sent to Lakeshore."

Calvin had wanted to press. He hated the way Father seemed to always have an ace up his sleeve. What important people? The Krufts? The ones behind the multimillion-dollar pharmaceutical grants? Or the ones who underwrote the research facility at Lakeshore? What connection did Kruft Pharmaceuticals have with any of this? Why would they care? What was in it for them?

The conversation had ended not with a slap or punch, but with a dismissal and a mission. "We will need leverage with the Fox," Father had said. "Of the available choices—mother, father, little sister, and grandmother—we should go with the old hag. She fooled me for too long. She's the one who helped him escape. Be careful; she's clever, and it's time for her to pay. You know what to do. She must be alive and healthy enough to last the duration of the experiments."

"How long will that be, Father?"

"No more than two weeks. If my predictions are correct, even less." He'd turned to Calvin and smiled. "I know I've been harsh, but think about it. In less than two weeks, possibly one, we will possess the key to life everlasting. We will take it from Fox, and we shall drink from the grail. Together you and I will walk through time everlasting. It is so close. Finally so close."

Calvin had thought about it as he'd assembled his needs for this excursion north and stowed them in the trunk's tire well. *An eternity with Father—the definition of hell on earth.*

There was, however, a more attractive option. And if he kept his emotions hidden, if Father never knew what ticked behind his eyes, then he would not see it coming. Life everlasting, forever young, forever handsome, forever with his heart's true love. And Calvin knew beyond doubt that, while he might be seventeen, what he felt for Miles Fox was no adolescent infatuation. It was the stuff of legend. He felt… no, knew, to the depths of his being, even though it was not rational… it had the ring of truth, and while other than a precious nod hello or humorous bit of banter over cutting apart their cadavers, and the one time when their eyes met and Miles smiled and held his gaze…. Calvin sighed. He had no doubt the feelings would be mutual.

Now, as he turned left off Highway 6, he cut the lights and checked the GPS. The electronic voice informed him, "You have reached your destination. It is on your right."

Trained since childhood on how to conceal physiologic arousal—*I am a machine*—he steadied his heart and willed his pulse lower. Like throwing a switch, he turned off the part of his mind that held all the soft emotions Father hated. "I am a machine. I feel nothing."

OBLIVIOUS TO the danger, Anna sat in her kitchen drinking coffee—her third pot of the day—and tried to comfort her daughter Rachel over the phone. "Of course he didn't do it," she said.

"I know, it's preposterous. But the way they're portraying things in the news…. How can he recover from this?"

Rachel's anxiety sparked Anna's higher. Her hands trembled from fear, caffeine, and elevated blood pressure she refused to get medicated. Her head throbbed, but even an aspirin would muddle her needed clarity. Her grandson was in mortal peril, and ultimately this was her fault. *I should never have had a child.* "Morris gave me the name of someone good in New Orleans. He'll need a lawyer. Do you have a pen?" she asked, listening over the line.

"Okay."

"It's Ben Conti," she said, and she gave her daughter the attorney's number. "I've already spoken to him. He agreed to take the case, and I've taken care of the retainer, so don't worry about it." She didn't want her daughter to know these details, but earlier that afternoon, she'd arranged a wire transfer of twenty-five thousand dollars.

"Mom…."

Anna sensed her daughter's struggle, but Rachel and Joseph Fox, while solidly middle class, did not have the cash reserves to handle what was coming.

"Thank you. When this is all over, we'll figure a way to pay you back."

"Not necessary. It's not like I can take it with me. Consider it getting part of your inheritance early. Not exactly the new kitchen you'd like, but…."

"Don't talk like that, Mom. They wouldn't let us see him. How is that even legal?" Rachel asked.

Anna, who'd spent hours on the phone with family friend and attorney Morris Brock and the newly retained Ben Conti, had some answers, none of them good. Her grandson was like the mouse in the maze, or more aptly, the fox pursued by the hounds. "The FBI took him by helicopter to Logan and from there back to Louisiana."

"But aren't there rules about extraditing from one state to another?"

"Apparently not when it's a federal case. And there was something too about Miles being on an active psychiatric commitment paper. According to Mr. Conti, once he landed in Louisiana, the judge would send him to a specialized psychiatric hospital. He said that even before being arraigned, he has to undergo a competency-to-stand-trial evaluation. So the usual rules, all the rights prisoners normally get, are at the discretion of the treating facility. It's why he hasn't been able to call."

"Oh my God, this is a nightmare! How can they—"

"How's Joseph handling things?" Anna asked, wanting to put a cap on her daughter's mounting hysteria.

"Better than me. He's convinced it's all a mistake and that the truth will win out. I'm not sure, and I don't think you are either. Everything about this is wrong. Miles is not crazy, and he's not a murderer."

"Of course not." Anna's attention was pulled by the flicker of the kitchen lights. They blinked once, and then she was plunged into darkness. "Not again."

"What is it?"

"The power went out." She held her breath and counted the seconds, waiting for the standby generator to kick in. It didn't. "Perfect. Dear, let me get off the phone. I have to call the power company and the generator man."

"Sure… but call me back."

"It's late," Anna said.

"As if I can sleep, and knowing you, you're on your twelfth cup of coffee."

"You're not wrong. I'll call you back in a bit. And Rachel, this is going to work out. Joseph is right. Miles will be okay."

Those words were lies, and she knew it as she hung up. She sat in the dark kitchen, the moon casting silver swaths across the table. With her oversized iPhone in hand, she tried to ignore the growing pain in her temples. It was 11:20. She felt a guilty pang, knowing she was about to wake someone, or at least interrupt their evening. Her fingers trembled as she pressed her contacts list and scrolled down to the contractor who'd installed the twenty-kilowatt generator. She'd picked him because he was close and advertised 24-7 repairs. The thing was less than five years old and had been serviced religiously, as blackouts in Truro could be a weekly event, especially during hurricane and nor'easter seasons. Fear gurgled in her belly. *The power goes out all the time. That's why you got the generator... so why didn't it kick in?*

A muffled noise from outside the kitchen door made her pause. She held her breath and listened, not to the distant surf, but something else. Probably raccoons or one of the skunks who used the space under her porch as a walkway. She stared at the door, the windowpanes covered by sheers. There were shadows. *Someone's out there.* With phone in hand and her fingers shaking, she pressed 911 just as the door exploded in. It seemed an eternity before the emergency operator picked up. In that eternity a hooded figure wearing night-vision goggles broke into her kitchen, ripped the phone from her hands, and tossed it to the ground. He grabbed her, hoisted her out of her chair, and wrapped her in a choke hold.

She tried to scream as he wrapped his right arm around her throat. Her years of going with Miles to Krav Maga classes made her act. She kicked back hard against her attacker's shin and let her weight collapse against his body. It threw him off-balance; his grip loosened as she stomped her foot up and down. She felt the hardness of his boots and knew she was no match.

He retightened his hold, and there was no swing room to jab back with an elbow. *Just get free.*

She heard her cell, always set on speaker phone, from the kitchen floor. "Nine-one-one, what is your emergency? Hello? Nine-one-one, what is your emergency?" His arm was like a python around her neck. She couldn't breathe. The pain in her right temple flared white hot. Her last conscious thought was the sound of her phone. "Nine-one-one, what is your emergency?"

And then there was no pain. She opened her eyes and stared up into her father's smiling face. She wanted to reach up and touch that ridiculous moustache but was unable to move, and for some reason, that didn't concern her. She felt no fear, just peace. She tried to speak and couldn't.

"It's okay, sweet Anya. Rest. No one can hurt you here."

Where am I? she thought.

"Between the two worlds," he said as he put a finger to his lips. *I will watch over you until you return to the mortal world or join your family in the lake. Would you like me to tell you a story?*

Yes, Papa.

Good. There are so many that I've wanted to give you. He winked as tears fell down his cheeks. One landed like a diamond on the pointed tip of his moustache. *You'll like this one. It's about a kind and beautiful princess and a dark sorcerer.*

CALVIN GRIPPED his arm like a steel band around the old woman's throat. *I am a machine. I feel nothing.* He would not think about the shooting pains in his right shin where she'd kicked him. If not for his steel-toed boots and her rubber-soled walking shoes, it would have been worse.

He squeezed harder and tried to still the rising panic as the 911 operator, unable to get a response, informed him and the now unconscious woman that an emergency response team would be dispatched to the GPS location of the phone.

This is bad. This is a mistake. I am a machine. I feel nothing. I need to get out of here. The old lady's body convulsed. Uncertain if this was another trick, he held fast, choking off her blood flow and air. *Don't crush her trachea. She must stay alive. I am a machine. I feel nothing.* Her movements grew more violent, but not like her earlier attempts to get free. Her arms shot out spastically as her head bucked back against his shoulder. *She's having a seizure. I am a machine.*

Holding her fast, he started to back toward the door. Her feet dragged on the floor, and a black shoe dislodged as he pulled her dead weight onto the back porch. Her spasms lessened as he reached in his pocket for the remote and clicked open the car's trunk.

He loosened his grip and grabbed her around the middle before she fell to the ground. There was no movement or resistance as he pushed her into the trunk. *Fuck, is she dead?* He yanked off his gloves and dropped them into the trunk. He reached for her neck and felt for the carotid.

You have to get out of here. You don't have time for this shit. He held his breath. *I don't feel anything. There's no pulse! Fuck, fuck, fuck!* And then he felt it. First one beat, and then a second and a third. *She's just unconscious. Get out of here, then stop someplace and dose her. I am a machine. I feel nothing.* He slammed the trunk and got back in the car, the 911 operator barely audible in the distance. "Help is on its way."

Not good. And with wheels spitting out crushed clam shells and gravel, he sped off.

CHAPTER 24

LUKE STARED at the diagonal blue and green stripes on his father's tie. He felt numb seated in Dad's dark-paneled study, his mother, Dina, off to the side, her hands folded in her lap. He knew she'd offer nothing other than the occasional sigh or throat clearing that punctuated her husband's tirade.

I'm twenty-three, Luke thought. *Why does this man still have so much power over me?*

"What were you thinking?" his father demanded. His face was red, and traces of spittle caked in the corners of his mouth.

Since being picked up by his parents and driven home last Thursday, these midday interrogations had become the norm. He quickly learned questions such as "What were you thinking?" "Do you intend to throw your entire life away?" and "How could you do this to your family?" were rhetorical, and it was best to say nothing. But it was equally important to not zone out, as occasionally his father would slip in "Are you even listening? Is any of this getting through?" To which some rejoinder was expected, even if it was in his mother's vocabulary of subverbal passive agreement.

As if his father sensed the wander of Luke's thoughts, he demanded, "Are you even listening, Luke? Do you understand what you've done? What you've done to us?"

Luke met his dad's gaze. *Just nod and agree. Yeah, and see where that's gotten you. Don't do it, Luke. You have another fifteen minutes to go, and then he has to get back to the hospital and round on his post-op patients. This will end. Don't make it worse.*

"Yes, Dad." He didn't break the gaze. Instead he pictured Miles. He saw his face and felt the ache of longing, regret for not having stayed with him, guilt for being such a coward. *I will not blink.*

"Do you have any idea what people are saying? Not to my face, of course, but what happened in New Orleans with that boy…. You have shamed your family. You have disgraced me. I will not have it. No son of mine is going to be a homo. Are you listening?" The tone of his father's voice shifted, and took on a hint of compassion. "Luke, this is not a way to live your life…. You have to believe me. Are you listening?"

And there was another question that demanded an answer. *To tell the truth or to continue, as I've done my entire life, and tell the man what he wants to hear?* "I'm listening, Dad."

"You'd better, son. Your mother and I have discussed what needs to be done to put this behind us."

Luke braced for the ultimatum.

His father closed the few feet separating them, leaving Luke the option of either staring at the ground, the pockets of his Dad's lab coat, or his dark, angry eyes. He looked up. *I will not blink.*

"You will not see that boy again. You will apply to MUSC, and I'll see that you're admitted. You will live at home, and when you are not at the hospital or in classes, you will be here. We will *never* speak of this again. But let me tell you this, if you think that your being gay is an option. It is not. If you go against me, I will have no choice. Please, Luke, don't do this."

Luke looked up and saw anguish on his father's face. "I'm sorry, Dad, but…."

Before he could get the words out, the coldness returned to his Dad's voice. "I will not have that filth infect my home. If you go down that road, you will not be my son. You will never speak to your sister or brother again, and if you attempt to do so, I'll have a restraining order filed. Are we clear?"

Luke blinked. He heard his Dad's words. *What century is this man living in?* He pictured Miles, who was never far from his thoughts. Those green eyes, his smile, the intensity of that first kiss… and what came after.

"I want an answer, Luke."

Luke knew anything other than total capitulation would be unacceptable. This was not a negotiation. He glanced at his mom. She looked from her husband to her son. She smiled and nodded, encouraging him to sign on to the wonderful deal he'd been offered.

"Well?" his father persisted.

The doorbell rang.

"I bet that's Jenna," Dina said, rising from her chair.

"Why would Jenna be here?" Luke asked.

His mother glanced nervously from him to his father. "We invited her, dear."

"You can make this right, Luke," his father said, his outrage damped by affection. "You need to do right by that girl. Our actions aren't just about us, son. You hurt that girl. You need to make it right." As soon as his mother left the room, his dad sank into the chair beside his, all traces of anger gone. "Look, Luke, men have needs… urges that aren't under our control. I understand that… I do. But we have to resist those urges; we have to be strong. And if we fall down and fail now and again, we have to put it behind us, and no one, absolutely no one, must ever know. I am not without sin… not even your sin, but I will not bring it home."

Luke was shocked. *What the hell did he just say to me?* Even more than the revelation of secretive hookups, he saw fear in his dad's eyes. *What is he so afraid of? Is having a gay son so bad?* His five years in New Orleans had shown him views that differed from those held by his family and their close-knit Southern Baptist church. Views that had been drummed home in eight years of summer bible camp and promises to keep the vessel pure. Their church's views on homosexuality were explicit. It was abomination.

Luke heard his mother open the door and muted voices.

"Make it right, Luke. Put this behind you. Tell her it was an accident. Tell her you were drunk. Tell her he forced you. I don't want to lose you, son. Make it right." And like a light switch being thrown, his dad stood, all traces of his momentary lapse gone.

There it is, Luke thought. The deal was clear. *If I do what he says, he will love me. If not, I have no Dad and no family. And he's not kidding.* He thought about his younger brother and sister, John and Cindi, and that at twenty-three, he was dependent on his parents for tuition.

"I'm late for rounds," his dad said. "We'll discuss this when I get home. I'll want your answer. If it's not the right one, you're to be out of my house by morning. Understood?"

"Yes."

"Good."

Dina reappeared in the study door. "Jenna's here, dear. She's in the sitting room." She glanced nervously from husband to son. "Talk to her, Luke. She's such a sweet girl, and so pretty."

Frying pan to fire. "I'll talk to her." The minute he said that, he saw triumph… relief… in Dad's eyes. *Why the hell did I say that?*

"Good. I'll be home for dinner. We'll talk then."

LUKE FOUND Jenna in the front sitting room, with its uncomfortable balloon-backed Victorian parlor set and the baby grand no one played. She wore a form-flattering blue knit dress, her blonde hair down and lustrous. She turned as he entered.

She's been crying. He noted her eyes were red rimmed, and she was wearing more makeup than usual. Used to seeing her in either scrubs and a white coat or jeans, Luke thought she seemed different… uncomfortable. "Hi," he said.

"Hello, Luke." She looked up and then away.

He struggled to find words. *What am I supposed to do here?* The answer that came was *Just tell her the truth.* "You want to take a walk?" he asked.

She nodded. "Sure."

As she gathered her purse, he wondered what his parents had done to get her there. It would have been Dad's doing. *What did he tell her? And what did he just tell me? Dad is a closet case… or a sometimes closet case?* He held the door to the King Street home where he'd grown up and looked across at the square, with its well-tended magnolias and live oaks dripping with spanish moss.

"I'm not sure why I'm here," she said as they walked across King and entered the park. "But before you say anything, I have to tell you this, because it's killing me. I'm sorry for calling the cops on Miles. It was a shit thing to do." She batted the back of her hand against her tear-streaked cheek.

As usual there were tourists taking selfies with the historic homes in the background and workers from the nearby post office grabbing a quiet lunch in the shade.

"Yeah, well… I think you get a pass on that, Jenna. Catch your boyfriend and GBF in bed together…. Yeah, you get a pass."

She nodded. "If I had an ounce of country, I would have pulled out a gun and shot you both in the butt." She cracked a smile. "And cute butts at that."

"It was Dad, right? He called?"

"Yeah, and he wasn't going to take no for an answer."

"That's Dad."

"To be truthful, Luke, I wouldn't have come for him… or for you after what you did. I need some answers. I don't think you can know how this is tearing me up."

"Fair enough."

"I loved you, Luke. I still do, although I don't think I've ever been so angry in my life. Your father says you didn't know what you were doing. Is that true? 'Cause I don't think it is."

Luke thought about Dad's ultimatum. Everything hinged on this moment. He stopped and looked back at the gracious 1850s weathered-brick home where he'd grown up, the windows framed with black shutters and tidy window boxes in which the flowering contents were changed quarterly. In a couple of hours, his brother and sister would be home from school, and a few hours after that, he'd have to give Dad his answer. Toe the line and be a part of a family he loved, or…. *Or what?*

"Luke?"

He looked at Jenna. She was beautiful and smart, and he'd hurt her… deeply. It was unintended, but there he had it. "I can't lie anymore," he said.

"You're gay, aren't you? It wasn't some experiment, or what your father said, that you were drunk…. You love Miles…. I mean, fuck it all, I love Miles. Everyone loves Miles. How can you not?"

"I don't know," he said, filtering his thoughts. *What have I done to her?* The truth was undeniable as his dad's ultimatum stood before him like a fork in the road. *Tell Jenna it was all a mistake. I was drunk, I didn't know what…. Hell no.* "I wasn't drunk, Jenna." *I'm in love with my best friend. I think about him constantly.*

She stared ahead. "So what were you doing with me? Was it a game? I feel like such an idiot. And at school all our friends are laughing at me." Her attempts to stay calm unraveled as hurt and anger flared. "You did a good job, Luke. No one knew. I told your father my coming here was a bad idea. He insisted that you were all fixed, that just by my showing up, you'd be better. I'm not an idiot. I know that's not how it works. But here's the thing…." She faced him, her jaw twitched, and she was fighting tears. "I love you, Luke, so I had to try. But there's no point, is there?"

"No." And with that one word, he'd made his choice. Not just about Jenna, but everything.

"Then I'm done here. Oh God!" She threw her hands over her face, barely able to speak. "And this is when I'd go to Miles… and I don't have him either." Sobbing, she turned on him. "I don't ever want to see you again. I don't want you to call…. Nothing. Just tell me this. You owe me that at least. Was it something I did?"

"No." In her eyes he saw horrible pain and knew he was the cause of her suffering. "I'm so sorry, Jenna."

"That makes two of us. Promise me something."

"What?"

"Don't ever do this to another girl. I don't know what you're calling it, but you lied to me. Both of you did. Luke, we made love. I thought you loved me. But it was all lies. How can you do that to someone? I just…." She spotted a cab and hailed it. "I can't do this." Without looking back, she ran toward it and got in.

He watched her drive off. "I never meant to hurt you." *But you did. So what now?* It was an odd mix of emotions: numbness, guilt, and something else, a lightness as he realized he'd made his choice. *I can't go home.*

He pulled out his cell and called the house in New Orleans. Joel picked up.

"It's me," Luke said. "You haven't rented out my room yet, have you?"

"No. Month's not over, and you've still got your first and last. We were waiting to hear from you before we did anything."

"Good. I'm coming home."

"I thought you were expelled."

"I am, but there's nothing for me here. I'll get a job. See if Marie will hire me at the Swamp Witch."

"Okay, but… what about the whole be-a-doctor thing?"

"I don't know. I'll try to get in somewhere else. Have you heard from Miles?"

There was a pause.

"Joel, you there?"

"Yeah, so you don't know," Joel said.

"Know what? What's happened?"

"He's been arrested. They say he killed one of his patients."

CHAPTER 25

M‌ILES SAT mute in the back of the locked, windowless transport van. The events of the last forty-eight hours felt surreal and horrifying, from his arrest on the beach and the chopper ride to Logan airport surrounded by armed agents in black flak jackets, to being presented in five-point shackles to a Louisiana judge, who did little more than uphold the commitment paper written last Wednesday by Gerald Stangl.

"Miles Fox, I remand you to the forensic unit at Lakeshore Hospital, where you will undergo an evaluation that is not to exceed thirty days to determine if you are mentally competent to stand trial for the murder of Mr. Antoine Dey."

Prior to his transport to Lakeshore, he had been allowed a one-hour consultation with attorney Ben Conti, a whip-thin man in a perfectly draped suit, with hawk eyes that studied him from behind frameless glasses. Grandma Anna had found and retained him via a family friend. The interview, with Miles chained to a ring in the floor, had underscored the deck stacked against him.

"It comes down to this," Mr. Conti said. "Competence to stand trial means you know what you did. If you're guilty you knew it was wrong, and you're able to effectively take part in your own defense."

"And what happens if they say I'm incompetent?"

"The good news is then the death penalty is off the table. The bad news is they can keep you locked up in a forensic hospital for the rest of your life, with no due process, no rights to appeal, nothing. The worse news is, if you're both competent and found guilty, this is a death penalty case."

"I didn't do this."

"I didn't think you did, and for the record, you don't sound like a whack job. They've got evidence, though, and they have to share it with your defense. Problem is they don't have to share jack until after you clear the competency assessment. It boils down to this: if you're incompetent—in the legal sense—you have almost no constitutional rights. It's a different rule book. There will be no trial, no jury of your peers, and no sentence. The judge will find you incompetent, and you will be sent to a high-security forensic hospital… most likely for the rest of your life. All *you* need to focus on is getting whatever shrink does the assessment to find you competent. That's it. Once that happens the prosecutor has to turn over every shred of evidence they've collected, and then I can mount your defense."

"And what if the shrink doing my evaluation wants me locked up in a hospital?"

Conti's gaze narrowed. "What are you saying?"

"Dr. Gerald Stangl. He's the medical director at Lakeshore. He's the doctor who wrote the commitment paper in the hospital last week."

"Go on. Tell me everything. You have some kind of bad blood with this Stangl?"

"Yeah. I don't know why, exactly. There's a weird history and coincidences that don't add up." He'd realized this attorney, whom he'd just met, was going to hear a story that might make him sound paranoid. "My parents brought me to see him when I was eight."

"Why would they do that?" Conti asked.

"It's all going to come out, isn't it?"

"Yes, and you need to talk fast, Miles. We get an hour, and that's it."

"Okay, when I was a kid, I heard the voice of my great-grandfather."

"I'm taking it he wasn't in the room at the time?"

"He died in nineteen forty-five in a concentration camp."

"Do you still hear his voice?"

"Yeah, sometimes. Mostly I see him in my dreams."

"Wonderful. So what does Great-grandpa have to say?"

"Mostly he tells stories."

"I know I'm going to regret this," Conti said. "What kind of stories?"

"I don't know, like, fairy tales. Twisted ones."

"Give me a for instance."

"Like the one with the fisherman and his wife where she keeps asking for more and more, only in this one, they kill the magic fish and eat it. Or this one where a girl's accused of being a witch, and the only way she can get out of it is by staying silent for seven years, breaking a magic spell, and then in front of everyone turning seven swans into her brothers… which supposedly proves she's not a witch."

Conti nodded. "There's a moral in there for you. Keep your mouth shut about this. So does Grandpa tell you to kill anyone?"

"No. Never."

"What about chopping off heads?"

"What are you talking about?"

"It's how they found Mr. Dey."

Startled, Miles stared at the attorney. "Why would someone do that?"

"Good question. Here's another, and tell the truth no matter how bonkers it sounds. You did something with Mr. Dey in the hospital. A nurse called security, and you went berserk when they tried to pull you off of him. All of which makes you look crazy as batshit. What exactly did you do?"

Miles, trained by years of Grandma's dire threats, hesitated.

"Just spit it out. I need to know everything."

"I healed him of stage-four cancer."

"That's quite an assertion. Can you prove it?"

"Yeah… sort of."

"How?"

"His records. Get his hospital records. He had been admitted for a last-ditch round of highly experimental and toxic chemo. He was filled with tumors."

"And you healed him?"

"Yes."

"They'll say it was the chemo."

"Probably, but anyone who knows how long it takes chemo to do its thing, kill off populations of cells, destroy bone marrow, then hopefully leave enough alive that's not cancerous, or do a bone-marrow transplant, it takes weeks, months. What I did happened fast. And don't ask me how, 'cause I don't know."

"So let's recap…. A psychiatrist who's out to get you, who's followed you from Boston to New Orleans. A magical healing ability, a great-grandfather who's been dead for seventy years telling you bedtime stories…. Anything else I need to know about?"

"It doesn't sound good, does it?"

"No, but I can work with it. And here's some information you need, and like I said, I don't have the details, but the prosecutor is pretty certain they've got you tried and fried. Apparently they've got DNA evidence at the scene, and the tip-off for the body came from your computer. Any idea how those two things might have happened?"

It felt like the floor had been swept out from under him. "Someone's got to be doing this."

"Yeah, a frame job. I got that," Conti said, his expression unreadable.

"I didn't kill Antoine. I just wanted to save him. He had two little children and a wife. I just wanted to save him. I made a promise to his little boy… and he's dead anyway." Miles swallowed back the horror and sadness that welled with Conti's revelations. Not only was Antoine Dey murdered, but it was brutal. *His poor wife…. Jasper.*

Conti shook his head as an officer rapped her knuckles on the door. "Time's up, gentlemen."

"Right." The attorney, who was jotting notes, closed his leatherbound pad and lowered his voice. "Here's my advice. Don't give this Stangl anything. He's going to tape you. No conspiracies, no dead greatgrandfather. More than that, if even a portion of what you've said is true and this psychiatrist has it out for you, he's going to try to make you look both crazy and dangerous. Whatever he says, whatever he does, do not take the bait. Where you're going, he's going to have all the power, and that's going to hurt like a bitch. The more I think about it, dead Grandpa's swan story makes sense. Keep your mouth shut and get through this. I can't do much if you're found incompetent to stand trial. What I will do, is get another shrink in to evaluate you. Her name is Amelia Raskin and she's sharp. Suffice to say, you will tell her none of this. Best case scenario, the judge will look at the two expert evaluations and one will cancel out the other, and he'll let your case go to trial. It's a risk, but I'm good at what I do. And crazy as your story sounds, and I'm not saying I believe this healing crap, I don't think you killed that man."

NOW ALONE with his thoughts and an armed marshal who sat across from him, texting, he listened to the traffic. They were on the highway, the vehicle slowed, and he braced against the bench and wall as they hit a sharply banked off-ramp.

DNA evidence, like what? Miles thought, unable to remember much of last Tuesday night. *The only way there was something on my computer is if someone broke in. That has to be what happened. It's got to be Stangl. This is all his doing.*

After a thirty-minute ride, the van pulled to a stop.

The driver got out. He was talking to someone. Miles's pulse quickened at the sound of Stangl's clipped syllables. While he could count the number of times on one hand he'd ever hit someone in anger outside of the Krav Maga studio, all he wanted in that moment was to slam a fist into Stangl's smug face. He thought back to the conversation with attorney Conti—and that would be playing into Stangl's hand. *He wants you here. It has to do with the gift and whatever he meant by "Do you believe in fate?"*

The back doors opened onto a steel-edged loading dock. The marshal unlocked the manacles threaded through steel rings beneath the bench and helped him up and out of the van. Miles looked back through the open bay door at manicured lawns and a dense mangrove swamp that edged the lake. He spotted Stangl with the driver. He was signing forms on a tablet. *Like a package from UPS.*

A pair of Lakeshore security officers grabbed him by his elbows. "This way."

As he ambled with chained ankles, he tried to calm himself and to gather details. While he couldn't see the building's exterior, he knew where he was, or at least he'd seen the ultramodern steel-and-mirrored-glass building in brochures for the medical school and from a distance at the annual Halloween bash. It contained the most up-to-date imaging equipment in the state of Louisiana.

So what am I doing here? It's beyond convenient. He knew Conti didn't buy his assertion that Stangl had been tracking him for fifteen years. *I wouldn't believe it. But if it's true, this building, the equipment inside…. How many millions of dollars?* Stangl was a research giant who had more active grants than any other member of the faculty. *How do I fit into this? How does he?*

One of the guards waved his key card over the pad and steel doors opened.

"Come on," he said.

Miles said nothing as they escorted him down a broad hallway with polished granite floors and textured steel walls that acted like fun house mirrors. He caught his distorted reflection, manacled in an orange jumpsuit and white-soled laceless sneakers. He hadn't shaved in days, and his eyes looked sunken. He heard the doors shut behind him, Conti's words in his head: *You have no power here.* He thought of Tomas's swan story. *Shut up and knit.*

The guards stopped in front of an elevator. The one on his right waved his badge over the keypad. The doors slid open, and they entered. The other guard placed his finger into a scanner while simultaneously pushing the button for B1.

Horrible speculations hounded Miles. *You're never going to leave this place. Why did he kill Antoine? There's no one to help you.* He thought of Luke and how he'd selflessly rescued him from the ER. It seemed so long ago, when in reality it was only days since this nightmare started.

From the elevator he was marched through a windowless corridor with the same distorting steel mirrors. It ended at a pair of transparent doors. Behind them he glimpsed a gleaming white modular nurses' station. What he didn't see was people, nurses, other patients…. *Where is everyone?* The guards and his footsteps and the rhythmic jangle of his chains were the only sounds.

They stopped in front of the doors. Miles observed two ceiling cameras trained down on them. One of the officers punched in a nine-digit code and again pressed his forefinger against a scanner. Seconds passed. There was the breathy release of hydraulics, and the doors swung in.

The unit before him was unexpected, like something from a sci-fi or James Bond movie. While Miles had completed his psychiatric rotation, he'd successfully avoided contact with Stangl's posh private hospital. His only trips to the grounds of Lakeshore had been at the almost mandatory Halloween bashes, and for those his costumes had included either thick makeup or a mask. *And this was not part of the general tour.* The walls were transparent, constructed of a thick polymer. As far as he could see, there were only two patient rooms, like human fishbowls. One was completely visible, with a platform bed made up with white linens, an exposed toilet in the corner, and a sink with a motion-detector faucet. The other room/cell was of identical size, but what, or who, might be inside was obscured by white curtains. There was not a speck of dust, no clutter on the expansive white nurses' station. *Where is everyone? And who is behind the curtains? What are they hiding?*

"In here," one of the guards said as a thick transparent door slid open. He nudged Miles's elbow as the second guard stood outside the cell.

I have no power here. He trudged forward, and his chains scraped the floor. He smelled bleach and the pine-scented antibacterial cleaner they used at the hospital. Years of Krav Maga training, both in Boston and during his summers on the Cape, caused him to wonder. *I could probably take the guards, but they're armed and I'm not.* He thought of ways his chains restricted his movements but could also be used as weapons.

As if reading his mind, the officer outside his show-and-tell cell shut the door. The one left inside unlocked his manacles. "Don't even think of running," he said as he undid the five-point restraint. "These walls are unbreakable. You're on camera 24/7, and between you and the world outside are a series of high-security doors…. But it's not all bad. The food's great."

"Who's behind the curtains?" Miles asked as he massaged his bruised wrists.

"Not a clue," he said. "We're just the hired help. Now I need you to take off your clothes. You have to be searched."

"Seems everyone wants me naked," Miles quipped, having already been through this with the FBI, his processing at the lockup in Boston, and his stint as the violin-playing angel.

The guard answered without humor, "Just do it. We've got a lovely pair of Lakeshore jammies. You'd be amazed how many of the paying clients stuff these into their bags."

Wordlessly Miles undid the snaps of the jumpsuit, toed off the laceless sneakers, and, staring back at the curtained room, he stripped.

"Everything," the guard said.

And off came the blue prison-issue boxers.

He had a good three to four inches on the guard, who was now snapping on purple propylene gloves. He felt numb, and beneath that, rage. *Just get through this, make it through. Don't give them anything to use.*

"Turn around and put your hands against the wall next to the sink. Now spread your legs. I'm sorry, but I have to do this. You'd be amazed at the kind of contraband people try to smuggle in."

The guard's apology struck him. It sounded genuine, a whiff of kindness while simultaneously violating his dignity. He controlled his breathing as the guard left no crevice uninspected. *You will get through this.* He stared between his hands toward the nurses' station. Where it had been deserted, there now stood a young blond-haired man in dark green scrubs and a crisp white lab coat. His water-blue eyes met Miles's. His cheeks colored, and he looked down at something on the counter.

What the fuck? That's Stangl's kid. What's he doing here? His gaze shifted from the blushing teen to a recessed display case behind the nurses' station. It was the only apparent decoration and was filled with a dozen or more silver goblets in various sizes. *Trophies?* They weren't engraved, and he was struck by their graceful lines, all the same form, perfectly symmetrical bells fused in the middle.

He looked back at the boy as the guard completed the search. He observed the teen's flushed cheeks and shallow breathing. *Calvin... that's his name.* He remembered how the teen had audited the gross anatomy lectures and labs. He'd been assigned to a cadaver two tables down from him and Luke. *Why is he here?*

Calvin glanced up.

Miles held his gaze. Aware of his nakedness but feeling detached from his body, his thoughts pulled in data. *Straight guys don't look at me like that.* Wanting to test his hypothesis, he kept eye contact and gave the kid a smile. The effect was immediate. Calvin swallowed and the red in his cheeks spread down his neck and up to the tips of his ears. *Interesting.*

"You can turn around," the guard said. He held a pair of folded white pajamas.

Miles complied, aware the kid was checking out his butt. *So Stangl's kid likes to look at naked men. Is this something I can use?* He took his time getting dressed, conscious of the kid's covert glances.

"That's it for us," the guard said as he backed out of the cell. Miles watched as he and his partner left the unit. Sensing the kid's attention, he held still. He thought of Conti's advice and Tomas's story. *Shut up and knit.*

CHAPTER 26

CALVIN STARED at one of the dozen flat monitors embedded in the modular station's backsplash. It was hard to think, to even catch his breath. *He's beautiful*, he thought, unable to take his eyes off the images before him, every inch of Miles's tall, lean body spread before him. Their brief moment of eye contact was almost too painful to manage. *You have to look at him.*

Screwing up his courage, he pulled his eyes from the charged images and stared at the man. *He's watching me. Is he smiling? He is. He's smiling at me. What does that mean? Does he like me? He's still smiling. What am I supposed to do? I can't just stare at him. So beautiful. Those eyes. He's smiling at me.* Calvin's throat tightened, and his dick was rock hard. *Stop staring. He's going to think I'm a creep. I don't want to look away. Those eyes, so green. He's still smiling.* Grateful for the station that concealed the physiologic effect Miles had on him, he drank in every inch of the man who had plagued his thoughts for over a year, since that first day in anatomy class. *He's more beautiful than anyone. And he's here. He's mine.*

The guard was speaking in Miles's room, but the sound was turned down to where Calvin couldn't hear. *Please don't look away.* But he did, and now Calvin was staring at Miles's backside.

He didn't know where to look first. Broad shoulders tapering like a V to narrow hips. *His ass, firm and muscular. He's perfect.* And while his mind and blood-engorged penis skittered from erotic image to erotic image, it was that smile…. *He smiled at me. Does he like me? Is it possible? He knew I was watching…. He smiled.*

Calvin riveted his eyes to Miles's back as he lifted first one long leg and then the other into the pajama bottoms. Calvin traced the smooth skin of his back to where it vanished into the fabric, the mounds of his butt clearly visible. *Beautiful… perfect.* Mesmerized, he watched Miles pull on the matching V-neck top.

The guard who was outside the cell called out, "Will you be needing us for anything else, sir?"

Startled, Calvin shook his head. "No. I'm good." But he wasn't. *What am I supposed to do? He can't see me like this.*

"Right."

The guards left.

I can't look at him. He glanced across the bank of monitors, four trained on Miles, four on the old lady in the curtained cell, one on the elevator, one showing the unit's front entrance, and the remaining two with split feeds of the building's exterior. He glanced down at the tent in his dark scrubs. Something sticky leaked from his penis into his underwear.

He can't see me like this. I'll go into the back room. His head filled with images of Miles stripped… naked… only it wasn't like Internet porn. This was real. This was Miles Fox. He pictured the yearbook he'd seen in his apartment. It had taken all his will to not add that to the other trophy, the jock hidden beneath his mattress. The words "Miles the Fox" scrawled under his name… probably by a girl. *I'll just go in the back and take care of—*

Lost in erotic reverie, Calvin's head shot up at the sound of the unit door. Like acid in his veins, fear replaced his prior plans. *Father! Shit! He'll see. He'll know. I am a machine. I feel—*

"Calvin," his father barked, "come out. We don't have time to waste."

"Yes, sir." He thrust his hands into the pockets of his lab coat to camouflage his arousal, although Father's presence had an icing effect. Fortunately his attention was not on him, but on Miles. *Miles the Fox. My Miles. He is mine. I am a machine. He smiled at me.* He glanced from Father to Miles. Miles was focused on Father, and where there'd been a smile for him—*he wouldn't do that if he didn't like me*—hatred now shot from those gorgeous eyes.

Father was in full gloat. "The Fox had quite a run. But in the end, the hunter is victorious. Now while you managed to escape the morons at the hospital and make it out of town, I hope you've taken the opportunity to observe your current surroundings. What appears to be glass is a polymer that can withstand several tons of impact."

Father chuckled, a sound Calvin associated with an attached slap or punch. Only the strike was not for him. He stared at Miles. *I'm sorry. I had to do this. Please don't hate me.*

Father continued, "Of course, none of that is necessary to keep our Fox in his cage. You see…. Oh, wait, I've forgotten my manners. Have you met my son?"

Calvin's breath caught as Miles met his gaze. The blood rushed from his head, and he felt frozen. *He's not smiling. He's angry. Please, it's not me. It's Father.*

"Calvin, did you introduce yourself to our guest?"

He swallowed hard. "No, Father…. We were in anatomy class together."

"Right…. Yes, good. The two of you will be working quite closely over the next week. It's odd, isn't it?" Father continued, his focus on Miles. "We know so much about you, Mr. Fox. I can see all those questions swirling in your head. Why is this happening? Why you? Although I suspect you know, and your recent adventures with the unfortunate Mr. Dey were the proof we needed. But back to my prior point, and why you need to recognize that escape is not an option. Calvin, lift the drapes behind door number two."

"Yes, Father." *He's going to hate me. He's going to know I did this. I had no choice.* He walked behind the counter and pressed a button. He stared at the monitors, his gaze moving between Miles, who stood transfixed by the rising curtains, and the ones that showed what… who… was being revealed.

"No! Grandma Anna! What have you done to her?" Miles gaped as the curtain rose on his unconscious grandmother. "*No!*" She lay on a hospital bed, a nasal cannula in her nostrils delivering oxygen, her vitals displayed on a monitor. Her head was shaved and dotted with EEG electrodes hooked to a second monitor, which displayed rows of wavy lines that showed her brain function.

Calvin swallowed. *He'll know I did this. He's so angry. He'll hate me. She wasn't supposed to fight me. She wasn't supposed to resist.* He pictured her cell phone lying on the kitchen floor. *"Nine-one-one, what is your emergency?" I had no choice.*

"What have you done to my grandmother?"

He's furious. Calvin, who'd been riding the euphoria of Miles's smile, plunged into despair. He caught Father's triumphant smile in the monitor. *This is his fault. I would never have done this. He made me do it. I had no choice.*

"She's stable," Gerald said. "Apparently, when Calvin picked her up, she had a bit of a hemorrhagic stroke. Possibly the excitement, possibly something that was set to happen regardless. She's stable… for now. The bleed is too deep to attempt an evacuation. And obviously blood thinners are out of the question."

No! Why did you have to say it was me? Calvin risked a glance from the screens to Miles, who stared at his grandmother, his hands balled into fists.

"Why?" he asked.

"Good question," Father replied. "Care to be more specific? Why kidnap your grandmother? I imagine you can come up with the reasons. But here's two. Whatever gene, or combination of genes, carries your unique abilities came from her. And the more practical reason is this. We have important work to do, you and I. What's involved is bigger than the two of us. Your cooperation is essential. If you don't do as instructed, she will suffer, and she will die. Yes, the stroke was unfortunate and unintended. I had so many things I wanted to ask her. I believe she met my father and my grandfather, both great men of science. I'd love to hear what she remembers of the old days. I'd like to know how she hid for so many years. Though from the scars on her wrists it's clear she was determined to stick to the shadows. You see, up until your display with the recently deceased Mr. Dey, I didn't have conclusive proof."

Calvin saw fury on Miles's face. *Why doesn't he speak? Why doesn't he demand to be let free?* Mesmerized, he watched Miles shift his focus from his comatose grandmother to Father. *Why isn't he speaking?* The silence was unnerving, and before Calvin could avert his gaze back to the safety of the monitors, Miles looked at him. Unable to resist, he stared back. *I should look away. I don't want to look away. Please don't hate me. I didn't want to hurt her.*

"Calvin." Father broke the trance. "Have you taken samples yet?"

"No, Father."

"What are you waiting for?" Annoyed, Gerald looked at Calvin, and then at their prisoner. "What is with you today?"

"Nothing, Father."

Gerald noted the color in his son's face, an unfortunate tell he'd tried to beat out of the boy. *He's too soft.* His emotions were too close to the surface. Then again, this was a landmark moment for the two of them. The culmination of a life's work. "Pull it together, son. I want a full panel for baseline. We have a single chance to do this right. I don't want shortcuts or sloppiness. Understood?"

"Yes, Father."

Gerald looked at the comatose old woman. She reminded him of a baby bird, with her bald head and blue veins visible below the thin skin stretched across her skull.

He turned to Miles. "If she dies, we have other options. Your mother, father… your sister, Maya. It would be so easy to pluck her on her way to class. We have her entire schedule; she's quite the budding young writer, although I can't imagine how your parents are managing the strain of both your tuitions. Wesleyan is quite pricey, and even with your scholarships here…. They're all fair game, Miles, so it's best you behave…. Huh?"

Gerald noted something on the old lady's EEG monitor.

"That's interesting." He walked to the edge of her cell, tapped in a pass code, and placed his finger on the scanner. The door slid open, and he entered. He studied the reading on the monitor and checked the lead placements on her head. "No, they seem fine," he said, prepared to discipline Calvin if he'd messed up something as simple as an EEG. He examined the wires to ensure there were no loose connections. Satisfied the equipment was correct, he studied the display and pressed the button for a printout. "Calvin?" he shouted.

"Yes, Father."

"In addition to blood and urine, get an EEG. Better still, when you put him out, hook him to a machine. There's something interesting here." Gerald felt the tingle of discovery. *What does this mean?* The old lady's tracing was unlike anything he'd encountered, a bizarre mix of REM and languid theta waves. Clearly she was dreaming, but against a background associated with trance states. *What is going on in your head, you tricky old bag? REM and theta do not go together… not ever.* "Tonight we'll do an fMRI on her. Something's happening."

Calvin stood in the open door. "What do you think it is?"

"I don't know. It's as though… as though she's… in a trance." Gerald pressed the machine's memory and scrolled through hours of data. "It's been like this since she arrived. This is not a coma. This is something else. A dream, only…."

"Only what, Father?"

"I'm not sure. But we will find out. Now get the samples and have them both prepped for the scanner. And you're clear on the first subject?"

"Yes, the man with AIDS, Kaposi's, and pneumocystis in the ICU."

"Good. We know it works on cancer. We'll begin with infections both viral and bacterial. We'll do him and then pluck someone with advanced rheumatic disease, or the fifty-year-old we talked about with ALS. I think a late-stage Alzheimer's would be good. Although now that I think this through, let's just do two. The AIDS patient ticks multiple boxes, then something end-stage and autoimmune, and that will be adequate." Gerald hated how little time they had. What should have been up to thirty days, now truncated to ten, unless he wanted to risk having Miles evaluated by Amelia Raskin, one of the world's top forensic psychiatrists.

"How long until we attempt the transfer?"

"Calvin," Gerald bristled. "There is no attempt. We will succeed. And soon." Calvin's doubt fueled his own. *This is going to work. We are so close. Just this one piece that's been missed. And missed, and missed.*

"I'm sorry, Father…. How long until the transfer?"

Gerald looked between the Fox and his grandmother. The key to life everlasting was in his grasp. Millennia of careful and not so careful experimentation had paved the way to this moment. Miles Fox was possibly the only living vessel of the grail. The jury was out on the old bag, and neither the mother nor the sister possessed the green eyes. "We are so close. Just one final piece."

"Yes, Father. I'll get the samples, and I'll have the infected nurse here and prepped by ten."

"We're going to witness something miraculous, you and I." Gerald turned from the old lady to Calvin. *Why does he blush like that?* "It will be the dawn of a new age. A world cleansed of impurity and of disease. We will usher it in; we will be its gods."

CHAPTER 27

CALVIN GATHERED his phlebotomy tray with its color-coded rubber-stopped tubes, needles, and tourniquet. His fingers fumbled over tasks he'd done countless times. If Father were here, his clumsiness would be met with corrective backhanded slaps. Fortunately he was off on rounds with the medical students and residents who rotated through Lakeshore.

He hazarded a glance at Miles. He hadn't moved, still up against the wall, focused on his comatose grandmother. *I didn't mean to hurt her. Why did Father have to say it was me?*

But that wasn't the worst of it. It was the plan itself. Life everlasting… with Father. Could there be a clearer definition of hell? *I don't want that. I want Miles. He smiled at me. That means something. It has to.*

He grabbed the tray by its molded handle, his arousal deflated by Father's Snidely Whiplash declarations and the realization Miles Fox probably hated him.

Pretending composure, he crossed the distance while Miles watched him approach. The weight of his stare and the growing proximity jumbled Calvin's thoughts like a twelve-year-old fangirl coming face-to-face with her boy-band heartthrob. Each step brought home how beautiful Miles was.

He felt giddy and tongue-tied. *Say something. He's going to think you're retarded.* "I need you to step away from the door and sit on the bed."

Miles didn't move.

Maybe the sound isn't on. No, it had to be because he spoke to Father. *Why isn't he moving?* "Please, I need to draw some blood… and get some other samples. You have to sit on the bed." *Don't look at me that way.*

There was a long pause. "Or?"

Calvin's breath caught on that single word and the way Miles arched his right eyebrow up. "Or I have to fill the room with gas, knock you out, and take what I need while you're unconscious."

Miles cocked his head, and the hint of a smile played across his lips. "Then I guess I'd better get on the bed." He turned, stopped, and looked back. "Would you like me with my shirt off?"

It wasn't necessary, but caught in his stare, Calvin nodded. *Yes, please, I'd like you with your shirt off.* As he pressed his forefinger onto the reader, he tripped and shot a hand against the cell wall to steady himself. *Pull it together.* He knew as soon as Father finished with his rounds, he'd return, and his every movement in this unit was recorded. *If Father knew....*

He watched as Miles, still standing, pulled the white V-neck shirt off and tossed it onto the bed. His lean torso had an immediate effect Calvin couldn't dampen. Frantically he ran multiplication tables and thought of the heads in jars. *His skin is like marble. I am a machine. I feel nothing.* He smelled Miles's musk, felt the heat from his body as his eyes feasted on Miles's taut muscles and the thin pajama pants that hung low on his slim hips.

Still standing, Miles said, "So…the bed…"

Oh yes, yes, please… I'd like you on the bed. I'd like you on the bed very much.

Miles held creepy Calvin in his gaze. He fought the urge to smash a fist into the teen's gut. His arousal was obvious, and beyond the ick factor of having Calvin Stangl paw him while he was unconscious, there was a glimmer of something that reeked of hope.

He perched on the bed as Calvin placed his plastic basket of supplies on the white molded table that rose like a mushroom from the floor.

"Which side?" Calvin asked.

Miles held out his arms and subtly flexed his chest, curious to see Calvin's reaction. It was immediate. He froze and then turned to his basket of tubes and needles. His skin from his neck to his cheeks flushed.

Okay, he's got the hots for you. He thought of Tomas's story about the magic trout, and remembering fishing trips with his dad on Cape Cod, he played out the line. He observed Calvin fumble over the tubes. *Put him at ease, get him talking.* He looked at the teen, blond and blue eyed, handsome in a psycho-twink sort of way. "Seems like your dad rides you kind of hard."

Calvin looked up from the cart. He chewed at his bottom lip and nodded.

Miles could almost read his thoughts. Keeping his voice to a whisper, he asked, "He's taping this, isn't he?"

"Yes."

Miles saw Calvin's hesitation, his flushed cheeks and shallow breath, a heartbeat away from a panic attack as he stood with his Vacutainer, needle, tourniquet, and fistful of tubes. "It's okay, Calvin." He held out his right arm and pumped his bicep a few times to raise the blood vessels on the surface. Like reciting lines from cheesy porn, he whispered, "Go ahead, I'm an easy stick."

Calvin gripped Miles's upper arm.

He's trembling. "It'll be easier if you sit next to me. I don't mind." But there was something else. Where Calvin's skin connected with his own, the sense of reading the boy's thoughts grew stronger. But it wasn't words that flowed into him…. *I can feel him, his emotions. What is this?*

Tentatively Calvin touched down on the bed, his body at a forty-five-degree angle to Miles. He wrapped the elastic tourniquet around Miles's bicep and swabbed a swath of skin with an alcohol pad.

Miles kept his eyes on Calvin as he held his emotions in check and focused on the weird flow of energy. The little bastard was responsible for kidnapping Grandma Anna, and God only knew what else. An obvious sociopath who happened to have a raging boner for him. *He thinks he's in love… with me.* Miles shifted forward, letting his knee brush against Calvin's. The connection grew. He felt Calvin's mounting panic… his excitement as he tried not to tremble while he brought the needle in line with the popped vein.

"I haven't seen you since anatomy last year. Do you go to school, Calvin?"

He shook his head. "No."

"Never?"

"I'm homeschooled, and then I audit at the medical school. But I can't do any of the clinical work till I formally matriculate."

Miles held still as the needle pierced his flesh. "So your dad plays the tune, and you march along."

Calvin struggled to line up the first of the glass tubes to place in the barrel of the Vacutainer.

"Here, I'll hold them for you," Miles said and pressed his leg against Calvin's inner thigh. It would have been so easy to wrap his hands around his neck. But such a move would do nothing other than ruin his one shot at leverage. And with the added physical connection, images formed.

"Thanks…. I'm sorry about your grandmother. I didn't mean for that to happen."

"What did happen?" Miles asked. *Show me what you did.* As if in answer, he glimpsed a moonlit view of Grandma Anna's house at the Cape. Only the colors were off, as though being viewed through a low-light filter.

"She had a seizure… and I guess a stroke," Calvin said.

"You went to her house in Truro?" he asked, testing the hypothesis. *Am I really inside his head?*

"Yes." Calvin flicked his tongue against his upper lip as he pressed the first tube into the barrel.

Miles watched his blood swirl into the red-topped container. From his rotations in the clinics and wards, he identified the samples being drawn: a complete blood count, metabolic screen, and the purple-topped tube for clotting factors. *What did you do to her? Show me.* It was all he could do to keep from beating this evil fuck to a pulp as he watched what happened. He saw Grandma Anna through her kitchen window. She was on her cell. The overhead light flickered and then went out. He saw her annoyance and a flicker of fear. She said something into the phone and hung up.

Calvin pressed his leg back.

Miles glanced at his grandma as images poured from Calvin. The kitchen door offered little resistance, and then he was inside her cozy home. He saw fear on Grandma's face… and fury as she resisted. *The little fuck is going to pay.*

Calvin gasped, his gaze riveted on Miles's chest, his right hand on the Vacutainer, his fingers splayed over the bicep, attempting to keep the inserted tube steady with his shaky left hand.

Miles let his focus drift, allowing Calvin's thoughts and emotions to wash over him. *Jesus!* The kid was all over him, replaying images of his naked body as the guard searched him, his pecs and abdomen, his ass and his junk. But more than cataloging his body parts, Calvin kept coming back to his face, his eyes and his smile. As Miles focused, he heard words inside the boy's head. *Listen…. Did he smile at me? Could he like me?*

Stunned by what he was experiencing, Miles remembered an embarrassing conversation he'd had with Grandma Anna when he was sixteen. "Girls are going to have crushes on you, boy. It's because of your looks… which you get from me." She'd chuckled and pulled out the photo albums. "You wouldn't think it to look at me now, but beauty gives you power. Your grandma was quite the dish in her day."

She wasn't kidding. Between her arresting eyes, raven hair, and flawless skin, she'd been starlet lovely. Even now with her head cruelly shaved, the planes of her face and high cheekbones gave her an ethereal beauty.

She had warned him. "Be careful with it, boy. Don't lead girls on that you don't like. You don't realize it, but just the way you look will cause pain. And you, my boy, are far too handsome for your own good."

Calvin nearly dropped the first tube as he held the Vacutainer with the needle embedded in Miles's vein steady. "It's okay, Calvin. Take your time. No need to rush." *Tell me all your secrets.*

The boy nodded and carefully placed the filled tube in the plastic tray. He turned back, and Miles handed him the second, letting his fingers linger against Calvin's. "You seem nervous."

"I'm okay," Calvin said, not taking his hand from Miles's.

"That's good. I don't want you to be nervous around me." He pressed the tube into his palm. The added skin-to-skin contact increased the flood of information. "I think you've got enough in your life to worry about."

With his voice barely audible, Calvin replied, "You have no idea."

Miles inched closer, letting Calvin drink in his smell and his body heat. A covert glance at the kid's crotch let him know his seventeen-year-old libido was headed toward the obvious. "You can tell me," he whispered and gently rubbed his knee up and down Calvin's inner thigh.

Calvin shuddered and dropped the tube back into the tray. He looked into Miles's eyes, all pretense at drawing blood gone. His breath was shallow and came in gasps. He shivered and pressed back against Miles's knee. He bit his lip as the climax came in repressed gasps.

Miles let the energy flow. *Show me, Calvin, show me everything.* Unfiltered images tumbled through his head: him naked, his apartment in the quarter, Antoine Dey naked and tied to a metal table… glass jars filled with human heads, one that was unmistakably Tomas. He held still as the boy's breath continued in staccato gasps. A dark stain blossomed in Calvin's lap.

As Calvin struggled to regain composure, Miles both saw and felt his desire turn to fear. The pictures that came were all of Gerald Stangl. Try as he might, he couldn't hear the words, but the emotions were painful— humiliation, dread, but something else…. Rage.

"It's okay, Calvin." He felt his panic and knew everything rested in the next few moments. The fish was on the hook; the net was out. Time to reel him in. "Your father doesn't need to know. I'm not going to tell. Now pick up the tube and get what you need."

Calvin's nerves hummed as the aftershocks of the most intense orgasm of his life subsided. He knew he should have felt embarrassed, and if Father ever.... *Don't think about that.* Dizzying revelations and hoped-for possibilities had left the world of pretend and become flesh. He gazed into Miles's eyes. *He's smiling... at me. He doesn't hate me... he likes me. I love him. And....* He felt the stickiness in his shorts. It was the closest he'd ever had to sex... at least with another person.

Miles whispered, his breath hot and moist on Calvin's neck, "It's okay. You get all the... samples you need."

"Yeah." He wanted the physical contact to continue, but everything was being taped. *Father must never know. What will he see?* Reluctantly he pulled off the tourniquet, placed a cotton pad over the needle, and pulled it out. He wanted Miles to keep his knee pressed against his thigh. It felt good. It felt like love. But he pulled it away, and a hollow ache flooded his chest.

"So what happens next?" Miles asked.

Barely verbal, Calvin looked into those eyes. "Experiments."

"What kind?"

He could feel Father's disapproval, and he didn't care. "To see what you can do. How far it goes."

"I see, and how will you do that?"

"We'll bring you people. People who are dying. You'll heal them." Calvin felt peaceful sitting with Miles, so unfamiliar and alien. *I'm happy. This is what happiness feels like. Do you know I love you?* And he realized a bigger truth. He stared at Miles, not wanting his thoughts to be clouded by emotion. *I need to know. Does he feel the same?*

"What happens after I heal them?" Miles asked.

Calvin barely heard, lost in those eyes and Miles's proximity. The look Miles gazed back at him with was intense, open, and caring. In that instant, doubt vanished. *Miles Fox loves me. I love him, and we will be together... forever. Of course.*

He gathered his blood samples and got up. He hid the dark stain in his lap with the plastic phlebotomy tray. "You have to sleep now." It was hard to tear his eyes from his beautiful torso. Fear and uncertainty nipped at his thoughts.

"I'm not tired," Miles said.

"I'll give you something," Calvin said as he backed toward the door.

"I don't like to take drugs."

"I know. It's mild. You have to be rested." Holding the tray firm against his lap with one hand, he reached back with his other for the keypad. He touched his forefinger against the reader, and the door slid open.

"Calvin, I don't want to be drugged."

"I'm sorry." And he was. *Please don't hate me, please love me. I need you to love me.*

Outside the cell he tore his gaze from Miles and glanced at the control pad. *I'm sorry, I'm sorry, I'm sorry.* He touched the menu key and scrolled to the therapeutics screen. He tapped on the sedative he wanted, the dose, and then hit Enter. There was a three-second pause, two beeps, and a thin white mist seeped through the vents into the otherwise sealed room.

He saw hurt in Miles's eyes. "Don't worry, I promise it won't hurt you. It's just a sedative. You'll sleep for eight hours, nothing more…. I promise." *Please don't hate me. I won't hurt you. I love you. I have a plan, and you and I—not Father—will be together… forever.*

Gas flooded Miles's cell, and with it came fury and panic. He stared at Calvin. *You little shit. I'm sorry, Grandma. I won't give up. I will find a way. I'll get us out of….* Within three breaths he was dead asleep.

"Quite the pickle," Tomas said as he popped up from the lake. "And I know of what I speak."

"I can't see a way out. Not yet," Miles admitted, struck again at how Tomas stayed dry as water shed from his clothes like oil from vinegar.

"I wish I could say that it turns out well. That's not been my experience." Tomas clapped his hands, and the wagon and matched black horses emerged from the forest.

"Another story?" Miles asked, unable to shake the fear that had followed him into sleep.

"Not today," Tomas said. "We've other important things to discuss." He climbed onto the wagon and picked up the reins.

Miles followed, his eyes drawn to the lake's roiling surface. Waves crested and broke against the shore. Dotted throughout were dark-haired heads, their green eyes fixed on the two of them. "Is there a storm coming?" He was still uncertain what these dreams represented, if they were an alternate reality, a figment of his imagination, a sign of insanity…. *Could Stangl be right? Do I have schizophrenia?*

"Of course you don't. And yes, the biggest storm we've seen since the last one," Tomas said.

"Last one?" Miles asked, reminding himself to find out about the weird telepathy he'd just experienced with Calvin.

Tomas grimaced. "The one that kicked this ball into play. The flood, perhaps you've heard of it? It wiped out our world. I wasn't there, but there are enough bobbing in the lake who can give you the blow-by-blow."

Miles groaned. He had let the seed of hope take root, and here his dead great-grandfather was about to drop another fairy tale on his head.

"It happened," Tomas said.

Right, I get it, you can read my mind. And apparently I can do the same sometimes… and not just here.

Yes. "But I enjoy speaking. I don't often get to hear the sound of my voice. We are a silent bunch, chattering in our heads. And we are frightened. I also thought we'd made some progress, Miles. Your doubt serves no good. I blame myself, but the past is past. My little Anya, with the best of reasons, kept you from our truths, and now she, and all of us, may pay the price." Tomas gazed from across the water at the single mountain that pierced the lake and the sky above. "She's between worlds," he said.

"She's in a coma, but she still has brain function. She's not dead."

"As I said, she's half there and half here. As her papa I'm eager to welcome her, to give her all the love that was stolen from her as a child. I will do that, it's just…."

"Just what?"

Tomas snapped the reins, and the wagon lurched forward. He pulled back with the right and turned the caravan to face the forest wall. "There's someone I need you to meet. Two someones, in fact."

"You just changed the subject… again. Tomas, please, what aren't you telling me? You drop hints like a stripper drops clothes. Just give me the whole thing. I don't know if I'm going to survive this. I don't know how I'm going to save Grandma. If there are things you can tell me that will help, I need them now before I wake and have to deal with whatever crazy they're serving on the other side."

Tomas chuckled without humor. *If you fail, if they kill you, and you have not passed on the gift, then we are at an end. Our world, all you see, will cease.*

How can you know that?

We all know that. We feel it. When my Anya refused to have a child, we sensed the end's approach. She was adamant to not have a child, and she was the only living vessel of the grail. He smiled. *Thankfully your Grandpa Henry loved my daughter and was a persistent lover.*

Miles perked at the mention of his beloved grandfather. "Is he here?"

"No. This place is just for us… and for the person we're going to meet."

"So if Stangl and creepy Calvin, who God only knows what he's doing with my sleeping body at this minute, kill me, this all goes away?"

"We believe so, yes."

"And if I survive and don't have a kid…."

"The same."

"What about my sister, Maya?"

"She doesn't carry the seed. Your mother did. She passed it on to you but not to Maya."

"And we've had the discussion about my being gay?"

"Yes, son…. You prefer men. One in particular if I've followed things correctly."

"And all my dead relatives become even more dead if I don't reproduce."

Tomas twisted on the bench and glared at Miles. *Do I look dead to you?*

No. Miles was struck by the intensity in Tomas's gaze. *Look, there's no use getting pissed at me when you're the one keeping secrets. Apparently you know everything about me. You, what, tap into my head at night for the day's recap?*

Tomas nodded. "You're right. The truth is big, and the stakes are enormous." He pulled back on the reins, and the cart veered down a wooded path. "I don't tell you things because of their weight. What you've learned in the past few days should have been taught over the course of years. But that didn't happen."

"We've covered this, Tomas. Grandma would just as soon everything about this ends. I'm sorry, but people live, and then they die. Maybe there's an afterlife. I guess this is kind of what this is…."

"We're not dead, Miles. But if the gift passes from the world, then yes, we are truly dead, but that's not what's at stake."

"Yes, and…?"

Tomas shook his head. "And you're not ready."

Miles wanted to scream.

Tomas continued, "But here it comes anyway…. You, of course, know the story of Noah and the flood."

Here we go again.

Don't be a smartass. The story is ancient, and it survives because of its central truth. The flood happened. It was the end of our world and the start of yours. It predates your written words by millennia. Its enormity kept it alive and close to the facts as humankind found their tongues and told the tale. The ark carried the seeds of our extinguished race. Noah, his wife, his sons, and their wives were not mortal, at least not of the human race. Even in the Bible it drops hints about this. How many people do you know live to be eight hundred?

Miles listened, having traded disbelief for a burning urgency for something… anything he could use to save Grandma Anna and himself. This story about Noah's yacht club wasn't cutting it. "Tomas, I get that this is important, sort of, kind of… but not really. I need something I can use, do you understand this?"

"I do. You want the punch line without the joke."

"Yes, please."

"Fine. The grail, of which you are the only living vessel, is the last vestige of our race on earth. But more than that, it is a counterweight to evil. It is the embodiment of hope and of the miraculous. That's the punch line, the whole point to the story. A world dies in flood and in fire, but hope and the spark of magic survives. *We have kept that flame alive through the ages. It is our sole purpose.* If you die without passing it on, if somehow Gerald Stangl extracts the gift and takes it for himself, then the world enters a new era. Like a clock that is reset to zero. There is power in the gift… the Holy Grail. Things you've started to glimpse. Things that should not be played with."

"Like creepy Calvin's fixation on me?"

"Yes," Tomas said. *Had you been schooled, you would have known. Instead your instincts… and I suspect desperation… have led you to truths. The boy is enamored of you. If you stay quiet around him, if you make physical contact, you'll be able to read his thoughts as you read mine now. It happens easiest with touch, but with practice and with time, and if you learn to be still and silent, you can read another's thoughts as they travel on the breath.*

"Thank you, that was useful. It would have been nice to know this sooner, but…." Miles flashed back through his close encounter with Stangl's son. *This makes sense.* He looked at Tomas and thought, *Is it just that I can read his thoughts, or can I influence them?*

It's both, and it's subtle, but the latter carries risk.

With anyone?

"Yes and no." The cart rounded a bend, and a charming cottage with a white fence and tangled thickets of red and yellow roses came into view.

"Fine. So when is it yes, and when is it no?"

"We can push people in directions they've started. But you can't turn love to hate. Or rather… you shouldn't."

"Hold up. Can't and shouldn't are different things."

"Yes, as are good and evil. We can use the gift to amplify what people feel. That boy is besotted with you. He started out well on his way. What you've done is taken a teenage crush—bad enough to start—and stoked it into a flame. How it will end…." Tomas pulled back on the reins, bringing the wagon to a stop.

Miles smelled the roses as the cottage door opened and a man with dark curly hair, a beard that reminded him of a toilet paper roll stuck to the end of his chin, and eyebrows plucked into sharp angles appeared. Behind him followed a smiling woman with wavy black hair and emerald eyes.

The woman raced past her partner and pushed open the gate. *Welcome, Miles. We've been wanting to meet you.*

He met the woman's smiling eyes and then the bearded man's. *Something's different about him.* His eyes… not green, almost black.

The man's thoughts entered his head. *Yes, I am the outcast here. The one who does not fit. I am Zosimus of Panopolus, and this is Marta. Welcome to our home.*

Why do I know your name? Miles tried to place the man's odd appearance, like someone who'd stepped from a museum's frescoed walls. *Egyptian? Roman?*

Zosimus nodded. *Greek and Egyptian. Born the one and spent the majority of my first life in Egypt. It's where I met Marta. And you've heard of me because I am very famous.*

And a braggart, Marta interjected.

Hush, woman. He walked behind her and wrapped his arms around her waist. She leaned into him, her head against his cheek. *I was a scholar and a scientist. Perhaps you've read my work, the* Khemia. *It's quite long.*

You're the earth, wind, and fire guy.

Zosimus's smile broadened. *See, Marta, they do remember me.*

The woman shook her head. *Wonderful! The man's ego is big enough. It will be decades before I shrink his head back to size.*

Miles pondered this improbable get-together. *You lived over two thousand years ago.*

And I am still alive. Come, we know of your plight… our shared jeopardy. Marta has set the table, and we've stories to tell. We are none of us strangers here. I am your brother, as Marta is your sister. Enter our home. Eat our food and hear our tale. Zosimus paused on the cottage threshold. *And unlike the rest of these fools, I won't speak in riddles. Someone needs to give you tools to stay alive. To keep us alive. The good news is that you already possess these. What you don't know is how to use them.*

CHAPTER 28

As Luke pulled into the empty drive of the house he shared, he was met by several truths. He had no money and no job. The career he'd worked toward since high school had been blown apart. The girl he'd dated for nearly two years hated him… and who could blame her? And to top it off, he'd fallen in love with his best friend, who'd been arrested for a gruesome murder. The last he found absurd. *Miles is no murderer. Which means what? Antoine Dey is dead; that's a fact. If not Miles, then who?*

But the worst part, which left him with an agonizing sense of helplessness, was the news that Miles was being held at Lakeshore, allegedly for a competency evaluation. "Stangl. It all comes back to that smug, lying sack of shit!"

He gripped the wheel of his aging Corolla, his thoughts on Miles and how terrified he had to be. He looked at the small white clapboard house with its pretentious columns, as though trying to measure up to the more stately homes on the block. "What now?"

In response, a dark sedan that had been parked across the street pulled in behind him. He turned as the two plainclothes detectives who'd interviewed him with Dean Strachey emerged. One approached the driver's side of his car while the other stood blocking the passenger's door.

"Luke."

He rolled down the window. "Yes, Detective… LeClerc?"

"Good memory. We'd like to ask you some questions."

"Sure." Luke realized they'd been waiting for him, which meant they'd probably called his father… or mother… who'd told them where he was headed. "Inside okay?" he asked, noting no other cars in the drive.

"Inside is good." LeClerc stepped back from the door. "You were in Charleston."

Luke's gut clenched. He hated this now familiar feeling of things spinning out of control. He was exhausted from the drive, and before he could stop himself, he blurted, "Why are you here? Am I being arrested?"

LeClerc paused and glanced back at Johnson. "Like I said, we've got questions… about Miles Fox."

Luke flipped through his key chain, much lighter since getting expelled from school. He'd turned all of the plastic e-badges in to security, along with his hospital IDs.

He unlocked the door. "Joel…. Justin." There was no response, not surprising for a Friday morning. He glanced up the stairs and was struck by memories of Miles. He thought of the silver angel with his violin at his back door, of that first kiss and an afternoon's lovemaking that had changed his world…. *And then it all went to shit.* "We can talk in the kitchen."

The detectives trailed in. Luke glanced out the back door, everything so familiar, and yet he felt like a trespasser. He braced back against the counter. "What do you want to know?"

Detective Johnson started. "Some things don't add up about your friend."

Luke resisted the urge to laugh or make a flip comment. "What in particular, Detective?"

Johnson nodded at LeClerc, who picked up. "The night you helped Mr. Fox escape from the emergency room, he had done something with Mr. Dey. The witnesses are split on what they saw, but that's not the kicker, and we've had our own experts review Dey's medical records…. The man was dying."

"That's true. He had end-stage liver cancer."

"But in the morning," Johnson added, "the cancer was gone."

"And?" Luke asked.

"The hospital doctor said it had to be the chemo. But everyone we've checked with says chemo doesn't work that fast…. It's not possible."

"That's correct." Luke realized these detectives, like himself, wanted an explanation for the inexplicable.

LeClerc shook his head. "So either Dey wasn't that sick to begin with, or the tests they ran were somehow messed up, or…."

"Or Miles Fox did exactly what he said he did," Luke replied. "He laid on hands and cured Antoine Dey of stage-four liver cancer."

"It's not possible," Johnson said.

"Then why ask me these questions? You spelled out the options. I'll tell you this—Miles couldn't kill anyone. If you knew him, you'd know that's crazier than thinking he's a miracle healer."

Johnson responded, "Let's say we're willing to follow you down this rabbit hole. If Miles didn't kill his patient, and there's damn good evidence saying that he did, then who else would have the motive? Antoine Dey was a family man with a solid business. Other than maybe overcharging a customer on a plumbing job and not showing up when he said he would, the man didn't have enemies. His wife loved him. He went to church on Sundays."

"It wasn't Miles."

"Then who?"

Luke held his tongue. Because as crazy as Miles's healing talents sounded, what ran through his head was worse. He looked at the detectives. They weren't bad men and were struggling with aspects of a case that made no sense. They could have just closed the book on Miles; after all, they'd said there was strong evidence. So why even look at the bits and pieces that didn't fit? "I saw his arrest on TV," Luke said. "The FBI brought him in."

"That's correct. They've taken the lead on the case," LeClerc said.

"Because he crossed state lines?"

"That and some other factors came into play that got them interested."

"Other factors?"

LeClerc looked to his more senior partner and then back at Luke. "Information that this might not have been a single event. That Mr. Fox might have done something similar in another state."

"Massachusetts?" Luke asked, getting more than he was giving.

"Yes."

"Okay, only one place that information could come from. You asked me who else might harm Antoine Dey? That's not the right question."

"So what is the right question?" Johnson asked.

"I think you know. I think that's why you're here. Antoine Dey was collateral damage. He was never the target…. It's Miles and what he's able to do." Luke knew this was dangerous territory. He was about to implicate a powerful member of the medical community.

"So who, then?" LeClerc asked.

Luke shook his head. It felt like a trap.

Johnson spoke up. "You think it's Stangl."

Luke startled at the mention of his name. *It's out there. I'm not the only one thinking this.* "Who gave the information to the FBI?" Luke asked.

The side of Johnson's mouth curved up. "Yeah, Dr. Stangl has been quite… helpful."

"From the start his hand is in all of this," Luke said. "He's the one who wrote the commitment paper on Miles. And all that crap… excuse me… stuff you were asking about Miles stockpiling weapons. That could only have come from Stangl. I mean, for God's sake, the man is one of the most powerful physicians in the medical school. He's a full professor. What the hell was he even doing in the emergency room at 10:00 p.m.?"

"That's not usual?"

"Hell no." Luke picked away at pieces of this nightmare that made no sense. Maybe these two could shed some light. "They have on-call psychiatrists and residents who cover the overnight."

"So let me get this straight," LeClerc said. "You're saying that Stangl showed up in the emergency room because he somehow knew Miles would be there, and he wanted to commit him and…. That makes even less sense than Miles Fox having magic fingers."

"I know." The implausibility stank. "It doesn't make sense. But there's got to be an explanation." *How the hell did Stangl know?* Luke desperately wanted to believe Miles, but this made zero sense. It hadn't from the start, and he'd ignored it. And if it wasn't true, then Miles's entire story unraveled. *Could it have been a coincidence?* Luke felt defeated. "There's got to be an explanation. Somehow Stangl knew."

"Luke." LeClerc's voice was gentle. "I'd be careful who you share this with. The last thing you need is to be accused of slandering Dr. Stangl. The doc's story is he was at the hospital rounding on patients on the psych ward. Apparently it's something he does every second Tuesday. He told us the resident in the emergency room asked him to consult on Fox. She was worried because Miles was a medical student, and she didn't want to screw up."

"You spoke to the resident?"

"Yeah… and her story syncs with Stangl's."

"And the fact that Stangl evaluated Miles when he was a kid?"

"That's the only coincidence we found. Yeah, it's a big one, but a psychiatrist seeing a mental patient in the hospital, and it happens to be someone he'd seen in another state…. Not so farfetched. Especially when you do the compare-and-contrast with your scenario."

Luke thought back to his earlier interrogation in the dean's office and the stuff Stangl had written on the commitment paper that made Miles look deranged and dangerous. He shook his head.

"What are you thinking?" Johnson prompted.

"Just trying to take it in," he said, not wanting to share the wander of his thoughts. Yeah, he heard what they were saying about Stangl, and he suspected there was more, which was why they'd come, wasn't it? They'd hoped he had answers, which he didn't. What he did have was fear, vast and gaping. Luke believed Miles. Yeah, it sounded crazy, paranoid, delusional. Bottom line was Antoine Dey had terminal cancer. Miles healed him, and that kind of power, the implications of it, could attract all kinds of crazy… and evil. Stangl had been gunning for him and now had him under his control. But for what purpose?

"Luke, let me give you some advice," LeClerc said. "I don't think you'll take it, but here goes. It's best you forget Miles. Sometimes when you care for someone, you get blind to the pieces you don't want to see. At the best Miles is a very sick man. At the worst, and I think this is how the story goes, he's both mentally ill and dangerous. You'll be lucky if you don't get hit with an aiding and abetting. So stay away, don't try to contact him, and for God's sake, don't share any of your theories about Stangl."

"Message received," Luke said.

"But," Johnson interjected, "if you come up with something solid"— he placed his card on the kitchen table—"call."

After the detectives left, Luke replayed the conversation. LeClerc and Johnson had doubts. He wondered at their roles in the investigation. If this was a federal case, did they have any clout, or was this them trying to tie up loose ends? Mostly he thought of Miles. LeClerc's advice was well intended but impossible. *Where are you? What kind of hell is Stangl putting you through?*

Fuck the pieces that don't make sense. Go with what you know. He started to pace.

"Miles healed Antoine Dey." *Check.*

"Gerald Stangl falsified a commitment paper on Miles." *Check.* *Why?*

"To get Miles locked up." *Check.*

"Miles escaped." *Check again.*

"Stangl ramped things up, and there was a manhunt." *Check.*

"Miles came here… dressed as an angel, and I had the most mind-blowing sex of my life, and pretty much undid my entire life's plan." *Check, check, check.*

…and it wasn't just sex. Check. He paused in his inventory. *LeClerc pretty much said love was blind and deaf and dumb. Maybe you don't want to see the truth.* Doubt crept in. *No, whether or not you're stupid in love, he's still Miles. You've known him for five years. Keep going. Right….*

"So his Grandma Anna drove from Massachusetts, got him out of town, and Stangl managed to turn this into a federal case. They captured him, airlifted him to Louisiana, and now he's locked up in Lakeshore."

Luke pulled apart the moves and countermoves; it felt like chess. The missing bits he guessed at. The biggest one being *What the hell does Stangl want? Miles, obviously.* But more pointedly his ability to heal.

Luke pulled at his temples with his fingers. The detectives had warned him to back off. Not an option. *So how do you fill in the missing pieces? How do you get Miles the fuck away from Stangl?*

He reached for his cell and flipped through the contacts list. Under Miles's name, he had numbers for both his family in Brookline and his grandma's house in Truro.

He stared at the numbers and thought of Miles's Grandma Anna, whom he'd met twice on parents' weekends. Once she'd come with his folks, and the second time it was just her. He pictured the two of them together, their green eyes betraying their relatedness. When Miles spoke about her, it was with a mix of love, humor, and fear. *"You don't mess with Grandma Anna."*

He dialed. It rang several times before a machine picked up.

He started to leave a message. "Hi, Mrs. Warren, this is Luke Paxton…. I'm a friend of Miles. I was hoping—"

A woman picked up.

"Luke?"

"Mrs. Warren?"

"No…. This is Miles's mom."

The distress in her voice was obvious. "Mrs. Fox, I was hoping to talk to Miles's grandma."

"She's not here," Mrs. Fox stated.

"What's wrong?"

"Just about everything. Have you seen Miles?" She sounded in shock, her voice disconnected.

"No."

"That's right. He's in a hospital. His attorney says it's nicer than the state hospital where they usually go."

Luke knew Rachel and Joseph Fox's home in Brookline was hours from the Cape. "What's happening, Mrs. Fox?"

"It's my mother."

Luke braced for bad news. Anna Warren had survived the holocaust. He knew she and Miles had a strong bond. *Please let her be okay.* "What's happened?"

"She's gone," Rachel said.

Luke pictured the white rental car that scooped Miles off the street. Was Anna returning for a second rescue mission? "You think she's down here?"

"No. The police don't know what to say. There was a break-in. Someone cut the lines on the power and her generator. She's gone. Someone took my mother."

Luke processed the surreal news. He bit back knee-jerk questions: *Why? Who would do that?* "Are the FBI involved? Have they connected the kidnapping to Miles?"

"No. Why? Miles would never hurt his grandmother. What are you talking about?"

"Of course he wouldn't. When was she taken?"

"I spoke to her Sunday night. The power went out. I tried to call her back, but the line was busy. I figured she was trying to call the power company… but she has a generator. I should have kept calling. I should have called the police."

Luke sensed Rachel's mounting hysteria. He thought back. If Anna went missing—kidnapped?—Sunday night, it would have been a day after Miles's arrest. Clearly it would be impossible to pin this on him, but what possible reason would someone have for kidnapping an eighty-year-old woman? "Was anything missing?" Luke asked.

"No, at least not that I can see. With my mom you never know. She's the hide-it-in-your-mattress type. It wasn't a robbery."

"Did they leave a note?"

"No… and no one's called."

Luke felt sick. *This is bad.* "Mrs. Fox, are you there alone?"

"Yes. Why?"

He resisted putting his thoughts into words. "I think you should stay with other people."

There was a pause on the line, and for a moment, Luke wondered if they'd been disconnected. "Mrs. Fox?"

"Luke, do you know what's happening? You have to know that Miles is not a murderer."

"I do."

"You think whoever took my mother has something to do with Miles."

"Yes."

"And you don't think I'm safe here."

"I don't."

"The police don't think there's a connection. They think this was a robbery gone bad. They haven't told me to my face, but they think my mom is dead. Luke, what aren't you saying?"

"Mrs. Fox." He struggled for words and ended up blurting, "Do you know about Miles's ability to heal?"

Silence stretched. Finally Rachel spoke. "You're talking about the dog."

"What dog?"

"When he was six, after my father died, we bought Miles a golden retriever—Amos. It got hit by a car…." Rachel's voice choked. "After, my mother insisted we give the dog away. She said it was the only way he'd learn. I didn't want to do it. He'd just lost my father. Why do you care about this, Luke? What does this have to do with what's happened?"

Luke batted back tears. "Mrs. Fox, do you know what Miles can do?"

"I saw," she said. "I never told my mother this, or Miles. But yes, I saw what Miles did. And I saw how terrified it made my mother. I knew it was something to keep hidden. I didn't quite know why, but you have to understand, my mom keeps secrets… lots of them. When that dog stood up…. Luke, he was dead. Even from where I was standing—and it was far enough away that I've always tried to tell myself it wasn't as bad as it looked—even if that were true, there wasn't a scratch on him. As horrible as I felt giving Amos away, as much as Miles begged us not to, I knew my mother was right. Luke?"

"Yes?"

"What does this have to do with what's happening?"

"Everything."

"Oh God. Tell me this…. Do you think he killed that man?"

"Absolutely not!"

"What aren't you saying?"

It was a loaded question, but at least with Miles's mother, he felt like he wasn't going insane, that he wasn't the only one who believed Miles. After all, the world was filled with stories of healers, of Indian yogis who did miraculous things. "When he was eight, you brought him to see a psychiatrist."

"How do you know this?"

"He told me."

"What does this have to do with things?"

He heard fear in her voice and knew he was making it worse. "The psychiatrist who saw him here, the one who had him committed, is the same doctor."

"What? That's impossible. You mean… Gerald Stangl?"

Hearing his name completed a circuit. Miles's story, piece by piece, was being verified. "Yes. What do you remember about that?"

Her voice sounded flat. "Everything. He wanted to lock Miles up. He said that he had early onset schizophrenia."

"And what did you do?"

"My husband, Joseph, was dead set against it, and my mother stepped in and took Miles to live with her in Truro."

"You mean not just for the summer."

"Yes. It was bad. When we refused to follow Stangl's advice, he filed a parental neglect allegation with the Department of Children and Families. Miles stayed with his grandmother and went to school in Truro while we dealt with the authorities."

"And Stangl backed off?"

"Yes, eventually. My mom found someone on the Cape to counter Stangl's evaluation. He had no choice… and he's the one who committed my son. Luke, how is that possible? It makes no sense." Her question hung in the air.

"I know," Luke said, careful to not voice his suspicions.

"This has to be connected. Why? Why would someone do this? Why would that psychiatrist be so interested in Miles?"

"Because of what he can do," Luke said. "I think that's what this is about."

"And my mom? What you're saying…. This is crazy."

"I know."

"You're saying that some psychiatrist has basically kidnapped my son, made it look as if he's a murderer, and then… kidnapped his grandmother. All because something strange happened with his dog nearly twenty years ago. Luke, I feel like I'm about to lose my mind. Please, if you're not telling me something, just spit it out."

Luke paused as Rachel connected the dots.

Finally he spoke. "The murdered man was Miles's patient. He was dying, and Miles healed him. A lot of people saw something strange, and when they tried to pull Miles off, he freaked out and hurt a couple of guards. It's like he was in some kind of trance."

Rachel let out an audible breath. "Oh God. Now it makes sense."

"What does?"

"My mom was dead set against his going to medical school. This explains it. She knew. She always knew, damn her. Damn her and her secrets!"

"Mrs. Fox, I have to go. If you think of anything that could help, call me."

She gave a humorless laugh. "No one's going to believe any of this, are they?"

"No."

"But it's the truth… and it won't set him free."

He hung up, his cheeks wet with tears. He looked at the cards the detectives had left and thought of calling. *They'll think you're a whack job. The hysterical boyfriend….*

He looked at his hands and the speckled kitchen table. He thought through what Rachel told him. "Miles's Grandma Anna, the person he loves the best, the one who knows his secrets, the one who dropped everything and flew to New Orleans to get him out of town, has been kidnapped. No note, and it's not a robbery…. Too bizarre." The thought that came was so farfetched his rational mind pushed it away. "But it's the only thing that makes sense…. Stangl took her."

But….

He startled at the sound of the front door opening.

His housemate Joel found him in the kitchen. "Luke, you're back."

"Hey, Joel," Luke said, noting his roomie's brightly colored bags from one of the downtown Mardi Gras supershops. "Having a party?"

"Halloween, man."

"Right." He looked at his curly-haired roommate, who seemed at an uncharacteristic loss for words as he dumped his bags on the counter and opened the fridge.

Joel pulled out a beer. "Want one?"

Luke hesitated. *Keep a clear head. Yeah, and one or two beers isn't the worst idea.* "Sure." He took the cold bottle and twisted off the top. The first swig and the taste of hops and malt helped. "So what you getting dressed as?"

"The killer clown from *It*."

"And that's going to get you laid?" he asked, aware of his roommate's three driving forces—architecture, booze, and women.

"Undergrad sorority party." Joel grinned. "Fish… barrel… shoot."

"It's a plan." Luke tried to sound like his old self.

"So what's up with you and Fox?" Joel asked, his expression serious. "It's true, right?"

"Which part?" Luke braced for whatever was about to come.

"You're, like, gay now?"

"I guess," he answered, hoping to avoid a round of twenty questions. "It just happened, Joel." He wasn't sure how his roommate, whom he'd hung out with for the last five years, would take this.

Joel cracked a smile. "Cool, more for me."

"Yes." Luke tipped his beer toward his friend. "You can have them all."

"Jenna sure was pissed."

"I feel like shit about that."

"Did you always know?" Joel asked. "Did Fox do something…. I mean, they say that guys know what guys like…."

"Please shut up."

"Just curious. I mean, like…."

"Don't." Luke felt a moment's normalcy. He looked at the bulging bags on the counter, filled with a shiny patchwork costume and fuzzy red wig. An idea formed. "Joel, can I buy that costume off you?"

"No way."

"A killer clown isn't going to get you laid. I may have gone over to the other side, but big red noses and butcher knives aren't what girls want."

"Pregnant nun?"

"Okay, who's the gay one here?"

"Fine. So what, then?"

"You give me the clown and take my Tarzan outfit from last year."

"Dude, that thing's obscene."

"Exactly."

"Right, I remember. Jenna was furious with those girls who kept trying to cop a feel at the medical school party. Now I'm thinking maybe it wasn't just the girls."

"Joel, get a grip. Do we have a deal?"

"Sure." Joel narrowed his gaze. "What are you up to, Luke? Fox is locked up, and you're going trick-or-treating?"

"Life goes on," Luke said, and unable to meet his roommate's questioning stare, he chugged the beer. "Life goes on."

CHAPTER 29

CALVIN WHEELED a frail woman into the room Miles had dubbed the Stangls' mad scientist laboratory. Although the state-of-the-art equipment, which included a coffinlike full-body fMRI, electron microscope, and desktop DNA sequencer, were beyond anything Dr. Frankenstein could have imagined.

The woman couldn't have been more than five feet, though it was difficult for Miles to tell from the tortured curve of her spine. Her light skin was taut and deeply lined from years of pain, her eyegrounds were muddy, and her hands shook from her medicine's toxic effects. Calvin, his blond hair gelled into a tousled boy-band do, looked up from the wheelchair.

"Miles, this is Daisy Osborn."

"Hi." He smiled at the woman, who had no idea where she was. As for his part in what he'd come to discover was a series of well-planned experiments, he was torn. He saw something akin to hope in Daisy Osborn's expression, and the familiar trust older people had around doctors. She believed she was there to get help, and that was all that mattered. As Miles grew still inside, he caught flickers of her thoughts: small children, a tabby kitten with tufted ears, a grown son and daughter.

He looked around the room where horrible things were set to happen, with its multimillion-dollar scanner along one wall, cameras that raised and lowered from the ceiling, and equipment he couldn't identify arranged around a complex medical bed.

"Daisy is a sixty-six-year-old mother of two and grandmother of eight, who has advanced ankylosing spondylitis; it's a rare autoimmune disease," Calvin explained as he wheeled her to the bed and helped her from the chair. He chatted while hooking her forefinger to the pulse oximeter and positioned the automatic blood pressure cuff around her skeletal upper arm. He glanced at Miles and grinned. "Are you familiar with it?"

"Yes."

Miles, who by now, whether he wanted to or not, could tap into Calvin's emotions, realized the new hairstyle was for him. Two days in, and between the drugs knocking him out and the revved-up activities in the dream world, it was a struggle to keep the days straight—*this has to be*

Saturday. Despite that, he'd begun to understand the rhyme and reason to his captivity. The morning had started with Dr. Stangl doing a pro forma psychiatric assessment for the court. He'd sat outside Miles's cell and shot questions.

Stangl prefaced the court-required interview with: "You will cooperate. That's not an option. That is, if you hope to ever see your grandmother wake up. As you can see, she has brain function. Quite a lot. There's no reason she shouldn't wake… unless something unfortunate were to occur. What's puzzling is her EEG reading. Similar to yours when you sleep. Obviously you dream, but it's not just REM. Where do you go when you sleep, Miles?"

"I don't know," he lied. "I never remember my dreams." He tried to find the internal quiet necessary to glimpse another's thoughts, but the sight of Gerald Stangl, the mocking tone of his voice, made him burn. He remembered Tomas's story. *Shut up and knit.*

Stangl narrowed his gaze. "A minor point, I'm sure. But as with all your secrets, you will reveal them, or…." He glanced at Anna and drew a finger across his throat.

"I get it," Miles said.

Stangl clicked a handheld remote and started to record. "This is Dr. Gerald Stangl at Lakeshore Hospital, interviewing patient Miles Fox. It's 8:42 a.m. on October 30th, 2015. Good morning, Mr. Fox. Did you sleep well?" Stangl's gaze met Miles's as though daring him to say something wrong.

"Yes."

"And your basic needs are being attended to? The food, adequate exercise, books, and television, all that sort of thing is being taken care of?"

"Yes, I'm not being maltreated." *That is, if you call being pawed by your seventeen-year-old son and gassed nightly humane treatment.*

"Very good. I'm glad that you're comfortable. Let's get started. This interview is part of your competency evaluation. As such everything you say is not confidential. Do you understand that?"

"Yes."

"Wonderful. So let's jump right in. How long have you heard voices?" Stangl asked.

"It's a single voice, and since I was old enough to remember." It triggered a memory. He couldn't have been more than four or five, and he was with Grandpa Henry. They were playing their violins, and Miles had wandered to a different tune.

"Where's that coming from?" Grandpa Henry had asked with a smile.

"Other Grandpa," Miles had said.

"The one in your head?" Grandpa Henry had asked.

The memory was crisp, the look on Grandpa Henry's face interested, amused, and not at all concerned. "Show me," he'd said.

And Miles had turned his fiddle so Grandpa Henry could follow his fingers.

"It's a mazurka," he'd chuckled. "You are a marvel, my boy." The two had improvised on the lively melody that twisted into a minor key before resolving the beat before the refrain.

"Whose voice is it, Miles?" Stangl asked.

"My great-grandfather's."

Stangl looked above Miles's head toward the camera as if making a point to an unseen judge and jury. "Your long-dead great-grandfather, is that correct?"

"Yes."

"A great-grandfather you have in fact never met, correct?"

"Yes."

"Tell me, Miles, what does this voice of your dead relative tell you to do?"

It was a leading question, and Miles felt like giving a wiseass remark like "That's not how you're supposed to interview a psych patient." But no, pissing off Stangl when he currently held all the cards was not smart. *Just knit.* "Mostly he wants me to join him."

"In death? Is the voice asking you to kill yourself?"

"No." Miles realized to answer yes would be a slam dunk for extending his commitment—dangerousness to self or others.

"Then where or how does he want you to join him?"

"It's hard to describe."

He glanced across at Grandma Anna. *She's so weak.* He'd watched as late yesterday Calvin inserted a feeding tube down her nose and into her stomach. It was a procedure Miles had done on patients at the hospital. Calvin had performed the steps as though it was something he did on a regular basis. The most important piece, getting an X-ray to ensure that the tube was positioned in the gut and hadn't taken a wrong turn into a lung, was handily completed. Calvin wheeled in a portable X-ray machine, checked the placement, and even showed Miles the film before he hung a bag of creamy nutritional supplement, and voila—calories to the comatose.

"We have time." Stangl shifted his pale eyes from the camera to Miles. "Tell me where this voice tells you to go."

He wondered if in her unconscious state Grandma could hear what he said, or vice versa. But no matter how still or quiet he became, he sensed nothing. Perhaps the walls of her cell prevented that, perhaps the physical distance. Perhaps the heartache he felt whenever he looked at her.

NOW, MEETING the terminally ill Daisy Osborn, Miles felt dread. *They're going to kill her.* The woman, who looked decades older than her reported age, smiled at him.

"That nice young man says you can help me," she said.

And here it comes. Like a serpent uncoiling in his gut, the gift—the grail, if Tomas and the others were to be believed—was wakening after a life spent pushing it down, not letting himself feel the suffering inside others. It… he was coming to life.

"I think I can." Streams of energy coursed up from his belly. He gazed into Daisy's eyes. *So much pain and so much effort to hide it from those she loves.* "I'll need to touch you quite a lot. Is that okay?"

Daisy's lower lip hung down and her breath grew shallow. "Yes." Hope blossomed in her eyes. "You can really do this, can't you?"

He reached across the space that separated them and gently touched the side of her face. Even before flesh connected with flesh, he felt it start. "Yes."

His belly expanded in and out with his deepening breath as waves of something he could only describe as electric juice pumped up. It raced down his arms and into his fingers, making them dance. Like yesterday his vision clouded, and the periphery grew hazy. He fought it, not wanting to lose his awareness, to at least bear witness to this thing inside of him.

Unlike the metaphor-spouting Tomas, Zosimus had been forthcoming with techniques to stay in control. "Find a spot on the wall and focus on it.

It works for me. Otherwise I'd do a healing and wake up hours later, robbed and naked."

To which Marta had added, "Think of making a tether to pull you back. I keep my attention on a spot inside my head, between my eyes."

Miles glued his gaze to Daisy's right ear as the juice sizzled and flowed. His fingers danced and trilled. It was tempting to abandon his focal point, to try to see what was happening. He'd done that with yesterday's subject—Trevor Owens, a forty-two-year-old with AIDS.

He'd immediately realized his mistake. Marta's tether analogy was apt, and the instant he'd shifted his attention from Trevor's ear to trying to catch a glimpse of his body's antics, he'd lost consciousness. He'd woken hours later in his cell, shirtless and with Calvin applying a cool cloth to his forehead.

Focus on the ear. It worked, like standing under a bridge in the midst of a tornado, a haven within the storm. More than that, as he focused on the curves and subtle colors of her ear, what were snippets of Daisy's thoughts turned into a live feed.

Something's happening. Please, Lord, I want to see my grandbabies grow up. Even a month more, Lord. I know I've no right to ask for a miracle, but a month, Lord, even a week… or longer if it's your will.

The force of her prayer, the wonder she experienced as the grail crackled through her ravaged body, all entered his head. Images and words flew through his mind's eye, children playing tee ball in the front yard of a shotgun house that still bore the watermarks of Katrina, a husband buried in a dark suit, a job as a school bus driver, another as a waitress, and still another where she tied on an orange apron and helped customers find the right nut, match a paint color, or puzzle out a home repair. Proud images of her in a blue dress beside her two children as they graduated college. Holding her daughter's hand as she birthed each of her four children.

Even one day more, Lord. Please, I'm not ready. They're not ready to lose me. I'll take the pain. I'll take more. I can handle it, Lord. But let me see them grow, just a day, a week, a month. It's wrong to ask, and I'm begging. Please, Lord. Help me. Hear me. Heal me.

He held her ear in his gaze and let her thoughts pass through. The edges of his vision cleared like clouds opening onto blue sky. Suddenly it was like surfing, unlike before, where it had pulled him under. The healing gift—*the grail*. He felt her illness and the molecules of her body as they met the force of what flowed from him. It was joy and it was light, and the atoms of her body danced with his. If not for her ear, it would have been easy to get lost in the ecstasy of it. A thought, not quite his and not coming from her, flew to mind. *This is the force of life. This is creation.*

The crackle and flow ebbed. Unwilling to risk it, he stayed fixated on her ear, noting the color had changed from a sallow yellow to pale pink. His fingers slowed their manic trills, and his hands, which had been tracing circles over her body, rested on her shoulders. His breath, like a bellows pushing his belly in and out, quieted. The rush of air in the back of his throat, which made a deep rasp, grew silent.

Cautiously he let his gaze leave her ear. He looked between his hands at her rapturous expression. Her eyes were shut, her lips parted. "You can open your eyes," he said.

As she did, tears came. She gazed up at him; the dull-yellow circles lining her corneas were gone. "Thank you."

He wanted to tell her it was not something he was responsible for; whatever just happened was beyond both his understanding and his control. More than that, for the first time in his life, he grasped just how wrong Grandma Anna had been. This was not something to be repressed.

"You're welcome," he said, his own wonder reflected in her eyes. The aftershocks, which held the connection between them, were like gentle waves cresting from the tips of his fingers into the softening planes of her face. Only now, instead of her disease's tangled energy flowing back, there came a champagne-like stream of bubbles.

"How long?" she asked. "How long until the pain returns?"

Having heard her prayers, he knew. "It's gone. Your disease is gone." As the words left his mouth, reality entered his head. *Your disease is gone, but you are in great danger.*

She nodded. *Can you hear what I'm thinking?*

Yes. He let go of her face, and like a switch being thrown, the connection dimmed and then was lost. *Can you hear me now?*

She shook her head. "It's gone."

"What's gone?" Calvin asked. He approached from behind Daisy's chair. "What are you talking about?"

Miles looked toward Calvin. He thought to lie, not wanting to hand the sociopathic father-and-son tag team any information. But the kid had done his homework and knew more about his abilities than he did. Chances were good this effect was already known. "It seems that along with the healing, there's a bit of telepathy."

"We could read each other's thoughts," Daisy said, following his lead.

"But just while you have physical contact, right?" Calvin asked with wonder and excitement.

"Yes."

Miles kept his expression neutral, hoping whatever horrors Daisy might have glimpsed in his head, she'd keep to herself. Especially those that came to him courtesy of Calvin's touch, like what had happened to poor Trevor Owens after Miles healed him. Even now, as the grail's joyful energy receded, he felt the horror of what they'd done, of what they now intended to do to Daisy. She was nothing more than an experiment. A test animal to be vivisected, her body's responses measured while alive, and then they'd cut her into pieces in an attempt to unravel the secrets of the grail.

"Then it's true…. Touch her again."

Miles turned to the grandmother who'd prayed for a bit more time to watch her grandbabies grow. She smiled, and he detected something false. He placed a hand on the side of her face, did his best to calm his thoughts, and let his mind reach hers. *You're frightened.*

He saw the effort in her expression as she reached for his thoughts. *I can't hear you.*

The current that had flowed and overtaken his body was nearly gone. Again Zosimus's tutelage kicked in. *"You don't make it happen, you let it happen. It starts on the exhalation, like water flowing out."*

Miles gentled his breath, and without effort, ripples of the grail fluttered up from his belly and trickled through his fingers. It was soft, and like plugging in a power cord, reestablished the connection.

Yes, I hear you now, Daisy thought, her eyes fixed on his. *You fear the boy and his father.*

I do. And rather than words, he let images flow. The cell where he was imprisoned; Grandma Anna's motionless body hooked to machines; a newspaper headline, Man Beheaded by Deranged Doctor in Training; and waking to Calvin's flushed face inches from his own. He saw fear blossom in her expression. *Say nothing.*

"What are you telling her?" Calvin demanded.

Miles pulled back his hands and the connection broke. "It's more impressions and pictures than anything else. I was seeing her grandbabies and how much she loves them."

"Interesting," Calvin said. He looked at Daisy. "And you, what did you see?"

She looked from Miles back to Calvin. "A man in love." The smile she directed at Calvin was guileless.

"Really?" Calvin asked.

"Oh yes," she said, "and trust me, I've been around long enough to know the real deal."

His face lit up. His eyes shone. "Really?"

"Yes," she repeated.

Miles risked a sideways glance at Daisy. She'd caught a lot in those few instants. He wondered how much. It wouldn't be enough to save her, and he wondered if it was crueler that she die knowing the truth or with the hope of a woman healed of a painful and fatal disease.

Chapter 30

His stomach in knots, Luke drove his aging Corolla up to the short line of cars in front of Lakeshore's guardhouse. Dressed in a purple, green, and orange satin clown suit, his face greasepainted white, with green eyebrows and lips and a red rubber nose, he waved an old and deactivated picture ID and a bloody plastic ax. The guard in blue barely looked at him, as though painted killer clowns were usual visitors to the sprawling nineteenth-century asylum's campus.

"Just follow the cars and lights to Parker Hall. You can't miss it; it's the one with the pumpkins…. The clients carved 'em this morning," the guard added.

Luke smiled, although unnecessary through his broadly painted lips. "Thanks. Been coming to this for years."

"Yeah, it's a big deal," the guard said, and going off script, added, "but you ask me, knives, pumpkins, and mental patients…. Gives me the willies."

Luke chuckled, and still clutching the ID so that his name was concealed by his white-gloved hand, he drove toward the party.

That was his first hurdle. He was also now past anything resembling a plan. Having not yet completed his psych rotation, his only exposure to Lakeshore was these Halloween bashes. Attendance was not optional, and the usually repressed medical students were almost expected to misbehave… within limits. The booze would flow, and his classmates, junior and senior faculty, along with select VIP Lakeshore patients, would have a night of masked revelry.

As he parked the Toyota at the edge of the lot closest to the swamp, he remembered years gone by. The last outing had been him, Miles, Jenna, and two other classmates crammed into his car. Only he and Jenna had returned in it, the three others having found Halloween hookups.

Gripping the wheel, he felt a pang of jealousy, and it wasn't for the first time. Yes, he'd gone home with Jenna. They'd joked about the dapper blond vampire who'd been all over Miles, who in turn had uncharacteristically succumbed to the free-flowing mojitos and Dracula's charms. With jealousy came guilt and perspective. *You really fucked that girl over.* Their last encounter was so clear, her accusations… her pain. *Enough. You can't undo the past.*

He got out, grabbed his knapsack filled with a hodgepodge of what might be useful, and headed toward Parker Hall and the raucous party. Since yesterday he'd made discreet inquiries and searched Lakeshore's website. In the latter were brief mentions of "forensic capabilities" and "court assessments." It didn't say where.

He'd done a literature search on Gerald Stangl. The man was a brilliant and well-connected academic powerhouse. His most recent papers on epigenetics, those things that caused a particular gene to be turned on or off, were remarkable. Much as he wanted to hate the man, his discoveries were Nobel Prize material. In the opening of one study on a family with early onset Alzheimer's, which didn't follow any established pattern of genetic transmission, he'd commented, "What is it inside the nucleus of our cells that one day says, 'Let's give ourselves a disease? Let's slowly kill ourselves.'"

In another large trial of a medication for schizophrenia, he'd posited the delusions and hallucinations associated with that disorder were analogous to a radio stuck between stations. "For us to say they are false is to miss the possibility that the individual is perceiving a reality beyond the collective awareness. Regardless, these voices, visions, and fantasies disrupt the patient's ability to function in society, and so we label their condition a disorder. Whether future generations of scientists will bear this out is unknowable."

One bit of information that had piqued Luke's interest was in recent articles, those where the authors had to disclose all funding sources and potential conflicts. There, among the NIH, NIMH, and SAMHSA grants, was listed Kruft Pharmaceuticals.

As he'd doggedly followed the trail of information, he'd discovered a division of Kruft owned Lakeshore and several other freestanding psychiatric and substance-abuse facilities around the country, including one in Brookline, Massachusetts—Miles's hometown. Like Lakeshore, they were mostly abandoned state hospitals on large tracts of land the company had acquired or leased on the cheap due to abatement issues from over a century's worth of toxic dumping, in-ground oil tanks, and buildings well insulated with asbestos.

He still struggled to understand the chain of apparent coincidences between Miles and Stangl. With those thoughts came doubt. *Don't do this. You either believe him… 100 percent… or you don't.*

"Right." He caught his darkened reflection in a windshield. Orange wig, gruesome, painted face. "Yeah, this is going to work…. Not."

His gaze tracked from Parker Hall to rows of tidy two-story brick buildings with white mullioned windows and weathered-copper gutters that housed the two-thousand-bucks-a-day patients. Toward the right of the party were larger, mostly abandoned structures, remnants of the hospital's earlier life as a self-contained city for the mentally ill. One building, far in the distance rang discordant with the crumbling nineteenth-century architecture—Stangl's research pavilion. The moon shone silver white against its mirrored walls, and along its lower stories were silhouetted reflections of twisted mangroves.

His Internet searches had provided publicity stills of gee-whizz equipment, which Stangl's grants and pharma connections had procured. He had the latest imaging equipment, far beyond anything the hospital or medical school possessed. Stangl did groundbreaking research into the workings of the brain and how drugs, stress, genetics, and disease altered its functions.

But nowhere on the Internet could he discover where Lakeshore housed any forensic patients. It seemed unlikely they'd be mixed in with the paying customers. Plus, if Miles was the crazed murderer they'd painted, there seemed little security in the homey brick buildings, euphemistically dubbed cottages. Those patients were voluntary. Miles was not.

He stared at the shimmering moonlit structure. *He's got to be in there.* From Google Maps he'd studied the oddly angled four-sided research pavilion and imagined its interior. The more he thought about it, the more he was convinced it was where Miles, and possibly his Grandma Anna, were being held.

So how the hell are you breaking in? He walked toward the party as the rapid-fire rhymes of Nicki Minaj blasted across the lot. As he neared he recognized classmates and a couple of the faculty and hoped that between the wig and the greasepaint no one would ID him. He spotted a red plastic cup half-filled with beer abandoned on a stone bench and picked it up. He glanced toward the side of the building and saw a couple making out under a dimly lit magnolia. As he studied the grounds to the left and right of Parker Hall, he spotted others taking walks along the paths or huddled in small groups, likely smoking weed.

With drink in hand, he veered from Parker and, keeping to one of the lit and paved walkways, made toward a covered dock that jetted into the lake.

As he neared the dock, he wasn't surprised to see a shadowy couple on one of the high-backed benches. What shocked the hell out of him was Jenna's voice.

"You just never know," she said.

Luke froze as a man responded, "Yeah, well, his loss, my gain."

"Don't push it, buddy."

"Just saying…."

He didn't recognize the guy's voice. *Good, let her move on.* But more than that, it wasn't jealousy, but relief. *You made a mess, and she'll get over it.*

An owl hooted from the swamp, and he turned his attention to the Stangl Research Pavilion. *He's got to be in there.* There were no lights on the upper floors and no signs of life around the building's base. The twinkling white lights strung along the walking paths stopped well before the pavilion and the surrounding husks of Lakeshore's abandoned structures.

He stepped off the path and kept far from Jenna and her new beau. *Maybe just a hookup. No, not like her…. Shit!* Two years of being her boyfriend, of thinking she was the one… the one he'd marry, the one who would maintain his standing as the good son… weighed him down. He stood frozen in the night. *She's not the one for you. Let her go. You've hurt her enough.*

"Right… so instead you pick a suspected psycho killer… who you love… who's a guy." He smiled. *Sounds about right,* he thought and headed toward the research pavilion.

As he neared, the futility of what he intended grew. *No guards, at least none that I can see. Because they'll be inside.*

He hid behind a hedge and took stock. The main entry was lit and would be locked. He spotted cameras, both on posts around the pavilion and embedded in the buttressed overhang that girded the structure's second story.

Any closer and he'd be observed. *There's got to be another way.* He pictured the satellite photos of Lakeshore, which he'd enlarged until they'd pixilated into undecipherable dots. *Think!* From the air, the sprawling Lakeshore complex was laid out to mimic a city, with Parker Hall at its hub and the rows of patient and staff residences and facilities arranged in blocks and streets that radiated out like spokes on a wheel. The larger and now abandoned buildings on this side of the complex had been for the wards of "incorrigibles," those patients deemed too ill and/or dangerous to ever leave.

As he gazed at the Stangl Pavilion—*one of these things doesn't fit*—he thought back through newspaper stories about the Kruft takeover of Lakeshore. While the parish had been eager to unload the toxic liability, there had also been community pushback. Some argued that the facility, with its vast tract of waterfront, should be turned into a community park. Others felt the decaying asylum needed to be preserved for its historic value. There were even thoughts of turning the sprawling real estate into a Mardi Gras theme park.

The articles reported on town meetings where Kruft executives, local politicians, and concerned community members had met. Promises had been made, and Luke suspected, palms had been greased. The deal went through, with Kruft making commitments to rehab what could be saved and to preserve anything of historic merit. Obviously the dying brick structures on this side of the property, with their crumbling mortar and wood-slat fences dotted with caution signs, didn't make the cut.

The only truly new structure on hospital grounds was the Stangl Pavilion. He stared at the shimmering building. No sign of life, no lights shining through its darkly reflective windows. He observed its position among the abandoned buildings. *Something else must have stood there.* He wished he'd had that realization before when he could have checked it out against older photos. A thought clicked. In among the articles he'd read about the wildlife impact and Kruft Industries' promises to protect the wetlands were rules. Something about how any new construction would have to be over existing footprints. If that were true, the Stangl Pavilion had been built over an earlier structure.

And this matters how? Hopelessness crept in. *This is ridiculous. And what? You're going to leave him?* "No, you're getting Miles out or are going down trying."

He tracked his gaze from the impregnable pavilion to its nearest neighbor, a four-story nineteenth-century brick building, which at one time might have been attractive, with its covered porches and turreted roofline. Now the porches had separated from the brick, their iron anchors rusted away. Chunks of the roof had collapsed, and the once-white mullions were mostly gone, having provided sustenance for decades of termites and carpenter ants.

Behind him music thumped as his eyes traced the distance from the bombed-out wreck of a building to its shiny neighbor…. *Maybe fifty yards.* The spark of an idea struck. He pulled at his memory of the satellite photos, the buildings arranged like spokes, but there was something more. Or did he just imagine it? *No, think.* Slowly he traced the terrain, the swamp providing a lacy mangrove backdrop between the pavilion and the ruins. Here and there orange contractor's barriers had been erected…. *They're connected. Of course they'd have to be… for wiring, plumbing… sewage. It's like a town.* He pulled for forgotten details, things he wouldn't have thought important that now seemed crucial. *What is it you saw?* Massive pipes, but bigger than that.

He approached the hulking brick building and headed around the side that faced the swamp. The waning moon, a few days past full, poured light into the exposed structure. Much of the back wall had collapsed, and an iron fire escape hung at a perilous angle.

He imagined even if there were tunnels connecting this to other buildings, they had been removed or destroyed by time and the elements.

He shrugged off his knapsack and retrieved a wire cutter. He snipped the ties between several of the slats and ducked through the fence. Thankful for the moonlight and not wanting to attract attention with his flashlight, he stepped carefully among fallen bricks and splintered strips of wood. One of the satin covers over his sneaker caught on a piece of rebar. He stumbled and nearly fell into a glass-sprinkled copse of swamp grass. His heart raced as he regained balance. He swallowed and fought back the thoughts that came with it. *Hopeless. You can't save him.*

He whispered into the night, "You're going to get Miles out of here, or you're going down trying." It helped… a little… and he stepped into the structure's hulking shadow.

The ruined building gaped like a mouth. He entered through a hole in the back wall. Climbing over loose mounds of brick, wood, and glass, he knew one wrong move and he'd be of no use to Miles. He came to what was once the building's back ward, the remaining windows laced with wire and framed behind iron bars. The moon's glow dimmed with each step.

He held still until his eyes adjusted. Above him a jagged section of the roof had collapsed, taking with it a portion of the floor below. *You need to go down.* He looked from the rusted beds to the floor, where weeds had sprouted among the cracked tiles. At the distant end of the ward, which had likely housed a couple of dozen patients, was a banded door that had dropped from its hinges but still blocked the egress. On the side closer to the Stangl building was an intact wall with a blackboard on which someone had drawn a grid. Most of what had been written was gone, but traces of patient names in thick white chalk—Tom, Ted, Nathan, Bill C, Bill W— could still be seen.

Torn between being discovered and taking a fatal misstep down a hole, Luke pulled out his flashlight. Careful to keep its beam low, he swept the room's periphery. Something slithered off to his right as a cluster of shiny black beetles scurried from the unwanted intrusion of light. The interior walls were intact. The door was his only option.

With shuffling steps to avoid a nail piercing his sneakers or a soft spot in the floor that would send him falling to whatever lurked below, he passed through the ward. He reached the door and examined the hinges, which had mostly ripped from the wood frame. It was massive, solid, steel-banded oak. He tucked his light into his waistband, and grateful for the gloves of the costume, he gently pushed. There was minimal give. He braced the palms of his hands against the door and rocked it. Before he could get out of the way, the remaining hinge bolts ripped free and the door canted toward him.

"Shit!"

Dropping the flashlight, he whipped his hands up as the weight landed on him. Trapped beneath it, he tried to distribute the load through his arms, his back, and his legs. He stayed like that for a few moments, and then, in tiny increments, moved his hands toward the right edge. It unbalanced the weight, and with a final shove, he let it fall away. He braced, awaiting the crash, but its landing was muffled by a bedframe that still had its mattress, albeit more of a nest for some now displaced and disgruntled field mice.

He held still, alert to the sounds of scurrying feet as baby rodents fell from the mattress to the floor. He could no longer hear the party as musky scents from the invading swamp filled his nostrils. Retrieving his light, he explored the building's once-grand entry. Here and there, where the ceiling and roof were still intact, he saw patches of a diamond-patterned floor, a sweeping central staircase with oak turnings, and carved urn-shaped balusters that shot upward toward the glowing moon. Unfortunately the stairs ended on the main floor.

Keeping his light low, he searched behind the stairs and found a door. He gripped the handle, half expecting it to be locked or again fall off. But protected by a bit of roof and the stairs, it turned, and with the squeak of unexercised hinges, it opened out.

The smell that rose from the narrow stairs that fell into pitch black was pure swamp, algae and decay, but also sweet, like garbage left to bake in the New Orleans sun.

He gripped the doorframe and trained the light into the dark. "I will get you out, or I will go down trying." He thought of Miles as he stared into the hellish pit. For a moment before heading down, he stopped and took stock of where he was, what he was doing, and what he intended. He thought of his father, mother, Jenna… and Miles. *I will find you. I will tell you that I love you.* The thought of seeing him again, of holding him, pushed through the fear and the stench.

He swept the beam across each of the wooden treads. And careful step by careful step, he descended.

CHAPTER 31

GERALD, DRESSED in white tie, tails, and a black-leather Zorro mask, made polite conversation with the short and stocky Dean Strachey, dressed as a 1940s female baseball player, complete with red-and-white striped hat and pleated skirt.

"Gerald, I think this is the best one yet," she commented.

As was the norm, the two of them, like most of the faculty, had migrated to the second-floor mezzanine, where they watched the dance-floor gyrations and drunken pairings of the medical students and their guests.

"Yes, well, if you feed them, they will come. Although I think it's less about the buffet and more about the booze." He glanced at the clock above the entry and calculated how much longer he'd have to remain before turning things over to the staff. *An hour, no more.* It was killing him; his cheeks ached from smiling. He envisioned at first a sedative gas and then a poisonous one sweeping the dance floor—it helped.

"A shame about the Fox boy," she said.

His attention perked at Fox's name. "In what way?" he asked, curious as to how this piggy little woman—*they say she's a lesbian*—put things together.

"You know, the usual. He'd have made a fine and caring physician."

What is she talking about? And what does she want now? He'd sat in too many of her agenda-free meetings, wondering if and when they would ever end, knowing her true purpose would emerge and boil down to one or two of three things—they needed more money, they needed faculty to spend less money, or she needed volunteers for some project no one wanted to be a part of. Other than the waste of his time, he was largely free from such demands, well-buffered by his grants, the financial success of Lakeshore, and his unparalleled publication track record. "Is that it?"

She plucked a mint leaf from her drink and looked up. "The boy had a quality about him. I went through all his evaluations to see what we'd missed. If there'd been warning signs, little freak-outs on call that no one had bothered to bring to my attention. When one of the students is a problem, it's typically not a single event, but there's a pattern. You know"—she twirled her drink—"where there's smoke…. There was none of that with Fox."

Gerald sensed her questions. She knew he was doing Fox's evaluation, and this was her attempt at a fishing expedition. Either that, or she was questioning his judgment. *The little bitch.* Tremors of rage rippled through him. He would not rise to this insignificant troll's bait. "So what *did* you find?"

"Near-perfect evaluations. He was consistently in the top ten percent of his class. Not quite valedictorian, but a number of his supervisors had included thank-you notes from his patients in his file."

"Is that unusual?"

"I've seen maybe one in the past twenty years. But with Fox, three separate faculty supervisors and one of the residents attached patient testimonials to his end-of-rotation reviews."

Gerald nodded. "Perhaps that's your smoking gun."

"That he's a caring human being whom patients seem to love?"

"Beverly." He gentled his tone. "You've done this a long time. You're describing the tip of what is likely a large delusional iceberg."

She blinked. "Oh… I see where you're headed. A Jesus thing."

"Exactly."

"Huh… I had not considered that." She gave a dramatic shudder. "How one gets from healing the masses to chopping off their heads, I don't think I want to know…. And I don't suppose you'd tell me if I asked."

He chuckled. "You know I can't, although all of my observations will be public record through the court."

"Yes, and that's, what, a month… maybe never if the case doesn't go to trial? You're a tease, Gerald. And I freely admit that I look forward to reading it…. Although I am not looking forward to the publicity for the medical school if he does stand trial."

Just as when he'd come to identify the moment in her abysmal meetings where the true purpose was revealed, he heard her tone shift as the real point to their tête-à-tête emerged.

"You know," she said, "all things being equal, and I don't want you to think I'm trying to influence your evaluation…."

"Of course not."

"It's just… it's just it would be so much simpler if Fox were found unfit to stand trial."

"True," Gerald said. "The media made quite a lot of how he killed poor Mr. Dey."

"Exactly. Not the best PR for the hospital, the medical school, or our fine city. A trial would only prolong things."

"Not to worry, Beverly. The boy is quite mad."

"You mean…."

He shook his head. "You know I can't give you more than that." He wondered what she'd do as his endgame neared. Before Dr. Amelia Raskin arrived to do her evaluation, Fox would go missing or be found dead, hanging in his cell. He hadn't decided which. The former would leave too many loose ends, and the latter would make it difficult to remove the boy's head. Although once cut down from his cell and an autopsy completed, who was to say what happened to the body?

Crucial pieces of the grail's transmission were slowly coming to light, how the gift traveled from Fox into the terminally ill subjects. The healing power obliterated advanced diseases in a matter of minutes and provided immunity from the most virulent pathogens for the next twenty-four hours before the body's normal immunity resumed. Case in point being the man with AIDS whom he and Calvin had vivisected earlier that afternoon. The HIV virus, which had been over a million copies per milliliter of blood, was undetectable. Even when they'd sliced into his brain and cracked open a femur to extract marrow, there were no hidden foci of disease.

"I'd love to know what you make of the Paxton boy's involvement in all of this." The dean's voice rose in a question.

"How so?"

"While I'm not entirely up on the who's with whom in our student body, I was a bit surprised. I did not see that coming."

"That he was gay?" Gerald asked, curious as to how the dean would respond, knowing the rumors about her and her long-term *roommate*.

"No, not that. There's more…. You're the psychiatrist. Could it be shared delusions? Is that even possible?"

"You lost me."

The dean looked out at the dance floor. "I was in the room when a pair of detectives interviewed Paxton after Fox went AWOL. I had no doubt of the boy's sincerity. But...."

He sensed her struggle and was curious for any light she might shed on Fox's accomplice, who thankfully had been expelled and shipped hundreds of miles away to his parents. "But what, Beverly?"

"Maybe it's just young love, but Luke Paxton didn't seem to care, or care enough, that he'd jeopardized his career. He was so certain he'd done the right thing by helping Fox escape. But more than that, his father is a bigwig surgeon back in Charleston. My phone conversation with him was not pleasant. When I discreetly let him know about the relationship between his son and Fox, he did not take it well."

"What did he say?"

The dean smiled. "Fine, I'm divulging privileged information about the students, and you're not even throwing me table scraps about Fox."

Gerald nodded. "Yes, but I give you other things, like this marvelous party, and my newest and soon-to-be-announced NIH grant includes a million dollars in administrative overhead."

"Really? How much discretion do you have?"

"I think you mean 'we.' How much discretion do *we* have with it? And the answer is quite a lot. I'll have my secretary set up a meeting, and we can discuss how to cut the cake. So... what did the good surgeon doctor have to say about his wayward son?"

"Let's see if I can reconstruct his words. 'My son is no queer. He must have been tricked.' At one point he even threatened me, that if this leaked out—the gay bits—he'd sue for defamation. And there was something about New Orleans turning his son gay." She laughed. "I don't like to be threatened. It made telling Dr. Paxton that his son was being expelled so much easier. Although I feel bad for the boy. I can only imagine what must be going on with a father like that." She looked at her empty drink. "I think I'd like another. Can I get you one?"

"I'm good," he said and watched her retreat to the bar. *Clever woman,* he thought, realizing nothing in their conversation was by chance. Fox was a liability and a PR nightmare for the school. Luke Paxton was another piece of that, and shipping him out of town was essential. Yes, Beverly's objectives were clear, and fortunately in lockstep with his own. Miles

Fox would never leave Lakeshore. He and Calvin would complete their experiments, unravel the last pieces, and then transfer the grail from one vessel to two. All that remained was how best to dispose of the old one.

Standing over the sweating, drinking, lusting youth, he imagined how it would be to finally possess the grail, to feel its power. *What will it be like? Like being God.* He thought back to that marvelous moment when he first suspected Fox was the one, that the years of waiting and watching had not been in vain. Staring at the brewing orgy below, he murmured, "Do you believe in fate, Dr. Stangl? Why, yes, I think I do."

"Hey, Doc!"

Gerald startled at the rasp of a familiar voice. "Louis, what are you doing here?"

Louis Drake, his silver hair slicked back, dressed in white Lakeshore scrubs, a blue bathrobe, and slippers, seemed right at home with the costumed throngs. "I know I'm not supposed to be at this shindig, but I gotta thank you, and you need to know what the dollar told me."

Gerald glanced to either side of Louis, wondering if there was a handy attendant who could escort him back to his cottage. Not seeing either a security guard or a hospital aide, he resigned himself to the inevitable. *Perhaps bringing him here was not a good idea.* "So what's it saying?" he asked, again struck at how from every angle Louis was Grandpapa Oskar's double.

Louis shot a hand into his bathrobe pocket and pulled out a crumpled single. "It's saying funny stuff, Doc. Look at this." He flattened the bill against the mezzanine rail. "It's another F, so fine, fun, flipper, find the fox."

Gerald stared at the bill. "In the last F bill you said 'fox.' How come?"

"Clear as day, Doc. You got to pay attention. Read the numbers. The eye don't lie. The last one things were set to reset, the clock is running, you know, the quick brown fox, it's running fast. One, two, three. See the numbers." Louis's excitement grew, and he smacked his lips as he read the serial number. "F, oh, oh, oh, one, two, three. It's a clock, Doc. Can you hear it? Tick, tick, tick, talk, talk, talk. Listen…."

"Louis, I kind of get it. Thanks. Not to be rude, but you probably shouldn't be here."

Louis looked Gerald in the eye and then out at the crowd. His tongue licked his dry lips. "Doc, you been good to me. I don't forget favors. I just needed you to know what the dollar said."

Gerald paused, having never bought the explanation that the ramblings of people with schizophrenia were nonsense. "Why is it important for me?"

Louis shook his head. "'Cause ain't nothing an accident. Read the numbers. This dollar just found me. It found me here, your place, the clock is here, it's running. It starts with an F. Look where it ends."

Gerald stared at the bill where Louis jabbed at the end of the serial number with his forefinger.

"It ain't right."

Gerald, who could usually follow the ramble of Louis's thoughts, had no clue. "It starts with an F, the numbers go up, they come down, and it ends with an F. What's it mean?"

"Shit, Doc. It's clear as the bell and the bats. The thing finds itself."

At that point Stangl was relieved to see the familiar face of Lakeshore's head of security. He gave a nod, and the man was at his side.

"Louis, thanks for the info. I'll visit tomorrow. The cottage is good?"

Louis narrowed his gaze, as he looked from the uniformed officer back to Gerald. He stuffed the bill back into his pocket. "You'll see. Things find themselves. The F wants to be with an F, not with an S." And he allowed himself to be led off without further comment.

CHAPTER 32

Calvin, his face smeared with fake blood, removed the gag arrow that gave the illusion of going through his head. His companion, a sophomore named Katie Swan, dressed as a ballerina zombie, braced a hand against a live oak. "I'm going to hurl!"

He didn't wait as a night's worth of rum punch, shrimp balls, and bile spewed forth.

"Where you going?" she croaked between heaves. "I thought you liked me."

"To get you a towel and some water."

"I'm fine." She puked again. "Just got to get it all out. Don't go away."

"I'll be right back."

Bent over, she caught his true intention like a slap. She turned her makeup-smeared face back, a bit of vomit stuck to her lower lip. "You're ditching me!"

"No, I swear, I'll be right back."

"I know when a guy's ditching me." She twisted her mouth as she tried to straighten. "Oh God, there's more."

He wanted to run, but something about the girl's distress fascinated him. He watched as she retched again and again. Oddly, it didn't seem to bother her.

"So what's wrong with me?" she asked.

"Nothing."

She narrowed her eyes to slits as though seeing him for the first time. "Why'd you bring me out here if you don't like girls?"

"I do so." *How can she know?*

"Yeah." She staggered toward him, her tutu torn, her eyes wild with booze and the ipecac he'd stirred into her punch. "Then prove it."

The smell of puke was too much as she pressed her body against his, deliberately rubbing her firm, full breasts across his chest.

Repulsed, he backed away.

"Thought so! OMG, Dr. Stangl's one and only son is queer bait. OMG!"

"I am not. Just shut up!"

"Nothing wrong with being a fag."

He balled his fists. *Not here; too many people.* The urge to put a fist into the middle of her face was intense. "You're drunk, and I don't like puke breath."

"Just what a queer would say. A real man could care less. So run away, little boy, go find what you're looking for. A nice big…." Before she could complete her crude accusation, a wave of nausea overtook her.

He backed away from her drunken insults and puke. He turned toward the pavilion and tried to focus on what needed to happen in the next hour. *You have time.* But it did nothing to calm him or quiet the fear. *What if it doesn't work? Father will know.*

Breaking into a jog and then a run, he raced across paths festooned with fairy lights. He passed couples necking on benches, and more advanced activities behind hedges and under the canopy of the pecan orchard.

All his thoughts were on Miles. His smile, the feel of his perfect skin as he slept, the little twitch of his strong jaw as he dreamed. It went deeper, far beyond the superficiality of looks. The way Miles encouraged him, as though he could reach into Calvin's mind and let him know that everything was all right… that he was all right. These were new and wonderful feelings, and nothing Father could say or do would take them away. He was in love with Miles Fox, and it was reciprocated.

This was going to work. The thing Father had scoffed at as fairy tale and legend was the single greatest truth in all those musty volumes and scrolls. The Zosimus configuration was the only known success. And unlike Father and the countless generations before him, he saw that the answer came not in shucking the grail from the green-eyed vessel, but something more intimate, and, as he thought about it, obvious. *How could they all be so blind?*

He sprinted across well-kept lawns, his purpose laser sharp. The grail was both metaphor and reality. Like the cups he forged and hammered, they were both tools and an indispensable ingredient—pure silver, free from contaminants. One drank from a cup, as one drank from the grail. One didn't destroy such a precious thing; one treasured it. One loved it. One loved him. Just as Zosimus loved Marta.

He cleared the path and ran toward the Pavilion. *You have time.* The party would last until the early-morning hours, and it was barely eleven.

Father would stay… wouldn't he? Doubt and fear crept back. *Will he wonder where I've gone? Will he look for me? Will he check up on the test subject? On Miles?* He didn't want to think about the hours he'd lost, or that the Zosimus configuration, as it needed the pure silver, also needed the moon, which was near full and high in a cloudless sky.

You don't have enough time. You should have left the party sooner. But he didn't dare, knowing Father was watching. As bad luck had it, this was the first time Father had insisted he attend the annual bash. "Lots of pretty girls, Calvin. Yes, a bit older than you, but for a first or second time that's a good thing. Save you a lot of unnecessary fumbling. Let them take the lead. Your virginity does neither one of us any good. It's easy to get one of the students into bed… or just go behind the bushes. You flatter them, say how pretty they look. You bring them drinks. You tell them I'm your father, if need be. You pay attention to what they say, even if they're boring." Father had laughed. "Yes, especially if they're boring." He'd handed Calvin two foil-wrapped condoms. "Wear one. When and if the time comes for you to create an heir, we'll pick the right carrier."

His ears burned at the memory of that awkward conversation and of the puking ballerina he'd used to conceal his escape from the party. *Let Father think I'm screwing that disgusting girl.*

A muffled explosion from off to his left halted him in his tracks. Breathing heavily, he tried to trace the source. Up ahead was the pavilion, to the left one of the brick ruins. *It came from there.* He held still and heard the soft lapping of the lake, the chirp of cicadas, a loon's cry.

He searched for movement in the moonlit wreck. He traced his gaze over the collapsed roof and down to the piles of rubble. *What was it?* He tried to match the noise he'd heard to something plausible, like a parapet falling to the ground. *Probably more of the roof.* He stood an instant or two longer. *There's no one there. The only one likely to stop you is Father…. You can't give him that chance.*

He did a quick 360 to make certain he hadn't been followed. Then he darted to the back of the pavilion, took the metal stairs two at a time, tapped in his code, and placed his fingers into the reader. His heart raced as he waited for the lock to click.

Once inside he took the elevator to the subbasement workroom where he'd honed his craft. Father had dropped a rare bit of praise on his most recent efforts. "I see you're finally taking this seriously," he'd said as he examined one of Calvin's efforts. It, and its four matched partners, were perfect.

"As above, so below," he whispered and packed the five goblets into a fitted stainless attaché. So much could go wrong. Horrible thoughts chattered in his head. *What if none of this is true? What if the Zosimus configuration is a fantasy, an urban legend spread through the centuries by the bitter remnants of a Teutonic religious order?*

Stay calm. He pictured Miles…. *My Miles. So what if it doesn't work? We're both young. I will save him from Father. We could leave this place… and Father… and run far away. But what if he won't leave? His grandmother…. He won't leave her.*

Stop! This will work… but what if it doesn't?

He closed the case and, clutching the handle, left the workroom and took the dark, narrow stairs up to the basement, up to his true love. *It's time.*

With case in hand, he opened the concealed panel that let him into the small med room behind the nurses' station. He closed it behind him and knew he stood at the point of no return. Everything would be taped. If he was unsuccessful, Father would know all. His anger and retribution would be extreme. *Will he kill me?* The answer rang in his head. *Yes. If Father learns about this, about any of this… he will kill me.*

CHAPTER 33

Miles awoke from a drugged sleep, his temples pounding as though he wore a hat two sizes too small. This time was not as bad, since he'd learned that if he held his breath as the gas was pumped in, he could lessen the dose.

He'd been to the lake, yet as he'd returned to wakefulness like a swimmer rising to the surface, another dream pursued him. A nightmare filled with wraiths, anguished faces—Antoine Dey, Jasper, Trevor Owens with his Kaposi's-ravaged face, others he didn't recognize. They'd chased him across a war-torn landscape. Just before waking he'd stopped to face them. "What is it you want?" There was no answer, and they faded.

Now, alone with his thoughts, he stared at Grandma Anna's EEG. The bright red LED oriented him to time and date, fast-approaching midnight on Halloween. He couldn't see her face in the dim light, just the shine off her shaved scalp… like a concentration camp prisoner. He bit back his rage. The anger did no good, and it clouded his thoughts. He needed clarity and stealth.

He remembered the last conversation with Zosimus, Marta, and Great-Grandfather Tomas. There had been no good-natured banter and no metaphor-laden stories as they'd gathered around Grandma Anna's crystal casket. There was only fear and warnings. But something more….

"She can't be saved."

No. The sleeping beauty gee-whizz of it was long past. "It's not that," he'd argued back with his dead but not-quite-dead relatives. "She won't be saved. She wants none of this."

Tomas had replied, "It's one and the same, boy. And if your head leaves your shoulders without passing the torch, we all perish."

A muffled clang from behind the nurses' station pricked his attention. Like Pavlov's dog hearing the bell, his pulse quickened. *Which freak is it?*

He knew he was being recorded. If they checked the tapes or were watching, they'd know he was up. Still, as the door behind the station whisked open, he feigned sleep. It was what they'd expect, having gassed him with sedative less than three hours ago. As he closed his eyes, he pictured Grandma Anna's oddly spiked EEG that had so fascinated Dr. Stangl.

He cracked a lid as light flooded the ward. *It's the kid.* His mind strained to hear Calvin's thoughts, but he'd discovered that ability was contingent on a state of intense calm and/or physical contact. The former he didn't have, and the latter he didn't want.

As Calvin neared he wondered at the blood caked in his hair and smeared across his cheeks. *Has something happened? Is it even real? Great, he's staring at me. Look all you want, kid,* he thought, having by now taken a few strolls through Calvin's noggin. The teen was a hormonal volcano. *Why are you here so late? Where's Daddy... or you've come alone. Awesome.* Although getting groped, he reasoned, would also be a chance to peek inside his head. As he puzzled over the visit's purpose, Calvin reached for the control panel.

Shit!

The vents in the ceiling hissed. Miles filled his lungs and held it. *Think about something else.* His thoughts skittered to his Krav Maga instructor, Ileana Glass, who between rounds of attacking her heavily padded students would instruct them to "be effective," "do what works," and "real fights have no rules. All that matters is survival, and when possible, eliminate the threat."

He wondered what the ex-Israeli operative would make of his current situation. Yes, he could overpower Calvin, but what good would that do? Between here and freedom were at least three locked doors. They held Grandma Anna and had threatened his family, going so far as to show him video of his sister Maya through her dormitory window at Wesleyan. He'd no illusion of the lengths the Stangls would go to to make him toe the line.

He also knew that doing what they asked and then going his merry way was not an option. He'd seen the heads in jars in Calvin's thoughts. How many had already died? They wanted what he had, and in the case of Calvin, it wasn't just his abilities as a healer. His lungs ached as pressure built in his chest. *Think of something else.*

He focused on long-ago martial arts classes in the Provincetown studio, remembering how Grandma Anna had first just dropped him off, and then she'd stayed to watch, and finally, after several heated discussions with Ileana, she'd suited up.

The hissing stopped, and the misted drug felt wet against his cheek. *Hold on.* He knew gravity would pull the aerosolized drug down. *Just a little longer.*

He replayed a memory of Anna covered in head-to-toe protective gear, laying into a pair of teens who'd been instructed to attack her. They'd started by going easy. She was having none of it as she'd stomped the instep of one while repeatedly hammering the groin of the other with a gloved fist.

The pressure in his chest grew, and his pulse hammered in his ears. *She tried to fight off Calvin…. Think of something else.* His mind fastened on Luke. He'd been trying in these past few awful days to not think of him. To not picture his eyes, the touch of his hand… his kiss. *Luke.* He imagined him back in Charleston, having sacrificed his career, Jenna. *Why, Luke?*

Tomas's voice shot back, "Because he loves you, moron. Now take a breath before you pass out…."

With Luke's face fixed in his mind, Miles cautiously sipped the air. He heard noises from behind the nurses' station and cracked his lids open, half expecting to find Calvin staring down at him. But he wasn't there. He was pushing a wheelchair with a stainless-steel briefcase on the seat and a pile of familiar leather restraints.

His heart sank. Much as he wasn't up for a touchy-feely session with the psycho teen, this was worse. This was how the experiments started. *How many people do they intend to kill?* He thought of that sweet woman from the morning, Daisy Osborn. He'd tasted her fear as she'd crept into his thoughts and seen what the Stangls intended. *Is she still alive?* Images of her grandchildren were still fresh in his head.

He shut his eyes as his cell opened. He braced for what was coming, wondering if it wouldn't have been better to let the drug do its thing so he wouldn't have to feel the kid creeping his fingers through his hair and copping feels of his chest, or worse.

Do what works. He used the physical contact to access Calvin's thoughts. What he saw was like soft-core porn where he was the star. It took all his will to not recoil. The teen's head was filled with him, his hair, his eyes, his mouth, remembered gropes, and stolen touches. *But what else, Calvin?* Feeling like an explorer, he poked around. He let his thoughts gently flow. *What are we doing tonight, Calvin? What's on the menu?*

Images of the Parker Hall Halloween bash passed between them. *Of course, it's Halloween and you're in costume. Where's Father?* He masked his own thoughts with Calvin's own pattern of speech—not "Dad," not "Pops." Father. *Where's Father?*

As he pressed the thought into the boy's mind, a wave of anxiety rolled back. He saw Gerald Stangl in tails and a black half mask, looking down over the party. He glimpsed a pretty underclassman puking into the bushes, accompanied by a snippet of Calvin pouring ipecac into a fruity drink.

What are we doing tonight? he wondered, realizing the boy was on his own. He was making his move.

Calvin skimmed his hands down Miles's sides.

He wanted to flinch. *Don't move.* He wondered if what the kid intended was to take his erotic musings to the next level… like raping an unconscious man. *What are you doing?* The flow of Calvin's thoughts was gone as his hands lost contact with Miles's skin.

Miles kept his body limp as the kid tugged at his legs and pushed them toward the edge of the bed.

Okay, we're going for a ride. Why? Where…?

With his lids cracked, Miles watched Calvin bend over him, his body pressed against his. He snaked his hands around Miles's waist. The flesh-to-flesh contact plugged Miles back into his head.

What he saw, amongst the strain in Calvin's back and legs and growing arousal, was difficult to decipher. Old books, cases of them, a table, and some sort of metal workshop… and a diagram on parchment. Calvin's thoughts kept returning to that as if checking off ingredients on a recipe. The chalices in the case, the moon, Miles laid out on an altar. In the parchment diagram was a man with a crazy beard and elaborately folded turban—Zosimus—his chest bare, his legs covered in a pleated linen skirt. Before him, surrounded by diagrammatic lines, almost like a blueprint, a bare-breasted woman lay smiling on a rectangular table…. No, an altar. Her eyes were a vivid green. There was no mistaking their identities—Zosimus and Marta.

What the hell? Like instructions.

Miles let his dead weight pivot up and onto the chair. He resisted the urge to pummel Calvin's head into the floor as the boy strapped a restraint around his waist and then secured his hands and feet to the wheelchair.

Although… his fingerprints work the locks. And then what? You're going to beat him unconscious, drag him and Grandma Anna through the hall, up the elevator, steal a car, break out through the front gate…. Not yet, Miles. You may not get another chance. Shut up and knit. Listen to his thoughts. He thinks he loves you. He thinks you love him. He… what the?

What he glimpsed in Calvin's thoughts, aside from the perv factor, was important. *Zosimus and Marta, the exception to the rule. What are we trying to do here, Calvin?*

And then it hit. As Calvin wheeled him past Grandma Anna's sleeping form, Miles realized he intended to do what Zosimus did with Marta. To split the grail. The problem was, at least according to Zosimus, the equation was based on not four elements, but five. The fifth being the only true magic in the human world… love, unconditional and absolute. It was how the grail passed from mother to child, father to daughter, always connected by love.

Miles tensed with the realization. *And when the spell fails and he realizes he's made a horrible mistake…. You've got to get out of here.* But tied down and unable to jeopardize Grandma Anna and his family's well-being, escape was not an option. *You have to knit. Just shut up and knit.*

Calvin stepped onto the unit, and there, in the dim light, lay Miles. His breath caught, and there was an ache in his chest. He stood and stared. *So beautiful,* Miles shirtless, the sheets tangled around his long legs as he slept in a drugged and dream-filled sleep. *This will work. This has to work. I love him so much.*

He crossed from behind the station to Miles's cell and took one final precaution. He pressed the button to release an additional dose of sedative. *Sleep, my love. Soon we will be together, forever and for always.*

He worried at his bottom lip as the aerosolized drug filled the space. With a second button, he turned on the reverse air flow and sucked back the residual.

He feasted on the sight of his sleeping love and retrieved a wheelchair from the nurses' station. He opened the cell door and wheeled it to the bed. It took all his effort to stay focused, to not get lost in expanses of silken flesh over hard muscle. He played his fingers through Miles's raven's-wing hair. It curled like silk.

He wrapped his arms around Miles's legs, and pulled them to the edge of the bed, and then over the side. He scooted beside him and leaned over. Calvin's nostrils filled with his wonderful smell as he spread his palm over his bare chest. He slid a hand up to Miles's right shoulder and placed his limp hand over his back. He grabbed the other and, wrapping his arms tight around Miles's waist, pulled him to sitting. Wrapped in those arms, Miles's head against his own, he had never felt such bliss. He let his lips brush against Miles's. It was a kiss, Calvin's first. Not a real kiss, but the sensation was more powerful than anything he could have imagined. *You have to hurry.* Wishing he could stay like this forever, he forced himself into action.

He pulled back, and with Miles's feet acting as a fulcrum, pivoted him out of bed and into the wheelchair. He fastened the strap around his middle, and with practiced efficiency he popped up the footrests and secured him to the chair with leather leg and ankle restraints.

He glanced at Miles's grandmother. The EEG readings were as odd as ever and nearly identical to ones Miles produced.

Calvin's plan had not extended to Anna Warren. She would soon be dead. And frankly that would be best. For a moment he considered ending her life now; one less loose end. But time was fleeting. He looked toward the ward's door and imagined Father stepping through.

Keep moving. Having never before attended the Halloween party, he tried to remember: *Does Father stay till the end?* He knew there was a costume contest with the winners announced at midnight. *He'd have to stay for that. He has to play the good host.* Calvin's mundane selection of a bloodied arrow victim was deliberate. It met the dress requirement without placing him in jeopardy of being considered for a prize. Father would have seen him leave the party with the pretty medical student, unaware Calvin had laced her drink with ipecac and that she was likely still puking in the bushes.

He picked up the case with the chalices and wheeled Miles out of the ward, not bothering to shut the door behind him. Moving fast, he headed toward the elevator. He pressed his fingers to the reader, pushed Miles in, and hit the button for the roof. He glanced at his watch—11:13.

"Soon." He brought his lips to the back of Miles's head. He inhaled the scent of shampoo and his soft hair, like some luxurious pelt, tickled his skin. "Soon we will be together forever. I love you, Miles, and you love me."

The elevator came to a cushioned stop. The doors slid open, and, pushing Miles out, Calvin arrived at their next hurdle; six metal steps that led to the roof.

Undeterred and prepared, he retrieved two ten-foot planks he'd left there that afternoon. It was one of the riskier parts of his plan, as he was invariably captured on tape. But being the son of the medical director had its perks, and it was unlikely anyone would have reported his behavior to Father.

He placed the planks at the width of the chair's wheels along the stair treads. They were barely long enough. He tilted the chair back and brought the wheels to the edge of the boards. He felt the top of Miles's head against his chest. The weight of it felt good. *I'm doing this for us, for our future.* Digging in with his legs, he pushed hard. The chair rolled up, and going slow and careful, he moved his precious cargo.

The boards slipped in tiny increments as the weight of Miles and the chair grew and the angle of ascent steepened. A gap opened between the top of the board on the left and the platform. The board on the right barely hung to its purchase. With a heroic surge, Calvin shifted the chair's weight to the right and pushed with all he had.

The left board flew out from under the wheel, and for what seemed an eternity, the chair perched on one plank. Calvin's straining arms and legs were all that kept Miles from falling backward down the steel steps.

"No!" Calvin grunted and pushed with all he had. The last board shot up, nearly catching him in the groin as the edge of the right wheel cleared the landing. The plank thudded back and slid down the steps. Calvin repositioned his feet and pushed the grounded wheel farther onto the landing before letting the other side touch down.

Calvin's heart pounded, and sweat dribbled down his back and chest. Carefully he moved first one foot and then the other up the last steps, never releasing his grip on the back of the chair. He fixed his eyes on the rear wheels, which still hung off the landing. Step by careful step, he pushed the chair, and Miles, to safety.

"Never fear." He let himself brush a trembling hand through Miles's hair. "I've got you. I always will."

He flipped up the brakes on the wheels. It wasn't necessary, but there'd be no more taking chances. He fished a key from his pocket and unlocked the roof-access door.

Cool air kissed his face, and the moon, a few days past full, was high. With the tip of his foot, he released the brakes, and with a grunt and shove, he pushed Miles over the threshold.

Calvin stared across the flat roof. The building's four walls were in perfect alignment—north, south, east, west. At its dead center was a raised diamond-shaped altar made to resemble an air handler. He rolled Miles up to the altar and set the brakes.

Giddy and nervous, he searched for the four concealed circular indents, each in perfect alignment with their direction and principal. He played the ritual in his head, the directions and the elements—north, south, east, west—that corresponded to earth, wind, water, and fire.

On this, if Father were present, he would have agreed. But the missing piece, the thing that had prevented all but one from attaining the grail, was neither a direction nor the calling of the four elements. Yes, those were necessary, but in the way a building needed scaffolding while the bricks and mortar were put in place. Only Zosimus had understood, which, considering he'd been the greatest chemist and alchemist of his day, was fascinating.

The missing piece, the thing that could both call the grail and allow for its transfer into a second living vessel, was the only magic mankind possessed. To Calvin it was obvious. It surprised him how Father and all the others had missed this point with their head-chopping attempts to force the grail into submission.

He glanced at Miles. *Is he awake?* He stared at that perfect face, pale in the moonlight. Were his eyes open? No. How could they be? *He'll sleep for another half hour, and when he wakes…. We'll call the grail, you and I. We'll give it what it wants. What I want… what you want. We'll give it love.* He paused. *His lids just fluttered…. No harm with a little extra.* Prepared, he reached into a lab coat pocket, pulled out a small syringe, uncapped it, and with efficiency of movement, injected the contents—the same fast-acting sedative he'd piped into Miles's cell—into his neck.

There, now everything is perfect.

CHAPTER 34

LUKE TRAINED the beam of his flashlight into the partially collapsed brick tunnel. The mortar of its seventy-year-old walls had disintegrated from the swampy groundwater and the Louisiana heat and humidity. His shoes and socks were soaked with mud and goo that sucked and slurped with each step. His wilted satin costume clung to his legs with sweat and filth. Around him he heard stirrings of life, mostly frogs disturbed from their mucky hollows, but also the slither of snakes and heavier doings of reptiles, maybe snapping turtles but probably gators.

He pulled out his cell and held it in the direction of a gaping hole in the floor above. He pressed the compass app, having determined the spatial relationship between his current location and the Stangl Research Pavilion. He stared into the tunnel, which bent in the right direction. From the articles about Lakeshore, he knew they'd been unable to break fresh ground due to the wetlands. Any new construction had to be on the footprint of existing buildings. Buildings that at one point, like most hospitals of this age, had been connected by service tunnels. The question was *Is it still connected? Or is this a tunnel to nowhere?*

Stepping over a mound of bricks that looked like a beaver lodge, he entered the tunnel. As he left the basement with its accidental moon roof, the air thickened. He bounced the light down at the slick floor. Grateful for his thick-soled shoes, he moved as quickly as he dared. Each step released dank gasses like rotting eggs and methane.

As he rounded a curve, the reception in his cell's compass app gave out. He ran the flashlight over the half-destroyed tunnel. Its cedar beams, like the ribs of a whale, were mostly intact. The swamp gasses and moisture, instead of destroying them, had started to ossify them. The bricks were another story, apparently not the best choice, as sections of the wall had caved under the weight of the swamp.

"Shit!" He stopped, or rather the tunnel did, his progress blocked by a wall of dirt and rock. "Now what?" Using both his cell's flashlight app and his Maglite, he did a 360. He shone the lights over the rocks and mud that had burst through the bricks. The cedar beams were intact, and he could see a section at the top where light passed to the other side of the obstruction.

Tucking his cell away, he toed into the avalanche. Rocks and bits of dried swamp mud skittered down. He inched up and felt the mucky layer on the floor start to give. He pressed his body in tight and hung on. Perched a couple of feet from the ground, he played the light over the opening. Gingerly he scraped at the top layer, trying to widen the gap. Dried mud crumbled in his fingers as he made a hole big enough to squeeze through.

Going headfirst, he pushed over the blockade, and his orange wig fell behind. Half-over, he felt the whole mess start to move, his added weight displacing the lower layers of mud. Bricks that had been wedged in place shifted and fell. One caught him across the back of his head, another in the cheek. *It's coming down!*

Pushing and pulling with his arms and legs, he hauled through and scrambled hands-first down the other face. He stuck the flashlight between his teeth as his once-white gloves sank wrist-deep in the ooze. Bricks tumbled, clobbering him in the back and the legs.

Gracelessly he belly crawled through the mud and pushed back panicked thoughts of being buried alive.

He scrambled to his feet and pulled the light from his mouth. The hole he'd made in the wall was gone. The mud floor was moving under the weight of the collapsing tunnel, pushing it out as more sections of the brick gave way.

He reached in his sopping pants for his cell. It was gone. "Shit!"

He turned away from the collapsing walls and swept the flashlight in the other direction. "No way!" Hope surged. Not twenty feet away was a steel door, and not an old one. As he approached it, he saw a moisture-crinkled specification label. Covered in greasepaint and swamp, he felt giddy as he read the date on the label—March 3, 2010. *This is it. This has to be the research pavilion.*

As quickly as hope blossomed, it shriveled as he searched for a handle. "What the hell?"

He moved his muddy hands over the metal door, leaving trails and tracks. He pressed and pushed and felt no give. Fear trickled through his veins. *You're going to die down here.*

"No!" Thoughts of Miles's peril hounded him. "You're not going to be able to save him. You're going to die here. And he'll never know." He replayed treasured memories. *You did tell him you loved him. Yeah, but like a friend. You really love him.*

He stared at the impregnable door. *You're going to die for him. Yeah, and that's not the problem. I'm going to die, and it's not going to help him. That's the problem.* He shone the light at the blocked tunnel. No going back, no going forward, and as he looked at the flashlight, which had dimmed and now started to flicker, he realized the batteries were on their last 10 percent. He berated himself for not putting in new ones.

"This is not going to happen."

He turned to the door in its galvanized steel frame. He traced each inch of the obstacle with his dying light and the palms of his hands. *A door without handles, just smooth steel… and hinges.*

The two barrel-shaped exposed hinges caught his attention. He felt for his pack. At least that was still there. Unzipping it, he retrieved a thin screwdriver and small hammer. Starting on the top hinge, he placed the tip of the screwdriver flush with the steel pin and tapped the screwdriver with the hammer. At first nothing, just the sharp ping reverberating through the tunnel. A few feet back, a section of brick crashed to the floor. He hit the hammer harder, and the pin moved. At first little more than a millimeter, and then another. The head of the pin rose up from the hinge as the screwdriver's tip traveled up. He quickened his blows, and the long pin cleared the last ring and toppled into the mud.

Without pause he dropped to his knees, sinking into the muck as he worked at the bottom hinge. The light was nearly gone, and as the second hinge pin came free, it died.

He rose from the mud and pressed against the door. Using his weight and pushing in, he felt it move. Without a handle to grab, all he had were the rings of the unhinged hinges. He gripped the top rings with his fingers as he rocked into the door. He felt the rings start to slide out of alignment. With his right arm against the outer edge of the door and his left on the top hinge, he pressed in hard. Back and forth he pushed and rolled with his hips and the weight of his torso.

He lost all sense of time, his focus on the door and the slowly separating hinge rings. The door canted as the top hinge separated.

Luke stepped back, repositioned his body, and with both hands, pulled at the exposed rings. The door held tight in its frame. He shifted his weight to the right and then the left. He kicked at the lower hinge and, using the back of his sneaker, knocked it free.

The door, suddenly free of its supports, fell onto him. *Shit! Not again.* It happened fast, and he wasn't ready. He'd not anticipated the weight, and he cursed for not having read the label. It was solid steel and hundreds of pounds. His arms strained to keep it from squishing him into the mud. His ruined clown gloves slid over the smooth metal as his feet sank ankle-deep into the goo.

Unable to see, he felt the door's heft between his flattened palms. He broadened his stance and tried to torque the door so it would fall off to the side. It wasn't working. The bottom of the door had sunk inches deep into the swamp, anchoring it in place.

He held still, his arms not able to take much more. He rethought his strategy, and feeling with his feet, he took shuffling steps back. As the door angled lower, its weight grew. He felt for the edge and knew that once he let go, if any part of him got caught underneath, he'd be trapped, injured, and food for whatever critters called this place home. The top edge slipped from his hands, ripping the surface of the cheap gloves. He stumbled back, his heel caught on a rock or brick, and he fell ass-first into the mud. He yanked his legs in tight as the door gave in to gravity, and with a slurp, settled into the swampy floor.

From behind he heard scurrying, slithering, and hopping as he wiggled his toes within his muddy socks, relieved his feet and all digits were still attached.

He stared into the darkness at where the door once stood. He saw a faint glow through the doorframe. Far from light, just less than pitch-black.

"Okay, then." Rising from the mud, he felt for his knapsack. He'd taken it off to get to the tools, and now it, like his cell phone, was gone. Beneath the clown suit, he patted the pocket of his jeans. His car keys and wallet were still safe.

But you're in. That's something. He walked across the sinking door and came to the open passage. As he crossed the threshold, cool air hit the sweat and mud on his face. He shivered and entered. He tripped a motion detector, and an overhead light went on. He blinked as he took in his surroundings, noting the dome camera in the ceiling and the white walls and floor he'd already marred with hand and footprints.

He stared at the camera and wondered who'd be watching late on a Saturday night. *Hopefully no one.* He jogged down the white hall, past three steel doors. He checked each. They were locked, and next to one was a keypad and scanner. *Keep moving.* For a second he heard a movement from behind the door.

"Miles?" He pressed his ear to the door. *Nothing. Keep moving.*

He bypassed the elevator with its keypad and fingerprint scanner and headed toward a final door with a sign overhead: Stairs.

He knew it would be locked, and as he placed his filthy hand on the lever, he wondered how he'd get through without any tools, with guards likely already aware of his presence, with…. Stunned, he looked at his hand as the lever pushed down and the door opened.

Thank you, Jesus. And with no clear plan other than to find Miles and get the hell out of there, he raced up.

CHAPTER 35

GERALD SIPPED Scotch as he edged around the lobby of Parker Hall. Near midnight the party was in full swing, and from experience, he knew it would last till either he put a cap on it or security swept up the stragglers in the morning and helped them into their cars, or cabs if they were too wasted to drive.

He'd stay through the stroke-of-midnight costume contest and then go back to the pavilion to follow up on the Daisy Osborn experiments. The woman with ankylosing spondylitis was immune to the first dose of the viral infection they'd injected immediately after her healing. Now, at the end of the grail's conferred protection, they'd see what the second dose of the virulent pathogen did. Chances were good she'd be dead by this time tomorrow. Yet these things could not be assumed; to understand how, and how long, the grail conferred immunity was important. For the AIDS subject, it had been twenty-four hours, and a bit shorter for Antoine Dey, eaten from the inside out by methicillin-resistant staphylococcus.

Pride swelled as he thought of his father and grandpapa. *What would they think of this? Of how far I've taken their discoveries.* Real strides, the science finally ready to take control of the grail. Not prone to sentimentality, Gerald knew his efforts rested on the shoulders of those who'd come before. *Father, Grandpapa, if only you could see this.*

His gaze fell on a pretty, young, and obviously drunk student with blonde hair, a mussed white tutu edged with feathers, and dark zombie eye makeup. She was barely upright, a condition that seemed to the liking of her companion, a medical resident dressed as a pregnant nun. What caused him to pause was the girl. *That's the one Calvin left with.* He checked the time. *And not more than an hour ago.*

So where is he? Through the eyeholes in his mask, he surveyed the rollicking scene. *This is useless. The boy could be anywhere.*

He approached the girl and her eager companion. "I think I know you," Gerald said, his tone casual.

The girl struggled to focus… and to stay upright. The horny nun wrapped a proprietary arm around her feathered waist and looked back at

Gerald. He was about to say something like "Get away, she's mine," but recognition set in, and the young doctor-in-training bridled his tongue.

"Dr. Stangl, great party… like always."

"Thanks." *He thinks I remember his name.* He looked familiar in that eager, fresh-faced way they all had. Bobby, Billy, Biffy. *I don't care. But why is this little slut here and not in the bushes with my son?*

The boy smiled. "You don't remember me. I'm Barry Leventhal. I spent a month out here my senior year."

Barry, right.… And Leventhal. "Thanks." Gerald eyed the girl and her dribbling drink. "And you are?"

"Huh?" She looked up and pointed her drink hand at him. "You're that TV guy. What's his name? Oh no, my drink." The smile turned to a comic frown as the last of her mojito's macerated mint leaves fell from her plastic cup. Like an on-off switch, she was back to smiles as she turned to the expectant… and expecting nun, Barry. "Get me another. Pleeeeeease."

Barry cast Gerald a worried look.

Moron. He thinks I want to poach his drunken slut. "Don't worry, I'll keep her safe for you."

"Thanks, Dr. Stangl."

"Please, it's a party. Call me Gerald." *And get the fuck out of here.*

"Right." The boy glanced across the mobbed dance floor at the distant bar, which was three deep with his colleagues looking to soak up as much free booze as their bodies could take.

"Can I get you anything?"

"I'm good," Gerald said. "Now go, get.…" He turned to the drunken ballerina. "What did you say your name was?"

"I'm Katie, Katie Swan." She looked down at her feather-trimmed outfit. "You know… from *Swan Lake.*"

"Lovely." He was a ball of curiosity. The girl was smashed. *So where's Calvin?* It was past time the boy shed his virginity… and that snippy attitude.

"You know.… *Swan Lake,*" the girl persisted. She flounced out her skirt with her hands, and white feathers floated to the floor.

"Yes, I can see you're a lovely ballerina."

"You don't get it.… No one gets it."

"Gets what, Katie?"

"I'm the white swan after she gets bitten by a zombie."

"Isn't that clever. So, Katie, I thought I saw you with my son a while back, a boy a bit younger than you, blond, had an arrow through his head." He watched the changes in her expression. Her booze-soaked brain and ghoulish makeup seemed to magnify her thoughts. He also detected an odor coming off her, and what he'd taken as a makeup effect dribbled down the front of her feathered corset and tulle skirt was vomit.

She gave him a wide-eyed smile. "You mean the little homo?"

Gerald froze. "What did you say?"

"Calvin, he's such a little cutie, but gay, gay, gay."

"You're mistaken."

Katie's flirty tone shifted. "And he's your son… and you didn't know. Oops. Think I let the cat out of the bag." She giggled. "Or the homo out of the closet."

"Come with me." He needed to get her away from the noise, to question her about this ridiculous assertion. *Calvin is not gay. How absurd… but he is soft, and….* "Now." He grabbed her by the upper arm.

"But my drink…. Where's Barry?"

"You can have as many drinks as you want. In fact… I'll take you to my private stash."

"Dr. Stangl, are you trying to get me drunk?"

You little whore, you're well past that. "Not at all." He glanced back and thought he saw the pregnant Jewish nun trapped at the bar. "Come on. A little fun, and then I'll get you right back to Barry the nun."

"Why would I want to bury the nun?" She let herself be pulled away to one of the dimly lit common rooms off the lobby. "Where are we going?" she asked.

"It's not much farther." He placed his fingers into the sensor, and the door to his administrative office slid open.

"Ooh, fancy," she cooed.

"Thank you." The door slid shut, sealing them in quiet. "So what happened with Calvin?"

"The homo?"

Gerald clenched his jaw and went to the liquor cabinet. This girl was a nightmare, her words like razors. "My son is not a homo."

"Look, Dr. Stangl. The kid brings me out back…. I figured, what the hell, he's cute, he's the big boss's son. What's the harm? Little Calvin didn't lay a finger on me."

"What?" Gerald poured himself a Scotch and selected a green-melon liquor for the girl. At the back of the cabinet was the bottle filled with the narcotic he'd given Calvin to help him get laid. Perhaps he'd given her too much. "Maybe you don't remember, Katie. You've had a lot to drink."

"Puh-lease, I remember puking my guts out in the bushes, and I remember your son running off like a rabbit."

"What? Where did he go?"

"Who knows? I do know this—any guy who's not gay would have taken what I was offering."

Gerald's fingers shook as he counted drops of the drug into the sweet green liquor. *One, two, three, four.* Each drop was enough to induce a dreamlike sleep. *Five, six, seven, eight…. Calvin is not gay, impossible…. Nine, ten, eleven, twelve….* Unwanted thoughts intruded—the way Calvin stared at the Fox boy… who was queer and made no bones about it. *Thirteen, fourteen, fifteen, sixteen, seventeen…. And there was something on the video. Calvin touched Fox more than was necessary to place the EKG leads on his chest. And his fingers were looped in his hair as he put on the EEG sensors. Eighteen, nineteen, twenty.*

"Here you go, Katie."

"What's that?" Her eyes were bright as she spotted the brilliant libation.

"It's delicious. Drink up."

"Mmm." She took the crystal tumbler and sniffed the contents. "Yummy."

Gerald raised his own glass in toast. "Bottoms up."

She giggled. "I bet that's what Calvin's doing right now." And she downed the contents.

He would have relished wrapping his hands around her pretty little neck, but he needed to move fast. He pried the drink from her hand and hustled her out of his office, back through the common room, and to the spot they'd been standing.

"Here comes the nun," he said, watching Barry's progress as he skirted dancers with two fresh mojitos.

"My hero," she slurred as the drug began to take effect.

"She's all yours, Barry." And with a smile and wink from behind his mask, Gerald headed off in search of Calvin.

The swan girl would go into respiratory arrest within an hour and be dead shortly thereafter. The drug, which was broken down in the liver into harmless components, would be undetectable at autopsy. With a bit of luck and timing, she'd drop dead beneath the rutting enthusiasm of Barry Leventhal. If Gerald weren't so plagued by her accusations, it would have made him smile. Nothing put the kibosh on a budding medical career like being caught with your pants down on top of a dead coed.

"You mean the homo?" Her words clanged inside his head. "Not possible… and where the fuck are you, boy?" And the answer that came back: "He's with Fox."

Barreling through the costumed revelers, he searched for Calvin. In his gut he knew she had told the truth. He felt sick as he headed into the humid night air. *I should have known. How could I have missed this? I should have smothered the boy in his sleep.* Nausea rose from his gut as he imagined Calvin mooning over Fox. He turned toward the research pavilion.

"What the fuck?" There was a light on the roof. At first he thought it must be the moon reflecting off metal. He squinted, ripped off his mask, and let it fall to the ground. "Not possible." What first appeared to be four sparkling lights were flames. Dumbstruck, he watched as they turned green, and then a fifth shot up.

"The little shit!" He tore off fast, realizing what Calvin was attempting. As his feet pounded the ground, he berated himself for his blindness. The soon-to-be-dead Katie was correct. *Calvin's queer. He's attempting the Zosimus configuration.* And that meant one thing. *He's in love with Fox…. The imbecile thinks Fox loves him back.*

Hounded by humiliation, rage, and nausea, Gerald ran. *Calvin… will fall from the roof. I do not have a homo for a son. I will have another son. I will take the gift and I will start again.*

CHAPTER 36

RESTRAINED ON his back, Miles stared into the night sky at a near-full moon and stars, a moist breeze against his face bringing faint strains of music. *Right. Halloween, big party.*

"You're awake," Calvin said. His pale face and ghost-blond hair hovered over him. "I'm glad. You have to be awake for this." He bit his lower lip.

"What are we doing here, Calvin?" *And why the fuck do you keep drugging me and tying me down?* He tried to move but was held fast by a strap across his chest and buckled leather ties that held him spread-eagled to the altar. He flexed his wrists and ankles; there was a little give. *I could probably slip the one on my right wrist.* "What's going on, Calvin?" He stared into his eyes. Something about him was not just nervous or excited, but… jubilant.

"It's tonight." Calvin placed a hand on Miles's shoulder.

Well past the creep factor, the contact was all Miles needed, and like watching a movie, he dove through Calvin's thoughts, where images of himself figured front and center, naked to the waist and strapped to an altar. The manuscript with Zosimus and Marta fluttered in the teen's head, and words, like an incantation: *Earth, wind, water, fire…. Love.*

"Tell me," Miles said, not breaking eye contact. "Tell me what we're doing." His use of "we" sent an expectant flurry through Calvin. With it came echoes from his own dreams and Tomas's stories. The wrong suitor, the magic fish who lost its head, and the girl—*Shut up and knit…. No, the time for that is over.* The boy's thoughts were fevered and disjointed, like a volcano set to blow. "It's okay, Calvin. Tell me. Everything is going to be okay. What are we doing?"

He faltered, gripping Miles's shoulder with his fingers. His thoughts spilled between them. *Earth, wind, water, fire, love. Earth, wind, water, fire, love.* Calvin struggled to voice a question…. The question.

And here it comes, Miles thought, knowing what was about to happen, and also not seeing a choice. Holding eye contact, he worked at the give in the restraints. *I could probably break free. There has to be a way off the roof… and then steal some clothes, get out of town. And leave Grandma*

Anna? And then what? Stangl will go after Maya, Mom, Dad. I can't run. He saw the intensity in Calvin's eyes and the words he so desperately wanted to say. *This is your shot… a sociopathic teen who's head over heels with you.* It was his only leverage, and in the spirit of divide and conquer, he read Calvin's fantasies of the two of them. What wasn't clear were his plans for dear old Father. *So bring it on, kid. Let's do this.*

"Do you…." Calvin swallowed. The words wouldn't come.

Miles drank in the boy's fear. He saw the words lined up in his head. *This is it, the trout is on the line. And what did they do with that fish? Come on, Calvin, it's time to reel you in and serve you up.*

Calvin averted his gaze. His fingers loosened on Miles's shoulder.

"Just say it, Calvin." He felt the boy's doubt, the paralyzing fear he was about to be taken for a fool. "Just say it." Miles saw the manuscript in Calvin's thoughts, the drawing of Zosimus and Marta, and more importantly, what he'd heard from the ancient alchemist's mouth. "Calvin. You have to. It's part of this." The latter was speculation, but Calvin's fear began to lose its grip. "I won't bite… unless you want me to."

The humor and promise in Miles's tone swept away Calvin's trepidation. His pale eyes, lit by the moon, stared down at his restrained beloved. "Do you love me?"

Are you fucking insane, you nut ball? "Yes, Calvin," Miles said, not breaking eye contact and placing as much sincerity as he could muster into his voice. "I love you." Sensing the cheesy teen script needed to go both ways, he pressed for the obvious. "Do you love me?"

"Oh yes, Miles. I do. I do love you."

Miles shuddered. The tapes running inside Calvin's head were a scary mix of Disney and wedding marches. And he knew what needed to happen to seal the deal. The kid was his, body and soul…. *As long as he thinks the same is true for you. Reel the fish in.* "Calvin?"

"Yes, Miles."

"If you love me, you have to kiss me." He braced and thought of Grandma Anna as Calvin bent over for his Sleeping Beauty moment. His thoughts flew to Luke, and just like that, he didn't have to fake it.

As their lips connected, he watched Calvin's thoughts fly apart, replaced by bliss. In truth Miles felt bad. While not up there with chopping off people's heads, tricking a seventeen-year-old boy in love wasn't something to feel proud of. Random thoughts and images spilled out of Calvin, and something dark as well, like a gaping hole inside of him.

Miles refocused on Luke, knowing he'd never see him again, glad at least he was safe from this nightmare. He pictured that first kiss… actually their second, but that one in the bathroom when Luke practically attacked him. That was love… and lust…. *And the best friend I've ever had. Have a life, Luke. Even if I survive this, you need to stay away from me.*

As Calvin tentatively reached for Miles's tongue with his own, Miles foraged through the boy's thoughts. It wasn't words or even images that flooded back, more a kind of knowing as though reading Calvin's essence, the years of indoctrination by his father, a crushing loneliness, a motherless hole in his heart, and something else. Hidden behind ebullient teen love lurked something reptilian. Trapped in the kiss, Miles dove toward the scary truth, the part of Calvin Stangl that was like an on-off switch for anything remotely human. It was dark and frightening, and Miles headed straight into it, needing to see, needing to know.

The images came fast. Antoine Dey strapped to a table as Calvin decapitated him with a surgical-steel bone saw. The attack on Grandma Anna in her kitchen. Injecting deadly toxins into Antoine, Trevor, and Daisy. Words hovered around the coldness and the cruelty: *I am a machine. These creatures are of no consequence. I am a machine. I will be immortal. They will bow before me. I will be their god. They will worship me.*

Calvin slowly pulled back. "I love you so much."

Miles felt the air between them, the kid's hunger like a ravenous animal. "I love you too, Calvin. So tell me, what are we doing up here?" And with Calvin's eyes fixed on his own, Miles flexed and relaxed his hands inside the restraints. The one on the right was definitely loose. *I think I can slip them.*

CALVIN'S BODY sizzled. His lips sparkled with the aftereffects of Miles, so different from the stolen kisses when he'd been drugged and unconscious. *This is real. This is happening. He loves me! He said he loves me.* "I'll tell you everything," he said, finding his voice. "I didn't before because I wasn't sure."

"Not sure?" Miles asked.

"Of us." Calvin glanced across the rooftop, and then like a honeybee seeking nectar, right back to that beautiful face, those eyes, those lips…. *"I love you."*

"There's nothing to be afraid of, Calvin. It's just you and me."

"Forever," Calvin whispered. It was hard to speak, even to breathe. "We have to move fast. If Father finds out… he'll stop us. He'll…. No, that's not going to happen." It felt so odd, scary, and also wonderful to finally confide in another person.

"What would he do?" Miles asked.

"You don't want to know. He's not a nice man."

"You have to tell me, Calvin. That's just one of the rules for people who love each other. They share everything. No secrets, at least not about anything important."

Calvin couldn't have held back; there was something so hypnotic about his beautiful lover. "From now on I won't worry about Father and what he might do. In fact…. Miles, we have to move fast. Tell me I can trust you, and I'll believe you."

"I love you, Calvin. You can trust me."

He felt like a balloon filled with joy. "This is what we're going to do. It's only ever worked one time before. It's called the Zosimus configuration. We've not talked a lot about your gift, but you know that's what this is about."

"Yeah, I got that. So who's this Zosimus, and what exactly are we configuring?" Miles smiled.

The effect on Calvin was immediate. "I want another kiss."

"Hell yes, me too, but if we're worried about Father interrupting, perhaps we should save that until after… whatever it is we have to do here."

Calvin stumbled, as he'd begun to lean over for the kiss. "Of course… you're right." He tried to tamp back the disappointment that spread like a cancer over his mood. He narrowed his gaze as he studied Miles's perfect face, those glittering eyes, those lips. Doubt blossomed in his belly, almost too painful to bear.

"It's okay, Calvin. A quick kiss."

The husk of Miles's voice, the brush of his breath against Calvin's face, pushed away the darkness. "Thank you," he whispered and clamped his lips to Miles's. *Even better.* Smells and tastes and feelings too wonderful to miss. Like an untapped fountain erupting with joy and love. Reluctantly he pulled back. "Thank you." Of course Miles was right. They had to be careful. *What would Father do if he saw that?* "We should start."

"Tell me what we're doing."

"Yes." With one hand hovering over Miles's restrained chest, he looked back at the steel case. "It's the grail, you know."

"What is?" Miles asked.

"You. It's not what people think. It's a kind of magic that travels in your bloodline. It's very ancient. It's what lets you heal people, and in some stories, there may be other abilities attached to it."

Calvin copped a last feel of that warm wonderful skin before turning away and retrieving the case. He clicked it open and pulled out the first of the chalices. "My family, like yours, is very old, but our bloodline is pure. Yours has been mixed and mingled. We go back to a sacred order of knights, and before that to a lineage of mages…. The Seekers." Calvin felt odd speaking the family history aloud to anyone other than Father. It was forbidden. He held the first chalice in the moonlight so Miles could see the perfect form and symmetry of his handiwork.

"What are the goblets for?" Miles asked.

That voice. It was hard to think straight. *He loves me. He really loves me.*

"Calvin?"

Love songs and poems flitted through his thoughts, all suddenly making sense. *If I could dive into those eyes, I would swim forever. But no. Stay focused.* A sliver of fear pushed him into action. *Father means to kill him. That will not happen.*

He placed the first of the goblets in the circular indent above Miles's head. "This points true north." From out of a pocket, he pulled a plastic baggie with a few ounces of soil and emptied it into the goblet. *North is earth.*

He got up to retrieve the second and third, placing them in the southern and eastern points. *South is air.* The chalice was left empty. Into the eastern vessel he poured water.

"These chalices, which have to be made of pure silver, are like you, a vessel for the grail. But unlike you"—and he placed the fourth goblet in the western position—"they can only hold the magic for a time. It needs a human vessel, and from all we can tell, it must be one that contains your DNA…. But there was an exception."

"Is that the Zosimus configuration?"

"Yes, that's right." *He's smart and he's beautiful, and he loves me. Yes, but stay focused.*

From his lab coat pocket, he retrieved a tightly sealed mason jar. He unscrewed it, and the smell of the kerosene-soaked rag filled his nostrils. *From the west comes fire. And with it the clock starts.*

He flicked his lighter, lit the rag, and dropped it into the goblet. The fire would burn for five minutes. *Five minutes from now, your life will have changed forever.* He pulled the final and slightly larger chalice from the case. Its upper and lower bell-shaped chambers were broader than the others and better suited for where it would be placed.

"Do you know who Zosimus was?" Calvin asked.

"No."

Calvin's hands trembled as he approached Miles with the fifth chalice, his eyes riveted to the lean torso spread before him. He swallowed, finding little moisture in his mouth. "He was a great scientist and the leader of the Seekers. He wrote a series of books, the *Khemia*. He was the father of chemistry. Over two thousand years ago, he understood the workings of molecules and the interplay of visible and invisible forces. He fell in love with a woman who carried the grail, and she fell in love with him. It was the one and only time the grail has ever been transferred, or rather shared, between two people. Some say it's a legend and that it never happened."

"And that's what we're doing," Miles said.

Calvin nodded as he approached with the final chalice and placed it gently over Miles's navel, its broader base giving it stability. "Yes." It took all his restraint to not splay his hands across that magnificent body, to press his own against it. But the passing of seconds weighed on him. *He loves me. There will be time for that… all the time in the world.* "You need to keep still. We have to hurry."

"Sure, what now?"

"Blood." Reluctantly he removed his hand, fascinated at how the chalice seemed rooted to Miles's abdomen.

"Whose?"

"Ours, but don't worry. I have yours already. Did you know it's darker than other people's?" *Shut up, you idiot.* He glanced at the fire chalice, its blue-and-orange flame dancing in the night. When he'd practiced this, timing how long the kerosene rag would burn, trying different textiles, it had always been away from breezes that would fuel and speed the incineration. *You don't have five minutes. It's burning too fast. Move!*

"Seriously?"

"Yes, it's subtle, not the kind of thing anyone would notice." *What comes next? Stay focused.*

"What makes it darker?"

"I don't know." He shuddered. "Father's obsessed with finding out. He thinks it might be how the grail travels…. Something in your blood." Nearly tripping over the eastern vessel, he removed an IV bag from the metal case. "I took this while you were sleeping."

He ripped the plastic stopper from the bag. *This is it.* Heart pounding and barely able to catch his breath, he portioned Miles's blood into the four directional chalices. He heard the sizzle and smelled the acrid smoke as it met the fire of the west, careful to hold back a few precious ounces for the goblet that covered his navel. *The chalice of love.* Like squeezing toothpaste, he watched the last drops pour out. He placed his hand again on Miles's chest, feeling the muscles and his ribs. The moon reflected off the blood's surface, making it appear not red, but white.

"You need to stay perfectly still."

"What comes now?"

"My blood." *You moron, you nearly forgot. You only get one chance. Don't fuck this up.*

He scurried back to the case for the tied bundles of dried sage coated with myrrh. Holding them bunched in his fist, he lit them. He watched the flames spread, the resinous myrrh fueling the fire. Once they caught, he blew hard, extinguishing them and filling the air with fragrant smoke. The five bundles glowed and he hurried around the altar, placing them beside the goblets. The fire goblet still burned, but not as bright. *You have to hurry.*

Without pause he laid the final bundle of smoldering sage beside Miles, careful to not let the embers touch his precious skin. *Think… think, Calvin. Have you done everything? The grail, the vessels, earth, wind, water, fire, love… his blood, the incense… it's done.*

He dug into his pocket and retrieved the capped ceramic scalpel. He ripped off the protective cover, and holding his left arm in the moonlight, made a decisive incision over his left wrist. *Too deep. Shit!* He watched as droplets of blood blossomed on his skin. He felt no pain, but there was something else happening. *It's starting.* He felt it, not just his own excitement, but something shimmered in the air. He looked at Miles as the droplets coalesced and a pulse of blood gurgled over his hairless wrist. *You hit an artery.*

"You're glowing. Miles, it's happening! It's not just the moon."

"It's your blood," Miles said. "The second you cut yourself, I felt the gift, the grail…. It's moving. I don't know if it's the pain or your blood, but something's happening."

"Yes."

Gushing blood, Calvin raced to the northern point and chanted in ancient Greek, the words worn familiar through untold hours of practice. He watched his blood mingle with Miles's and the dirt of the swamp, and for the briefest instant saw a flash of green light shoot from the goblet. *This is going to work. It's going to work.* Not stopping, he repeated the same at the southern, eastern, and the fiery western vessel. The barely perceptible spark grew as his blood joined Miles's and the elements. Suddenly the flashes of green, like friends joining hands, found one another and formed a floating band of emerald luminescence. *The color of his eyes.*

With the four directions complete, he turned to his true love, the man he would join for eternity. They would march hand in hand through time; they would witness the rise and fall of civilizations. Never breaking the chant and holding his bloody wrist in front of him, he approached Miles. *This is our wedding. We are being joined.*

His blood gurgled forth, soaking the cuff of his jacket. It splattered to the ground. His lips never stopped their chanting as the vibrant green danced around them. *Earth, wind, water, fire.* He held his now shaking wrist over Miles. His blood spurted all around, mostly missing the goblet. Taking his other hand, he steadied his damaged wrist, needing the blood in the chalice but aroused by the sight of it on Miles's bare chest. *Earth, wind, water, fire, love.* Green flames shot from the fifth goblet. The emerald fire flew up, and then, like a fountain, it sparked out to the edges, joining the band of light that encircled them.

Still chanting, Calvin looked up in wonder. The moon was nearly obscured by the dome of sparkling green. He gazed back at Miles. Perhaps it was the blood loss, or the excitement, or the magic. But standing there, his blood pulsing out onto his beloved, he had never felt such bliss. There was a moment's revelation, not just that this was joy… or even love, true love… but that this was his. Miles was his, and there was one final step to be accomplished. Now, just like in the fairy tales Father once read when he was very young…. *Now the kiss.*

CHAPTER 37

LUKE OPENED the stairwell door marked with the letter B. Aware his movements were captured by cameras, he was alert for the sounds of security.

He stared down the hall. *That one's open.* He ran toward a patient ward with an odd transparent front wall. Inside, he looked from the gleaming-white nurses' station to….

Too late. Hope surged and crashed with the beating of his heart. He stared at the empty room… cell. He saw the mussed-up bed linens. *Too late.* A rubber tourniquet littered the floor along with the wrappings from a needle. It was discordant with the sterility of the cell. *Someone was in a hurry.*

And then he saw Anna Warren, Miles's grandma, unconscious, helpless, and her head shaven. He noted the feeding tube down her nose. *And Stangl put her there so Miles would see, so he'd do whatever sick thing they wanted…. Where are you? What have they done to you? Are you even still alive?*

He circled the space, his movements captured on camera.

He needed to get out of there, but something didn't add up. Someone had left the door to this futuristic ward wide open. *Why?* Stangl was brilliant and calculating. If getting his hands on Miles and his abilities was the plan, it had been hatched over decades. *That doesn't fit with leaving a door open… at least not by accident. Something's happening.*

Behind the nursing station, he discovered the array of monitors. There was movement in one that showed the approach to the building. *Stangl.* He was running toward the camera and then got picked up on a second monitor entering the building. His mouth was twisted, his jaw tight. His fury was obvious. Luke watched as Stangl stopped and stared up. He reached into his breast pocket and retrieved something dark that reflected for a brief instant in the moonlight.

A gun! Luke had seconds at best to get out of there. Whatever had happened here involved someone else. *But who? Did Miles escape?* He scanned the monitors, his attention pulled by something his brain at first registered as a defective screen filled with static. But no…. The black-and-white image behind the thick lines of… *whatever the hell that is. That's Miles. What the—?*

Nearly obscured by the weird static was Miles, bare-chested and restrained on a platform. *The roof.* There was a blond man with him, his hair white on the screen. It took a second for Luke to make the connection with the shy but talented teen who had audited anatomy—*Stangl's son.* He was climbing on top of Miles. *Get off him.* But that wasn't the strangest part; it was those lines. *What the hell are those?* One shot out from Miles's belly like a cresting fountain. He glimpsed the blond's rapturous face. *What is that shiny liquid? He's bleeding.* The young Stangl lay on top of Miles, and Luke saw the drenched sleeve of his lab coat, and blood, spasming arterial blood. The boy was hurt. *But deliberate. He did that to himself.*

He glanced down the row of screens. Stangl the elder was no longer visible, probably on his way to the roof…. *Or here.*

Luke bolted from the all-white unit. At least now he knew where Miles was… under some bleeding teen son of a sociopath. *Like father, like son. Why is the kid bleeding? Calvin, his name is Calvin.* He slowed as he approached the elevator. Just beyond it was the stairwell. The light above the elevator showed it was headed up. *Stangl's going to the roof.*

He grabbed the stairwell door and hauled ass. He took the steps in twos, his thoughts tortured by what he'd just seen. *Why is Calvin Stangl bleeding? He cut himself… but why? Why does Dr. Stangl have a gun?*

His long legs pounded up the stairs, his emotions too hot to think smart. There was so much blood. *That's it! It's not the blood. The kid is wounded. He did it to pull the healing gift from Miles.* That was the source of the lines on the screen. Miles had been right all along. It was what Stangl was after. *So he's using his son… like some sort of bait, to pull it out of him? Then why wasn't Stangl there? Why was he running? Why does he look furious? Why does he have a gun?*

The elevator stopped overhead, and he heard footsteps on metal stairs. A door banged open, and then less loudly, it shut. Winded but not stopping, Luke strained to hear.

He cleared the last flight and cautiously opened the door. He saw the two long boards on the floor and thought about grabbing one as a club. *Way too big.* He ran up the short flight of steel stairs to the roof. He paused, his ear to the door. *He has a gun….*

Cracking the door open, he blinked and tried to make sense of the brilliant green swirl before him. Sparkling lights hummed and danced across his vision. They came from the center of the roof. Their luminescence made it hard to focus. There was a pulsing dome, and he could make out Miles's prone form. Calvin Stangl was on top of him. *What the hell? Is he kissing Miles?* He squinted, searching for Dr. Stangl. And then he heard a shot.

GERALD'S AIM was off, his mind fixed like a laser on the scene before him. *My son is a homo.* He aimed again, sighting the barrel at Calvin's shocked face, his lips plump from kissing, his eyes wide and sparking with the reflected green. Gerald's revulsion welled. *I have no son.* He squeezed the trigger.

Calvin dropped off Fox and vanished behind the altar. *I have no son!* Gerald saw blood on the ground and smelled it burning in the air as the green fire sparkled around the tied-up Fox. *I'll get to you soon enough. You did this to my boy. And now I have no son.*

The lights from the grail were blinding and beautiful. In any other circumstance, this would have been a moment of triumph. The grail was exposed, ripe for the taking… which was just what Calvin had attempted to do…. *Without me! My son is a queer.*

With the small-caliber Colt raised, Gerald edged around the dancing lights. *So beautiful.* He noted the placement of the chalices and the one still balanced on Fox's navel. *The fool. I have no son. Where are you? Come and taste lead, you little queer.* It took all his restraint to not turn the gun on the scum responsible for this. But Fox could not be wasted…. *Not yet… but maybe. Everything was prepared. The grail was exposed.*

He edged around the altar, his focus down the barrel. *I have no son. I will make a new one… a better one. One who is perfect.* He spotted droplets of wet blood. *Come out, come out, wherever you are.*

There was a flash of movement behind an air handler. Placing one stealthy foot in front of the other, he approached. He tasted bile, his mind poisoned by the image of Calvin kissing Fox. It was all that was sick in the world, the Fox boy an amalgam of Gypsy, Jew, and queer. And Calvin fell in love… with that. *I have no son.* A humorous smile crept over Gerald's lips as the back of Calvin's lab coat came into view. The boy was huddled behind the air handler. He was shaking. It sickened Gerald further. *He's sobbing. I have no son. This abomination will not continue.* He aimed, inhaled, and squeezed on the exhalation.

As if sensing the killing shot, Calvin turned and faced his father.

He knew he was going to die. He stared at Father's masklike face, hatred etched in his smile. "Shoot me, Father. Just do it." Death was preferable to this horrible pain that spread through his chest. *How could this have failed? I love him.* The feel of Miles's lips was still on his. *I love him, and he loves me.* "Do it!" he shrieked.

Gerald stared at Calvin's huddled and pathetic form. His smile grew as he voiced the thing Calvin most feared. "He doesn't love you, you fucking little queer. You're weak, and you're soft, and you're stupid. He doesn't love you. He tricked you. That's why it didn't work."

Worse than any bullet, the truth ripped through Calvin. *I want to die.* He shut his eyes. *I want to die.*

Concealed behind a vent stack, Luke knew he'd get one chance. He'd heard that first shot and knew he was too late. It took all of his will to not rush Stangl, but it wasn't Miles at the end of Dr. Strangelove's barrel; it was his son. The thought of gunning down Stangl's son who'd stolen kisses from Miles, after tying him down and doing God knows what, didn't seem so awful. And from a pragmatic perspective, one Stangl to deal with versus two seemed like better odds.

Luke followed Stangl's progress as he pursued his son. The green lights around Miles danced before him, sparkly and hypnotic. And inside them Miles was alive and no longer lying down. He had worked one of his hands free. He'd also unfastened the restraint around his middle and was furiously twisting his left wrist to get it free. His chest was covered with something dark and slick…. *Blood. What have they done to him?*

A second shot ripped the air, and the green lights sizzled and flared. Behind them Luke heard the music of the party. He knew there'd be no rescue, no SWAT teams to swarm the roof. It came down to him and his actions in the next few seconds. *Go after Stangl or try to free Miles? No, too risky. Take out the threat.*

He heard Stangl's voice. "He doesn't love you, you fucking little queer. You're weak, and you're soft, and you're stupid. He doesn't love you. He tricked you. That's why it didn't work."

Luke used Stangl's rant—*sounds like my father*—to track his location. He crept past the altar, glad to put himself between Miles and the madman trying to gun down his child. It took all he had to not go to Miles, but the risk was too great.

He focused on Stangl, his gun raised, his son crouched before him on the ground. There was blood on the side of the boy's head. *Is he hit?* Without pause Luke sprinted toward Stangl, who was primed for the kill. Years of Pop Warner and high school football, combined with hours with Miles at Krav Maga, kicked in. He tackled low and hard. The impact caused Stangl's knees to buckle as his finger, poised on the trigger, took the shot.

Stangl grunted as Luke's velocity and forward momentum pitched his face into the roof's rough surface. Stangl twisted beneath Luke's weight and freed himself.

The move was unexpected and threw Luke's balance. Grasping for Stangl's waist, he glimpsed the gun in his hand. To let go would mean death.... *Take out Stangl!*

Luke pressed his legs into the ground, and throwing his weight against Stangl, he pushed with all he had. With his head and shoulders against the crazed doctor's chest, he never saw Stangl's raised gun hand as he brought it down. The steel grip of the Colt hit behind Luke's ear. The impact was strategic and effective.

No! Luke fought to hold on as the blow to his head rippled down his spine. He felt his nerves and muscles lose control, his legs weakened, as blackness washed over him. *No.* His last thought before losing consciousness was of Miles. He'd failed them both, and unable to fight it, he fell into the dark.

MILES, SURROUNDED by the eerie green lights, worked feverishly at the last leather restraint around his right ankle. The time to shut up and knit had passed, and knowing that Luke was there brought a war of hope and fear. His fingers bled as he worked the tough leather, yanking it back and forth. Slick blood that had spilled from the goblet made it hard to get purchase on the buckle, but as it dribbled onto his ankle, it worked like a lubricant. Pushing past the pain, he yanked back on his foot, twisting one way and then another until it scraped out of the still buckled manacle, ripping skin in the process. He pivoted on top of the altar. There was smoke and the acrid smell of burning blood.

He saw Luke and Stangl silhouetted in the moonlight, like wrestlers, and then Stangl's raised hand came down. The barrel of the gun glinted. There was the thud of impact, and horrified, he saw Luke fall. *No!*

It happened in an instant, but time lost all sense. It seemed forever to cross the few yards that separated Miles from Stangl. There was no more reasoning, no more weighing the pros and cons of his actions. There was only fury as he threw his fist into the back of Stangl's head, striking the soft spot where the skull connected to the spine. He followed with his left a millisecond later in a crippling kidney punch. Miles did not stop; to do so was death. He couldn't pause to see if Luke was alive, but he glanced once in Calvin's direction to make certain the boy was down and would stay down.

Stangl, still clutching his gun, attempted to turn. Miles kept to his back, throwing rocket punch after punch, his focus on the sweet spot at the base of Stangl's skull. He landed blow after blow. *Why won't he go down?* His knuckles bled as Stangl whipped back his gun hand in an attempt to throw him off.

Miles dodged, but was unable to keep to his back as Stangl took the opening, turned, and with an unsteady hand, brought the gun between them.

Before he could fire, Miles slammed his bare foot onto Stangl's instep while shooting the palm of his right hand into his throat with full force. It was a maneuver he'd practiced thousands of times. Always with padded opponents, always pulling the punch… but not now. He felt and heard the cartilage in Stangl's throat as it cracked. He saw Stangl's eyes bug in shock and pain. But the gun was still there, and without pause, Miles blocked with his elbow and grabbed Stangl's wrist. With blood-slick fingers, he dug deep for the release point. If Stangl could have screamed, he would have. The Colt fell to the roof, followed by Stangl, who clutched his throat, unable to breathe through his crushed trachea.

Miles caught his breath as he stared at the dying man. Stangl was trying to speak, but no words came through his shattered airway.

Fueled by blood and pain, the green lights swirled. The dome of luminescence that centered around the altar and the goblets now followed Miles. He stepped back from Stangl, seeing how the green glow wanted to attach itself to the man's wounds as Stangl's legs kicked, and his fingers clawed at his ruined throat. *That's not going to happen.*

He stepped away, pulling the lights with him. *Where's Luke?* The awful image of him falling beneath Stangl's blow was fixed in his mind. *Where's the gun? Where the fuck is Calvin?* He'd been right in front of him, half-hidden behind the air handler. With an eye on Stangl but far enough away to not inadvertently heal him, he glanced to where the gun had fallen, or he thought it had fallen. *Where the fuck is it? Where's Luke?* The green blurred his vision, like being inside a glowing fish tank. *Where's Luke?*

He heard movement behind the air handler. Edging back, feeling with his bare feet, he circled to the right. Stangl's movements grew less frantic. *He's dying. You killed him.* A part of his brain had to shut down, the part that wanted to help. *No, he needs to die.* As he moved back and off to the side, he spotted all three missing things—Calvin, Luke… and in Calvin's hand, the gun.

All thoughts of Stangl's death throes fled. There, captured in the moon's glow like a twisted pietà, was Calvin, Luke bleeding and smeared in clown makeup clutched in his arms, with the gun pressed to his temple.

Calvin's face was streaked with tears and blood. He looked at Miles. His breath came in short gasps, his trembling gun hand steadied by Luke's temple.

Miles stopped as the green lights hovered and danced. The edge of the dome pushed out like fingers or the plasmid movement of an amoeba sensing food. Only it wasn't food this thing inside him wanted. It wanted to ease pain, to stop the blood, and to calm suffering. Like a beggar at a banquet, the grail swirled about him. Miles stopped. "Let him go, Calvin. Please…."

The boy seemed in shock. His hand shook. Miles held his breath. The distance between them was at least forty feet, too far to attempt a frontal attack. By the time he could clear the distance, Luke, who was breathing but unconscious, would be dead. *Not even the grail can bring back the dead.* "Let him go, please."

Calvin bit his lip as he tightened an arm around Luke, clutching him like a blanket. "No."

"Please." Miles risked the tiniest of forward steps.

"Stay back!"

"Calvin." Miles's gaze bore into him. He searched for the kid's thoughts, but without the physical connection, there was nothing. *Say nothing and knit.* He stopped. *It's the grail. It's thinking... no, feeling.* Without knowing what he was doing, he rode the alien sensation, like an arm that started in his gut and extended beyond his physical body. As he did, the glow that surrounded him sent out a whiplike projection. It lashed forward and touched down on Calvin's face. In that moment Miles was inside his head. Calvin's thoughts were jumbled and disconnected. Most of them were of his father, gun raised, spewing words of hate. But that wasn't the worst, the thing that fueled a pain worse than anything Miles could have imagined. At first he wasn't certain if he was reading thoughts, but no, Calvin moved his lips, and his anguish filled the space between them.

"You said you loved me," he said, his words both question and accusation. "You said you loved me!" He pressed the barrel of the gun into Luke's temple.

Miles was trapped. He had no words to calm the storm inside Calvin. *So much pain.* None of it was physical. *This is heartbreak.*

"Say something!" Calvin demanded as he hugged Luke's limp body. "Say something, please, please…."

The grail, like a giant green amoeba, engulfed the three of them. The space between them sparked with energy. Like flipping between channels, Miles tapped the disconnected dreams inside Luke, and more…. Stangl's blow had shocked his spine. When… if… he awoke, his legs would be paralyzed. *But no.* The grail had begun its magic. Its bubbling essence flooded into Luke and danced along his damaged spine.

Miles held Calvin's gaze, but the words that might have calmed the teen would not come. He thought of Grandma Anna and how easily she told lies. Her entire life she had concealed who she was and the gift she possessed.

"Please… talk to me," Calvin begged.

"You know the truth," Miles said as he used the dazzling green to conceal his feet as he inched closer. There was calm inside the shimmering dome, as though the three of them had been transported to a world where only they existed. "Calvin, put the gun down. Don't let anyone else get hurt. No one else has to die. That was your father. It doesn't have to be you."

His words touched Calvin.

"Do you love me?" Calvin repeated, his thoughts filled with precious images of Miles, of kisses stolen and well-worn daydreams of a life together… of eternity together.

The lies would not come; the grail would not tolerate them. *I love Luke, and if I say that, what will he do?* "Calvin." *Huh, there it is again.* The sound of his voice was doing something to the kid, like gentling a frightened animal. He tested the theory. "Calvin, you're in shock. You're going to get through this. We're all going to get through this." His words acted like oil on the troubled seas of Calvin's thoughts and emotions.

Inch by inch Miles shuffled forward, his eyes never leaving Calvin's. He kept moving his lips. "Everything, Calvin, everything is going to work out. You'll be happy. You'll be free."

As Calvin relaxed, the shimmering green swelled. Miles felt it flow inside Luke and soothe Calvin's heartache. It was doing something to him as well. It flowed down his arms, and his fingers started the dance he'd come to associate with the healing gift. Like flying over the arpeggios of a violin concerto, he let it take control. *Only I'm still here.*

"Calvin, it's going to be okay." *Why do I believe that? And what the fuck is happening with my feet?* Torn between looking down and maintaining the contact with Calvin, he tried to make sense of the fact that he'd stopped shuffling forward. Or rather his feet weren't moving, but he was. *Keep talking. Don't think about it. Just shut up and knit.* "You're going to be okay. You're smart. You'll figure this out." And realizing the grail was fueled by all that was positive and true, he threw Calvin a bone. "We'll figure this out. It's going to fine. You're going to be okay."

Like a cobra with a snake charmer, Calvin was entranced. His breath came in shallow gasps through his parted lips. He relaxed his gun hand and fixed his focus on Miles.

Yes, Calvin thought, repeating Miles's words inside his head, *we'll figure this out. I'm going to be fine. I'm going to be okay. So pretty*, he thought of the dancing green lights. *But wait!* Something inside Calvin resisted. *No, go away. You're trying to trick me.* This voice was dark and carried traces of Father's venom. *"You're soft. He doesn't love you."*

"Calvin, I need you with me. I'm going to help you. We're going to get through this."

The dark thing in Calvin struggled to the surface. *He doesn't love you. It's a trick to save his boyfriend. Turn the switch, Calvin. Do it. Turn the switch. Pull the trigger. I am a machine.*

"Calvin, stay with me." Miles sensed the change, and with less than two yards between them, he sprang. As he did, the reptilian thing that allowed Calvin to chop off heads and kidnap old women and terminally ill patients took control.

Miles wrapped his hands around Calvin's throat and used the forward momentum to break his grip on Luke. He both felt and heard the gunshot.

He screamed as the bullet entered Luke's brain. "No!" Miles grabbed for the gun. With an iron grip, he caused Calvin to drop the firearm as he forced him to the ground.

The grail struggled for control. There was so much pain, so much blood. It twisted and howled. It did not want Miles to hurt the boy.

"No!" Miles shouted into the night. He would not give up control. "No!" And as much as the grail fought, Miles brought his fist down hard against Calvin's temple and his other fist under the jaw with practiced efficiency, shattering teeth and knocking him out.

The grail howled at the violence.

Miles rolled off Calvin and saw Luke unmoving on the ground. "No!"

The green was all around, but where it had sparkled, it was now like the dying embers of a winter's fire. "No…." He scrambled on hands and knees to get to Luke. "Oh God, no."

He smelled gunpowder and the singe of burned hair, bone, and flesh. He felt the sticky blood that oozed from Luke's scalp.

"No." He wrapped his body around Luke's and felt for traces of life. *Please, please.* The grail thrashed inside of him. *Please! Don't be dead.* He tried to focus, to calm his despair. *Please.* He pressed his head against Luke's. He felt slick greasepaint and blood against his cheek. *Please.* He hugged Luke tight, feeling through the bare flesh of his chest for any spark of life. *Please.* He listened, not through his ears, but through the grail. *Show me. Show me what I have to do. I love him. Please help me. Help him. He can't be dead. He can't be*.... He kissed the side of Luke's face, and that's when he felt it. Like halves of a live circuit, there was a spark… a heartbeat, and then another.

Barely able to breathe, Miles felt at the base of Luke's neck for a pulse…. *He's alive. Please help me. I love him. Show me.* The grail swelled and poured from Miles into Luke and back again. Miles's fingers danced as he gave himself in to the miracle.

Luke shuddered in his arms. Then he took a breath, and then his thoughts returned.

Luke opened his eyes and found Miles's. "I love you." The air crackled between them. "I think I was dead… or almost, and that's what I most regretted. I never told you. I never said I love you, Miles. Not like a friend, but like…."

"I know." Miles would have said more, a lot more, when Luke's lips found his.

They kissed, and as they did, the green dome exploded like a Fourth of July chrysanthemum firework.

Calvin awoke to the sight of their kiss. He wailed, "No!"

His shrieks, far louder than the gunshots, carried over the sounds of the party and alerted hospital security that something was wrong.

Lost in each other and the kiss, neither Miles nor Luke heard it. Nor were they aware they had completed the Zosimus configuration. The brilliant energy danced between them. It healed Luke and expelled the bullet from his brain. It wove its magic, like a bridge, between the two men.

ON THE ground, hospital security, including those doing overtime for the party, raced to the research pavilion, followed by a costumed and drunken swarm. The crowd knew something had happened, but what they witnessed was bizarre. A light show on the roof, someone setting off green fireworks, and a man screaming. One witness would later say, "It wasn't really a scream, more like an animal in pain…. Like a howl."

CHAPTER 38

THE KISS with Luke—the element of unconditional love—completed the spell. The green lights rocketed into the night sky, crested in two, and dove back into Miles and Luke. Then it was gone, leaving neither shimmer nor sparkle.

Calvin held his knees, sobbed, and wailed. His self-slashed wrist and whatever physical injuries inflicted by Father had been healed, their presence marked by his blood-soaked jacket and clumps of matted hair from the grazing shot.

Luke pocketed the gun, his thoughts crisp in Miles's head. *He's down, but he's not out.* They held hands and waited for what seemed hours, but it was less than five minutes for the guards and the trail of partygoers to make it onto the roof. Those minutes together were precious and strange, starting with the realization that they could read one another's thoughts. Strongest when touching, but still present without physical contact.

And while spoken words weren't necessary, Miles felt compelled to say, "I love you, Luke."

"Yeah, I know."

"They're going to lock me up. I killed him." The palm of his hand still tingled from the blow to Stangl's Adam's apple.

"It was you or him. We'll tell them the truth… or something they'll believe. I will get you out. You know that?"

"Yeah, I do."

"Or we could run… right now. They'd never find us."

"No." He squeezed his hand, needing to feel the solidness of Luke. "We can't run. We have to face this. It's the only way. And even then…."

"I know."

They kissed, not caring who saw, wondering if it would be the last time.

I'm in your head, Luke thought with clarity and amazement.

Yeah, welcome to my world.

Nowhere else I'd rather be.

THE FIRST guard arrived through the roof-access door. She was followed by others, and then came sirens, the police, paramedics, and the familiar detectives, Johnson and LeClerc.

Costumed revelers swarmed the roof, too drunk to heed the officers' warnings to stay back. They wondered if the green fireworks and Calvin's agonal screams were a Halloween amusement.

The medics, seeing the blood, went first to Calvin. They cut away his lab coat, not understanding how there could be so much blood when the underlying flesh was pink and intact. Miles and Luke stood back, knowing a hammer was set to fall. They felt the watchful eyes of the detectives as a second team of medics found Stangl and confirmed what Miles knew. Dr. Gerald Stangl was dead.

LeClerc and Johnson isolated Miles and Luke to a corner of the roof.

"Start explaining, and let's dispense with the bullshit," LeClerc began.

Miles knew that the time of silence had passed. "They have my grandma," he said, uncertain where to start.

"Where?" Johnson asked.

"In the same ward where they kept me. She's in a coma. They did something to her."

"Okay." LeClerc looked across the unruly crime scene. He appeared torn as the crowd on the roof compromised evidence. He shook his head and muttered to his partner, "Secure the scene, or try to make sense of this madness?"

There was one dead, and Calvin had started to howl again.

Johnson shrugged. "I want to know. Let the uniforms handle this."

"Awesome. So what's with blondie?"

"Heartache," said Luke. His voice throbbed with urgency. "Miles's grandma needs to go to a hospital."

"There's more," Miles said. "Somewhere in this building is a woman named Daisy Osborn. I don't know where they're keeping her. Like my grandma, they kidnapped her. They did experiments on her, horrible things. And she wasn't the only one. We need to find her."

"Fine," LeClerc said as a crime-scene unit arrived and attempted to shoo the dozens of drink-spilling partygoers off the roof. "Show us."

They left the moonlit crime scene and took the stairs, bypassing the packed party elevator.

Johnson noted mud and blood smear on the handrail. "Whose is that?"

"Mine," Luke said. "I came in through a tunnel and up this way."

Johnson paused. He looked at the two men. "You guys are tight, aren't you? Not a lot of people would take that risk for someone. And it's not the first time you've gone to the mat for Fox."

Luke grabbed Miles's hand. "Yeah, is that a problem?"

LeClerc chuckled. "Don't go looking for enemies where you don't have them. We could care less about the gay thing. What you need to do is explain this freak show and have it make sense. Got it?"

"Easier said than done," Miles replied as they continued down. His thoughts bounced between Grandma Anna, Luke's hand in his, the nightmare they'd just survived, and the fragile Daisy Osborn.

I'm here, Miles, Luke's voice spoke in his thoughts. *We will get through this. One question, though....*

Yes?

So there's a hot guy in your head who kind of looks like you with a weird moustache. He told me he's got some stories "just for me."

Miles snorted.

"What's so funny?" Johnson asked.

"Nothing." *That's my great-grandfather, Tomas. How can you see him?*

He's in my head right now. He's trying to tell me something. Can't you see him?

No.

Miles, something's happened.... He's with your grandma.

As they came to the basement door, Miles stopped. He looked into Luke's mind and saw Tomas and Grandma Anna, and before they arrived at the locked unit with its transparent walls, he knew.

But seeing her lying there, hooked to a monitor, with a flat line on the screen, was a shock. "She's dead."

"Don't touch anything," LeClerc ordered.

Ignoring him, Miles went to her. Her cell was locked, only able to be opened by one of the Stangls. He stared at her chest to see if there was any rise and fall of breath. But he knew. For an instant he fostered the hope of breaking in and healing her. But now Tomas was front and center in his head. *Don't bring back the dead, Miles. It never goes well.*

"No." Miles stared at his grandma, and tears fell. "She's dead." It was impossible to wrap his head around this, as she lay with her shaved head like some twisted version of Snow White in her crystal coffin. "This is my fault."

"No." Luke wrapped his arms around Miles and held him as they stared at the monitor's endless flat line. *This is not your fault. None of this is your fault.*

"They kidnapped her to get to me."

"Why would they do that?" LeClerc interjected.

"The truth?" Anger surged from under his sorrow.

"Yes," LeClerc replied.

"It's because the stuff you're trying to tell yourself couldn't be true is all true. I healed Antoine Dey. And Dr. Gerald Stangl and his son kidnapped him, did a series of horrible experiments to see how long he'd stay healed, and then they chopped off his head."

"Why? Why would they do that?" Johnson asked.

Miles paused, wrapped in Luke's arms. He stared at his grandma, a woman he loved and who he knew loved him back, though she had a weird way of showing it. She'd hate this… him talking to the cops. He heard Luke's thought: *Best to leave this piece alone.*

"I don't know why. But Antoine Dey wasn't the only one. There was a man with AIDS—Trevor Owens—I think he's dead. And they brought a woman to me this morning. Her name's Daisy Osborn."

"What was wrong with her?" LeClerc asked.

"Ankylosing spondylitis. It's an advanced autoimmune disease. She was dying."

"Do you know where she is? Is she even still alive? Because I have to tell you boys, none of this makes sense, and if you can find a witness…."

Miles turned from his grandma and faced the detectives. He struggled to keep the emotion from his voice. "They recorded everything." *These cops are not the enemy.* "Daisy could still be alive." He steadied his breath. "It was just this morning…. A lot of it's blurry—they kept drugging me— but I think she's still alive." Realizing how bizarre what was about to come from his mouth would sound, he barreled ahead. *I have to make them understand.* "They were experiments. Calvin kidnapped terminal patients from the hospital. They'd have me heal them, and then they would try to make them sick again."

"Seriously?" LeClerc asked. "No one noticed patients disappearing?"

Miles looked him dead-on. "Our boy Calvin has some serious skills. Probably drugged the patient, and pretended he was transporting them to some test. As to how they covered things up, I've no clue."

"Where would they be holding her?"

"I think I know," Luke said. "I came in through a tunnel. There's a floor below this. It's like a bomb shelter. There were rooms off a corridor. I tried a couple of doors. They were locked. But I thought I heard something from behind one of them."

"Show us," Johnson said.

"Sure. Miles, I'm so sorry." *I know you loved her. This wasn't your fault. They did this, not you.*

Miles batted back tears. "They went after her because of me."

"I know. And it's not your fault," Luke said. "Let's go find this Daisy."

"Right." Feeling a dull ache, he thought, *I'm sorry, Grandma.* Then he followed Luke and the detectives toward the stairs.

As they passed the elevator, LeClerc stopped it and looked inside. He observed the smeared palm prints by the buttons. "This says we're in the basement. But what's this for?" He pressed a blank button next to the B. Nothing happened.

"I'll show you," Luke said. He opened the stairwell door. Inside were stairs going up, but having entered this way, Luke knew what appeared to be a solid wall concealed a door. He pressed his hands against it and felt the tiniest give. His heart sank. *Not again.* "It's here. It opens in. There's some kind of mechanism." He played his hands over the surface.

"It moved." Johnson stepped in and helped Luke press in and back. Each time the wall moved farther, only to spring back to its original position. "Wait a minute… I think I know," Johnson said. "Stand back." He brought the heel of his foot down hard on the wall. There was a click, and the door moved enough that Luke could grab the edge before it sprang shut.

"Help me." He strained to hold on to it.

The others grabbed the exposed edge and pulled. The hydraulic mechanism was strong, but between the four of them, they got it open enough for Miles to duck through, followed by the detectives, and then Luke. Once they were inside, it shut behind them.

"It's easy to open from this side," Luke offered as he caught the detectives' worried expressions. "See." He pressed against the door; it swung open, stayed like that for several seconds, and then closed.

"Good to know," Johnson said as they hurried down and out into the brightly lit, steel-walled corridor. "It is like a bomb shelter."

Luke pointed down the hall. "I came in through there." He called out, "Is anyone down here?"

The four men held still but heard nothing.

LeClerc shouted, "Anyone down here?"

They listened, the seconds stretched, and then they heard a woman's barely audible cry. "Help me. Help me."

Miles pointed to a door in the middle of the corridor. He rapped on it. "Hello?"

"Please, help me." She sounded exhausted and far away. "Help me."

Miles felt across the door's surface. There was no handle, just a pad for print recognition.

The four of them attempted to do what they had just done in the stairwell. The door didn't budge.

Miles looked at the keypad. "Calvin." He turned to the detectives. "The kid's fingers will open this. You have to get him."

"Right," LeClerc said. He pulled out his cell. "Son of a bitch."

"What's the matter?" his partner asked.

"No reception. I'll be right back…. Do me a favor. One of you stay by the door to let us back in." And tearing off, he vanished up the stairs.

"Daisy?" Miles called through the door.

"Yes." She sounded exhausted, her words choked by a fit of coughing.

"This is Miles. I'm here with the police. We're going to get you out."

Her cough worsened. Miles felt the grail strain through his fingers, but the steel door stopped it from reaching the dying woman. "We're going to get you out of here, Daisy. I need you to hold on. It won't be much longer."

He heard her battle to get the cough under control and the gurgle as she brought up blood. *What have they done to you?*

"Hang on, Daisy…. Tell me about your grandchildren." It seemed an eternity as he stayed at that door. He cajoled and promised. "We're going to get you out of here." *What the fuck is taking them so long?* The grail roiled in his gut, desperate to get to her. "Stay with me, Daisy. You know I can help." He felt Luke's hands on his shoulders. "Just hang on."

The coughing worsened, and with a choked sob, it stopped. "Daisy…? Daisy?"

There was nothing. He pressed his ears to the door… nothing.

They turned at the sound of a scuffle from the end of the hall. LeClerc had returned with Calvin, whose hands were cuffed behind his back. "You can't make me…." Calvin froze midrant when he spotted Miles. "You! This is your fault. You tricked me. You said you loved me!"

Miles rose from his crouch by the door. He looked from Calvin's twisted and tear-streaked face to LeClerc pushing him down the hall. "His fingerprints open the door."

"You can't make me!" Calvin shrieked.

LeClerc looked to his partner. "Give me a hand." He uncuffed Calvin, and the two detectives forced the teen's hand onto the reader.

"This is illegal!" Calvin was in tears. "You have no right to do this. You need a search warrant."

The door swung in to a darkened room.

"We don't need shit," Johnson said as he grabbed Calvin's hands and recuffed them. "It's called probable cause." A stench of bodily fluids and rot spilled out of the darkened room.

"What the hell? Something died in here," Luke said.

"Not something," Miles answered as his eyes adjusted. He lowered his voice. "Someone."

"It wasn't my fault," Calvin moaned as they entered the slaughterhouse.

"Where are the fucking lights?" Johnson barked.

"By the door… on the right. This wasn't my fault. It was Father. He made me do it."

Miles tuned out Calvin and the detectives as he edged across the floor. The grail pressed up from his belly.

Luke was at his side. "What's happening?"

Miles reached with his thoughts. *Best to use our inside voices.*

Luke snorted and choked on the poisonous air. Bile rose in the back of his throat. *What's happening, Miles? This thing is like a Doberman who needs to go for a pee… now!*

It's the grail. "Daisy, where are you?"

Lights flooded the room. The scene was horrific. The half-dissected remains of yesterday's patient, Trevor Owens, splayed out on a stainless-steel morgue table. Red, blue, and green anatomical flags, like cocktail skewers, had been planted in his flesh, his abdomen and chest spread open by surgical retractors. And perched next to his body was his severed head.

"Not my fault. It was Father. It was Father," Calvin whimpered.

"Daisy?" Miles called, searching first with his eyes.

No, she's over here, Luke's thoughts spoke in his head. *And this is how we use our inside voices.*

Yes. Miles followed Luke to what looked like a futuristic tanning bed but was, in fact, the latest in fMRI technology. "Daisy." He sank to his knees. "Daisy, it's Miles. Can you hear me?" He strained and thought he heard a wheeze. "We have to get this open."

"Tell us how!" LeClerc barked in Calvin's face.

"Hit Menu," Calvin said, as he pressed back against the wall.

"Then what?" Luke asked.

"The Clear button."

The machine's lid lifted with a whisper. Inside lay Daisy, naked, her flesh covered with draining pustules and dark-purple bruises.

LeClerc put a hand to his mouth. "It's what they did to Dey. What did you do to that woman? You little shit, what did you do to her?"

Calvin sobbed. "It was Father. It was Father."

"Daisy." Miles stared at her face as the grail surged from his belly, down his arms, and into his fingers.

It knows she's alive, Luke marveled as he, the detectives, and Calvin watched.

Daisy. Miles placed first one hand and then the other on her shoulders, his gaze on her face, aware she'd been robbed of all modesty.

Son, it doesn't matter if they see my naked old bones. Do this thing. I don't fear death, just, please, not like this. He felt her fear, but more, tenderness and love for her children and her grandchildren. *I don't want to die like this.*

You won't. And while he hated to admit his stay with the Stangls had any upside, there was no denying his leapfrogged skills. He did not lose consciousness, and he kept the twinkling dance in his fingers to the barest necessary to allow the grail to flow. It spread like champagne bubbles into Daisy's body. He braced as her disease flowed into him. *What the hell did they do to you?*

"Needles" was her first word aloud. "It was something in the needles." Her voice gained strength. "The boy did it." *Is it okay to speak?*

With her question and also her disease inside him, Miles focused on the hardest part. He felt Luke's hands on his back, but more than that. Luke was taking a piece of it, of her pain, of the damage done by whatever disease Calvin had injected into her.

Daisy turned her head as her strength grew. She smiled through cracked lips. "You have a friend," she whispered. Her gaze bounced from Luke to Miles. *He's cute.*

I know.

You should tell him that.

Think I just did.

Any chance I get to keep this mind reading thing when you're done? she asked.

No, Miles replied as her disease mixed with the grail and shattered into light.

Too bad.

And like the tide pulling back against the shore, the grail did a final run through Daisy's now pink flesh as though checking for hidden pockets of disease. Satisfied, it returned through his fingers, up his arms, and spiraled down into his belly.

"I can't hear you anymore," Daisy said.

"I know. So how do you feel?"

She paused and took a moment to assess. "I feel good. A little chilly." Her smile was infectious.

Both detectives removed their jackets as Luke ripped open the Velcro closures on the remnants of his clown costume.

"Yours is disgusting," LeClerc told Luke before he could give his muddied and bloodied outfit to Daisy.

Miles unstrapped the bands across her chest and abdomen and helped her sit up. Blocking her nakedness with his body, he eased her arms into Johnson's suit jacket. She pulled it closed in front, and with steady fingers, did up the buttons. Her eyes landed on Calvin.

"I don't understand," she said, her words directed toward him. "How could you do this to me? To anyone?" She bit back tears, unable to avoid the horror of poor Trevor Owens's dissected remains. "That was going to be me. You were going to do that to me? Why?"

All eyes turned to Calvin. His face was streaked with tears, and he opened and then closed his mouth like a landed trout. His gaze landed on Miles. "I did it for him. It should have worked. You said you loved me. You said you loved me."

CHAPTER 39

THE FOLLOWING morning, Miles and Luke sat across from Judge Miriam Gonzalez in her crowded chambers. In addition to them were Detectives LeClerc and Johnson; a pair of federal agents propped against the wall by the door; Miles's attorney, Ben Conti; and prosecutor Garrett Keyes.

With no sleep but showered, shaved, and in ill-fitting navy suits they'd purchased years back for their medical school interviews, they had a single objective—get all charges dropped. Miles turned to his attorney. "What happens now?"

Conti lobbed it to the judge. "Your Honor. We have a confession, hundreds of hours of digital footage, and a mountain of physical evidence that my client had nothing to do with the murder of Antoine Dey. I move for immediate dismissal."

The county prosecutor, a morbidly obese man in his fifties, snorted through his nose. "It's all a steaming pile of horseshit!"

"Garrett," the judge snapped, "you know how I feel about that language. Do it again and I'll have you removed."

"Sorry… Your Honor." The words came through a pleasant smile but sounded like a sneer. "What I meant is that a confession from some deranged, twinked-out kid doesn't seem to be worth a lot. Seriously, how are we supposed to believe any of this? Heads in jars? Nazi conspiracies? Laying on hands to heal the sick? This isn't a court case; it's a party trick."

Detective LeClerc, who with his partner stood behind the seated Luke and Miles, spoke up. "Your Honor, may I?"

"Please. You and Detective Johnson are closest to the case. As best I can tell, your testimony makes or breaks any case the parish might have, and the feds have made it clear that they're out. I've read your reports, and I appreciate how little sleep any of you have had. They tell quite a story. Is it the full story?"

"Yes, Your Honor. Miles Fox had no hand in Antoine Dey's murder, the murder and kidnapping of his grandmother Anna Warren, or the murder of Trevor Owens."

"You'll testify to that?"

The detectives responded in unison. "Yes, Your Honor."

"Which leaves the murder of Doctor Gerald Stangl, which Mr. Fox alleges was in self-defense. Calvin Stangl gives the same story, and Mr. Paxton… speak."

"He did it to save me, Your Honor. Gerald Stangl tried to kill his son, and he tried to kill me. If Miles hadn't stopped him, we'd both be dead."

She shook her head. "Then I see no choice…." She looked at Miles. "Mr. Fox, you are a free man."

"Thank you, Your Honor." He found Luke's hand with his own. *I'm free.*

Yeah, but let's not get jiggy till we're out of here.

The judge fixed her gaze on the two handsome young men, so obviously in love. She smiled. "I've lived here my entire life," she stated. "I've seen some… stuff. I know in my heart you had nothing to do with killing those people, but, Mr. Fox, if even a fraction of what that Stangl boy is rambling about is true, people are going to be interested in what you're able to do. Or at least what Calvin and Gerald Stangl thought you could do."

The mention of the Stangls was like being dunked in ice. "I'm aware of that, Your Honor."

"Is it true?" she asked.

Miles felt all eyes on him as he gripped Luke's hand. *What am I supposed to say?*

There is no good answer.

Gee, that was helpful.

I love you, Miles.

Okay, but I don't think that's what she wants to hear.

He looked into the judge's dark eyes. "Am I still under oath?"

"No," she admitted. "The case is dropped."

"So I can lie now?"

"Yes."

"Good, then here's my answer. I can't heal anyone. Never could."

She nodded. "Mr. Fox, if I were you… I'd stick to that story."

CHAPTER 40

WITH A yellow-and-black-striped prisoner's belongings bag in one hand and his other clasped in Luke's, Miles headed for the courthouse stairs. His anxiety ratcheted up with each step.

"It's okay. You heard the judge," Luke said, sharing Miles's fear and wondering who might try to stop them.

I still feel them… the Stangls.

I know. I can see it inside your head.

Is that a bad thing?

Not usually, and stop fishing. I love you, but it's more than that now, isn't it? It joined us.

Seems so.

They crossed the threshold into an unseasonably warm November day. Hot sun beat down on their faces and their dark suits. Luke looked across the courthouse steps to the planter spruced up with purple asters and ornamental cabbages. Beyond that were Tulane Avenue and the parking lot with his Corolla. He squeezed Miles's hand. *We should have gotten married while we were in there.*

"Did you just propose to me?" Miles turned, not caring about the looks being shot their way.

Luke faced him. *I did.* "I do. So what do you say we get out of this town. Go somewhere new…. Say yes, Miles."

Miles gazed into Luke's soft brown eyes. With his free hand, he pushed back a lock of sandy blond that had fallen across his lover's brow. "Yes, and…." *Although we're kind of already married, don't you think? I mean, how many couples have "indoor voices"?*

Luke clasped the back of Miles's neck and twined his fingers through his hair. "Let's make it legal." And standing on the courthouse steps in suits they'd outgrown, they kissed.

"For the love of God, get a room." LeClerc's voice broke the moment.

Unwilling to stop, Luke and Miles gave the detective the finger as he and his partner looked on.

"Fine," Johnson said, "we can wait, and considering we're the ones who convinced the judge to drop the charges, it better not be *too* long."

Reluctantly Miles pulled back. *We can go to Boston and get married. My parents could probably swing it for our rabbi to conduct the ceremony.*

Luke snorted. *Awesome. That should send my dad totally over the edge. Not just gay, not just marrying a dude, but wearing one of those beanies on my head.*

It's called a yarmulke… or kipah *if you prefer.*

"What's so funny?" LeClerc asked.

Miles looked at the detectives and wondered how they were piecing it together. "Nothing, really. We're making plans."

"To leave town?" Johnson asked.

"Yeah, why?" Luke interjected. "You heard the judge. 'Free to go.'"

"Not saying anything different… just this. If I were the two of you, I'd not only get out of town, but I'd consider dropping off the grid."

"Not possible," LeClerc contradicted his partner. "Not anymore…. You boys take care of yourselves."

"Thanks," Miles offered as the detectives headed toward their car.

"That was ominous," Luke said, noting a small circle of onlookers.

"Yeah." Miles pulled back his hand, breaking a piece of their connection. "We should get out of here. I mean, way far out of here."

"I've got your violin in the back. You left it at my house. You want to stop at your apartment and…."

"No. You, me… my fiddle. Nothing else I want. Nothing I need. We'll go to your house, you can pack what you want…."

"No." Luke retrieved Miles's hand, feeling a loss without it. *You're all I want. You're all I need. Let's just leave.*

To where?

Does it matter?

No. And they held each other and kissed. Horns honked from the avenue, some for, some against the pair of handsome men in navy suits making out on the courthouse stairs.

A gruff voice intruded on their moment. "Give me a dollar."

"Huh?" Miles pulled away. His pulse raced as he stared into a pair of water-blue eyes. For an instant it was as though Gerald Stangl had returned. But no, this man was older, his clothes rumpled, his silver hair disheveled and thinning. *But those eyes.*

"Give me a dollar," the man repeated.

Recognition blossomed. This was one of the psych patients who'd been through the ER when Miles had his rotation. "You're Louis."

"Give me a dollar."

Luke reached into his pocket and pulled out a buck.

"No." Louis Drake shook his head. "Not you, the fox. Give me a dollar."

"Okay." Miles fumbled in his pockets. "Here."

Louis took the bill and thrust it into the sun. His lips smacked, his tongue twisted and protruded from his mouth as he concentrated on the numbers and the messages. "Starts with an S and ends with an F. But no… that's not right." He looked at Miles, and then back at the bill. "Starts with an S and ends with an F… you killed the doc."

Miles held his tongue, not thinking this old man who obviously had schizophrenia was a danger, but not about to take chances.

"He was good to me. Know that. He was good… he had issues." Louis chuckled, and his head bobbed up and down. "There we go, there we go, there we go, give it a second, and the numbers march into place. It's not a start and not an end. It's a hunt, hunt, hunt. You killed the doc, and the numbers keep on marching, keep on hunting, hunting the fox. See." He thrust the bill in front of Miles. "You cut off the head, and they keep on marching, marching, marching. But maybe you get a head start. Get it? A head start, head start. Did you cut off the doc's head?"

"No." Miles twined his fingers with Luke's. "Keep the buck. Let's get out of here."

They backed away and headed down the courthouse stairs. Louis stayed behind, fixated on the bill, lips puckering and smacking, his tongue twisting in and out of his mouth. "Numbers keep marching, keep hunting, hunting, hunting. Cut off the head, doc, doc, doc, and they keep on coming. They always find the fox. S is for Stangl, S is for the seeker, and the sneaker and the sleeper."

ALSO WATCHING from the second-floor courthouse window were the two federal agents who'd been in the judge's chambers as the case was dismissed. They eavesdropped on Miles and Luke's exchange through a high-powered device dubbed "Little Brother."

"What's with the whack job?" the fairer of the two asked.

"Stangl's pet patient."

"Where you think they'll head?"

"Boston."

"Yeah, he'll go for his grandmother's funeral. Sad about that. Wasteful."

"True, and not our place to question."

"You don't think things will go back to the way they were before…. Watch and wait?"

"Can't see how. Too many know what Fox can do, and the Stangl boy is unpredictable. God knows who he'll blab to."

"Not to mention the tapes."

"Yeah, but those will go missing by morning."

"You don't think they made copies?"

"Stangl, possibly; the cops, too soon. They'll have to bring in an expert. By the time they do…."

"Right. I am surprised they let the kid live. Wonder how long that will last."

"Yeah, well, ours is not to wonder why." He pulled out his cell, pressed his forefinger over the sensor to unlock it, and clicked on the GPS tracking app. The homing device they'd placed under the front axle of Luke's car showed red. "You up for the first shift?"

"Sure."

They watched as Luke and Miles crossed the avenue to the parking lot. Without further discussion they packed up Little Brother, bypassed Louis Drake, who stood rambling and rhyming with his dollar bill on the courthouse steps, headed to their car, and followed the fox.

CALEB JAMES is an author, member of the Yale volunteer faculty, practicing psychiatrist, and clinical trainer. He writes both fiction and nonfiction and has published books in multiple genres and under different names. Writing as Charles Atkins, he has been a Lambda Literary finalist. He lives in Connecticut with his partner and four cats.

Website: charlesatkins.com

Blog: calebjamesblog.wordpress.com

Facebook: www.facebook.com/Caleb-James-536765356387453

ALSO BY CALEB JAMES

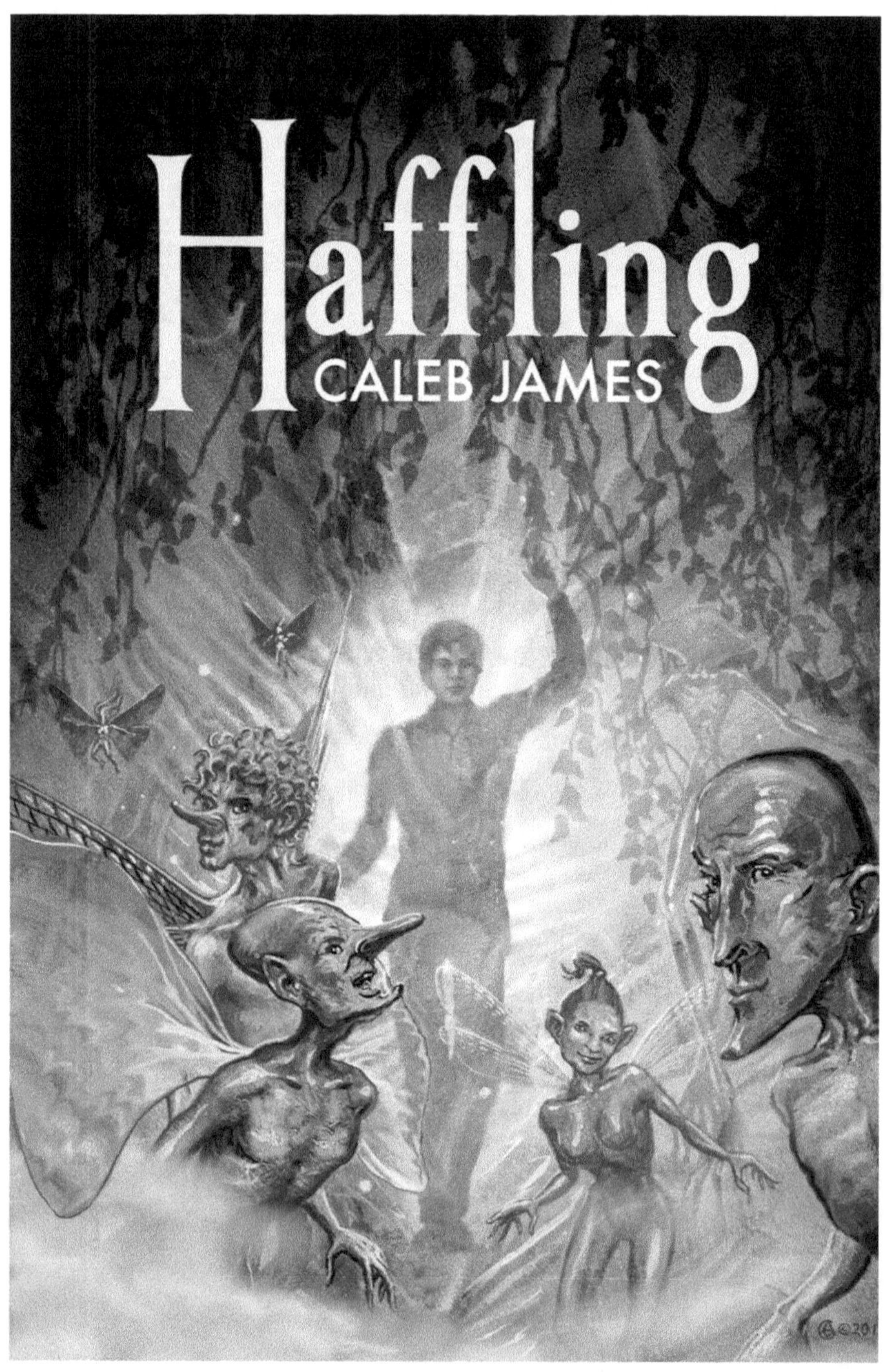

All sixteen-year-old Alex Nevus wants is to be two years older and become his sister Alice's legal guardian. That, and he'd like his first kiss, preferably with Jerod Haynes, the straight boy with the beautiful girlfriend and the perfect life. Sadly, wanting something and getting it are very different. Strapped with a mentally ill mother, Alex fears for his own sanity. Having a fairy on his shoulder only he can see doesn't help, and his mom's schizophrenia places him and Alice in constant jeopardy of being carted back into foster care.

When Alex's mother goes missing, everything falls apart. Frantic, he tracks her to a remote corner of Manhattan and is transported to another dimension—the land of the Unsee, the realm of the Fey. There he finds his mother held captive by the power-mad Queen May and learns he is half-human and half-fey—a Haffling.

As Alex's human world is being destroyed, the Unsee is being devoured by a ravenous mist. Fey are vanishing, and May needs to cross into the human world. She needs something only Alex can provide, and she will stop at nothing to possess it… to possess him.

www.dsppublications.com

BLUE
ON
BLACK
CAROLE
CUMMINGS

Lurking in the digital
underworld, he lures,
seduces, and charms.

IM

RICK R. REED

9 781634 768399